SHADOW
HUNT

By Melissa F. Olson

Disrupted Magic series

Midnight Curse
Blood Gamble

Boundary Magic series

Boundary Crossed
Boundary Lines
Boundary Born

Scarlett Bernard novels

Dead Spots
Trail of Dead
Hunter's Trail

Nightshades series

Nightshades
Switchback

Short Fiction

Sell-By Date: An Old World Short Story
Bloodsick: An Old World Tale
Malediction: An Old World Story

Also by Melissa

The Big Keep: A Lena Dane Mystery

SHADOW HUNT

DISRUPTED MAGIC BOOK THREE

MELISSA F. OLSON

47N**O**RTH

Text copyright © 2018 by Melissa F. Olson

Published by 47North, Seattle

www.apub.com

Amazon, the Amazon logo, and 47North are trademarks of Amazon.com, Inc., or its affiliates.

ISBN-13: 9781503949102
ISBN-10: 1503949109

Cover design by Mike Heath | Magnus Creative

Cover photography by Gene Mollica

Printed in the United States of America

See with what heat these Dogs of Hell advance
To waste and havoc yonder World.

—John Milton, *Paradise Lost*

Prologue

Three years ago

From the age of five or six, Petra Corbett had been told that she had bitter in her blood.

This was not surprising: even as a small child living just outside Paris, she had collected grievances as easily as other children obtained toys or trading cards.

In some families this attitude could have been a problem, but in Petra's world, animosity and resentment were practically the family trade. Her natural pull toward hostility in all its forms—verbal, physical, magical—actually wound up making Petra her grandfather's favorite, despite the unfortunate circumstance of her not being male.

Petra's mother hoped that time might mellow her youngest daughter's rancor, but instead Petra's capacity for hatred only seemed to expand. And expand. Until she was on her first scouting trip to America, and she realized that her entire lifetime of dislike had just been a long and arduous escalation to that precise moment. Because the reality was that Petra Corbett had never loathed *anything* as much as she hated driving in Los Angeles.

For the first four days of her stay, that was all she had done: drive the streets, getting to know the city and the shallow idiots who lived in it. It was bad enough that Americans insisted on driving themselves everywhere, but Los Angeles in particular seemed to depend on individual cars the way other, more intelligent cities depended on public transportation. And their reward for this individualism was to spend hours of every day in gridlock. Petra thought it was a perfect example of American "independence"—selfish, lazy, and with a complete lack of foresight.

Still, Grandfather felt that she needed to understand the city, so she gritted her teeth and drove, usually accompanied by the bargest Belle. Belle couldn't be trusted to ride up front untethered, so she stayed locked in the back of the rental van, inside one of the two massive steel crates that had flown to the city with them in Grandfather's private jet.

Occasionally, Petra would pull over, her whistle in hand, and let Belle out of the crate to run drills. This was only possible, however, when she could find a stretch of unpopulated land. Petra did not want too many people to get a look at the bargest, whose bizarre appearance was simply too memorable. Some members of the Family had actually argued that Belle should not receive the bargest curse for this very reason, but Petra's father, who was in charge of training the potentials, had insisted that Belle was the most intelligent and athletic of all the current crop. Petra hated her father—of course—but in this case she had to admit he'd been right. Belle was an excellent specimen. And it was easy enough to exercise her at night, when Petra could also keep an eye out for any signs of the local werewolf pack.

By the fifth day of their scouting trip, Petra had run out of the ostrich steaks that the bargest required for protein. She used her laptop to find a pet store that specialized in large animals: horses, mostly, but also goats, sheep, and very large dogs. After a moment's consideration, Petra opted to leave Belle in her second crate at the apartment complex. Petra didn't *think* Belle would forget her training and decide to hunt and kill a horse for fun, but the bargest *was* hungry. No need to risk it.

So Petra followed her phone's GPS to Freddy's Feed and Supplies in an area called Altadena. The store itself was dusty and understaffed, which was just fine with Petra. Small and insignificant meant no one would bother with video cameras, and understaffed meant Petra wouldn't have to deal with salespeople who didn't understand her limited English.

She had brought a couple of five-gallon pails from a hardware store, and went straight to the freezer section, filling both pails with frozen ostrich steaks. Then she lugged them to the counter herself, sneezing from the dust. There was one customer ahead of her at the register, and while Petra waited, her eyes wandered to a nearby rack of expensive, durable dog toys. It would never have occurred to Petra to "play" with the bargest, but she could see the value in keeping Belle's instincts honed by having her track and destroy a ball. It was the same reason greyhounds chased practice rabbits.

Petra absently scanned the racks of rubber and thickly stitched canvas, and then her gaze landed on the leashes hanging from a hook at the very top of the shelf. Her breath caught, and she dropped the buckets and stepped closer. Petra could read English better than she could speak it, and after a few moments of concentration, she understood the small sign above the leashes: HANDMADE IN LOS ANGELES.

But that didn't make any sense.

"It can't be," she whispered to herself. She grabbed the middle of a leash, holding it two inches from her face so she could examine it: the same nylon used in fishnets, braided and twisted over and over again in a unique pattern that formed a series of interlocked knots. Petra had once seen the hitch on a pickup truck detach from the truck bed while testing one of these leashes.

"Miss? Can I help you find something?"

Ignoring the confused-looking clerk, Petra ran out to the rental van and scooped up the thick fishnet leash she'd brought with her from France. She carried it back inside and held it up to the new item, comparing them. Her own leash was black, and the other was brown, but there was no mistake: the design was identical, down to the intricate braiding near the handle attachment, the length, and the number of knots.

A rare grin spread across Petra's face. She pulled out her cell phone and called her grandfather in Paris. It was two in the morning there, but he would forgive her. While she waited for the connection, Petra turned to look at the young man behind the counter. He was tall and gangly, an uncertain-looking teenager with acne and braces. Oh, this was going to be easy.

No, this was going to be *fun*.

The phone rang three times, and then Grandfather's gruff voice came on the line. "What is it, Petra? Have you found the nova wolf?"

"No." She didn't bother to keep the satisfaction out of her voice. "But you will never believe who I *did* find."

PART I

Chapter 1

It started with an overprotective bargest, and what I assumed was the flu.

For weeks, Shadow, the bargest who had adopted me, had been obsessively glued to my side, following me so closely that it was hard for me to make sudden turns without stumbling over her. And I do mean *over* her: at about a hundred and eighty pounds, Shadow was roughly the size of a Great Dane, but shorter and more muscled. There were several times when I came close to belly flopping over her back and face-planting into the carpet.

At the time, though, I was moody and grieving, so if I noticed her unusual behavior at all, I chalked it up to her being worried about me.

Then, in the middle of April, I got sick, with what I thought was a normal flu bug. But one night, a few days into it, I went on a vomiting spree that legitimately frightened me. Usually when you get the flu, you stop puking—or at least slow down—when there's nothing left to come up. But I couldn't seem to get it under control. That's when I started to worry that there might be something seriously wrong with me.

No, I'm not a complete moron, and yes, I do watch television—I'm aware that by then, any reasonably informed, sexually active woman would have suspected a pregnancy. But it honestly never occurred to me, because although no one completely understands why nulls are the way we are, there's one thing that everyone agrees on: nulls are sterile. It's just a fact. Vampires need blood, werewolves have to change during the full moon, and nulls can't procreate. We're like zonkeys: a weird anomaly in nature that happens every once in a while, but can't reproduce itself.

So instead, I was worried that I might have, I don't know, a tapeworm or stomach cancer or, God forbid, an actual gluten allergy. Okay, fine: I was worried that I'd done permanent damage to my body months earlier, when I'd used my abilities to cure a human of vampirism. Dashiell and the others had warned me that there could be physical ramifications, but I hadn't listened. What if saving Hayne had done something to my insides?

The next afternoon, I called my doctor's office, but the nurse insisted I needed to take a pregnancy test. I rolled my eyes but decided to humor her, just so I could call back and figure out what was *really* wrong. I went out and got a box of three tests, read the instructions—and then realized I wasn't supposed to pee on them until the next morning.

It was a Thursday evening near the end of April. Thursday was the regular movie night at my house, and I was helping my vampire roommate, Molly, pick up the living room. It was Molly's turn to pick what we watched, and she had surprised me by opting for an Ingrid Bergman mini-marathon instead of her usual romantic comedies. Jesse, who often joined us if the movies weren't too girly, was coming by for the second feature, *Notorious*, after he finished having dinner at his parents' house.

"Scarlett!" Molly's voice was exasperated, and I blinked myself back to attention.

I realized she'd been talking to me. "Sorry, what?"

"I said, are you okay? You're pale again, and you've been folding the same blanket for, like, five minutes. Do you need the puke bucket?"

I made a sour face. I was very over the puke bucket. "No, it's not that. I was just . . . thinking of Jameson."

This was actually the truth. A month and a half earlier, I'd gone to Las Vegas on a freelance job and encountered a fellow null, Jameson. He had been killed, for a lot of reasons that weren't my fault, but also a little bit because I'd been too slow and dumb to save him. For weeks, I'd been struggling to come out of the worst of my grief and guilt, but having the pregnancy tests in the house kept forcing my thoughts back to Jameson. Stupid tapeworm.

Molly looked contrite. "I'm sorry. Do you want me to hold off on the movie?" She held up her DVD copy of *Gaslight*.

I'd ruined a lot of the week for both her and Jesse with my illness, and I didn't want to ruin movie night, too. Fuck it. "No, it's fine. I'm just gonna go to the bathroom." The tests were going to be negative whenever I took them, so what did it matter what time of day it was?

A few minutes later, I swung the bathroom door open, shuffling into the living room like the living dead . . . which was appropriate, since my ability to form thoughts had suddenly vanished.

"Scarlett?" Molly's voice seemed to come from far away, though it was just the other side of the room.

I shook my head, not really hearing her. "I don't know how to . . . this is so . . . so." I didn't have the words. I didn't have *any* words.

Looking panicked, Molly vaulted off the couch and rushed over to me, grasping my arms. "What happened?" she asked, searching my face. "Did someone hurt you?"

In answer, I held up my fist, clenched so tightly that my knuckles ached, so Molly could see the test.

"I'm pregnant."

It's remarkably difficult to leave a vampire speechless, especially one who's lived for more than a hundred years. After so many decades of witnessing the best and the worst of humanity, it's practically impossible to surprise them.

At least, I always thought it was, until I found the two words that got the job done.

Molly just stared at me for a looooong moment, her eyes huge. "You're *pregnant?*" my roommate repeated, completely dumbfounded. "With a baby?"

I blinked. "God, I hope so."

"But nulls are sterile," she insisted. "Everybody knows that."

"Except, apparently, my uterus." I sat down heavily on the couch, drawing my knees up to my chest. "I guess maybe things change when two nulls . . . get together."

"Oh. *Oh.*" Her eyes widened. "You and Jameson."

I nodded. Molly knew that I'd been upset over his death, and she wasn't stupid: she'd probably suspected that we'd slept together. But I'd never actually confirmed it, and she hadn't put me on the spot by asking.

"It's gotta be a false positive, though," Molly said doubtfully. "That's a thing, right? That happens on TV all the time."

"I took three tests. And I've been sick." And come to think of it . . . "And I guess I missed my period."

"You don't keep track?"

I gave her a look. "Why would I? Nulls are sterile."

"Right." She sat down next to me on the edge of the couch. "Um. Are you . . . okay?"

"No, not really."

At twenty-seven, I had finally gotten used to the idea that I would never be a mother. For years, I had told myself that I didn't really want kids anyway, and that my life was too complicated and dangerous. I had thought I was past wanting a child of my own . . . but even now, a terrifying joy was enveloping me from the inside out, like water spreading across ancient paper. The strength of it scared me.

"Are you gonna keep it?" Molly asked. Trust her to get right to the crux of the problem.

"I don't know," I said honestly. "Right now I'm just kind of scared shitless."

Molly looked at me in that way she had, as though I were a science experiment in her personal lab. "Why? I mean, I get why women are afraid of never sleeping again and gaining weight and all that. But isn't this pretty much what you've secretly been wanting?"

I shook my head. "You don't get it. This isn't a Lifetime movie, and I'm not a human. What if the baby is a null, like me? Or what if it's born a witch? Hell, what if it's born with no magic at all, but someone uses it to get to me?" I hugged my knees closer to my chest. "Any way you slice it, this baby would be in danger for most of its life. And that's completely apart from the fact that I'm single, there's no such thing as nocturnal day care, and I haven't so much as held an infant since I was about twelve." Emotions rose up in me, and I found myself suddenly trying to swallow sobs. When I was sure I could speak, I added softly, "And Jameson is dead, and I'm scared that every time I look at this kid, I'll remember that I didn't save him."

She looked at me for another long, quiet moment. "Okay," Molly conceded. "You make some solid points."

I sniffed a little, trying to calm myself down. "Besides," I went on, swiping at my eyes with the back of a hand, "what do you think would happen if Dashiell and the others find out they've got the world's only pregnant null?"

Molly thought about that for a moment. "They'd try to keep it quiet," she said finally. "They'd lock you away until the baby's born, and then Dashiell would pressure you to give it up for adoption, for its safety and yours."

This was pretty much the same conclusion I had reached, but it didn't help to have it confirmed. "Exactly. And if I give up my baby to strangers, I can't protect it if it *does* turn out to be Old World." I held out my hands. "I'm stuck." Tears threatened to spill down my cheeks again. "Unless I get an abortion. Then this whole thing goes away."

She gave me a sympathetic look. "And you'll never get another chance to have a kid."

That wasn't true, of course; I could still adopt a baby someday. But I knew what Molly meant: I would probably never get another chance to have my own personal uterine miracle. I only knew of a handful of nulls on the planet, and the only other male of reproductive age was (a) in Scotland, and (b) married.

"What do you want to do?" Molly asked softly. "I mean, you're not very far along, right? You've got time."

I gave her a pitying look, and she shook her head, not needing me to say it. "No, you don't. Because you told *me*, and Dashiell will expect me to report this to him ASAP. I don't really give a fuck if I get in trouble for keeping your secrets, but I'm guessing you do care."

"Damn right. You can't lie to him."

She slumped so her head was nearly level with the back of the couch. "Probably not, no."

We were being literal. Molly had sworn allegiance to Dashiell, the cardinal vampire of the city. That kind of oath had actual power in the Old World. If he really pushed her, and I wasn't there to keep everybody human, he could actually *force* her to tell him the truth.

A tide of hopelessness threatened to overwhelm me, and I felt myself trying to swallow back tears. This was too much. This was all way past too much.

Molly saw the look on my face and pushed out a breath. She sat up again. "Okay. I think we need to figure out what you're having. If it's a normal human baby, that's a very different prospect than . . . something else."

"Okay, but how do we find out?"

"That, I don't know. Ordinarily I'd ask the nearest cardinal vampire, but that's Dashiell. Even if you were ready to tell him, I think he's too young to know."

Most vampires get power with age, but every once in a while, a vampire is reborn with way more than his or her fair share. Dashiell was one of those anomalies, which meant he was powerful enough to hold a city, but not even two hundred years old.

"Yeah, if he's ever heard of a pregnant null, he would have at least hinted at it by now," I reasoned. It would be just like Dashiell to dangle null secrets in front of me and make me bargain for them. If he hadn't mentioned null reproduction, he didn't know about it. "Same goes for Kirsten." The witch leader of Los Angeles had a toddler, and I trusted her a lot more than Dashiell. If she'd known of a way I could have kids, she would have said something.

We could ask Kirsten to do some research, but she'd have to talk to people, if for no other reason than to explain why she needed to access the witches' library of magical knowledge. And I couldn't afford to let any more people know about this than absolutely necessary. Besides, Kirsten, Dashiell, and Will were all my partners in the city's leadership, at least in theory. Asking Kirsten was the same as asking Dashiell, and I was back to square one.

Talking to a vampire wasn't a bad idea in itself, though. I could claim I was in a relationship where the guy wanted kids, and I was curious if it was possible. But Molly was right—it would need to be someone a hell of a lot older than Dashiell, and I mostly just knew the vampires in LA, who were a fairly young group. There weren't a lot of vampires willing to swear loyalty to someone who was younger than they were.

"Who's the oldest vampire you know?" I asked Molly.

"Uh . . ." She held out her hands, palms up. "Most of my sisters were turned when I was."

"Shit." I thought about the vampires I'd met in Las Vegas, but other than Wyatt, who was only about two hundred, they all either hated me or had been killed. "Wait." A memory nagged at me. Not a vampire, but I'd had a conversation with Sashi, a healing witch in Vegas. We'd been talking about Sashi's friend Lex . . .

I stood up. "I know what to do," I said simply. "Get your overnight bag. We're leaving in five."

Molly rose, too. "Where are we going?"

"Boulder, Colorado," I told her. "To see maybe the oldest vampire on the planet."

Chapter 2

I threw clothes and toiletries into a small duffel bag, more or less on autopilot. My thoughts were still flying around faster than I could grasp them, but at least I sort of had a plan, however flimsy.

"Can I drive?" Molly yelled from the other room.

I started to say no, but paused to consider. Molly drove like a maniac. Or like a person who can heal from almost anything and has already faced down death once. But if she drove, we would get there a hell of a lot faster. Besides, I was already sick to my stomach.

"Sure," I called back, making a mental note to grab some of my heavy-duty ziplock bags. I was pretty much guaranteed to puke before we got there, but just in case, I went to the bedside-table drawer and popped a Dramamine.

Molly leaned into my doorway, looking hopeful. "Can we take Eleanor?"

I rolled my eyes. Eleanor was what Molly called her 1967 Shelby Mustang GT500, a muscle car she kept in a storage unit a few miles away. Molly rarely drove it, and I'd only been in it once. I didn't know anything about cars, but it was *very* pretty. And very conspicuous.

But Eleanor was fast, and it didn't have GPS or LoJack, which meant Dashiell wouldn't be able to track it. Besides, it wouldn't matter if we had a flashy car between LA and Boulder. Everyone I was worried about was within the city limits. "Yeah, okay."

Her face lit up. *"Yesssss!"* She turned and disappeared back down the hall, closing my door behind her.

"Let's take a cab to the storage center, so it looks like we're both still home," I yelled after her. Then I stopped, my hands frozen in the act of zipping my bag. I hadn't thought about how to cover my job. Or about Shadow, who was currently pressed against my right leg, doing her best to mirror my every movement. She was looking up at my face with obvious anxiety. Not about being left, I knew. Shadow didn't get afraid of things like that. She was afraid I'd be hurt while I was away from her.

"I'm sorry, but you know you can't come," I told her, starting toward the bedroom door. I'd left my cell phone out in the living room. I pulled the door open. "We'll call Jesse—"

At that moment, a familiar figure stepped into the hallway. "Somebody say my name?" Jesse leaned in my doorway, looking gleeful. Before I could answer, he added, "Oh my God, that was amazing. I've always wanted to have sitcom timing when I walked into a room. Now I can check it off my—oh. Hey."

I had thrown my arms around him, tears pricking my eyes. I don't know which of us was more surprised. "Hey," Jesse said again, awkwardly patting my back. "What's wrong?"

"You're here," I mumbled into his neck. He smelled the way he always did, of Armani cologne and oranges. It was immensely comforting.

"Yeah, my dad is working late, so we had to postpone family dinner until Sunday. Molly let me in . . . what's wrong?"

Ignoring the question, I forced myself to pull back. I straightened my shirt, embarrassed, and glanced down at Shadow. "You didn't feel the need to warn me about a visitor?" I asked her.

She looked at me and gave a huge, deliberate yawn, showing off a row of enormous, glittering white teeth. The message was obvious: Jesse didn't count. He spent too much time here, and she loved him nearly as much as she loved me.

"Scarlett?" Jesse had taken in the bag behind me, and the look on my face. "What's going on?"

"I need your help. *Again*," I said, sniffling a little. Jesse had made a ton of money from writing a book about his time as a cop. He didn't need to work for the time being, which made him conveniently available. This wouldn't be the first time I'd taken advantage of that. "Can you stay here and take care of Shadow and the Batphone for a couple of days?" My cell phone number was the one the Old World leaders used when there was an emergency for me to clean up. It was also an easy way to track me.

"Of course, but why? Where are you going?"

I opened my mouth to tell him—after all, Lex was really *his* friend—but snapped it shut again. That was thinking like a null. But Jesse was just a human.

"I can't say," I said, my voice pleading. "If you don't know, they can't make you tell."

He took a step closer. "*Who* can't make me tell?"

"Dashiell."

"Scarlett . . ." His painfully handsome face clouded over. "Is this about curing Hayne? Did it . . . do something to you?"

"No, it's not that."

"Then what kind of trouble are you in?"

I almost laughed at his phrasing. *In trouble.* I was definitely in at least three kinds of trouble. "It's going to be okay. I think. I'm not, like, staging a coup or anything. But I need to go ask someone for help, and it means leaving the county, which is against the rules for Shadow. I should be back . . . day after tomorrow? I hope?" Okay, I was starting to sound loopy as hell, even to me.

Looking worried, Jesse pulled me close again so he could plant a kiss on my forehead. "Okay. What do I do if someone calls the Batphone?"

"Tell them . . . tell them I still have the flu," I answered, brightening. Sometimes I went nearly a week without getting called in to clean up some kind of supernatural mess. "I'll text Dashiell and tell him you're helping me because I'm sick again." With luck, I might actually get away with this.

But I needed to do it either way.

Jesse looked in my eyes, and whatever he saw made him nod and step back. "Molly!" I yelled. "Do you still have extra burner phones?"

A brief pause, then: "Does the pope shit in the woods?"

"Uhhh . . ."

"Of course I do!"

"Great." I picked up my cell phone off the nightstand and handed it to Jesse, who put it in his pocket. "I'll get you the burner number before we leave. That way you can call me if there's a serious issue." One of the vampires would also be able to press Jesse to get my new cell number, but if it came to that, we'd already be screwed.

"Okay. What about Shadow?"

"Right." I glanced down at the bargest, who was glaring at me again. I had never left Shadow with anyone but another null, at least not for more than a couple of hours. I sat back down on the bed, which put my face more or less at eye level with hers. "I know you're not happy with me," I told her, "and I know why. But can you please try to be good for Jesse?" The one thing I absolutely couldn't do was leave Shadow alone during the full moon. She was magically driven to pursue and kill werewolves, thanks to the spell that made her a bargest, and during the full moon, the werewolves in LA had to change. Luckily, that was almost three weeks away.

Shadow kept the glare going for a few more seconds, but then her clubbed-off tail lifted and slowly began to wag. She dipped her head and gave my hand one regal lick. I scratched her ears. "Thank you." I looked back up at Jesse. "And thank *you*."

He nodded, still looking worried. "Go do what you need to do."

Chapter 3

Jesse drove Scarlett and Molly to a storage unit a couple of miles away, where Molly supposedly kept a muscle car. Under normal circumstances, he would be interested in seeing it, but he was too worried about Scarlett. She had been off ever since she'd returned from Las Vegas, her eyes distant and haunted. Then the flu, and now whatever this was. It was a lot of stress.

The ride was quiet, with only the low buzz of the radio and Shadow occasionally shifting around in the back seat, where she was scrunched in next to Molly. When they arrived at the storage facility, Molly got out of the back seat with a quick, "Thanks, Jesse," closing the door behind her. Scarlett put her hand on the door handle, then paused, looking over at him. She looked worried and pale, and she'd lost weight during her illness. Jesse had to stop himself from nagging her to eat regularly and drink lots of fluids.

"You look . . . um . . . not back to full strength," he said instead. "Are you sure about this?"

"No," she said quietly. "But I don't know what else to do." He opened his mouth to ask what she meant, but Scarlett just shook her head. "I'll explain everything when we get back, I promise."

She leaned over and kissed his cheek before exiting the car.

As he drove back to the cottage, with Shadow now comfortably stretched across the back seat, Jesse had to wonder about that kiss. It hadn't been romantic or anything, but Scarlett was so rarely affectionate, and that was the second time she'd touched him in one night, as though she was seeking comfort. Something had to be really bothering her, and it made him crazy that he didn't know what it was.

Back at the cottage, Jesse wandered around the living room, straightening couch cushions and folding up throw blankets while Shadow draped herself across the couch, watching him with what might have been amusement. Jesse wasn't a particularly neat person, but the night's events had left him with too much nervous energy. Really, he should get his gym bag out of the trunk of his car and take Shadow for a run. It'd be good for her—Scarlett hadn't exactly been a marathoner during her illness—and on the off chance that someone from the Old World spotted him, it would be easy to use the excuse that he was exercising Shadow while Scarlett was sick.

But the cop in him was tugging at his attention. Scarlett thought she was protecting him by keeping him out of whatever was happening, but that just wasn't like her. She had called on him for help plenty of times, and Jesse knew that she trusted him. So why was she suddenly afraid that Dashiell or one of his vampires was going to press him?

Then Jesse realized, too late, that he had a way around that.

Scarlett was a null; she never remembered that there were other ways to block vampire mind control. Months ago, Jesse had asked Kirsten for a stash of witch bags, which could protect him against different Old World species.

This had been while Scarlett was still recovering from healing Hayne, and Jesse was helping her. Kirsten had been so grateful that a few days later she'd given him a small box of witch bags, no questions asked. He had it hidden in his old bedroom at his parents' house, where there was no chance that Scarlett would come close to it and negate the magic.

Jesse could collect one of the witch bags to protect himself from being pressed, so there was no reason Scarlett had to keep whatever this was from him. He picked up his phone, where he'd programmed in the burner number—but then he stopped himself.

"She's still not going to tell me, is she?" he said to Shadow. He was mostly just thinking out loud, but she lifted her head from her paws, watching him attentively. "She's spooked, so she's going to keep it from me on reflex. But what if I can help her?" He stood up, pacing the length of the small cottage. Then he went back into the living room and looked at Shadow, who hadn't moved.

He felt a little ridiculous, but he went over and sat next to her on the couch, scratching her ears. "Okay, I'm never sure how much of this you're getting, but . . . is it okay if I search the cottage?"

She tilted her head back to study his face. "It's just, I want to help Scarlett, and I can't do that if I don't know what's wrong."

Shadow just looked at him for a long moment, making Jesse feel like even more of an idiot. What was he doing? Shadow was smart, sure, but she was a dog. A very protective dog. She wasn't going to understand the nuances of human—

But before he could even finish that thought, Shadow shifted gracefully off the couch—she was too big to jump down, so she just slid her paws off—and padded toward the kitchen. Jesse followed her to the cupboard next to the sink, where Scarlett and Molly kept a small garbage can. The cupboards didn't have any handles, but Shadow looked up at him and pawed at the door a little.

Jesse opened the cupboard, but Shadow continued to stare at him until he pulled the can out. The garbage was about half-full, with a wad of tissues on top. "What?" he asked the bargest.

Had she actually rolled her eyes?

She hooked the edge of the can with one big paw and tipped it over. "Hey," Jesse protested, but the spill revealed what was hidden under the tissues: a piece of blue plastic the size of a Magic Marker. He crouched down and flipped it over. "No fucking way," he breathed.

It was a digital pregnancy test, the kind that had actual words instead of plus and minus signs. And it said PREGNANT.

Jesse toppled sideways, landing hard on his butt. "She's pregnant?" he said stupidly. "How is that . . . I thought she couldn't . . ." He closed his mouth and swallowed hard, grateful that Scarlett couldn't see his face just then.

His first thought was, *That's why she's been sick.* His second was, *Who's the father?* To his genuine surprise, jealousy bubbled up within him.

Then the implications hit him. Oh, God, no wonder she was freaked out. Would the baby be a regular human? Even if it was, nulls were valuable, and a baby would be an easy lever to control Scarlett. That had to be why she didn't want Dashiell to know. But it didn't explain her leaving town . . . unless she was going somewhere to abort the baby. Why would she need to leave LA to do that, though? Humans in LA terminated pregnancies all the time, and it was unlikely to get back to anyone in the Old World.

He felt warm moisture and realized Shadow had licked his face with her enormous tongue. *Ew.* He gently moved her face away. "Thanks, girl, but . . . wow." No wonder Scarlett was so shook.

Jesse sat there on the kitchen floor, feeling like a fool. He'd been so cocky, assuming he could help Scarlett with whatever was troubling her. But this was bigger than him. He should have trusted her decision to keep him out of it.

Who was the father? Was Scarlett seeing someone?

Abruptly, Shadow's head whipped around to face the kitchen doorway, and a low growl rumbled out of her chest. "What is it—" Jesse began, but she was already racing out of the room, barking at top volume. The sound was deafening—and surprising. Had he ever even heard her bark before?

Then Jesse wondered if she was trying to warn him that Scarlett had come back for something. He swept the garbage back into the can and replaced it in the cupboard, making sure the tissues covered the pregnancy test. As he hurried toward the front door, Shadow's barks echoing around the house, he could just make out the sound of the doorbell ringing. Not Scarlett, then.

"Shadow, hush!" Jesse said. His parents' dog reacted the same way whenever the doorbell rang, but he hadn't expected it from the bargest. Jesse nudged her aside with his leg and stepped up to the door, looking warily through the peephole.

A young girl stood on the doorstep, her eyes red and puffy from crying. She was maybe twelve or thirteen, and her short summer dress was torn and bloodied. "Can you help me?" she said in a wavering voice.

Jesse instantly reached for the dead bolt. Shadow snarled at him—actually snarled, with the full command of her deep voice and bright teeth—but Jesse didn't even stop to process it. "She needs help," he insisted.

He'd flipped the lock and had one hand on the knob when Shadow lunged forward, knocking him to the side so he sprawled on the floor. She'd stopped barking, but a desperate whine was now coming from the back of her throat. Jesse looked up at her in shock. "Shadow? What is it?"

She planted her feet between him and the entrance, teeth bared toward the door. He had never seen her like this. His cell phone was on the floor near his hand, and Jesse reached for it without thinking.

Before he could dial Scarlett's burner phone, the doorknob above him turned. Shadow lunged at the door, but she was too late this time. A shotgun blast exploded into the sudden quiet, striking Shadow right in the face.

Chapter 4

As soon as we left LA traffic behind, I squeezed my eyes closed. Eleanor may have been pretty, but it wasn't exactly comfortable, on any level. The car—I was refusing to refer to it as "she," no matter what Molly said—didn't have modern shocks or padding or whatever the hell made normal car interiors so cushy, so the ride was very bumpy. And, since Molly was driving, it was also terrifying. She wasn't a *bad* driver, necessarily, but she was sure as hell a reckless one.

Which is probably why it took less than an hour for us to get pulled over. Molly practically giggled when she saw the flashing lights behind her. She pulled to the side of the road and looked at me expectantly.

"Do we really have to do this again?" I said, but my heart wasn't in it. The sooner we got to Boulder, the better.

She held up a hand and snapped her fingers and thumb together like a lobster closing its claw. "You know the drill. Rein it in."

I sighed and pulled my radius in as small as I could, leaning into my door to make sure Molly would be far enough away from me. Even in the dim light from the dashboard and the city, I could actually *see* her change back into a vampire: her cheeks grew rosy and her eyes brighter, and when she tossed her head, perfect blonde curls seemed to float back over her shoulder. She winked at me, and I wondered what the effect of all this must feel like for poor, unsuspecting humans.

The cop was a razor-thin Hispanic man in his early fifties, and he leaned down into Molly's window with an expression devoid of personality. "License and regis . . . oh. Hello." He blinked hard at Molly, who beamed at him.

"Hello, Officer," she purred. "We're traveling on important government business."

I didn't know of any government organizations that traveled by muscle car, but the guy was already gone by then. Molly wasn't the most powerful vampire I'd met, but she was old enough to press a mind *hard*. "Yes, of course," he said, eyes glazed over.

"You will get on the horn to all your friends and let them know our vehicle is in a hurry," Molly went on. "Tell them not to stop us, or make any official record of our presence."

"Yes, ma'am," the officer said eagerly. "Is there anything else I can do for you? Anything at all?"

For a second, I was afraid she was going to mess with him. I'd once seen Molly make a state trooper tap-dance after he called her "honey." The guy was *terrible* at it.

But Molly just smiled at him. "No, I think that will do," she said. "Go now. Make those calls."

The cop scrambled back toward his vehicle. I waited until Eleanor had roared back into traffic before I released my radius back to its normal size. "Just don't kill us," I warned her. "I couldn't take the irony."

Molly scoffed, but she did keep the car below a hundred after that. She asked me a couple of questions about whether I was hungry (no) and if her driving was making the nausea worse (not really). When it was obvious that I needed to sort through my feelings, she went quiet.

Which was good, because my thoughts were still whirling around my head fast enough to make me dizzy. I. Was. Pregnant. I almost burst into giggles, it was all so surreal. *It's gotta be the hormones*, I told myself.

Pregnant women in movies were always blaming things on hormones, right?

Then I caught myself. Pregnant women in movies? That was my point of reference? If I did decide to keep the baby—which I couldn't, because that would obviously be stupid and reckless and irresponsible, not to mention cruel to the child—I would have to read that *Expecting* book, take vitamins, go to the doctor, take birthing classes. Plus buy all that baby gear and figure out a place for the kid to sleep and eat . . .

It was overwhelming. It would have been overwhelming for a normal human woman who didn't have to worry about her baby being in mortal danger from her enemies.

I suddenly felt a great crash of grief for my mom. When I was a teenager and I'd pictured my future, my mom had always been there to help me with my baby. And now my parents were dead. Jameson was dead. I was on my own. Another reason why I had no business keeping it.

"So I have a question," Molly said, breaking me out of my funk. "You know it's going to be morning by the time we get to Boulder, right?"

"Yes." I'd looked up the drive. LA to Boulder was about fourteen hours, though Molly's driving would take a sizable chunk out of that.

"And sunset won't be until seven or eight p.m.," she continued. "Which means we won't be able to see this Maven until nighttime. So what are we going to do all day?"

"I have no idea," I admitted. "Hipster stuff?"

She nodded thoughtfully, as though I'd suggested we attend a reading of Proust followed by high tea. "I bet I could come up with a point system," she mused. "Like, one point for an ironic fedora, two points for a man bun—"

"Your system is already flawed," I said, leaning back and closing my eyes. "At this point I think all fedoras are ironic."

Molly chattered on about Boulder, mainly just to entertain me. Eventually, the rhythm of the car and her comforting voice lulled me to sleep.

"Scarlett. Wake up!"

I sat up with a start, jerking myself out of a tangled dream that was instantly forgotten. Sunlight was streaming into the car through the windshield, warming my skin where it was exposed. "What? What happened? Cops?"

Beside me, Molly smiled. "Nope. The sun rose around six; I had to drop down to the speed limit. Besides, I wanted you to get some sleep."

I blinked, still drowsy. "Oh. Right."

"You told me to wake you up when we got to Idaho Springs," Molly reminded me.

"Yes. That is a thing that I said." Yawning, I checked my watch. It had been a little after ten when we left LA, and we'd stopped twice to get gas—and so I could stagger into gas station bathrooms to pee and/or throw up. Now it was eight thirty in the morning. Damn, Molly drove fast.

I reached down and fumbled on the floor of the car for the burner phone, which had fallen as I slept. Before we'd left, I'd had the presence of mind to program Lex's number into it.

After careful thought, I had decided not to warn Lex we were coming until we had crossed the Colorado state line. I'm a big fan of the "better to ask for forgiveness" thing, and delaying the call would lower the chances of her turning me away. Besides, it wasn't like her boss, Maven, would be on vacation in Belize or something. The Old World is like the Wild West. If you own territory, you damn well better stick around to defend it.

The phone rang several times before I heard Lex's groggy voice say, "Luther."

"Lex, it's Scarlett. I need a favor."

There was a pause, and I could picture her sitting up and rubbing her face. "What the hell, Scarlett? It's morning." Lex worked for a vampire and was dating another vampire. Like me, she was borderline nocturnal.

"I'm sorry, but this can't wait. Can we meet up?"

Another pause, then, cautiously, she said, "You mean, like, in person?" She didn't seem at all surprised that I was calling from an unknown number, or that I didn't want to discuss things over the phone. We lived strange lives.

"Yeah. I'm going to be in Boulder in—" I glanced at Molly, who mouthed an answer. "About an hour."

There was a beat, then: "*Goddammit*, Scarlett! You can't just barge into my town—into *Maven's state*—without permission!" She was practically shouting. At least she was awake now. "What the hell were you thinking?"

I opened my mouth to say, "Man, you're cranky in the morning," but I swallowed it just in time, reminding myself I was about to ask for a favor.

Besides, technically, she was right. "Remember the time you came to LA without going through channels?" I said in a quiet voice.

Lex went silent. Years earlier, she had come to *my* city to find out what had really happened to her twin sister, Samantha. She'd learned the truth—that a rogue werewolf had killed Sam, and that I had destroyed the body as part of my job. She'd been really unhappy with me—okay, that was an understatement; she'd literally punched me in the face—but Jesse and I had gotten her back out of town before Dashiell or anyone else was the wiser.

We had helped partly because Jesse was sort of Lex's friend, and partly because neither of us could blame her for wanting answers. "There are extenuating circumstances this time, too," I said gently. "Personal circumstances."

I hoped that bringing up her trip to LA would help her make the connection I needed: that in this case, *personal* meant *family*.

In the background, I heard what sounded like a dog whining. "Ow. Get down!" Lex ordered, away from the mouthpiece. To me, she finally grumbled, "This better be *so* good. Meet me at Foolish Craig's in two hours."

"Foolish Craig's? Is that a restaurant?" I asked, but of course she'd already hung up. I sighed and looked at Molly.

"I've heard Boulder has really good brunch!" she said brightly.

Chapter 5

When the shotgun blast hit her, Shadow let out a startled yelp and fell back, but Jesse wasn't worried about her. He'd once seen her take a similar injury when she was close to Scarlett, who impaired the bargest's speedy healing.

He and Shadow scrambled to their feet at about the same time, but the door had swung all the way open by then, and the girl stood framed in the doorway.

No, not a girl—a woman. She was slender and wispy, with long, sort of colorless hair, but she was definitely in her twenties. She wore the same beige summer dress, but there was no sign of blood now. She had transformed, and Jesse realized it must have been magic. She hadn't pressed his mind, and werewolves couldn't mess with your brain, so it had to be witch magic.

The woman lifted a hand and wiggled her fingers at Jesse, her smug smile baring crooked teeth. She was obviously unarmed, in the thin dress, which didn't explain the gunshot—or why Shadow was frozen next to him with her feet planted. "What the hell?" Jesse started to say, but then he saw the long barrel of the shotgun move out of the shadows next to the woman. The short, wiry man who appeared behind the gun had the same pale hair as the woman. He was about thirty, and wore jeans and a military-style olive jacket with bulging pockets. The shotgun was braced against his hip, with the muzzle pointed right at Jesse's chest. Shadow had seen the gun before Jesse had. The few tufts of hair on her back stood straight up with anger. Jesse cursed himself for not bringing his own weapon in from the car.

"I do not want to shoot this man," the man said to Shadow. He had a heavy French accent that Jesse recognized from his high school language classes. Jesse still spoke a little French, but they didn't need to know that. "Back up so we may enter." His eyes flicked briefly to Jesse. "Both of you."

Shadow snarled again, a sound that would have made an ordinary man urinate on the spot. But the Frenchman just rolled his eyes and raised the shotgun to his shoulder, pointing the muzzle at Jesse's legs. "Have it your way. I will cripple him first."

Shadow growled and began to step back. Totally lost, Jesse did the same. The man gestured with the shotgun, and Jesse raised his hands. The man stepped close enough to kick Jesse's cell phone away, then retreated to a safe distance.

"What do you want?" Jesse demanded, though he had a sinking feeling that he knew.

"Kneel down," the man ordered.

Jesse slowly knelt down, trying to think of something. Why had he opened the door? Why hadn't he listened to Shadow, goddammit?

"Sabine," the man said, not looking away from the bargest. He knew that Shadow was the true threat here. The wispy woman—Sabine—sort of floated toward him, pulling something out of the back of the man's waistband. When she stepped aside, Jesse saw that she was holding a handgun, her finger resting casually along the trigger guard. That worried him. Most people, Jesse knew, were naturally a little wary of guns. In America, guns were a regular part of life, but that just meant everyone knew to be afraid of them, and treated them like they were practically otherworldly. This attitude usually extended into the Old World, where guns were considered not only alien, but also gauche and unnecessary.

But this witch, as weird as she looked, held the weapon with almost careless comfort, like a veteran cop—which made Jesse's stomach clench with fear.

Who *were* these people?

Sabine circled the man and came around to Jesse's back, carefully staying out of the shotgun's line of fire. Then Jesse heard the click of a safety, inches behind him. He started to turn his head to look at her, but the man ordered, "Stop. Look straight ahead."

To Shadow, he said in French, "What is this man's life worth to you, Belle? If you want him to live, be very still."

Belle?

The first *ping* went off in Jesse's brain, but he didn't have time to think it through before the man pulled something long and silvery from his jacket pocket. In a quick, practiced flick of his wrists, he turned and threw it at Shadow. "Shadow, run!" Jesse yelled, but the bargest just bowed her head as the heavy metal net flared out over her. She seemed resigned, as though it was something that had happened many times before.

That was when Jesse realized who they were. The French, the net, the name *Belle*—these two were part of the Luparii, the witch clan that had originally created Shadow and used her to attack and kill were-wolves. They had come back for her.

Fear gripped him as the man crouched down and pulled a strand connected to the net, cinching it shut around Shadow. She yelped, flipping sideways, and struggled on instinct before forcing herself to go still.

The man squatted down next to Shadow, pulling a capped syringe out of his other pocket. Jesse was taken aback—surely the Luparii witches would know that Shadow's skin was all but impenetrable?

But the man removed the cap and slid the needle into her open mouth, squirting in a liquid. Shadow allowed it—she'd obviously been through this before.

"What is that?" Jesse demanded. "What are you doing to her?" Could a bargest be poisoned? Wouldn't her healing abilities prevent that?

"It is elephant tranquilizer," the man replied, pronouncing it carefully. "No amount will kill her, unfortunately, but enough of it will put her into a deep sleep."

Sure enough, a few seconds later, Shadow's eyes drifted closed. Through the net, her stiff body pressed against Jesse, as if for comfort, and then finally began to relax. She slumped onto the floor.

Jesse's heart sank. He had seen the bargest rip the throats out of vampires. It was horrible, seeing her get taken down by one asshole. And all to save him.

The Frenchman turned to Jesse. "Now, where is Scarlett Bernard? Why did she and the vampire leave without taking their vehicles?"

Jesse blinked. If these guys were here to steal Shadow back, why would they care about Scarlett? "I don't know."

The man scoffed. "You are her best friend. You are watching the bargest for her."

"And I'm human, which makes me vulnerable to spells and vampires," Jesse shot back. "She kept it from me on purpose."

From behind Jesse, the woman finally spoke, in French. "Shall I shoot him now?" She came around to stand next to the man, but kept the gun pointed at Jesse. His knees were beginning to ache. "Perhaps in the shoulder or leg, to make him talk?"

The Frenchman studied Jesse's face. Finally, he shook his head and replied in French. "No, my love. He might be lying, or he may know something else we can use. You must put him in—" And then a phrase Jesse had never heard before: *le sommeil tordu.* He had to work through it for a moment to get the meaning.

The twisted slumber.

The woman pouted. "Killian! You know how it tires me!"

"I know." The man—Killian—checked his watch and answered her in the same language. "But we have time. You can afford the distraction. Besides, retrieving Belle is only half our task. Do you want to tell Grandfather that the null slipped through our fingers?"

Jesse couldn't see the woman's expression, but when she spoke, she sounded subdued. "No. I will do it."

Jesse desperately wished for those witch bags. He was still trying to think of something to convince them to go away when Sabine's pinched face clouded over with a vacant look that creeped him out. She held out her hands toward Jesse and began to chant.

"You don't need to do this . . ." Jesse began, but he couldn't finish the sentence. Something was wrong. His chest felt . . .

He crumpled to the floor.

Chapter 6

Foolish Craig's Cafe was situated right on Pearl Street, which was apparently the main drag of commerce in Boulder. We found street parking a few blocks away, and had to wander through an outdoor mall area packed with various kinds of restaurants, bars, shops, and public art. It reminded me of the Third Street Promenade in Santa Monica: one of the few parts of town that was equally friendly to tourists and locals. Molly stuck close to me, to stay in my radius.

On the inside, Foolish Craig's was a pretty good miniature reflection of Pearl Street, with exposed brick and funky colors. There was also an overall feeling of coordination to it, like the effect had been carefully planned by shrewd developers.

The smell in the restaurant was overpowering. I could tell, intellectually, that it was probably a really nice, breakfasty smell, but it was all I could do not to hurl again. I tried to breathe through my mouth. "You need to get some food in your stomach," Molly advised. "Some crackers or something. It'll help the nausea."

I stared at her. "How do you know?"

She held up her new burner cell phone. "While you were sleeping, I was listening to *What to Expect When You're Expecting*," she declared, looking smug. "The audiobook."

"Oh," was all I managed to say.

The waitress was walking past, so Molly reached out and touched her wrist. "Excuse me, do you have any crackers?"

The young woman gave us an apologetic look. She was about twenty, with green streaks in her hair and one of those cartilage nose piercings that unfortunately reminded me of cows. "I'm sorry! We usually carry organic, gluten-free crackers baked by a local artisan shop, but we're out at the moment."

"Dry toast?" I said weakly.

"Of course!" she chirped. "Wheat, rye, baguette, gluten-free, challah, or twelve-grain?"

I blanched. I hadn't known there were even twelve different grains out there. "Um . . . bread toast?"

When she'd gone back to procure my toast—probably by, I don't know, harvesting the wheat from a field behind the restaurant and crushing it with a mortar and pestle she'd hand-carved out of marble—I looked around the crowded restaurant, deciding it was a minor miracle that we'd managed to hit the right lull to get a table. I'd never been to Boulder before, but everyone looked so . . . healthy. They were chatting and laughing in variations of hiking boots and shorts, practically glowing with wholesome good humor. Nearly every patron had a reusable water bottle in front of them or peeking out of a purse. They were also almost exclusively white.

"Man, I don't get this place," Molly declared. She was studying the people around us with obvious curiosity. "I mean, LA has plenty of rich hippies, but it's like we're stuck inside a commercial for the world's happiest and most expensive summer camp."

"I think it has something to do with the fact that their tans are real," I suggested.

Lex walked in a few minutes later, moving through the restaurant with confidence and purpose, like the soldier she used to be. She was about my height, with reddish-brown hair and blue eyes. Her face was surprisingly youthful, and I realized that she didn't look a day older than when I'd first met her, three years earlier. This probably had to do with her witchblood: boundary witches age *very* slowly. Something about their cells not wanting to die.

She wore jeans and a gray tank top under an unbuttoned flannel shirt, and I could see the cords of muscle on her forearms and shoulders. As she entered my radius, I was amazed, once again, by how powerful she was. Kirsten was easily the most powerful witch in LA, but Lex left even her in the dust.

I half-rose from my chair and waved. She nodded and came over, looking a little irritated. As she got closer and took in my appearance, though, her face blanched. "What happened to you?" she asked me, taking a seat. "You look terrible."

"Hello to you too," I said dryly. "I just got over the flu." The lie came out of my mouth fast and easy . . . but then, covering shit up is what I do for a living.

Lex shrugged, her eyes cutting over to Molly. They'd met a few months earlier, during the Vampire Trials in LA. "I didn't know you were coming along," she said, her voice neutral. "Isn't that . . . kind of dangerous?"

"Because of the sunlight?" Molly said, cheerful as ever. "Nah, Scarlett's got my back. She expands her bubble to make sure I stay human. She's really good at it."

"Huh." Lex looked sort of wistful, and I remembered that last I heard, she still had a vampire boyfriend. I wanted to ask if the two of them spent time around Lex's niece, who was also a null, but I had the feeling that bringing Charlie into the conversation wouldn't go well for me. And besides, it wasn't really any of my business.

The waitress dropped off my toast and wrote down orders: coffee for Lex and a giant stack of pancakes for Molly. When she'd disappeared back to the kitchen, Lex turned to me. "So? What's going on?"

Right. Lex wasn't exactly known for small talk. I pushed out a breath. "I need a favor. I'd like you to get me an audience with Maven. Tonight."

She arched an eyebrow. After a moment, she said in a low voice, "Couldn't your cardinal vampire have set that up?"

"Yeah, well, that's the other part of the favor. I don't want Dashiell to find out we came here."

Lex leaned back in her chair, regarding me. "You know I have to ask you what this is about," she said eventually.

"It really isn't complicated. I have a question about nulls. Maven is very old; therefore, I'm hoping she'll know the answer."

Lex stared me down. "You sneak into Maven's territory to quiz her without your boss knowing, and you think I'm going to buy that this *isn't* complicated?"

"Well . . . yeah."

"What's the question?"

"I'd rather not say."

She didn't roll her eyes, because Lex is too scary for that. Instead, her expression suggested I was on my way to a serious ass-kicking. "You're a null, Scarlett. I would be a complete idiot to put you alone in a room with one of the world's most powerful vampires."

"Look, I don't even need to be close enough to turn her human again. It's just a question."

"Mmm-hmm," she said sarcastically. "Just a question that you drove fifteen hours overnight to ask at the spur of the moment. Presumably because it's too sensitive to discuss over the phone. And you expect me to take your word that you won't turn her human?"

We went silent as the waitress returned with the other orders. Molly, who had been watching our exchange with undisguised interest, gleefully attacked her plate of pancakes and hash browns. Lex took a sip of her coffee and then set it down, temporarily distracted by Molly's obvious enjoyment. She watched her with frank curiosity.

I leaned forward. "Lex . . . come on. This isn't us. I *know* you place as much value on vampire political shit as I do, which is zero units of value. So how about we *don't* do the political negotiation dance, and instead you just ask your boss if I can have five minutes of her time?"

She opened her mouth to answer, but just then her eyes flicked sideways, taking in the woman making her way toward our table. She was in her late thirties, with dark blonde hair and tired brown eyes, and she carried a thick binder with scraps of paper sticking out.

"Oh, shit," Lex muttered under her breath. "My cousin. She's a civilian." She pushed back her chair and stood up. "Hey, Brie," she said as the other woman came over to give her a hug. "What are you doing here?"

"Hey, yourself," the woman replied. "I'm meeting Elise for brunch, so we can do wedding planning." She glanced at us with open curiosity. "I don't think I've met your . . . Army friends?"

"No, they're, um . . ." She started to look panicked, so I stood up, pasting on a smile.

"I'm Scarlett," I said politely, standing up and holding out my hand. "Actually, Lex and I don't know each other too well, but we have a mutual friend in Las Vegas. I was passing through town with my roommate, Molly, on our way to Denver." Molls dutifully stood up and shook hands, too, still chewing a mouthful of pancakes. "We thought we'd spend a day seeing Boulder, and Sashi suggested we get coffee with Lex."

There, that covered all the details, right?

Lex was staring at me, her eyes bugging out a little, but the moment I said the word *Sashi*, her cousin was instantly smiling. "Well, I'm Brie, Lex's cousin. And we all *adore* Sashi. And Grace, of course." Her face brightened, and she looked at her cousin. "Lex, you should invite them to May Birthdays tonight."

"Oh, I don't think—" Lex started, but Molly perked up, swallowing her food.

"What's May Birthdays?" she asked.

"The Luthers get together every few weeks to celebrate the birthdays from that month," Brie explained. "Usually it's the first weekend of the month, but our cousin Jake and his family will be on vacation, so we're doing it a week early. And Grace will be there."

"I'm sure Scarlett and Molly want to explore Boulder—" Lex began, but Molly interrupted again.

"That sounds like fun," she said brightly. "If you're sure we wouldn't be imposing."

Huh? My head swiveled toward her, and I recognized the gleam in Molly's eye. What was she up to?

"Not at all," Brie assured us, her eyes sparkling. "There are always plenty of friends of the family there." She seemed to be suppressing a mischievous smile as she added, "Of course, they're not usually *Lex's* friends . . ."

Lex looked like she was about to argue, but Brie turned to her and said, "Are you bringing Quinn too? Or does he still have that weird work schedule?"

Lex looked at me, and we had a perfect mind-meld moment. I nodded at her, and a tiny, unguarded smile broke over her face. Probably the first one I'd seen from her. "Yeah," she said to Brie. "Yeah, he's coming."

"Great. Five thirty at your mom and dad's," Brie reminded Lex. "Don't forget this time."

"I won't."

Brie waved and went off to a table near the window. Lex perched on the edge of her chair. "I should go before my other cousin gets here," she said, taking a final sip of coffee and putting it down. "She's a cop; she'll have lots of questions." She hesitated for a second, looking at me. "You'll really wake Quinn up to come with us?"

"If you're sure he won't mind," I said. "Most vampires flip out when I wake them without express permission."

The same tiny smile. "Quinn isn't most vampires."

"And Maven?" I pushed.

The smile faded. "I'll leave word at the coffee shop. She'll get it when she wakes up. But even if she agrees, I need to be in the room. That's nonnegotiable."

I chewed on my lip for a second, but when Lex said "nonnegotiable," she meant it. We were going to have to trust her. I nodded.

"I'll text my address to your new number. Quinn's there now. Come around five." She turned to go, then paused and looked back over her shoulder. "Stay out of trouble today." The phrase *This is* my *town* was clearly implied.

"Oh, we will," Molly said cheerfully.

When she was gone, I turned to Molly. "What was that about? Why do you want to go to a family party for a family you don't even know?"

Molly rolled her eyes. "Come on, don't tell me you're not curious about Lex's life. And I want to meet the baby null. Besides, we've got time to kill before sunset."

"These points are not bad points," I admitted. It *would* be interesting to see Lex in her natural habitat. And if enabling Quinn to attend the party ingratiated me to her a little, that couldn't hurt my case later. "Okay. Family party it is."

Chapter 7

When Jesse Cruz opened his eyes again, he was lying on the floor of an LAPD evidence room.

That's what it looked like, anyway. He didn't recognize the specific lockup—the LAPD had twenty-one separate division stations, and he'd only visited a handful of them—but there were metal shelves surrounding him on every side, and they were loaded down with overflowing boxes, each one stamped with the official LAPD seal.

How the hell could the Luparii witches have gotten him this deep inside an evidence room? Were they capable of teleportation?

Jesse sat up slowly, checking himself for injuries. His mouth was dry and his head ached, but otherwise he felt okay. He reached for his phone, but it wasn't in his pocket. How long had he been out? He checked his watch, but that was gone, too, along with his wallet.

He stood up, intending to find his way out of there, or at least someone who could help him. The Luparii had taken Shadow, and Scarlett needed him. Jesse had no idea what he was going to say to whatever cops he found, but he couldn't just sit around waiting for everything to resolve itself. "Hello?" he called. "Can I get some help?"

There was no response, and nothing for Jesse to do but start walking. Which way was the exit, though? The room was dimly lit, and the shelves seemed to stretch on endlessly. He squinted in either direction, picked one, and started walking.

He only passed a few of the shelves before realizing that something was very wrong. It was too quiet, for one thing—evidence rooms weren't usually soundproofed, and he should have been able to hear the endless bustle of one of the busiest police forces in the world. But after he noticed this, he began to realize that other details were off, too. None of the boxes had lids, and there were no case numbers written on the sides. He stopped and pulled out a box, peering inside to see a Glock and an older-model cell phone. They were open to the elements, not even wrapped in plastic. Jesse reached in and touched the phone. It crumbled in his hand, turning into a chunky dust that somehow left his fingers greasy. He tried the gun next, but the same thing happened. Jesse pushed that box aside, wiped his hands on his jeans, and reached for the box next to it. This one held textbooks and clothes, the kind of stuff Jesse himself had owned as a high school student. He reached for them anyway, but everything crumbled again.

When he turned back, the first box was in its original position, with the intact gun and cell phone sitting in their original spots.

Jesse paused. Was he losing it? Had someone replaced the box with magic? He was really starting to wish he'd kept some of Kirsten's witch bags close at hand. "Hello?" he called again. "Who's out there?"

If this had been a movie, he would have heard a sudden malicious giggle, but there was nothing but empty silence that seemed to go on forever. How big *was* this room?

Jesse reached for the cell phone again. This time his fingers went right through it, like it was a ghost—or *he* was. His fingers felt cold where they touched the non-phone, and he jerked his hand back. "Nothing is real," he muttered to himself. He tried touching the shelf itself, wondering if he could walk through the damn thing, but no, of course *that* had structure.

With no better ideas, Jesse resumed walking. It was a little ridiculous, but the lidless boxes were making him more edgy than anything else. Jesse had spent years having proper procedure drilled into him, and the sight of open evidence boxes was jangling his nerves, like seeing someone chain-smoking inside an elementary school. It was just *wrong*.

Every now and then he pulled out boxes and tried to grab whatever was inside, just for the hell of it: key chains, old trophies, children's toys, ticket stubs. Everything disintegrated.

Next, he tried leaving boxes out to mark his path, but every time he looked away and then back again, they were gone.

He walked and walked, sticking to a straight line so he wouldn't risk going in circles, but the aisle he was in simply didn't end. He was thirsty, and his empty stomach rumbled, but there was nothing to eat except cardboard boxes, and Jesse had a feeling even that wouldn't work.

After what felt like hours of this strange limbo, he caught movement out of the corner of his eye. A woman was curled up on the waist-high shelf, arms around her knees, watching him placidly.

Jesse jumped. "Jesus!"

She smiled at him, twisting sideways and unfolding her limbs like a giant insect. She stood up and tossed back her colorless hair, and Jesse realized it was the Luparii witch, Sabine. "You!" he said, darting forward to grab her. "Where—"

But his hand passed right through her frail-looking arm. "Hello, Jesse," she said with a smirk. "Welcome to the twisted slumber."

"You can speak English," he said, the first thought that came to his mind. She didn't even have an accent.

But Sabine shook her head. "I control this space. If I want you to understand me in your dream, you will."

"This isn't a *dream*," he scoffed. "I feel hunger, thirst." Lightly, he smacked the back of his hand against a shelf, getting a quick flare of pain in response. "I can even get hurt."

"This isn't a *normal* dream, no. This is one that I twisted for you, using a piece of my magic. You should feel special. I don't do this spell for just anyone."

"Seriously?" He crossed his arms over his chest. "And *this* is your best shot at me? Miles of shelves? Wow. You sure showed me."

Her smile just widened. She stepped closer to him, seeming to grow taller with each step, until she didn't have to look up to meet his eyes. "Ah, but the tedium is the whole point. You're a man of action, but here there's nothing for you to do." She spread her arms, indicating the endless rows. "There are no dragons to slay—or vampires, for that matter. And no way to get yourself out. You can walk, or run, or climb the shelves. You can lay down and wait to die. It doesn't matter. *Nothing you do will matter.*"

Jesse felt it then: the hopelessness, the futility. Despite his bravado, his shoulders slumped. "*Why?* Why are you doing this to me?"

"Where is Scarlett Bernard?"

"I. Don't. Know," he said, enunciating each word.

She studied him for another moment, then sighed. "You are telling the truth. That is unfortunate. But we will see if you have other information we can use. Killian has some ideas."

They could get information from him? That meant Jesse had to be careful. He imagined building a wall to block off the most recent information he'd received about Scarlett. He didn't even let himself think about what it was.

"What do you want from Scarlett?" he said to the woman. "You've got Shadow."

Sabine hesitated for a moment, then shrugged, as if realizing it didn't matter what she told Jesse at this point. "Los Angeles needs to be taught a lesson," she said calmly. "Taking back our bargest isn't enough. Don't worry, you'll be dead very soon. It won't matter for you."

Well, that wasn't going to get him anywhere. Jesse thought of Killian's earlier questions. "You were tracking Scarlett's van, and Molly's car."

The corners of Sabine's lips turned down in a "whatever" expression. "To her credit, she has become good at examining her vehicle for tracking devices. But we are better."

"And yet she left town without you knowing."

Sabine bared her teeth. "She'll come back. Especially if someone finds your body."

Fear threatened to overwhelm him then, but he wasn't going to let himself freak out in front of this witch. "So you're going to kill me."

She edged even closer to him, and Jesse could feel her hot breath on his face. How could this *possibly* be a dream? "I am killing you now. The twisted slumber is a fever dream, emphasis on the *fever*. Even now, your body temperature is rising past what a human being can survive. A day, maybe two, and your organs will begin to shut down from dehydration." She clucked her tongue. "So sad. But the null will return when she learns you're missing, and we will be waiting for her. There is enough time."

"That makes it sound like you're in a hurry," Jesse guessed. "Why? What's coming?"

This time Sabine frowned. As quickly as she had appeared, she blinked away again.

Interesting. But now he was alone, with infinite miles of shelves on all sides. Nothing to do, nowhere to go, just like Sabine had said.

Jesse felt panic rising in his chest, and he resolutely began to walk again, trying to think this through. The Luparii wanted Scarlett, obviously, but why? There were plenty of horrible things you could do with a null, including assassinating powerful vampires. But if all they wanted was to kidnap Scarlett and take her back to France, they could have done that anytime. Scarlett didn't take Shadow *everywhere*; there would have been opportunities to snatch her away.

And the same went for killing Scarlett. If they'd been tracking her, they'd been watching for long enough to just shoot her when no one expected it. No, timing was definitely a factor here . . . which made it likely that Killian and Sabine had been watching in anticipation of something: a signal, maybe, or a certain date. Scarlett had thrown them off by skipping town.

His thoughts kept going in circles, although they seemed to end up in the same place: was his body really dying? He certainly wouldn't put it past Sabine to lie to him, but he *was* thirsty and hungry . . . it was worrisome. On the other hand, if he was dying anyway, why hadn't they just shot him?

Killian had specifically mentioned wanting to know more about Jesse. But how would the fake LAPD station help them learn about him? Unless . . .

He grabbed the closest box and looked inside. To his surprise, the top layer was hardcover copies of *Wunderkind*, the nonfiction book he'd co-written. Jesse hadn't been able to interact with the contents of the boxes, so he didn't bother touching the book itself. Instead, he tipped the entire box sideways onto the floor. Many more copies of the book spilled out, along with a small gold band. A wedding ring. Jesse crouched down for a closer look. It was *his* wedding ring, from his brief marriage to the book's ghostwriter.

It was like a fog clearing. The textbooks *were* his textbooks. The Glock was his first gun, and the ticket stubs were from concerts he'd seen.

He looked in another box, and this one held plastic claws and giant wolf paws made from plaster. This was the evidence he'd planted to frame the Luparii witch for Henry Remus's murder.

Excited, he grabbed at the next box—the charred remains of a human body, with a silver Rolex still clinging to the wrist. Lex's sister, Sam, whom he'd helped Scarlett cremate. The faint stink of charred flesh was still rising from it.

Jesse yanked his hand back from the box, looking around him. This wasn't just his deep history, at least not anymore.

These were his sins.

Jesse looked up at the mundane ceiling, raising his voice. "This isn't a dream," he accused. "It's a raid. You're going through my memories. What are you looking for?"

There was no answer. Of course.

Chapter 8

Molly and I spent the afternoon exploring Boulder, which was kind of a cool little town once you got past its intense and all-encompassing animosity toward gluten. Molly quizzed the restaurant hostess on the best places to visit, and an hour later we were boarding a converted school bus for Banjo Billy's Bus Tour, which was much less cheesy than the name implies. We got a pretty good overview of the town's history, and by the time the bus returned, Molly knew exactly where she wanted to go next. She dragged me up and down Pearl Street, into shops that ran the gamut from quirky kitchen supplies to extreme-sports gear.

The whole time, Molly kept forcing small amounts of bland food on me, and I had to admit, it helped: the nausea abated enough for us to get a big lunch at a taco place, where I made Molly move outside so they wouldn't kick us out from her moans of ecstasy. The food *was* pretty good. In the early afternoon, I tried to check in with Jesse, but he didn't answer either his phone or the Batphone. I frowned and checked my watch. Could he be napping? Or maybe he took Shadow for a run? I made a mental note to try again later. And we were off to another store.

I may have complained a little—okay, a lot—about the shopping, but it really was nice to spend a few hours on just another weird shopping adventure with Molly. I stopped thinking about the pregnancy and just enjoyed myself.

And then it was time to go meet Lex's vampire boyfriend.

She lived well outside the Boulder city limits, in a little cabin in the middle of nowhere. It was neat and unadorned, at least on the outside. I suspected the lack of decoration was more Lex being guarded than Lex being boring.

As soon as Molly and I climbed out of Eleanor, I could hear the barking of what sounded like an entire pack of dogs. She and I exchanged a look and shrugged.

"Nice house," Molly commented, knocking on the door. "Can you feel the boyfriend yet?"

"That would be impolite," I informed her. I was reining in my radius a bit so I wouldn't turn the boyfriend—Quinn—human until Lex was ready.

She opened the door, looking a little breathless. Her hair was loose and slightly damp, and she'd changed into nice jeans and a long black top that was pulled in at her waist with straps that tied around the back. She'd even put on a little makeup. It was probably the most dressed up I'd ever seen her. "I should have asked if you were okay with animals," she shouted over the barking, but Molly and I had both already crouched down to greet the four dogs, which included a couple of Lab mixes, a tiny and sort of vacant-looking Yorkie, and a slightly calmer mixed breed who hung back a little, protecting his mistress. That was what I noticed, anyway, before one of the Labs knocked me over so he could better reach my face for licking. I lost my grip on my radius, but wherever Quinn was, it wasn't close enough for me to turn him human yet.

"Cody!" Lex admonished, looking scandalized, but I laughed, rolling away and climbing to my feet. "I'm sorry," Lex said, and she actually looked kind of guilty. "They're a little . . . exuberant. They don't meet new people very often. Come on in."

When they realized we were coming inside, where they would have even better access to us, the dogs calmed down and trotted happily alongside us as Lex led the way to a large, high-ceilinged space that served as a combination dining room and living room.

Lex turned around, looking at me a little nervously. It was strange to see her look uncertain. "So . . . how does this work?"

"I'm kind of assuming Quinn has been around your niece before?" I asked.

She nodded. "Usually just at evening family functions, though, when it's natural for them to be together. We keep it as normal as possible. I don't ever want Charlie thinking we only love her for what she can do for Quinn."

It was a good attitude. I cleared my throat. "Okay, well, if he knows what a null feels like, this should be pretty simple." I pointed to a couch. "Molly and I will sit here, and you can go be physically near him. I'll expand my radius, and when he wakes up, you can explain what's going on. Take whatever time you need."

Lex was wringing her hands. "And you're sure he'll be okay?" She glanced at Molly, then back to me. "I mean, I know you've done this before, but can you really keep more than one vampire in your radius at a time, during the day?"

I blinked, surprised. "You . . . don't know a whole lot about nulls, huh?"

She started to look defensive, and I shook my head. "Sorry, forget that. If you're used to witch magic, and Charlie's a little kid, I can see where this would be confusing. Look, neutralizing magic doesn't affect me. It can't tire me out, and as long as they stay within my radius, there's no limit to the number of people I can . . ." I flapped a hand, looking for the right word. "Nullify, I guess. Like Molly said earlier, I can expand my radius to keep both of them in it. The only way Quinn could get hurt is if he, like, took off at a dead sprint when my back was turned, so I didn't know to widen my area."

Lex nodded, looking pacified. "Okay. Let's do this." She disappeared down a hallway, and I heard a door open and close, probably to the basement. I counted to ten before pushing out my radius until I could feel a second vampire. He was below us, deeper into the house. Some kind of basement hidey-hole, probably.

Ten minutes went by, and then I heard footsteps on the stairs.

Lex emerged, trailed by a tall vampire who looked to be in his late thirties, wearing worn-looking jeans and a fitted gray tee shirt. He was handsome, with blond hair and the kind of craggy face that would age well—if, that is, he could age. He started over to us, hand outstretched, but got distracted by the sunshine pouring in through the window behind me. "*Whoa,*" he breathed.

Molly grinned, jumping up from her chair. "I know, right? Hi, I'm Molly."

"Quinn," the man said absently. He had stopped just short of where the sunbeam hit the floor. Lex hung back, watching him with a little smile. Quinn looked over at me. "And you're Scarlett. Can I . . ."

I waved him on. "Go ahead. It can't hurt you."

Impulsively, he turned and grabbed Lex's hand, pulling her with him into the sunlight. She put her arms around his neck, laughing, and I looked away, feeling an ache in the pit of my stomach. They were so obviously in love. Molly reached over and squeezed my hand.

"So," Quinn said, turning so Lex's back rested against his chest. His arms were still wrapped around her. "I hear there's a party."

Chapter 9

Half an hour later, the four of us were climbing out of Lex's Subaru in front of a very large house in a very nice neighborhood. I didn't know anything about architectural styles or whatever, but it was brick and there were arches and Molly muttered the word *tony*, so I figured Lex's parents were rich. That was interesting. She had never given off a "spoiled rich kid" vibe.

Molly and I let Lex lead us in, and she gave me a wink over her shoulder. Okay, she had been right: this was fascinating.

Inside, the noise hit me first, followed by the food smells. We went through a small foyer into a huge dining/kitchen area, where dozens of people were milling around, talking and laughing. As the door closed behind us, the number of people in the room instantly made me nervous. I wasn't claustrophobic, but I hadn't grown up with any extended family around. Even when my parents were alive, there were never more than four Bernards in a room. This was taking "family birthday party" to a level I hadn't experienced.

The Luthers all had that fresh-faced look I had learned to associate with Boulder, and even if I hadn't known that many of them were related, I probably could have guessed by their similar features: honey-blonde hair, brown eyes, high cheekbones. It was like walking into a commercial for multivitamins. It made me want to drink a gallon of diet soda and eat a whole gas station pizza.

A couple of them looked up as we came in, waved, and went back to talking. An older woman with silver hair and a stout figure came bustling over to hug Lex. "Hi, honey. Oh, Quinn, you made it. That's wonderful." She smiled up at him, and then her eyes turned to Molly and me. "And you must be Sashi's friends. I'm Lex's mom, Christy."

Molly nudged me, and I stepped forward to shake hands and introduce myself.

Lex got pulled into a conversation with a short-haired woman, but before I could even feel uncertain of myself, Christy Luther reached out and snagged the arm of a passing girl holding a loaded appetizer plate. She was college age, with olive skin, thick dark hair, and Sashi's features. I felt a jolt of recognition. She might have looked like her mother, but the confident stance and capable broad shoulders—those were purely from her father.

From Will.

Not many people knew that Will Carling, the alpha werewolf of Los Angeles, had a daughter. In fact, I was pretty sure Will himself didn't know. I'd only stumbled onto the secret by mistake, and now I felt myself gaping at her.

"Oh, have you already met Grace?" Christy said. "She goes to CU, and she's an honorary Luther."

The girl turned toward us, her expression friendly and open, but held up a finger as she finished chewing something. "Sorry," she said after swallowing, laughing at herself a little. "Hi, I'm Grace."

The laugh was eerily familiar. I wasn't imagining that: out of the corner of my eye, I saw Molly's eyes narrow slightly, her head tilting a little. She looked like she was trying to remember the name of a song stuck in her head. "Hi!" I said, way too loudly. I cleared my throat and shook the girl's hand. "I mean, it's nice to meet you."

"This is Scarlett and Molly," Christy went on. "Scarlett is friends with your mom." Her voice was gentle, but Grace's face instantly froze over, and she took her hand back without shaking Molly's.

"Oh," she said coolly. "How do you know Sashi?"

Whoa. Calling her mother by her first name? "Through mutual friends," I said noncommittally. "I was just at your house a few weeks ago, in Las Vegas. She has pictures of you everywhere."

"Yeah. Well." The girl looked down at her plate, which still had a pile of chips and salsa. "Excuse me, I think I need more salsa."

After she'd departed, Christy sighed. "I'm sorry about that. I was hoping drawing her into a conversation about her mom might help."

"They're . . . estranged?" I asked. I didn't want to blow my "friends with Sashi" cover, but I couldn't help myself. "Sashi didn't mention anything."

"No, she wouldn't," Christy said wryly. "Sashi and my former son-in-law, John, dated for a few years, but it didn't work out. Grace took the breakup hard."

"Oh," I said stupidly, as pieces of information fell into place. When I was in Vegas, Sashi had told me she'd tried—and failed—to move on from Will. Grace Brighton wasn't a witch, which meant Sashi had also kept that part of her life away from her daughter.

Jesus. I knew more about these people than they did.

The conversation moved on. Christy introduced us to several other people, but even as I shook hands, I knew I had no hope of remembering all their names. I did take note of John, Lex's brother-in-law and Charlie's dad. He was . . . noteworthy. Very handsome, with bronze Native American coloring and an easy, likable demeanor that made me inwardly cringe with guilt. He was friendly enough, asking questions about the places we'd visited in Boulder, but I had trouble concentrating on the conversation. In the back of my mind, I couldn't stop seeing his wife's dead body as it went into the furnace.

Suddenly this wasn't so fun.

Molly, who'd been quietly working her way through a plate of food, saw the look on my face after John excused himself. She knew what I'd done to Samantha Wheaton's corpse, and reached out to squeeze my hand. I shot her a smile, but I was a little rattled at the emotional overload. Goddamned baby hormones.

After introductions, Christy encouraged us to go get food, and I was grateful for the excuse to get away. As we approached the buffet table, however, the smell of cooked meat hit me wrong. Molly saw the look on my face and winced. "Bathroom?" she asked in a low voice. I nodded, struggling to keep down the contents of my stomach. "Go. I'll cover for you."

Panicked, I wove my way through the crowd toward the nearest hallway. There were several closed doors, but one of them was standing open, and I could see a tiled floor and a toilet. I beelined toward it, not even pausing to flick on the light. I practically dove for the toilet.

I don't know how much time passed while I was throwing up, but after a while the light snapped on, and I blearily lifted my head, expecting to see Molly. Instead, a Native American woman with a long gray braid was scowling at me with her hands on her hips, as though I'd burst in on *her* in the bathroom and not the other way around. "You could at least close the door if you're gonna do that," she snapped. "Or do you get off on people walking in on you puking?"

I fell back on my butt. The vomiting was done, I thought, but I didn't have the strength to get up yet. The older woman closed the bathroom door and practically stomped over to the toilet. She "hmphed" and hit the flush lever, then unceremoniously lifted her dress and plopped down to urinate. I scooted away, embarrassed.

She snorted. "Oh, sure, you're happy to let the whole world see you puke, but one old woman peeing is an outrage." She was probably only in her late fifties, and moved like she was ready to play college football, so the "old woman" thing was just perturbing. "How far along are you?" she demanded.

I looked back, surprised. "What?"

"How far along?" she repeated. "Six, eight weeks?"

"I don't know."

She stood up, flushed the toilet, and went to the sink. "You don't even know how far along you are?" she said scornfully.

Okay, she was starting to piss me off. And it was only then, when I stopped thinking about the nausea and really focused on her, that I realized the woman was registering in my radius. She was a witch, but there was something weird about her magic. It was *extremely* faint. In fact, I'd have guessed it was just dormant witchblood, except I can't feel that at all.

"You girls these days," she groused to herself, scrubbing her hands with expensive-looking lavender soap. "Half of you act like no one in the world has ever had a baby before you, and the other half tries to pretend like nothing is happening."

That was enough. Using the tub for support, I climbed to my feet, glaring at her. "Listen up, *old woman*. I'm sorry I startled you, but you're *obviously* not in a position to lecture me about etiquette, and I don't owe you any personal details about my life. Back the fuck off."

For the first time, a tiny smile appeared on the woman's creased face. She wiped her hands on a towel and thrust the right one at me. "I'm Blossom," she said. "John's mother."

"Scarlett." I shook her hand.

"You want me to get your partner for you?" she asked, nodding at the door.

I was confused for a second, then got it. "Molly? Oh, uh, no. She's just my friend."

"Is your baby daddy here?" She looked pointedly at my stomach.

"He's dead," I said flatly.

"Oh." She leaned back against the counter, looking . . . well, not contrite, exactly, but thoughtful.

"Is there anything else I can help you with?" I said sarcastically. "Perhaps you'd like to discuss my history with yeast infections, or the times I've been groped on public transportation. My parents were murdered; wanna talk about that?"

Now the old lady grinned at me approvingly. "I like you," she said. "The rest of these white people are scared of me. But you push back."

I went to the sink and rinsed out my mouth. "The old witch likes me," I muttered. "Lucky me."

I turned toward the door, but Blossom stepped in front of it, looking wary. "Why'd you call me that?"

"Old?" I asked, just to be a dick.

She waved a hand. "The other thing."

I lowered my voice. "Because you've got witchblood." I watched her face for recognition—and got it. "You don't practice magic, and you haven't for a very long time. But you activated it, when you were a girl. It's still inside you."

The woman's mouth dropped open. "How do you know that?"

Shit. I'd opened my big mouth to show off, and now I was stuck. This woman already knew I was pregnant; if she found out I was a null too . . .

I took a leap. "Sam told me," I said at last. "I knew her in LA."

Blossom's face slowly relaxed, although she still looked wary. "I didn't think she knew." When I didn't say anything else, she shook her head. "John must have told her." Suddenly anxious, she met my eyes. "You won't tell anyone?"

"If you don't mention that I'm pregnant," I said sweetly.

That approving grin again. "Deal." Blossom stepped away from the door, waving me on. "Go get some crackers or something." I sidled around her and escaped through the door.

What was it with everyone and the damned crackers?

Chapter 10

When I went back into the hallway, I felt a familiar sensation in my radius, sort of like light being bent through a crystal. I turned around just as a line of children stampeded through the room, laughing as they knocked into grown-ups and furniture. "Charlie!" Lex called, a little stern. "Come here, please."

A small girl near the back peeled off from the group and turned to face us, pushing long, dark hair out of her face. My breath caught. She was probably around four, wearing a green sundress and Chuck Taylor sneakers spattered with paint in primary colors. She gazed up at Lex with bright blue eyes. Except for the darker hair and olive skin, she could have been Lex's younger clone.

Then the little girl frowned, tilting her head sideways as her eyes took in the rest of us. "Hi, Auntie," she said, drawing closer. Her eyes landed on Molly, widening with interest. "Hey, you're different. Like Uncle Quinn."

"Charlie, this is Miss Molly," Lex said. Molly held out a hand for the girl to shake. Charlie took it, looking amused at the adult ritual. "And this is Miss Scarlett," Lex said, pointing at me.

For the first time, the girl turned all her attention to me. "You're pretty," she said.

I blinked. "Thank you. I think you're very pretty, too." Wait, that was wrong, wasn't it? I'd read somewhere that we were supposed to praise little girls for their accomplishments, not their looks. Goddammit, I'd messed this up already.

Charlie was still studying me. I felt incredibly awkward, like everyone in the whole room must be staring at my embarrassing attempts to connect with a child, but really it was only Lex and Molly.

The little girl grabbed my hand and tugged down. Obediently, I knelt on the floor in front of her, Lex hovering anxiously over us. Charlie's face screwed up with concentration, and she pushed hair away from my face and leaned toward me so she could whisper in my ear. "Why do you feel different?"

"Because I'm like you," I said quietly. "Those feelings you get around certain people? I get them, too."

Charlie looked startled and glanced up at her aunt. "My daddy says I'm not supposed to talk about them," she said, just loud enough for Lex to hear.

"It's okay, Charlie," Lex assured her. "It's safe to trust Miss Scarlett."

The little girl studied her aunt for a moment, as if she thought Lex might be testing her. Then she shrugged and turned back to me.

"*Why* do we get them?" she asked.

I glanced up at Lex, who was chewing on her lower lip as she watched us. Until she was older, it wasn't safe for Charlie to know about the Old World—she wouldn't understand that she needed to keep it a secret, which could put her friends or family in danger. "Because we're very special," I told Charlie. "When you get older, you'll learn more about what those feelings mean."

Her face brightened. "'Cause you'll teach me?"

There was suddenly a lump in my throat. Stupid hormones. Lex started to say something, to make an excuse for me, but I said to Charlie, "It might be me, or it might be your aunt Lex."

With no further ado, Charlie climbed into my lap, her tanned arms loose around my shoulders. I held very still, like a butterfly had just landed on my arm. Small hands picked up a strand of my hair and began twisting and curling it around her finger. "Auntie Lex feels different too," Charlie confided, low enough so Lex couldn't hear.

I nodded. "She's very strong."

"'Cause she was a soldier."

Well . . . close enough. "Right."

"When I grow up, I might be a soldier, too," Charlie went on. "But I'm definitely gonna be a paleontologist. And have a lemonade stand. And I'll ride horses and have six dogs. That's more than Aunt Lex has, but she has cats, too." She wrinkled her nose. "I don't like cats."

"Me either," I told her. Nearby, Lex's phone buzzed, and she stepped a few feet away to answer it.

Molly was still watching Charlie and me, looking amused. I tried to think of something else to say. "I have a dog too," I finally offered. "Her name is Shadow. She's really big."

"And really ugly," Molly added.

I glared up at her, but she just lifted an eyebrow to say, *Well, she is.*

"Can I see a picture on your phone?" Charlie asked me eagerly.

I started to reach for the phone in my pocket, but remembered it was the burner. "I don't have any on my phone right now," I told her regretfully.

"Oh." She looked at me with disappointment and judgment. Ah. So there was some of her aunt in her too.

Luckily, at that moment Lex hung up the phone and turned back to us. "We're on," she said to me. "She's expecting you."

I nodded. "Charlie," Lex said, "Miss Scarlett and I need to leave now."

Charlie looked up with obvious displeasure, squeezing the strands of my hair closer, like she was protecting them. "But she's like me!"

"I know. We still need to leave, though. Besides, it's almost your bedtime."

Charlie pouted, but turned back to me. "Do you have FaceTime?" she demanded.

That threw me for a second. I hadn't realized four-year-olds were aware of FaceTime. But then again, what the hell did I know about kids? "Um, yes. I do."

"So we'll talk on FaceTime," Charlie decided. "That's what I do with Gramma Blossom, or with Auntie when she has to be gone for days."

"Okay," I said, bewildered. "We can FaceTime."

"Then you can go, I guess." Charlie released her death grip on my hair and climbed out of my lap. "Bye!" she yelled over her shoulder, racing off to find the rest of the kids.

I blinked. What had just happened?

Molly was grinning as she held out a hand to me. "So that was Charlie," Lex said, with a smile I hadn't seen from her before. It was proud and a little embarrassed and sort of fierce. Like a mom. "She's kind of a force of nature," Lex added.

"Yeah." I used Molly's hand to pull myself up. "I'm getting that."

The sun had gone down while we were at dinner. Lex drove us back to the Pearl Street Mall area, parking near a funny little coffee shop with a weird setup. Most of the coffee shops I'd been to shared the same basic layout—one big room with a counter somewhere—but the front doors at Magic Beans opened into a short hallway with multiple doors leading off in different directions. There were Day-Glo arrows painted on the floor that eventually led us toward a counter, where a bored-looking teenage boy looked up from a textbook. "Oh. Hey, Lex, hey, Quinn," he said.

"Is Maven around?" Lex asked.

"She's waiting for you in the back," he replied. "Do you guys want coffee?"

"Sure," Lex said, looking at Molly and me. We both nodded.

"Make it four," Quinn said, looking suddenly enthusiastic.

"Whoa, Mr. Quinn drinking the coffee. Crazy," the kid said in a monotone, and I suddenly remembered that marijuana was legal in Colorado.

He handed out the full cups, and Quinn took a couple of sips, looking fascinated. "Huh," he said, wrinkling his nose. "I don't remember it being so . . . gross."

"You get used to it," I told him.

He put the cup down on the counter. "Or not."

"Ready?" Lex asked me.

I nodded and she looked at Molly. "Wait here, please. Just as a security thing."

Molly rolled her eyes, but gave Lex a little salute. "I'll stay out here, too," Quinn said, locking eyes with Lex. "Give you guys some privacy."

I pulled in my radius as we entered a large room with a concrete floor and a small stage. Folding chairs were set out around a card table, and a young woman was perched on a chair with one foot folded under her. Maven was very young-looking, with a fashion sense I would describe as eclectic, if I needed to be polite: she wore a baggy denim dress that hung to the floor, along with huge, eighties-style glasses that somehow clashed with her bright orange hair. And she had layers and layers of cheap costume jewelry that reminded me of Mardi Gras beads.

Lex introduced me, and Maven gestured for us to sit. I took the seat farthest from her so I could keep her out of my cinched-in radius.

"Thank you for meeting with me," I said formally.

She smiled. "You certainly piqued my interest," she said, her diction completely at odds with her appearance. She sounded like people in old movies, with that fancy, mid-Atlantic kind of accent. She waved at me. "It's all right—you can release it. I wouldn't mind being human for a little while."

Surprised, I released my grip on my radius. Maven gasped, clutching at her chest as her heart started beating and her lungs struggled with the sudden need for air. Vampires usually do those things anyway, to blend in and to speak, but they don't *have* to devote energy to it, any more than I *have* to devote energy to walking on my tiptoes.

So Maven's shocked reaction was typical of most vampires, but for once, I was equally floored. When a vampire is in my radius, I get a vague sense of their power and age. Dashiell was powerful, but not very old. Molly had average power, average age. Quinn was young, and a little stronger than most vampires his age.

But *this* woman . . . "Holy shit," I breathed out, feeling the sudden compulsion to stand up and curtsy. She really was the oldest vampire I'd ever felt, at least a thousand years old. *A thousand years old.*

And she had every bit of power those years afforded.

Chapter 11

There was a long silence. Lex perched on the edge of her seat, looking back and forth between us like she didn't know who to protect from whom. It would have been funny if I wasn't so gobsmacked. Wait, had I really just used the word *gobsmacked?*

"It's okay," Maven gasped, smiling at Lex. "We just need a moment."

After a few minutes, we were both more or less recovered, although I now had a thousand questions. This woman was powerful as *hell.* What was she doing in Boulder, Colorado? She could literally be running the world.

Stay on task, Scarlett. I took a sip of my coffee, and Maven's nostrils flared.

"May I?" she said hopefully.

"Um, yeah. Of course." I slid the cup over to her, and she took a tiny sip, looking intensely thoughtful.

"Hmm," she said, nodding her head a little. "I usually keep a cup lying around as though it's mine, but I've never actually tasted this stuff."

"Have you been around nulls before?" I asked, hoping the answer was yes. She wouldn't be much help to me if I was the first null she'd encountered in all that time.

"Yes, but it's been decades, and coffee wasn't what it is now. Lex," she said, turning to face the boundary witch. "Can you go get me a frappe . . . and an espresso, and maybe some of those scones we just baked?"

Lex paused, looking wary, and I couldn't entirely blame her. Her one job here was to protect Maven, which she couldn't do from another room. She sort of trusted me, but leaving Maven unguarded with a null went against all her instincts. "I don't think—"

"It's okay," I reassured her. I trusted Lex. And now that I'd met Charlie . . . well, whatever Maven told me was going to apply to her too someday. To Maven, I said, "My friend Molly is waiting outside. Why don't I text her to bring it in?" Lex shot me a grateful look.

After the text was sent, Maven raised her eyebrows at me. "So. What was it you needed to ask me?"

I took a deep breath. "Okay. I don't know very much about the history of nulls. Dashiell, my cardinal vampire, is relatively young. Most of the leadership in LA is young." This was common knowledge, and Maven nodded, gesturing for me to continue. "Everything I've ever heard, however, suggests that nulls can't have kids. I want to know if that's true." I had a further explanation ready—the thing about a boyfriend who wanted to have kids someday—but I decided to keep it as simple as possible.

"Ah." Maven sat back in her chair, regarding me. I tried not to squirm.

"You're pregnant," she said softly.

I winced, and Lex's gaze shot toward me, her eyes widening.

Before I could answer, Molly walked into the room carrying a small round tray of beverages and scones. Her path brought her straight into my radius. "Hi," she said cheerfully to the other vampire. "I'm Molly. Love your dress."

Maven blinked, then looked down at herself and back up in a thoroughly human gesture. "Thank you."

Molly glanced at Lex and me, trying to gauge the mood. "Is . . . everything okay?" she asked.

"Um . . ." Of course, it had occurred to me that Maven might figure it out. Not because she could smell it on me or anything—even if vampires could smell pregnancy, like dogs, it wouldn't apply to a null—but because I'd come on such short notice, in secret, and I looked very much like I'd spent the last week vomiting.

But I knew enough about Old World politics to know that if I didn't confirm it, and there was no proof, Maven wouldn't have to act on it. "Let's speak hypothetically for a moment, can we?" I said carefully.

"Of course." The vampire began lifting beverages, taking small, appreciative sips. She looked up at Molly and gestured to the last empty chair. "Will you be joining us?"

Molly glanced at Lex, who shrugged her assent.

"Thank you." Molly perched on the edge of her chair, picking up a coffee from the tray that was already marked with her lipstick.

"Hypothetically," I started again, "if a null wanted to get pregnant, would it be possible?"

Maven finished a sip and set down her cup. "Yes," she said simply. "But very difficult."

Something inside me uncurled. Maven knew something about this. We had been right to come here. "Have you heard of it happening before?"

She nodded. "In . . . let me see . . ." She glanced at the ceiling, squinting. "It was the 1240s, I believe."

Molly actually spat out some coffee, though she managed to turn her head at the last moment so it would land on the floor. "Holy shit," she blurted.

I raised an eyebrow at her, widening my eyes to say, *Dude, we knew she was old.*

Molly nodded and sent a contrite look toward Maven. "Sorry, um, ma'am," she said. "I didn't mean to interrupt. I'll just go get napkins—" She started to stand up, but Maven waved her off.

"Don't worry, we'll take care of it later."

"Did you actually meet a null who was pregnant?" I asked, trying to get her attention away from Molly's gaffe. Lex was still silent, but she was looking at me like I'd sprouted another arm.

"Just north of Istanbul—it wasn't called that then, of course—there was a small village called Azad, and it was populated almost entirely by witch clans," she began. "This was shortly after the Inquisition began to spread across Europe, and many witches fled east to Azad, just as many Jews fled to Istanbul.

"In Azad, witchcraft was practiced . . . well, *openly* is too strong a word, but Istanbul was in a period of decline, and no one was much bothered by the actions of a small village, not when western Europe was in such turmoil. And so Azad became a sanctuary for magic." She took another sip of one of the drinks. Her eyes were distant. "I was in Istanbul at the time, on business"—Maven cast a furtive glance at Lex, then continued—"but I kept hearing stories about a city of magic, and decided to investigate. When I arrived in the village, it didn't take me long to learn that there were three nulls living there."

"Three?" I asked, shocked. Most of the time nulls are divided by thousands of miles. It's been theorized that this is an evolutionary imperative. "What was the population?"

She shrugged. "Five, six hundred people. And yet, three of them were nulls. One was a woman in her fifties, another a man in his early twenties, and the third was a teenage girl, maybe seventeen. Before you ask, they were not related. In fact, they were from three different clans." Another glance at Lex. "Three different *witch* clans."

My mouth dropped open. "They were all from witch families?"

Maven nodded. "That was when I began to suspect that all nulls are descended from magical lines. The most *powerful* lines."

It was too much. I scooted back my chair and got up to pace, trying to absorb the implications.

Lex, meanwhile, was looking at Maven. "Why didn't you tell me?" she asked softly.

Maven blinked. "Honestly . . . I thought you knew. Because of your niece."

Lex was a powerful witch, which meant her twin sister had inherited witchblood as well. "But John," she began, and then faltered. "He doesn't have magic."

I paused in my pacing, turning to look at Lex. "His mother does."

All three of them looked up at me. "*What?*" Lex said, as incredulous as I'd ever seen her. "*Blossom* has magic?"

"Yeah. She activated it as a teenager and then stopped using it, probably shortly after it kicked in. I can still feel it, though."

"And men often miss out on the active gene," Maven said mildly.

Now Lex looked as stunned as I felt, which . . . okay, if I'm being honest, made me feel a little better. At least I wasn't the only one who'd barely known my own family.

Wait. *My own family.*

"You're saying my *parents* were witches?" I said to Maven. "That's . . . that's ludicrous. They were the most normal humans I've ever met."

I thought back to the last few times I'd been with them. I'd never felt anything strange, anything I would later recognize as witches in my radius. It wasn't possible.

Maven spread her hands. "They might not have been active. They might not have even *known*. But if you're a null, your parents both came from extremely strong magical bloodlines. Unless you were adopted."

I was fairly certain I wasn't adopted. I looked just like my mother, and I'd seen pictures of her pregnant with me. Jack and I both had our father's green eyes.

Which meant they'd had witchblood. I dropped back into my chair, feeling suddenly faint.

"You should eat something, Scar," Molly murmured. After looking to Maven for permission, she slid one of the scones over to me. I picked at it absently.

My parents had had witchblood. Both of them. What were the odds? Actually, wait. The odds were miniscule—that was the whole point. For thousands of years, witchblood had become more and more diluted as witches married humans. How often would two descendants from extremely powerful witch bloodlines find each other?

Almost never. Which explained why nulls were so rare. "Can you please continue your story?" I said to Maven.

Looking sympathetic, she said, "In Azad, the two younger nulls eventually fell in love."

"And then she got pregnant," I said.

"Yes. They had a little girl, which was a shock—even back then, anyone who knew about nulls knew they were barren." Maven broke off a piece of scone, chewing blissfully. "Mmm. Anyway, I came to town when the girl was about three. I met the family briefly, and then I had to report to the Vampire Council to decide if we needed to do something about the child, or about Azad in general. Too many people knew about witch magic for the council's liking."

"And?" Molly asked.

Maven's expression clouded over. "Ultimately, it never came to that. A small army of radical Christian humans learned about Azad, and they burned the village to the ground. Some escaped, but not the two nulls or their child."

We all fell silent then, but after a moment, I had to ask. "The baby," I said quietly. "What was she? Was she human?"

Maven's eyes were sad. "She was a witch. The most powerful witch I have ever met."

Chapter 12

They wanted to learn something from him, that much was obvious, but Jesse couldn't tell if the Luparii witches had something specific in mind, or if it was a fishing expedition. Time for an experiment. Jesse squeezed his eyes shut. *Sabine*, he thought as hard as he could. *I'm ready to tell you everything.*

There was no reaction. Which didn't prove anything, of course, but it made Jesse suspect that perhaps she couldn't read his immediate thoughts. Jesse had no idea how much of this spell was Sabine and how much was his own . . . what, projections? Creative input? Was *he* putting the items in the boxes, or were they already there, waiting to be discovered? Was it really like a raid, where the Luparii could look through his memories like a file cabinet, or was she just trying to trick him into thinking about whatever he wouldn't want them to know?

When the Luparii had first come to Los Angeles, years ago, it had been because the city was being terrorized by a magical aberration: a nova wolf, driven to kill and turn as many people as possible. Werewolves were one thing, but a nova wolf was a rare occurrence. Someone in Will's pack had used his connections to alert the Luparii, trying to make a deal to get Will out of the way.

A Luparii scout *had* come, but not to make a deal. In fact, she'd ended up double-crossing the werewolf who'd made the offer, using Shadow to kill him. After that, she'd gone hunting.

Before the Luparii scout could find the nova wolf, however, Jesse and Scarlett had stolen Shadow and arranged for the Luparii scout to be sent to prison for the nova wolf's kills. Shadow had then helped them kill the nova wolf, Henry Remus. Afterward, Dashiell had brokered a deal with the European Luparii witches to stay the hell out of LA. It had been a very neat solution, all things considered. At the time, even Scarlett had thought the deal seemed a little too pat, but they'd had more crises to deal with, and none of them had expected the Luparii witches to return.

So why *had* they come back? And why the focus on Scarlett's whereabouts?

Jesse could think of a few possibilities, but he wasn't going to get answers unless he got out of here.

Or was he? What had Killian said about this spell? "You can afford the distraction." That implied that the twisted slumber required a little bit of her active concentration . . . which would mean that the Sabine who'd appeared in the evidence room wasn't just part of a dream. She was part of the real Sabine's active consciousness. Maybe *Jesse* could learn something from *her*.

It was a hell of a leap of logic, but it gave Jesse something to hold on to. And something to do. Time for part two of the experiment. Making sure his mind was clear, Jesse called, "I know you're with the Luparii."

Suddenly, Sabine was there, leaning against the nearest shelf with a bored look on her face. "Congratulations on being slightly less of an idiot than we thought."

"You used some kind of illusion spell back at the cottage," Jesse went on. "That's your whole thing, right? You twist things into darkness."

She didn't answer, so Jesse tried a new tactic. "You're supposed to stay out of Los Angeles," he said. To his own ears he sounded like a petulant child. "There was a deal."

Sabine smirked. "I think it's safe to say the deal is off."

"Because you couldn't stand to have someone else take your toy?" he scoffed. "All this is about you being a sore loser?"

She didn't like that. "This is about the natural order," she hissed. "And yes, we want what is owed to us. Our *birthright*."

Shadow? "The bargest is your birthright?" Jesse said without thinking.

Her expression grew cagey as she realized he was trying to keep her talking. "Clever, clever," she sang, giving him a little mock bow. "But that won't work. And we've already got what we came for. You are quickly running out of usefulness, Jesse Cruz."

"So first you let Scarlett get away, and now you're going to murder a mildly famous ex-cop? Won't that get you in trouble with your superiors?"

That annoyed her. "You forget," she snapped, spreading her arms. "This is my world. Here, I have no superior."

"Then why did you run away before?" Jesse taunted. "You were scared I'd learn something from you, because this connection goes both ways. If you're so confident about killing me, why not tell me the plan?"

Her fists clenched. Suddenly the shelves around Jesse seemed to grow, rising to tower threateningly over him. Boxes rattled toward the edges of their shelves, poised to fall right on him.

"If this is you trying to show me you're not scared," Jesse said in a bored voice, "you really do suck at it."

She grew again, her body distorting and leaning into him in a horrific parody of human behavior. It was as though someone had taken everything in Jesse's eyeline and stretched it like Silly Putty, first vertically, and then horizontally. Only Jesse stayed the same size.

The now-giant woman leaned down, wrapping her oversize fingers around Jesse's neck and *lifting*. She slammed him against some of the shelving, his spine making impact. It hurt like hell, even though it seemed ridiculous that it would.

When she touched him, though, it was like a window opening. Jesse could feel the anger and crazed intentions leaking out of her. There was something *wrong* with this woman, aside from the obvious. She had a screw loose.

There was something else there, too: a longing, a wish that occupied part of her mind at all times. Jesse had a brief image of riding a horse, carrying a sword. Violence and viciousness and unimaginable power.

What, she secretly dreamed of being a warlord?

Then she tightened her fingers, and Jesse immediately forgot about the sensation of riding. "Little boy," she thundered, "you have no idea what's coming. It's a shame you won't live to see your friends suffer and die."

Jesse clawed at her hands, trying to get air, which he somehow still needed.

Then she smiled. "But I can help with that."

She let go of his neck, and Jesse tumbled to the floor, dazed. It was eerily quiet, and when he finally managed to sit up, he saw that Sabine was gone—and so were the endless shelves. He was back inside Scarlett's little cottage. Everything looked just as it had when the Luparii witches had knocked on the door.

Had he really woken up?

He noticed that Scarlett's bedroom door was closed. She usually left it open so Shadow could go in and out as she pleased. Had it been closed when he'd gotten back to the cottage with Shadow?

He couldn't remember.

Jesse staggered to his feet, leaning against the wall. He felt feverish, and he was desperate for water, but first he had to know. Lurching toward the bedroom door, he knocked lightly. "Scarlett?"

There was no answer, so he turned the knob and pushed the door open.

Scarlett's lifeless eyes stared at him.

She was lying upside down on the bed, her head hanging over the foot, pointed at the door. Her clothes had been slashed and shredded, and blood soaked the sheets around her, running down her neck and into her hair, soaking the carpet.

Jesse gasped and yanked the door shut, trying to control his breathing. Was it real? It couldn't be real . . . could it? He was still in the twisted slumber . . . right?

He opened the door again, hoping it had vanished like a hallucination in a horror movie, but no, her body was still there. Still staring at him.

Jesse closed the door again, distantly hearing his own whimpers. He wanted to run outside, to fight something, to *move*, but he felt weak and light-headed. And so hot. His clothes were soaked with sweat. Did that mean he was awake now? He couldn't be.

It's still the spell, he told himself, even as he slid down the wall, his sweaty clothes aiding him. *Scarlett will call to check on you. When you don't answer, she'll realize that something is wrong.* He'd have to wait for that. She would come for him. She was still alive.

She *was*.

Jesse felt a rush of despair, and then there was only black.

Chapter 13

"A witch? You said she was *three*," I protested. "Witches don't come into their power until they go through puberty."

"Regular witches, yes," Maven answered. "But the little girl in Azad had activated her magic before she could walk. She was a witchling."

Lex looked up sharply. "What does that mean? My"—her expression soured—"*biological father* called me a 'deathling.'"

"Because you're nearly a purebred conduit," Maven told her.

Conduits were the first humans—well, whatever was before humans—who bonded with magic. They are also the ancestors of every magical race on earth: vampires, werewolves, witches, and—yes—nulls all descend from them. I didn't really understand what she meant about Lex, but I was too wrapped up in the story to ask. "Please," I said to Maven, "why were those nulls able to get pregnant? And why was the baby a witch?"

Maven sighed. "This part is all theory, you understand? I can't prove it, and short of Lex's friend the scientist"—she glanced at Lex—"no one has ever even tried. But we know that witch bloodlines have become more and more diluted, which has caused the ley lines to fade, which has caused all of magic to diminish."

This was all news to me, but Lex was nodding. "That's why vampires and werewolves are having a hard time reproducing," she explained to me.

"Ley lines," I repeated. Were there ley lines in LA?

I had about a dozen follow-up questions on that alone, but Maven continued, "I believe that nulls are an evolutionary response to the diminishment of magic. When two nulls have a baby, that child is born with power nearly equal to a conduit. A witchling."

"Which is why the parents are nulls," Molly supplied. "Because they can keep the baby from hurting anyone with magic."

Maven nodded again. "Witchlings may only come once in a thousand years, but they restart the bloodlines, boost the ley lines. They *keep magic going.*" She held out her hands, palms up. "That's my theory, anyway. But the witchling in Azad was the first I'd met, and the last." She gave me a sad, complicated smile. "Unless, of course, you were to hypothetically become pregnant."

Without thinking, I leaned forward and let my head thunk on the card table. Little exclamations of surprise came from Maven and Lex, but Molly just patted my back. "She does that," she explained.

I was in so much trouble. I mean, I hadn't felt great about the future when I was just a single twenty-something who'd gotten knocked up by her dead lover, but now I was also carrying the frickin' *savior of magic?*

Above me, Lex was asking Maven, "Is this why you brought me on? So you could keep an eye on Charlie through me?" Her tone was completely neutral.

"You're a tremendous catch in your own right, Lex," Maven answered, sounding a little amused. "But I'll admit, I want to keep an eye on Charlie, too, to make sure she stays safe. When she grew older, I always planned to have a word with you about this."

"Why?" Molly asked, practically. "I mean, no offense, um, ma'am, but do you even have a horse in this race?"

Maven sounded just the slightest bit offended. "Of course I do. We *all* do. Magic is dying, which could result in all of our species dying out. A witchling who grows up to have her own babies and boost the ley lines will help all of us."

My forehead was still plastered to the table. Great, now I felt like a broodmare. A broodmare who *was supposed to be sterile, goddammit.*

"This can't be happening," I said into the tabletop. Molly patted my back again.

I sat up and looked at Maven. "What do I do?" I whispered.

I'm not sure why I was asking her. I barely knew her, and I had no reason to think she cared about my best interests, or the baby's. But she had given me the information freely, without demanding a favor in return. And she seemed to actually care about the fate of the whole Old World, not just herself or her little domain.

Maven gave me a faint smile. "At the end of the day, a pregnant null has mostly the same options as any other pregnant woman. You can keep the baby, or you can abort it."

"Adoption?" Molly asked.

Maven pursed her lips. "That, I would not advise. The witchling will be nearly impossible for anyone else to care for. Or protect."

"I don't protect things," I squeaked. "I mostly break them."

Molly squeezed my hand. She looked at Maven. "Are you going to tell anyone?" she said in a low voice. "Dashiell?"

Maven made a show of furrowing her brow. "Tell anyone what? I thought we were speaking hypothetically."

Molly grinned. "I like the superpowerful vampire lady," she told me.

"Thank you," I managed to say to Maven. "I owe you one."

Maven shook her head. "No, you don't. If you were to get pregnant— someday—we would all benefit."

At that moment, the burner phone buzzed in my pocket, making me jump. I dug it out and looked at the screen, which displayed my own cell phone number, the one for the Batphone. At least Jesse was okay.

I was about to ignore it, but it occurred to me that he wouldn't be calling from this number if it wasn't urgent. I answered the phone. "Hey. This isn't a great time—"

"Scarlett? Oh, thank God." It wasn't Jesse's voice. It was Kirsten, and she sounded panicked. "I don't know where you are, but you need to get home, *right now*."

Fear churned the few contents of my stomach. "What happened? Where's Jesse?"

"I had a witch problem, and Dashiell said Jesse was covering for you," she said in a rush. "He wasn't answering the emergency line or his personal cell, and I got worried, so I had Abby track your phone and then I saw the missed call—"

"Kirsten, slow down! *Where's Jesse?*"

"He's right here," she said, her voice almost a sob. "But he's been attacked. I think he's dying."

Chapter 14

I stood up, ignoring the curious looks from Molly and Lex. "What do you mean, he's dying?" I demanded, turning my back to the others. "What kind of attack?"

"Magical," Kirsten said. "Someone hexed him and dumped him in the Ballona Wetlands reserve. Teddy and I found him."

Teddy was Theodore Hayne, Kirsten's husband. But a magical attack would be *her* department. "Can't you undo it?"

"I've been trying!" she said, nearly wailing. "I've never seen anything like this—it's like he's in a coma, but he's burning up. His temp is a hundred and *eight*. If I had a couple of days, I could reverse engineer it, but he's losing fluids too quickly. *Where are you?*"

"A hundred and eight?" I repeated. I had turned around and twirled a finger at Molly, our signal that we needed to leave. She stood and started gathering our things. "Is that even possible?"

"Apparently it is. We took him back to your place—it was the closest—and the carpet around him is soaked with sweat, and I can't figure out *why*." There were tears in her voice. The witch leader of LA was usually good in a crisis, but I'd seen her break down when people she cared about were in mortal danger. Jesse was her friend, too. And the fact that her magic couldn't fix him had to be terrifying. It was certainly terrifying *me*.

I could hear Hayne's low, soothing voice murmuring to her in the background. She took a deep breath. "I don't think I can solve this before he dies from it, Scarlett. He needs you to break the hex."

Shit, shit, *shit*. "How long does he have?" I demanded.

"I'm not a doctor, Scarlett. Can't you just get here?"

But I wouldn't be deterred. "Best guess?"

She hesitated again. "Hours. Two, maybe three."

Jesus. No wonder she was panicking. I wanted to burst into tears, but I needed to focus. I couldn't help Jesse if I was falling apart. "Call Matthias, get him there," I urged. Matthias was the witch-born human doctor who helped us with medical stuff when we couldn't use the human health-care system. "I'll pay his bill myself."

"I already called. He's on his way," she said more clearly. "When can you and Shadow get here?"

"Shadow," I echoed. "Jesse was taking care of Shadow."

A pause, and then Kirsten said, "She's not here."

I swallowed hard. I needed to be there, but even if Molly drove like a bat out of hell, we'd never make it back in less than eight hours. "Hang on." I spun around and looked at Maven. "Do you have a plane?" I demanded. Dashiell had a plane.

Maven blinked. "Excuse me?"

Lex shot me a *be careful* look. My words had been too flippant for someone so powerful, but I didn't care. "A private aircraft. Do you have one, or have access to one?"

"One of my Denver vampires owns a Gulfstream," Maven allowed.

"Can I borrow it?"

Unhurried, Maven leaned back in her chair and crossed her arms over her chest. "Why?"

I forced myself to take a breath before saying, "Someone under my protection has been hexed. He'll die if I don't get back in time to break the spell. *Please.*"

Maven just studied me. In that moment, I realized I would do anything to save Jesse. "I'll owe you a favor," I said.

She nodded. "All right."

Lifting the phone, I said to Kirsten, "I'm on my way. Meanwhile . . ." I hesitated, but made myself say the words. "Call Will and see if he'll come be on standby."

There was a pause, then Kirsten whispered, "Are you serious?"

"Yeah." There was no guarantee that Jesse would actually change from a werewolf bite—as Maven had explained, magic was fading and the odds were against him. And being a werewolf was considered a last resort among last resorts. Maybe I was being selfish to even consider it, but I wouldn't let Jesse die if I could find any way around it. "Did you tell Dashiell?" I said to Kirsten.

"No, he's my next call."

I wanted to ask her to keep it from Dashiell, but this was way too big. Jesse being hexed was a magical crisis on its own, but if Shadow was loose in the city . . . "Let me do it," I said, my stomach turning into a rock. "Please. I'll call him in ten minutes, from the car."

Kirsten wasn't happy about it, but she agreed. I hung up the phone and turned to face the others. At some point, Quinn had come running into the room. He was still breathing hard. I gave him a blank look, then got it: I'd extended my radius to the front of the building, alarming him. Oops.

I looked at Maven in a daze. She was so powerful. Did I need her to dismiss me? Should I curtsy or something?

To her credit, she waved us off. "No need."

I ran out of the coffee shop at a dead run, with Molly and Lex at my heels.

There are serious advantages to knowing an ex-soldier with Old World connections. Before we even made it to the highway, Lex had made the necessary calls and arranged everything. She would drive us to the airport, introduce us to the pilot, and take care of Eleanor until we could send someone to drive the car back to Los Angeles.

As soon as we had the plan in place, I called Dashiell and ran him through an abbreviated version of the last twenty-four hours: I was still sick, but I'd gone to Boulder to speak to Lex about an urgent personal matter. I'd left Jesse in charge of Shadow, and they'd been attacked.

There was really no way to sugarcoat it, so I didn't bother trying. As I had expected, his response was so curt it was practically a snarl. "I will connect with Kirsten and do what I can for Mr. Cruz. You and I will discuss this the moment the crisis has passed." And he hung up.

I stared at the phone, half-afraid it would bite me. "Was he pissed?" Molly asked from the back seat.

"You could say that," I said dully. Dashiell had sounded like he genuinely wanted to kill me, but at this point it was hard to care.

Jesse. My knuckles ached, and when I looked down, I realized that my hands were clenched into fists.

We arrived at the airport, but before I could even open the door, Molly said suddenly, "Wait."

Lex and I both turned to look in the back seat, but Molly's focus was on Lex. "Press me," she said hurriedly. "Press me to forget she's pregnant."

"Molls, no!" I said, at the same time Lex said, "It won't work."

"Why not?" Molly asked her, ignoring me.

"You've known about it for too long," Lex explained. "It's too deep in your mind now. I can't take away the knowledge without taking away the last two days, and that's too much. Your brain would work too hard to fill in the gaps."

"Just like when vampires press humans," I said, understanding.

"Then press me to think it was a false alarm," Molly insisted. "We came here and got answers, but Scarlett got her period while we were here."

Lex looked at me, questioning. As soon as I started to shake my head, Molly said, "Scar, it'll protect us both. It'll buy you time to figure out what to tell Dashiell and the others."

I felt myself wavering. "I don't like the idea of rewiring your brain for me."

She just gave me a look. "I do it to other people all the time. Consider it karma."

I chewed on my lip for a second. The pregnancy had seemed so terrifying and all-encompassing only an hour ago, but Kirsten's phone call had put things in perspective. I had months to figure out what to do about the baby. Jesse had hours. "Okay," I said. I looked at Lex. "Do it. Please."

"You'll have to get out of the car," she reminded me.

Oh, right. Null.

Relieved, and ashamed of it, I opened the car door and climbed out. Lex called after me, and I turned and looked through the door at her.

"About Jesse," she said, and for the first time I realized she was afraid for him, too. Duh, Scarlett. He and Lex were friends. "Will you call me and let me know?" She hesitated for a second, and added in a hard tone, "Either way." She gave me a long, meaningful look, and I actually understood. If Jesse died before I could save him, Lex would help me get revenge.

"I will."

Chapter 15

I've been in some horrible situations, where lives were at risk, but I can honestly say those two hours of flight time were the longest in my life. Molly tried to talk to me a few times, I think, but I barely heard her, and probably only grunted in response.

Jesse.

This was all my fault. I had dragged Jesse into the Old World to begin with, and I'd put him in personal danger any number of times—but usually I was at least *with* him, to level the playing field. He could handle danger as a human up against humans, and I'd taken for granted that he could handle my job for a couple of days, like he'd done before. I'd taken *him* for granted. And then I'd abandoned him, leaving him vulnerable to magical attack.

Now someone had hexed him with some kind of lethal spell, and Shadow was . . .

I frowned. Wait. Where *was* Shadow? When Kirsten first said the bargest was missing, I'd assumed Shadow had gone for help, but maybe she was trying to track Jesse's attacker? Or maybe she was trying to find *me*. Shadow was as smart as some humans, but she wouldn't try to run to Colorado, would she?

I had a sudden, terrible thought. Saying a prayer of thanks for the private plane, I pulled out my phone and called Kirsten. First, of course, I asked about Jesse.

"We still can't get him to swallow water, and Matthias couldn't get an IV in," she reported. "His veins just won't take it, like he's in stasis or something. But we've had another idea."

"Which is?"

"Hayne and I filled your bathtub with ice," she said. She had calmed down a lot now that there was a doctor on hand. "His fever is down to a hundred and four. He's still dying, but I think we can keep him alive until you get here. And Will is here, just in case."

"Okay. Okay." Molly was looking at me inquisitively. I gave her a weak smile to show that things were looking better.

"Scarlett . . ." Kirsten continued.

"What?"

"I want to prepare you," she said in a hushed voice. "There could be brain damage. From the fever."

"Could be?" I echoed. "So not for sure, right?" Now I sounded hysterical, and Molly's eyes widened. I looked away from her, out the dark window.

"It's a magic-induced fever, so we don't know if it'll have the same effects as if it was from an infection."

Brain damage? For a second I was too choked up to speak, but I forced myself to remember my reason for calling. I cleared my throat. "Listen, when you got to my place, was the door unlocked?"

A pause. "Yes. It was standing open."

Okay, that worked with the theory that Shadow was pursing the attackers. But I had to be sure. "Look around," I said. "Do you see a purple leather collar anywhere?"

A brief pause, then: "Hang on."

I waited. Considering her size and how she looked, it was hard for Shadow to blend in. Having a girlie purple collar helped, at least a little.

Shadow didn't like wearing it, but she accepted that it was a necessary part of disguising her as an actual dog.

Kirsten came back on the line. "I found it," she reported. "It was outside in the driveway."

My stomach dropped. "Is it damaged, like she clawed it off?"

"No. It was just unbuckled. Why does this matter?"

Molly was looking at me again. "There used to be a tracking device in her collar," I explained. "Shadow kept scratching at it and shorting it out." Which was *possibly* accidental, but I wouldn't put it past the bargest to decide she didn't feel like having an electronic tag. Her claws were as sharp as my throwing knives. "Abby's been working on a new scratchproof design, so the purple collar has no tracker—I just sliced off a tiny bit of it, so I could get a witch to find it." As a supernatural creature, Shadow couldn't be found with a tracking spell—magic usually couldn't work against itself, for some reason. But any decent witch could track a fragment from a larger piece, like the collar. "But if someone took her . . ."

"They took the collar off," Kirsten finished for me, "knowing you could get us to track it."

"Is the house trashed?" I asked. "Like there was a fight?"

"No."

Molly, who had heard most of the conversation, put in, "Couldn't Jesse have taken the collar off?"

"Maybe," I admitted. "But why would he have left it in the driveway?"

None of us had a good answer for that. If the collar had been some kind of message, I wasn't getting it. Meanwhile, we had to proceed as though whoever had attacked Jesse had also taken Shadow. "Just . . . focus on getting here," Kirsten said finally.

So I did.

He may have been mad at me, but Dashiell still sent a car to get us from the airport. As we pulled up to the house, I was already extending my radius as far as I could. I felt the *bzzt* sensation of a spell fizzing out . . . but this wasn't like the spells I was used to dealing with. It was powerful, for one thing, and there was almost a *taste* to it, something thick and green and toxic. It made me want to shower and throw up at the same time. I pushed away the thought and hurried out of the car toward the cottage, Molly rushing along at my heels.

I heard hushed voices as I walked in, but they went silent as Kirsten heard me coming. "In here," she called from the bathroom.

Our bathroom was small—and not particularly clean—but Hayne, Kirsten, and Matthias had all managed to cram inside. Hayne leaned against the counter, while Kirsten and Matthias crouched in front of the tub. They'd taken off the shower curtain, and I could see Jesse lying inside, covered in a mound of ice. He was facing away from the door, but as I squeezed into the room and rushed to his side, it struck me that he looked . . . dead. His eyes were closed, and I couldn't tell if his chest was moving. Someone had stripped him down to his boxer shorts—I could see the red color glinting through the ice—and his sickly yellow, bare skin only heightened the appearance of death.

"I felt the spell break," I blurted. "Is he—" Matthias was feeling for a pulse at Jesse's neck. I held my breath.

"He's alive," Matthias announced, after what felt like an eternity. "Good. But he's not out of the woods yet."

"What do you need?" I demanded.

Matthias raised his eyebrows at me, but didn't comment on my sharp tone. "A bed or cot. We need to set up a saline IV."

"When will he wake up?"

Matthias shook his head. "That, I don't know. I've never seen a fever induced by magic before. If it caused brain damage, he may not wake up at all, or he may have lost any number of functions. Or"—he shrugged—"he may be fine as soon as we get him rehydrated. But right now, the dehydration has its own threats. Let's move him."

I had a thousand more questions—would a werewolf bite fix brain damage?—but I swallowed them and went to pull back the covers on my bed, grateful I'd changed the sheets a few days before. I laid down a clean towel, and watched anxiously as Hayne and Matthias hauled Jesse out of the tub and got him positioned on the right side of the bed.

Hayne then retreated to the living room to make more space, and Kirsten and Molly hovered in the hall. I couldn't take my eyes off Jesse.

"Why is he shivering?" I cried out. "His lips are blue!"

"It's the ice," Matthias explained, his eyes focused on getting an IV needle into Jesse's arm. There was curiosity and a little interest in his voice. "It shouldn't be affecting him so much. When a regular fever breaks, it goes down slowly."

When the IV was inserted and taped down, Matthias took an instrument out of his jacket pocket and sort of swiped it across Jesse's forehead, studying the results. "Ninety-three degrees," he announced. "Mild hypothermia already. Interesting."

I really don't know why it happened in that *particular* moment, but suddenly I burst into tears. Great, hiccupping sobs erupted out of me while I stood there. Kirsten and Matthias stared at me in shock, and Matthias, who rarely had a hair out of place, sputtered, "He's going to *live*, for Christ's sake. It's very mild."

But I just kept bawling, and as if that weren't enough, I suddenly realized that I was about to puke.

I ran into the bathroom and started heaving, while in the other room I was dimly aware of Molly telling the others that I was still getting over the flu, that I'd had a really hard day with no sleep and not much food. Or something like that. I wasn't really listening.

Then Molly was there, in the bathroom, handing me toilet paper to wipe my face and helping me get to the sink, where she gave me a bottle of Listerine. Somehow, even as I rinsed out my mouth, I was still crying.

"You okay?" she asked quietly. I just shook my head. Molly gave me a sympathetic smile. "Look on the bright side. At least you're not pregnant."

I let out another choked sob, which I think she took as a laugh.

"Come on," she said, putting an arm around my waist. I let her steer us back into my bedroom, which was now empty except for Jesse, who had an IV drip in his right arm. Matthias had even set up what looked like an extendable IV tree on the side of the bed. Jesse's color was a little better, but his lips still had a bluish tint. I could hear low voices in the living room.

"Matthias said we just have to wait and see about the brain damage," Molly said softly. She pulled back the covers on the empty side of the bed. "Get in," she ordered.

I just looked at her, completely overwhelmed. "I know, you have to find Shadow and face the music with Dashiell, but you can't do any of that if you can't stand up," she said, not unreasonably. "And you need to be with Jesse right now. It's only a little after midnight. You can sleep for a couple of hours before you go see Dashiell. I'll call him and buy you some time."

She was right, but I still shifted my weight from side to side, looking at Jesse. "I'm afraid," I whispered.

"Afraid of hurting him, or afraid to touch him?" Molly asked in an amused voice. I gave her a startled look, and she rolled her eyes at me. "Just get in, Scarlett. God knows he needs the warmth."

Guilt lanced through me again, and I crawled onto the bed next to Jesse. "You wanna, you know, take off some of your clothes?" she suggested, but I just shot her a glare. Molly gave me a little *have it your way* shrug and departed, closing the door behind her.

Despite all the insane things that were happening around me, I suddenly felt like an awkward teenager. Jesse and I had been friends for years. We had once gone out on a date and even kissed a couple of times, but we'd never shared a bed, especially when one of us was nearly naked. Cautiously, I put my hand on his arm. I was still flushed from all the crying and vomiting, and I was startled by how cool his skin felt. It was scary.

"Jesse?" There was no response. I shook the arm gently, and said a little louder, *"Jesse."*

Nothing.

Oh, God. What if he didn't wake up? What if he really *had* suffered brain damage? I'd come so close to losing him, and I still could.

Forgetting my awkwardness, I scooted closer to him. He was so *cold*. I moved his arm and nestled into his chest, pulling the blankets close around us. I tried to think warm thoughts.

And then, despite the whirlwind of madness that still swirled around us, I drifted to sleep.

Chapter 16

Jesse woke up slowly.

He first became aware of a woman's body pressed against him in an unfamiliar dark room. The only light came from a crack in the doorway, creating a limited stripe of visibility that just showed him sheets and a cloud of long, dark hair. It was disorienting. Had he had a one-night stand? He hadn't done anything like that in years. On the other hand, he did feel sort of hungover . . .

Jesse caught the familiar smell of Scarlett's shampoo, and felt something sticking out of his right hand, and—wait . . .

Scarlett was pressed against him? And was he . . . naked? Jesse shifted a little. Okay, almost naked.

Then it all began to come back to him. Shadow. The twisted slumber.

He had seen her dead.

Panic struck him for a second, but he carefully curled his hand to brush the dark hair away from her face. She was deeply asleep, one arm thrown across him, her slow, regular breathing warming the skin on his chest.

For a long moment, Jesse just lay there, fighting the tears of relief that threatened to overwhelm him. She was alive. She was okay.

And so was he. The twisted slumber had felt so real while he was in it, but now it had no more power than a bad nightmare. Trying not to move too much, he flexed his right hand and felt the sticky tape and the tube connected to it. An IV. That made sense, if he'd been dehydrated.

Low voices were coming from the hallway.

"Matthias checked on them a few minutes ago," said a familiar voice. Kirsten, the witch leader.

"What did he say?" This was Molly.

"Jesse's recovering well—*much* faster than he would from normal dehydration, which lends weight to the idea that the hex was boosting the condition. But they're both still out." Her voice turned wry. "Matthias said he's half-wondering if Scarlett should be getting saline fluids as well."

"She'll be fine. She just needs rest."

"Yes, well, Dashiell has called three times in the last hour. We'll have to wake her up soon."

"I know." Molly sounded glum. "Ten more minutes, okay?"

"Fine." There was a pause, and then Kirsten added, "You should take a picture first. They're absolutely adorable in there."

Jesse smiled faintly as footsteps moved away down the hall. He gingerly reached over and turned on the bedside lamp, careful not to tangle the IV tubing. The flare of light hurt his eyes, but Scarlett didn't even stir. He looked down at her arm on his chest and saw that her fingers were curled into the sheet on the other side of him, like she had been afraid he would be taken away while she slept. Despite this, she looked so peaceful.

"Scarlett," he whispered. Her arm tightened around him, but she didn't stir. Jesse kissed her forehead.

Her eyes fluttered open, her face only inches from his, and he felt her whole body tense. He'd sort of expected her to pull back, but for a long moment she just regarded him with her unnaturally green eyes. When she spoke, her voice was hoarse.

"Are you brain damaged?"

Jesse smiled. What a perfectly Scarlett question. "No more than usual."

He could feel her body slacken with relief. "Thank God."

"Did you change my clothes while I was unconscious?" he asked, mock-angry.

A small smile lightened her face. "Matthias did it, but I saw the whole show."

"And?"

She shifted so she could push the hair out of her face, but she still didn't move away. "Hey, man, you can read my Yelp review like everybody else."

Jesse grinned, but it faded quickly. "You're pregnant," he said.

She did pull away from him then, a series of complex expressions flickering across her face. Fear. Guilt. Shame. Hope. But all she said was, "How did you know?"

"Shadow led me to the pregnancy test. In the garbage can."

"Oh. That."

"Where did you go?"

"Boulder. To ask Lex's boss about the baby."

Jesse nodded. It made sense. She could have told him, but it didn't really matter anymore. Although he knew it wasn't his business, he couldn't stop himself from asking, "The father?"

"Jameson."

That . . . explained a lot, actually. "Another null."

She searched his face. "Aren't you going to tell me how stupid and slutty I was?" she challenged. "That I was reckless, that I should have known better?"

His heart wrenched. "Scarlett . . . do you really think *I'm* going to judge you for a . . . romantic miscalculation?"

He could tell she was fighting a smile at that, but she said, "The old Jesse would have."

He thought that over. He and Scarlett hadn't spoken for a long time after she'd gotten together with Eli for real. During their time apart, he'd had a brief, ill-advised marriage and a bout of self-loathing and depression. "Maybe you're right," he admitted. "But I would have been wrong. Right now, more than anything else, I'm just relieved you're not going to run back to Las Vegas to be with someone." He stopped himself before using the word *else*. He had no right.

She turned onto her back so they were side by side, not looking at him. "It doesn't matter anyway. I can't keep the baby. After we find Shadow, I need to make an appointment."

He didn't know what to say to that. They lay there quietly for a few minutes, and then she glanced at him. "Don't mention the pregnancy to anyone, okay? Even Molly."

He wanted to ask about that, but Scarlett abruptly sat up, looking down at herself. Her jeans and tee shirt were wrinkled, and her hair was hanging in big limp tangles. Her face was blotchy, and she looked thinner than ever. "I'm a mess, I probably smell . . ." She started to rake her fingers through her hair, avoiding his eyes.

"Scarlett." He reached out with his free hand and caught her hand gently.

She looked up at him then. "I thought you were gonna die," she said, her voice cracking. "Because of me." There was guilt on her face, and he knew she was thinking of Jameson. And probably her parents and her friend Caroline. All three had been killed by Scarlett's former mentor. Scarlett had come a long way, but he knew she still blamed herself some for that.

"I didn't die," Jesse contended. "And I'm not going to."

Her jaw clenched, and she gave him her stubborn glare. "You can't promise that."

"Watch me."

Her lower lip trembled, and for a second he was sure she was going to either cry or hit him, or both. Instead, she stood up, wobbled a little, and went over to open the bedroom door. "He's awake," she called into the hallway.

It was a pretty effective way to shut down the conversation.

Twenty minutes later, Jesse was sitting at Scarlett's small kitchen table, dressed in the spare outfit from the trunk of his car, which was thankfully still parked at the cottage. The Luparii witches hadn't bothered to hide it, and since they'd taken his personal cell phone away from him, they hadn't bothered to search him for a second phone. Jesse didn't want to think about what would have happened if he hadn't pocketed the Batphone. He'd been lucky.

Hayne was sitting on Scarlett's counter, with Kirsten standing next to his dangling legs. Matthias had checked Jesse's blood pressure and temperature, given a brief lecture on hydration, and departed. Molly was uncharacteristically quiet, puttering around the kitchen making chicken noodle soup. Scarlett sat at the table, fidgeting with Shadow's purple leather collar. Jesse, who had been unconscious for nearly twenty-four hours, was too hungry to wait for the soup. He munched on handfuls of cereal while he told them all the story about Shadow and the Luparii witches.

"You're sure it's the Luparii?" Kirsten asked him, for the third time.

"Yeah. Killian and Sabine are their names. They didn't know I could speak some French."

"They used you against Shadow, didn't they?" Scarlett said.

Jesse nodded. "She allowed them to take her, to save my life."

"Why not just kill you, once they had the bargest?" Hayne asked. Kirsten gave him a look, and he shrugged. "No offense."

"None taken; I asked the same thing. I think they were hoping they could search my memory to find out where Scarlett had gone."

He told them about being put in the twisted slumber, about Sabine's taunts.

"I've gotta call Will," Kirsten said softly. She pulled out her phone and stepped into the hall.

"Why did they come back?" Molly asked. "Just to take Shadow away?"

"Shit." Hayne stood up and began dialing his phone. "Shadow wasn't the only one they left behind." He paced toward the back door, already speaking into the phone in a low, urgent voice.

"Who is he calling?" Molly asked Scarlett and Jesse.

Then Jesse got it. He closed his eyes, feeling like a fool.

"He's calling the women's prison in Chino," Scarlett said. She'd put it together too. "That's where they're holding the Luparii scout, Petra Corbett."

Hayne hung up the phone and turned back to them, looking grim. "Not anymore," he said heavily. "She broke out three hours ago."

PART II

Chapter 17

A little over an hour after Jesse woke up, I sat watching as Dashiell stalked back and forth next to the enormous oval table in his atrium, his lips compressed with anger. I opened my mouth to say . . . something . . . but Will gave me a quick little headshake, and I snapped it closed again.

Earlier that evening, while I was still rushing home from the airport to break the hex on Jesse, Petra Corbett had walked out of the minimum-security area at the California Institution for Women . . . despite the fact that she had been lodged in a higher-security level. According to sources from both Jesse and Dashiell, the prison was currently scrambling to figure out how Petra Corbett had ended up on the completely wrong side of the prison. But it didn't really matter to us at this point. She was gone.

Hayne had been the one to call Dashiell, who had immediately summoned us to the mansion. Now Will, Beatrice, and Kirsten were all sitting at one end of the oval table, while Jesse and I had taken the first two seats on the long side. Dashiell was pacing on the opposite long side, and I, for one, was really glad for the minor safety of the table between us. I was expanding my radius just a bit to keep everyone human, but I wasn't sure if that was helping or fueling Dashiell's rage.

The cardinal vampire had been pacing for ten minutes already, and it was nearly five in the morning, which meant we only had about an hour before sunrise. Every minute that went by without him speaking felt like a ratcheting up of tension.

And yet . . . I felt strangely calm. Seeing Jesse almost die had snapped me out of my pregnancy-news frenzy, forcing me to be present for the current crisis. Shadow, whom I loved, was missing, and we were facing an unspecified threat from some very bad people. I could put the whole abortion thing aside until we found Shadow and stopped the Luparii.

Shut up. I *could*.

"You left town without telling us," Dashiell finally ground out, though he didn't bother to slow down or even look at me. Yeah, I think we all knew who he was talking to. "You invaded another cardinal vampire's territory. You left the bargest with a *human*. The Luparii, who are back in my city, stole the bargest back and broke Petra Corbett out of prison. And now they're all loose in my city." He finally stopped, turning to glower at me, and spat out, "You irresponsible *child*."

Jesse sat up straighter, about to defend me. I reached for his hand under the table and squeezed it to stop him.

"I made a mistake," I said to Dashiell. Despite the two-hour nap with Jesse, I was more exhausted than ever. "I'm sorry."

"What was so important that you had to run to Colorado without telling anyone?" Kirsten broke in. She seemed more surprised and curious than anything else.

"It's a personal matter," I said.

They *really* didn't like that. "*Your* personal matter, or Allison Luther's?" Kirsten pushed.

I didn't answer. Dashiell looked like he was ready to yell again, but Will, who had been fairly quiet thus far, stepped in. "This is getting us nowhere," he said in his calm voice. Will looked like a lovable sitcom dad, and he was the most chill werewolf I'd ever met. But that only meant he was calm for a *werewolf.* "I understand there should be consequences for Scarlett's actions, but I suggest we put a pin in that until Shadow and the Luparii can be found. Agreed?"

He gave Dashiell a pointed look, and the cardinal vampire probably realized the same thing I did: with the Luparii running around LA, Will and his pack had the most to lose.

"Agreed," Kirsten said readily.

"Fine." Dashiell didn't exactly sound gracious, but he'd managed to stay just shy of begrudging.

"Are we sure they're even still here?" Kirsten asked. She looked like she couldn't decide whether or not to be hopeful. "They've got Petra and Shadow. They put us in our place. Why not take their toys and go home?"

"Shadow is *not* a toy," I said through gritted teeth. Now Jesse reached over to squeeze *my* hand. "She's basically a person."

Dashiell let out a little disgusted snort, but didn't deign to respond to my outburst. "That is possible," he said to Kirsten. His gaze moved to Jesse. "Mr. Cruz? What was your impression?"

"Well . . . they *definitely* wanted to kill Scarlett," he said, shooting me an apologetic look. "I got the sense that it was a priority."

"But what about now?" Will asked. "Would they stick around just to kill her?"

His phrasing made me bizarrely indignant, but Jesse answered before I could. "I can't really explain it right, but I got the sense that there was a bigger play happening. It's something that Sabine was looking forward to. It was like . . ." He paused for a moment, searching for the words. "Like they were working through a list, and Scarlett *needed* to die before they could move to the next item. Whatever their plan is, I don't think Scarlett's supposed to be around for it."

Everyone looked at me—Kirsten and Will, at least, seemed worried. But I was still enjoying my strange new sense of calm, so I just shrugged. "Happy to disappoint."

"Even if that's true," Will said, "there's nothing to suggest the next part of their plan doesn't take place back in France. They could be cutting their losses."

"It doesn't have to be France."

Dashiell's voice was uncharacteristically low, like he was thinking out loud. Since no one else was willing to question him, and I was already in trouble anyway, I said, "What do you mean? Isn't that where they live?"

"Some of them, yes." He stood up, as if to pace again, but instead he wandered over to the patio door and stared at whatever was inside. Without turning to face us, he said, "There's something you all should know. After the first time the Luparii came to my city, I thought it prudent to have my contacts in Europe gather more intelligence on them. As it turns out, our previous information had become . . . outdated."

Jesse and I looked at each other. Somehow I didn't think Dashiell meant the Luparii had shriveled up and died in the last three years. "Are they still a big-ass family of werewolf hunters?" I asked, because sometimes my mouth just does things.

Now Dashiell did turn and come back to the table, though he stood in front of his chair and leaned his fists on the edge. "Yes and no," he answered. "The Gagnon descendants still run everything—and it sounds like this Sabine, at least, is one of them—but they have been accepting additional witches into their ranks. Witches with different or no specialties. The Luparii name has come to encompass the entire . . . organization."

Out of the corner of my eye, I saw Kirsten nodding. "My aunt has heard similar rumors," she reported. "They are very secretive, though, and Scandinavia isn't considered part of the Luparii territory."

"Not yet," Dashiell muttered. Ignoring Kirsten's startled look, he finally sat down in his chair. "The Luparii have been growing in size over the last few decades, and they now have large cells operating in Portugal and Romania, as well as their main base of operations just outside Paris. They have become less a family and more of a . . . brotherhood."

"Hang on, what are we talking about here?" I said. "Is this like the Mafia kind of brotherhood, or some kind of witch fraternity?"

"I was thinking more along the lines of the Freemasons," Jesse told me. "But evil."

"*More* evil?"

The others ignored us. "My aunt said they were even employing vampires now," Kirsten put in. "Why do they care so much about expansion?"

Will, who had been texting—probably to warn his pack about the Luparii—looked up and added, "Especially since the wolves have been staying out of Europe."

I wondered for the first time how dialed in he was to other werewolf packs. Wolves are territorial by nature, and communication across large distances is difficult in the Old World, because we don't exactly trust the Internet or phone lines, and we're not allowed to bring any outside humans into the know. Did Will keep in touch with other alphas anyway? I'd never thought to ask.

"What about the Luparii's ideology?" asked Jesse. Out of all of us, he was probably the most accustomed to dealing with organized criminal wackos. "Has that changed, too?"

"I'm not sure," Dashiell admitted. "I know that they are still devoted to the eradication of werewolves. Still, as Kirsten said, I don't understand why they've been making a point to expand."

We were probably all thinking it, but it was Will who said, in a carefully level voice, "You didn't think it was necessary to tell us about any of this?"

Dashiell didn't seem offended, which surprised me a little. He spread his hands. "In truth, I thought we were done with the Luparii. Three years ago, when I negotiated with Aldric, their leader, I was unaware of the organization's scope. By the time I found out that they had grown to a much larger force, we had already made the deal to keep Shadow in Los Angeles and allow Petra Corbett to take the fall for the nova wolf. And I haven't heard a word from them since then." He shrugged, looking at me. "What is that phrase you've been using? 'Not my circus, not my monkeys'?"

I pushed out a breath, nodding. I could tell by the way he hadn't shot down Will for questioning him that Dashiell felt a little bad about not warning us. I couldn't find it in me to blame him, though, even though he'd come down on me hard about going to Colorado. Dashiell had been alive for over a hundred years, and he could theoretically live forever. Of course he knew big-picture stuff he didn't tell us about.

"So why make the deal with us in the first place?" Kirsten asked, worrying at her bottom lip with her teeth. "Why not just come here three years ago and put us in our place?"

"To buy time," I suggested.

Jesse nodded. "I agree. The timing of this latest attack is bothering me. Scarlett has never left Shadow with a human for more than an hour or two, and her trip to Colorado was unplanned." He glanced sideways at me, and I nodded, confirming it. I don't care how good your evil empire is, no one could have known I was going to Boulder before I did. "I doubt the Luparii witches randomly showed up the night Scarlett left town—it's too big of a coincidence. They've been watching her. There had to be a reason."

A chill spread through me. They'd been watching me? Watching the cottage? "For how long? Since we captured Petra?" I asked.

Jesse shrugged, "There's no way to know for sure, but I doubt it. Three years is a long time to surveil someone without them noticing."

I nodded, trying to push away the sensation that my skin was crawling with bugs. "Okay, so they've been keeping an eye on me, waiting for a chance to take Shadow. But they could have attacked well before now. I had no idea they were in town; I wasn't expecting it."

"But if they put you out of commission first, Shadow wouldn't have gone willingly, and it would have tipped off Dashiell and the others to their presence," Jesse pointed out. "That's why I think there's a larger plan here."

"Explain," Dashiell demanded. Yeah, he was still mad.

"Killian said something about 'them' needing a couple of days," Jesse said. "I think they originally planned something for a few days from now. Like I said, killing you and taking Shadow was just one part of that." He glanced apologetically at me. "But then you left, and they panicked when they couldn't find you. They also probably saw an opportunity to remove Shadow from the equation early."

In a weird way, it actually made me feel a tiny bit better that the Luparii were planning something before I blew town. What had happened to Jesse was still my fault, but I didn't deserve credit for the *entire* mess.

"Beltane is in a few days," Kirsten offered.

Dashiell and Beatrice made little "hmm-ing" sounds, but Jesse shot me a confused look. "It's the Wheel of the Year," I explained. "Remember a few years ago, when Olivia and Mallory attacked Kirsten's solstice party?" He nodded. "The winter solstice in December is the shortest night of the year. The summer solstice in June is the longest night of the year. If you picture the face of a clock, with winter solstice at twelve and summer solstice at six, that forms the Wheel of the Year."

Kirsten was watching me with a tiny amused smile, probably wondering how much I'd been listening all the times she'd needed to explain this to me. "A regular clock has twelve points on it, but the Wheel of the Year has eight, which are the eight strongest times to use witch magic. Halfway between December and June is late March, which is called . . . um . . ." I looked at Kirsten for support.

"Ostara," she supplied.

"Right. And halfway between Ostara and the summer solstice is Beltane. And that's in two days."

"Ostara and Beltane are the pagan names, from a western European tradition," Kirsten added. "Very few traditions celebrated all eight holidays, until as recently as the 1950s, when British pagans finally put the Wheel of the Year together—"

"But they're a convenient shortcut to describe the days when magic is objectively the strongest all over the world," I broke in. I knew from past experience that Kirsten could go on for hours about how different cultures used different witch traditions, and we didn't have that kind of time. "Bottom line: there's symbolism, and there's what works. For whatever reason, those eight days of the year work."

"If they're planning something big with witch magic, they might be aiming for that night," Kirsten said.

"Or they might be using it as a misdirect, to attack the night before or after," Dashiell pointed out.

"Well, whatever they might be planning, we need to find Shadow," I said, making eye contact with each of them.

"Have you considered the possibility that they've already killed her?" Dashiell said, in a voice that was surprisingly gentle.

"How?" I asked. "Short of a nuke, I don't know how you could kill a bargest quickly. If the Luparii have a simple way to do it, they would have killed her back at the cottage and saved the trouble of transporting her."

"What about drowning?" Will offered. He said it suspiciously fast, and I wondered how much time *he'd* spent thinking about how to kill Shadow.

"How are you going to hold her under?" I countered. "She's dense—heavy—but she can swim, and she can hold her breath a long time. Even if they still have her in that metal net, they'd need a way to hold the net underwater. Otherwise, there's a good chance she could struggle out of it and kill them." I took a deep breath and voiced my biggest fear. "Look, I've thought about this, back when Shadow first came to me. As far as I can tell, there are two ways to kill her. One would be to undo the bargest spell, but that requires a human sacrifice and a whole bunch of competent witches, not to mention some of the nightshades. It's complicated. The other way—" My voice suddenly caught in my throat.

"Would be to starve her," Jesse finished for me. His voice was grave.

I nodded. "She needs food and water like any other living creature. Her body requires fuel, and lots of it. It can heal itself, so she can probably last longer than ordinary dogs, but eventually she's going to dehydrate or starve. All they have to do is put her in a cage somewhere and leave her."

My voice was starting to tremble, so I forced myself to remember who I was talking to. Dashiell didn't care about Shadow the way I did. I needed to use the things he *did* care about. I lifted my chin and looked at him directly. "There's no reason for them to fly her back to Europe to starve her," I told him. "Shadow is a powerful weapon. And I think she's still here, at least in California."

He nodded, understanding. "We may be able to recover her. And if they leave behind a group of witches to guard her, as I would do in their place, we can catch some of those who did this. All right. We go after Shadow." He bared his teeth in what was really not a very nice smile. He was human in my presence, so it wasn't vampire-scary. But it was still Dashiell-scary. "Where do we begin?"

Chapter 18

Where *do* you begin looking for a kidnapped dog monster?

My first thought was to try and trace the equipment necessary to contain a bargest, but that metal net Jesse had described wasn't something you could get in LA—the werewolves would have found out by now and raised a stink—which meant they'd brought their own gear. And if they were planning to starve her to death, there was no point in trying to trace purchases of her specialized food.

That left trying to figure out where the Luparii might be staying, but we didn't have any confirmation that they were still in LA County, and even if they were, thanks to Airbnb and the like, they could be anywhere. We didn't even know how many people the Luparii might have brought with them to Los Angeles.

Dashiell said he would spend the remainder of the night looking at ways in and out of the city—given the heavy equipment, it seemed likely that the Luparii had arrived by private plane or ship, and Dashiell did a lot of business at the ports—and Kirsten agreed to put out feelers among her various contacts in the witch community, both here and in Europe. She'd also put all of her witches on alert for the Luparii magic.

Will would be busy trying to evacuate as many of his werewolves as he could from LA County, but he'd also have a couple of his best pack members sniff around, starting near the cottage and where Kirsten and Hayne had found Jesse's unconscious body. They all knew Shadow's scent. Even so, I didn't have much hope for that panning out. Los Angeles was an insane amount of ground to cover.

Which left Jesse and me. I was ready to start driving around the city with my head out of the window screaming Shadow's name, but Jesse suggested that we interview a friend of his who worked at the prison, in case the Luparii had left any evidence behind. Short of a hotel room key or a signed confession, I had no idea how that was going to help, but neither of us had any other ideas, and sitting at the cottage worrying about Shadow wasn't going to get me anywhere.

And so, everyone went about wasting the day.

Jesse and I went down to Corona and met his friend Dan Cohen over early-morning coffee, but he couldn't help much. He did tell us one thing that was being kept from the press: one of the other guards had walked Petra into the minimum-security part of the prison and basically waved her goodbye, all of which appeared on the surveillance footage. That same guard, Cohen said, now claimed he had no memory of why he'd done it.

I looked at Jesse, who nodded to say he got it too. The guard had probably been pressed by a vampire, which confirmed what Kirsten had heard about the Luparii: they were expanding their ranks.

Jesse asked Cohen if Petra had left anything behind in her cell, and he frowned. "I work in a different area, but I've filled in a couple of shifts on that ward," he said. "That chick was an ice queen. No personal effects, no books, nothing. She was careful . . . and scary. Every other woman in there left her alone, which is saying something."

"Did she have computer privileges?" Jesse asked. "Visitors?"

Cohen shrugged. "They're looking into that now, but there certainly wasn't anything that stood out as unusual. In a way, she was a model prisoner: left everyone alone, didn't cause trouble. But she creeped everyone out. She didn't even have a cellmate, because they kept trying to commit suicide."

Jesse and I exchanged a look. The Luparii magic tended to twist things toward evil. Why not minds?

Cohen misinterpreted our expressions and said emphatically, "Yeah, see what I mean? Creepy."

So the prison was a dead end. At noon, we checked in with Kirsten and Will, who were both busy dealing with informants and/or panicky werewolves, and didn't have any new information on Shadow. I was racking my brain for ideas about finding Shadow, but I kept coming up empty. Finally, we went back to the cottage—I kept my radius expanded so I'd have plenty of advance warning if the Luparii decided to try another run at me—and started making calls. Jesse phoned his old contacts at various police stations to ask them to call if there were any sightings of a *very* unusual dog, or noise complaints about a bark loud enough to shake the ground. I called shelters. It seemed like a very long shot, but Shadow was as smart as some people, with magic-enhanced strength and healing. I had to believe there was a chance she could get away from the Luparii on her own.

At 7:45, shortly after sunset, Jesse and I were sitting in my living room, trying to figure out our next move. I had just gotten off the phone with Dashiell.

"Any new info?" Jesse asked.

I shook my head. "More of a confirmation. The vampires in Europe have noticed that the Luparii are expanding. They've kept an eye on it, but the Luparii have made it clear that their continued goal is eradicating werewolves."

"So the European vampires don't really care," Jesse concluded.

"Exactly."

He opened his mouth, but his cell phone rang before he could say anything. He checked the screen and then paused, frowning like he couldn't decide whether to answer.

"Who is it?" I asked.

"A former friend," he said briefly, and answered the phone. "This is Jesse Cruz."

Then he listened for a long time, interjecting only the occasional "Mmm-hmm," or "Yeah, probably." At one point he looked at me and made a little writing motion, and I got him the pen from the coffee table. He scribbled something on the palm of his hand.

Finally, Jesse hung up and turned to me, looking grim. "There was a murder in Long Beach that could be supernatural," he reported.

I needed a second to take that in. His friend was in the know, and worked with the LAPD. While helping Hayne with his security measures, I knew the (very short) list of humans who were allowed to know about the Old World despite not being attached to it. And one of them was a criminologist in Jesse's old division. "Is this Gloria Sherman?"

"Yes." Jesse looked tense. "Years ago, Dashiell told her to call me if she got a case that looked supernatural. But I haven't actually heard from her since the Luparii murders."

"Huh." That didn't surprise me, given how quiet things had been in LA. Well, maybe not "quiet" so much as "we keep our shit contained."

Then a terrible, terrible thought struck me. "Is it . . . are there jaws missing?"

Back when the Luparii were hunting wolves for the king of France, they would save the wolves' jaws as proof of death. On the Luparii's last visit to LA, they'd killed two of Will's werewolves and taken their jaws.

Shadow. Shadow had killed them.

Were the Luparii making her kill again?

Before I could follow that thought down the inevitable rabbit hole, Jesse said, "No, no. He definitely wasn't mauled."

"Then how did he die?"

He made a face. "By beheading."

Oh, gross. "Who *does* that?"

He glanced at me, a little amused. "I was going to ask you the same question," he said. "Even in a city with as much crime as LA, you don't get a lot of people who *die* by beheading. Sometimes a body will be decapitated in a traffic accident, or someone will cut a head off *after* death, but it's really hard to kill someone by chopping off their head. Even if you've got them unconscious, there are easier ways to do it."

"What's the victim's name?"

Jesse checked his hand, where he'd written the name. "Karl Schmidt."

I turned the name over in my mind for a few minutes, but came up with nothing. "Never heard of him. But I'll check with the others."

I texted Dashiell, Kirsten, and Will. Neither Kirsten nor Will had heard of Karl Schmidt. Dashiell called me back about ten minutes later. I put him on speakerphone at his request.

"I don't know this Karl Schmidt," he said crisply. "But I have arranged for the two of you to go look at his residence."

I was surprised that he was taking the whole beheading thing so seriously. "Do you mean you want us to go see the body?" I asked. "My understanding is that it's at the coroner's building now."

"I spoke to the coroner," he said curtly. "The body has gone through a preliminary examination, but they are unable to do the autopsy until the morning. There is nothing to see except a naked body and a detached head."

"What about defensive wounds?" Jesse asked.

"There were none."

Jesse's eyes widened. "That's . . . unusual."

"Which is one of the reasons why I'm sending you two down there." Dashiell was starting to sound impatient with us. "The house is your best source of information. I have arranged for one of the forensics people to meet you there and walk you through the scene. I will also send a vampire so you can erase his memory, and the memory of anyone else you need to speak to."

Ugh. This was annoying, though not really unexpected. Most of the time, my job didn't involve human witnesses—or rather, they'd already been pressed and sent home by the time I was called in. But from time to time I dealt with a situation that was still ongoing, and required the aid of vampires. "Can it just be Molly?" I tried not to sound whiny, considering the thinness of the ice I was standing on. "I hate working with people I don't know."

There was a long pause. "No," Dashiell said finally. "I think you and Molly have had enough adventures for one weekend, don't you?" His voice hardened with every word.

I winced. He didn't want Molly and me colluding, or conspiring, or whatever c-word meant we weren't team players. I was irritated by the lack of trust . . . but I also kind of deserved it. Either way, I wasn't stupid enough to answer him. Go me.

"However," Dashiell went on, "considering the current circumstances, I concede that you'd do well with an ally at your side. I'll call Wyatt."

I brightened. Wyatt was the cowboy vampire I'd brought back with me from Vegas. Only six weeks ago, he'd been suicidal after the death of his wife, but since coming to Los Angeles, he'd found a job and a place in Dashiell's service. I went and checked on him a couple of times a week at the bar where he worked, and he seemed to have found a degree of peace. He'd even stopped announcing his running countdown of the days left before my agreement to kill him kicked in.

Long story.

"What about Shadow?" I said.

"Everyone will continue their current efforts, Scarlett, but until we get more information, there's not much else we can do," he said, not unkindly. "Get back to me when you know whether or not this murder is Old World."

I wondered if he was sending us to a crime scene just to keep me busy, so I'd stop pestering him about the search. But he was right—I couldn't think of anything else to do.

After we hung up, Jesse looked at me. "So he can just arrange a tour of an active LAPD crime scene?"

I shrugged. "The man has juice."

We got ready to leave, which felt strange without Shadow hanging out by my leg, nudging my thigh to remind me that she wanted to come too. After I grabbed my keys and jacket and made sure I had a knife in each boot, we headed out to my van, the White Whale. I started toward the driver's seat, then stopped in my tracks, putting a hand on the hood. The morning sickness was making itself known again. "Change of plans," I mumbled, holding out the keys. "You drive."

He didn't comment, but when we got on the road, Jesse pulled into a gas station instead of heading for the freeway. The tank was already pretty full, but before I could ask what he was doing, he was out of the van and jogging into the store. He returned a few minutes later with a small box of saltines. "You need to eat," he ordered, thrusting the crackers at me.

"Dammit, you too?"

The whole idea of eating was repulsive at the moment, but I reluctantly tore open the package and bit off a cracker. It tasted like crunchy dust, but I kept mechanically chewing anyway. "So what's the significance of no defensive wounds?" I asked. "Dashiell seemed surprised, and your eyes went all 'ooooh.'"

"I've never had a beheading case, but we studied one at the academy," Jesse replied. "Let's say I've got an ax."

I blinked, swallowing a chunk of wet sawdust. "Sure. Kind of a left turn there, but fine. Ax."

"If I swung it toward your neck, what would you do?" He took his right hand off the wheel to pantomime the swing.

I thought for a second. "Step into the swing so I'm too close for you to use the ax."

"And that's not a bad choice, but then I could punch you, and you'd stagger back far enough for me to cut off your head."

I nodded, understanding. "Which would at least give me a bruise. What if I grabbed for the ax?"

"You'd probably get in the way of the blade and get cut. If you tried to wrestle it away from me, or hit me, that would show up somewhere: abrasions on your hands, cuts on your knuckles. Something."

"What if I never saw you coming?" I suggested. "Ax ninja?"

"That's pretty much the only possible way, but it takes a lot of force to remove someone's head in one clean blow. Unless the killer is a complete badass with brass balls, he probably wouldn't use enough force on the first pass. He'd have to hack at you, and if you could move at all, you'd get your hands up and your fingers would get cut, *or* you'd try to crawl away from him, which would likely result in carpet burns or broken fingernails. Defensive wounds."

Huh. I thought that over for a few seconds. "Not if I was unconscious. Or pressed," I reminded him. "It seems possible if there's a vampire involved."

"Maybe one of the Luparii's vampires?" he suggested.

I groaned. "God, I hope not." That would really be the pickle on this shit sandwich of a situation.

Chapter 19

Half an hour later, I threw my arms around a tall, lean vampire with a mustache that looked like it had arrived from 1890 in a time machine.

Jesse and I had parked just down the block from the crime scene house, and Wyatt pulled up behind us a second later, ambling over to greet me in his long duster jacket and cowboy hat, his big handlebar 'stache turned up in a smile. I jumped out of the van and hurried over to him. I'm not generally a hugger, but Wyatt always seemed like he needed it. And he was sort of my responsibility.

I stepped back and looked at Jesse. "Wyatt, this is my friend Jesse. Jesse, Wyatt."

The men gave each other nearly identical wary looks, and then Wyatt looked down at me with concern. "Miss Scarlett, are you all right? You look a little peaked."

"I'm fine, Wyatt. Let's get this over with." I stepped toward the house, then paused and looked back at him. "There might be a lot of blood in there, and I'll need to shrink my radius so you can press the human. Did you, um, already eat tonight?"

Wyatt looked surprised, but gave me his slow, lazy grin. "Yes, ma'am. Don't you worry about that."

We trooped toward the house, a yellow stucco bungalow with crime scene tape wrapped on little sticks to block off the whole yard. The yard itself was tiny, maybe ten square feet total, with some of those goddamned bird-of-paradise plants lining the little footpath leading to the front step. I *hate* those flowers. They always look like they're about to come to life and peck me to death. At the very least, they're all definitely planning something.

There was someone waiting on the front stoop: a black guy in his late thirties, short and lithe-looking. He stood up as we approached, and his eyes narrowed. "Jesse Cruz?" he said in a voice with a soft southern accent.

I looked at Jesse out of the corner of my eye, and caught the way his shoulders slumped. "Hey, Aaron. I didn't know you were working this case. How's it going?"

The other man ignored the question, looking pointedly at Wyatt and me. "And who are you?"

"Jay Aaron, this is Scarlett and that's Wyatt," Jesse said. "Aaron is a crime scene investigator."

Aaron made no effort to shake hands. "I was here from eleven o'clock this morning until half an hour ago, then I get called to come back and show around some consultant team," he said coldly, his gaze moving back to Jesse. "That your new gig? *Consulting?*" He managed to imbue that one word with an impressive amount of scorn.

Jesse started to answer, but Wyatt glanced at me. I nodded and shrank my radius down to a couple of feet. Wyatt stepped forward, making eye contact with Aaron. "You don't want to ask us any more questions about why we're here," he said smoothly. "You want to take us inside now."

Aaron blinked a couple of times, then turned to the door. "Right. Let's head in."

Behind his back, Jesse shot both of us a glare, but I shrugged, unrepentant. We were going to erase this guy's entire memory of us anyway. Might as well move things along.

Besides, he was kind of being an asshole.

We put on gloves, hairnets, and booties—Wyatt had to take off his cowboy boots to get his on—and then Aaron led us silently through the tiny foyer into a small, tidy living room that had last been decorated in the late seventies. There were splashes of blood everywhere, but they were especially concentrated around a blue velvet La-Z-Boy. Jesse went straight toward it, then looked quizzically over his shoulder at Aaron. "Was he sitting in the chair when someone cut off his head?"

"No." Aaron still looked sullen. "Blood spatter indicates he was kneeling in front of the chair."

Not unconscious, then. "Clean slice, or was there hacking?" Jesse asked.

"One slice," Aaron said, with the tiniest bit of relish in his voice.

While Jesse questioned Aaron, Wyatt leaned sideways in the doorway, where he had a clear view of both the living room and the foyer with the front door. His job wasn't detecting clues so much as watching our backs and pressing Aaron when we were done. He caught me glancing at him and gave me a slow wink, his moustache turning up at the ends as he grinned at me. I smiled back. It was good to be working together again.

I turned back to the living room. I wasn't sure how useful I would be on the clue front either, since all my experience with crime scenes involved trying to destroy them, but I wandered around the room, taking it in. I kept an ear on Jesse's conversation with Aaron, but the forensic details didn't really interest me. Besides, Jesse would translate the information into whatever I needed to know.

When you got past the death stench, the whole room had an underlying smell that I naturally associated with *old man*. Karl Schmidt had been in his eighties, which made his odd death even stranger. If you want to kill a man that old, there are a hundred easier ways to do it, all of which would get less interest from the police.

I scanned the titles on the bookshelf, which looked like standard old-man picks: Louis L'Amour, Agatha Christie, and a decent amount of nonfiction covering two subjects: baseball and World War II. At the end of the shelf, I picked up a photograph in a simple oak frame: an elderly man sitting at a picnic table, the kind of thing they had at every public park in LA. He was surrounded by children: mugging on the bench next to him, laughing at his feet, even a couple hanging over his shoulder. The youngest, a girl of about three, sat in his lap looking content as hell. Schmidt and his grandchildren, probably. I counted twelve of them, ranging in age from toddlers to maybe twenty or twenty-one.

I studied Schmidt's face. While the children had light brown skin, he was alabaster-pale, with faded blue eyes sunk into a deeply wrinkled face. He appeared to be in very good shape for his age—I could see the muscle definition on his forearm, where it was looped carefully around the girl in his lap. The old man was smiling, but it was a worried, protective smile, like he needed to stay on guard lest someone run up and snatch the children away from him.

I realized that the voices behind me had risen in volume, and turned around. Aaron and Jesse were still standing near the armchair, but their body language was combative. "—which you'd *know* if you hadn't decided to cash out of doing your job," Aaron was snapping.

Jesse didn't take the bait, but he looked like he was losing patience. "You know this isn't about that, Jay."

"Isn't it?" Aaron waved his arms to indicate the room. "How do I know you're not just here to write a *sequel*?"

Wyatt was raising his eyebrows at me from the doorway, asking if it was time to press Aaron. Jesse caught the look and shook his head. "I just want to understand," he said to Aaron. "Schmidt was sitting in the chair, watching TV, and someone came in and made him kneel down so they could behead him. But what was the weapon?"

"You tell me, supercop," Aaron said snidely, crossing his arms over his chest.

"Okay, that's enough," I said, rolling my eyes. "Wyatt, if you would help Mr. Aaron with his cooperation skills?" I pulled in my radius.

Wyatt, now a vampire again, took a step toward Aaron . . . but he paused, his nostrils flaring briefly. I was about to ask, but he shook his head a little and advanced on the criminologist, who shrank away from him, backing up toward my end of the room. Unfortunately for Aaron, eye contact was all Wyatt needed. "Answer our questions," he said in a perfectly level voice, his eyes drilling into Aaron's. "And keep a civil tongue in your head."

The smaller man sort of went slack, then nodded. Jesse sighed, not liking any of this. I couldn't really blame him. "What kind of weapon was used?" he asked. "An ax?"

"No," Aaron said in a wooden voice, his eyes locked on Wyatt. "We have to do further testing, but the angle of blood spatter suggests some sort of machete or sword."

Jesse and I exchanged a bewildered look. A sword? Like an actual motherfucking *sword*? I knew lots of vampires who carried knives so they could make a quick little cut to feed from instead of using their teeth. But a sword was impractical and raised too many questions. Everyone in the Old World took pains to blend in, not stand out. This whole thing felt fishy.

"Was the lock on the front door damaged?" Jesse asked Aaron next. "No."

"Did you find any physical evidence from the suspect?"

"There were several sets of fingerprints, but no hair or fibers that didn't come from the victim," Aaron replied, still in that unsettling monotone.

"Who's in charge of the case?"

"Abramowitz."

Jesse gave a tiny headshake, mostly to himself. He didn't know the name. "Is he any good?"

"No, not really."

The answer came as fast and dispassionate as the others, and for some reason I had to stifle a snort. Jesse looked at me and shrugged, done with questions.

"Okay, Wyatt," I said in a low voice, but he didn't break the press yet.

"Did your people find the drops of blood in that corner of the room?" Wyatt asked, pointing toward the doorway where he'd been standing.

"Yes."

"Whose blood is it?"

"We don't know. Same blood type as Schmidt, but we don't know how it could have gotten all the way across the room. We'll know more when the DNA goes through."

Wyatt looked at me, which broke the press. "That blood isn't Schmidt's," he said quietly. Aaron was swaying a little, looking unmoored.

"How do you know?" I asked Wyatt.

The vampire went back to the corner and put his nose right over the carpet, taking a long inhale. "It *is* male," he reported. "But it's young—I can smell the hormones." He sat back on his heels. "I can also smell the magic in it."

Aaron's confused face somehow clouded over even more. "Magic?"

I ignored him, focused on Wyatt. "Are you saying—"

He was already nodding. "Witchblood."

I had no idea what that meant, but there wasn't much else we were going to learn from the house, so Wyatt took Aaron out to his car to get a new evidence seal and to do his final press on Aaron's memory. Jesse and I waited in the house so he wouldn't spot us after he'd been pressed.

"You okay?" I asked Jesse when we were alone. "He was kind of a dick to you."

Jesse nodded. "Most of the cops feel like that," he said, peeling off his gloves with great concentration. "They think I'm a traitor, that I sold out for money and fame. Which is only half-right, I guess."

I stepped closer to him, forcing him to look down at me. His eyes were sad. "I thought you were going to be done with all that," I reminded him. "The pity party ended ages ago."

He sighed. "This isn't me feeling sorry for myself, Scar. I'm just . . ."

"Guilty?"

He scrubbed the palm of his hand through his short hair. "More . . . sad, I guess. I really liked being a cop." Before I could think of a response to that, he changed the subject. "Male witches are pretty rare, right?"

"Uh, yeah. I need to call Kirsten and find out if the witch who was here tonight was part of her group, but . . ." I made a face. "I think I would remember seeing a teenage male witch at one of their gatherings. As much as I hate to say it, I think this may be connected to the Luparii thing after all. They could have brought the witch with them."

"Then how was he injured?"

"No idea."

Wyatt knocked on the door to give the all clear, and Jesse and I went out onto the front step. Wyatt handed Jesse the new seal, and he spent a lot of time putting it up, very focused on getting the lines exactly right. I edged sideways a little so I could see his face in the dim lights from the street. He looked . . . distraught. I was missing something.

"Jesse . . . what else did you see, in your dream?"

He flinched away from me, as though I'd struck him across the face, but didn't answer. Shit, I'd been right.

Wyatt looked back and forth between us for a moment, and then wandered into the tiny side yard, pretending to be interested in the creepy-ass plants.

"You said they were rifling through your memory," I said softly to Jesse. "But not where you were or what you saw. I'm sorry. I should have asked."

For a moment, Jesse looked like he was going to answer, but then he just shook his head tightly.

Impulsively, I stepped forward and hugged him, breathing in his scent. Stupid baby hormones. Jesse hesitated for a second, and then his arms went around me. We stayed like that for a long moment. I hoped that the shadows would hide us from the occasional car driving past.

When he finally stepped back toward the door, his eyes were just a tiny bit pink. "What now?" he said. He obviously didn't want to talk about the Luparii's attack anymore.

I pushed out a breath, increasing the space between us a little. A car turned onto the street, and I realized we needed to get out of there before someone called the police. "I'll make that call to Kirsten, just to cover our bases. Then we can check in with Dashiell and—"

"Scarlett!" Wyatt was suddenly running toward me with a wild look on his face. He slowed down when he hit my radius and then abruptly changed direction, heading across the yard instead of toward me. I stared at him, confused, until I finally registered that the car on the street had slowed down, and the window was lowering.

Jesse had put it together a half-second before I did, and was already pushing me down, but not fast enough. A quick *pop-pop* of gunshots rang out in the night.

Chapter 20

I instinctively tried to reach for the knives in my boots just as Jesse was shoving me toward the ground, and the two of us ended up going down in a tangle, my shoulder scraping hard against one of the narrow pillars framing the front door. Jesse drew his gun from a side holster, propped himself on his elbow, and began firing at the car's open passenger window, causing the driver to peel away down the street. The noise of Jesse's gun seemed deafening.

When he was sure the car wasn't coming back, Jesse put the gun back in his holster and turned to me, yelling, "Are you hit? Are you hit?"

"I think I'm okay," I mumbled, trying to disentangle my arms and legs. Then I saw Wyatt lying on the front lawn.

He was on his back, his eyes closed, holding what looked like exit wounds in his stomach. That was when I realized he had changed his trajectory across the yard so he would be between the bullets and me. "Wyatt!"

I fought the natural urge to run to him and instead began scooting away on my butt. I could still feel him in my radius, which meant he wasn't dead . . . but he would be if he stayed human.

My response had been too quiet, so Jesse was still yelling at me, but I cut him off. "I'm fine! Wyatt jumped in front of the bullets. Help *him*."

So he stumbled to his feet and staggered toward Wyatt, pulling his jacket off along the way. I backed all the way off the front step and into the side yard, until the birds-of-paradise leaves began pricking at the backs of my bare arms. Then I hugged my knees to my chest, closed my eyes, and concentrated as hard as I could on shrinking my radius away from Wyatt.

It was more difficult than it should have been. When I'm overwhelmed by emotion—a.k.a. anytime I totally lose my shit—my radius flares outward. Getting shot at certainly qualified as overwhelming. On top of that, the nausea was flaring back to life, but I could *not* throw up at a crime scene. I just couldn't. I tried to slow down my breathing.

Think it through, Scarlett. I had no doubt that the attack had been intended for me—Jesse had been behind me, closer to the house. If Wyatt hadn't gotten in between me and the car, I'd be the one bleeding out on the grass. I shivered.

Okay, so someone had tried to kill me. I was protected in Los Angeles by Dashiell, so it was probably the Luparii . . . which meant they were still in town. Which meant Jesse had been right about them being committed to killing me. I just didn't really know why. Yeah, I had helped kidnap Shadow from them, but plenty of others had helped me do it. Why not take a run at Dashiell, or kill Jesse properly? Why was killing *me* worth the risk of sticking around now that they had Shadow?

They'd found me at the crime scene . . . which meant they'd known I'd be coming. So they *were* involved with Karl Schmidt's murder, but why? Had they set up a random weird crime scene just to lay a trap for me? That seemed ridiculous—there were plenty of easier ways to trap me. They could have just pretended to be an animal shelter that had found Shadow, and I would have raced over without thinking.

At the same time, though, I couldn't see any other reason for them to attack some elderly human in Long Beach who had no ties to any of us. I didn't get it . . . but I'd be willing to bet if we went and talked to Gloria Sherman in person, we'd find that a vampire had pressed her to call Jesse. Or a vampire had pressed someone at the coroner's office to call in Gloria, knowing she would call Jesse and me. Vampires were working for the Luparii now, and the Luparii wanted to kill me; therefore, non-Jesse humans couldn't be trusted.

"Scar?" Jesse yelled from the front walkway.

I stood up so he could see me, still holding in my radius. "Is he okay?"

"I'll be fine, Miss Scarlett," Wyatt called back. "But do you hear that?"

My ears were still ringing, but when I focused on listening, I heard it too: the sound of sirens in the distance. The damn neighbors must have called the police.

I groaned. Between Wyatt pressing humans and Dashiell's influence with the LAPD, we could get out of this fairly easily, but it would take forever. I reached for my phone to call Dashiell—but it wasn't in my pocket. I'd been so pleased to see Wyatt that I'd forgotten to take it off the charger in the van when we arrived. Goddammit. What a rookie mistake.

Jesse had stood up and was hurriedly unbuttoning his shirt, which was stained with blood. I started toward the yard to get the phone, but there was no way to get down the walkway and through the metal gate without getting close to Wyatt, who was only now struggling to his feet. I stopped ten feet away from him, my radius clenched tightly around me. "I left my cell in the van," I told them, in a voice that was probably louder than it needed to be. "I need to call Dashiell and get us some help."

"Here, use mine," Wyatt offered, and tossed me a slim black iPhone. "I'll fetch yours while you make the call."

I wanted to protest that he was still healing from a bullet wound, but we didn't have time, so I shrugged to myself and tossed my van keys at him, pointing left down the street toward the White Whale. He turned to go. "And Wyatt?"

He looked over his shoulder. "Thank you," I said. "I know you moved into the path of those bullets."

The cowboy grinned. "You do keep things interesting, don't you, Miss Scarlett?"

As Wyatt took off at a light jog—slow for a vampire, damned fast for a vampire healing from bullet wounds—Jesse wadded up his bloody shirt and put his jacket back on over his undershirt. He looked like he was about to audition for a mob movie in the early nineties. "That was Killian shooting at us," Jesse said grimly. "I saw his face. Sabine was probably driving."

"Shit." I turned my attention to Wyatt's unlocked cell phone. Dashiell's number was one of only a handful in the contacts folder. I touched the number and held the phone to my ear, waiting for him to answer. Wyatt was far enough ahead now for me to wander down the little walkway toward the sidewalk. I looked idly in the direction of the van, parked about half a block away.

"Hello?" Dashiell said.

The sirens were very close now. "It's me!" I practically yelled, but I was distracted by the van. If the cops saw Wyatt, they might stop to talk to him first.

But they never had the chance, because as he opened the driver's door, it exploded outward in a dazzling burst of fire.

Chapter 21

When the van door exploded outward, I instinctively dropped to the ground, feeling the rush of escaping heat. It wasn't as big or colorful as a movie explosion, but that somehow made it even worse, more real and terrifying. As soon as I could, I staggered upright. "Wyatt!" I screamed, lurching toward the van. It looked like a giant had wrapped one enormous hand around it and squeezed. Bright orange flames were rising from the shattered windows, and I couldn't see any sign of Wyatt.

I ran into the street, vaguely aware of Jesse shouting something right behind me, trying to get me to stop. Neighbors were running out of their houses, many of them holding cell phones. Shit. Any second someone was going to start taping, if they hadn't already.

But I still had to know.

When I circled the van, I saw the body right away. Wyatt was lying facedown in the street, his body blackened, his right leg completely missing. My searching eyes found it a few feet away, the pants leg still on fire. I skidded to a stop and closed my eyes, forcing myself to feel for Wyatt in my radius.

"Scarlett!" Jesse came panting up behind me. "We have to—"

"Shh!" I held out a flat hand to silence him.

There.

My eyes popped open as I felt the little spark of vampire magic. "We have to run," I said, dazed. I was too upset; I couldn't rein in my radius. I needed to get farther away from Wyatt if he had any hope of making it.

Jesse came around to my front, looking exasperated. "That's what I've been *saying!*" Grabbing my hand, he practically dragged me back toward the Schmidt house. There was a tiny amount of space between it and the building next to it, and he led me through the side yard, around to the next street. None of the neighbors were watching us—to them, we probably looked like two more spectators who'd run out after the explosion; their attention was focused on the van and the body.

Oh, God, *Wyatt's* body.

When we were two streets away, Jesse slowed down and put his arm around me like we were just any couple out for a stroll. Now and then he would crane his head to see if we were being followed. I had dropped Wyatt's phone in the yard, and my own cell had exploded in the van, but Jesse still had his. When he was sure no one was tracking us, he called Dashiell.

It probably should have been me, but I was too . . . Poor Wyatt, he'd gone through so much just to protect me, and now I had no idea if he was going to survive the next few hours, much less whether he'd be able to grow his leg back. Werewolves could do it, I knew, but why had I never thought to ask about vampire limbs? And what if Dashiell treated him and he *did* survive? After losing his wife, Wyatt had wanted to die. Would he be angry if we didn't let him move on?

And there was also my van. God, I loved that stupid van. I'd paid it off myself, one of the first adult things I'd ever done. I'd taken such pains with it, and now it barely qualified as scrap metal.

"Okay," Jesse was saying into the phone. "I do . . . I will . . . Well, where do you suggest?"

After a couple more minutes, he hung up the phone and looked down at me. "We're going to a hotel," he announced. "Dashiell will send Molly over with some clothes. And he said you already have an extra phone at your place."

I nodded numbly. I'd trashed so many cell phones over the last few years that Abby had started buying them for me in bulk. Dashiell insisted on getting good ones—I'd once tried buying my own older model, but he insisted on good phones with GPS tracking. Dashiell was very big on GPS tracking.

"Does he have people at the scene?" I managed to say.

Jesse nodded. "When he heard Schmidt's house was in Long Beach, Dashiell put a couple of the vampires at the Copper Room on standby. They're already there talking to the cops. And they'll recover Wyatt . . ." Jesse hesitated for a moment, then added softly, "Either way."

The Copper Room was a vampire hangout in Long Beach, only a couple of miles away. It was popular among the younger, newer vampires. "Okay," I mumbled. "That's good, I guess. What does he want us to do?"

"Nothing for the next few hours," Jesse said. "He said he'll be busy making sure everyone who witnessed it gets pressed to think the car fire was an accident. He wants to meet an hour before dawn. Meanwhile, we should get some rest."

Rest. It seemed like I'd been doing so much of that lately, but then I never seemed to get more than a couple of hours. It was taking its toll. Also, didn't pregnancy make women more tired than usual? I should have asked Molly for more of her *What to Expect* knowledge before Lex pressed her.

My thoughts wandered around like that for a few more minutes as we strolled along the sidewalk. Then a dark red Lexus pulled up alongside us, and Jesse steered me toward it. "I think this is our ride."

To my surprise, the car's driver was Beatrice, Dashiell's wife. She was wearing tight jeans and a blousy white shirt, which was about the most casual I'd ever seen her at night. She still had five-inch stiletto heels, though, which clicked on the pavement as she came around the car and tossed Jesse the keys. "Hi, Bea," I said. My voice came out woozy. "You got here fast."

"I was at the harbor on business," she said as she strode up to us. She paused, gave me a critical look, and took me by the shoulders. "You can't go into shock right now, Scarlett," she said sternly. "Someone is trying to kill you. You must keep it together."

I blinked hard. "Someone is trying to kill me," I repeated. "And Wyatt might die. My van is gone. My home isn't safe."

"And you look terrible and smell like smoke," she added, "but this list isn't helping you stay alive." She pressed a rectangle of black plastic into my hand. Curious, I looked down and saw a very fancy-looking credit card.

"It's a corporate card for a shell company," she said. "For the hotel. Call Molly when you're settled. She can bring your things. Don't give her your room number over the phone; she'll call up from the lobby."

I had lost the thread of the conversation by then, but Beatrice looked at Jesse. "Get her out of here. Keep her safe."

"How will you—" Jesse began, but then a second Lexus, this one black, pulled up behind Beatrice's car. She'd had a security team with her, of course. I couldn't see the driver through the tinted glass, but Beatrice was already waving us on. "Go now."

Jesse drove us to the biggest hotel nearby, the Long Beach Hyatt. I don't remember anything about checking in or getting up to the room. The next thing I really registered was Jesse handing me a robe and pushing me into a bathroom with shiny new fixtures.

I showered and washed my hair, letting the hot spray blast me in the face, and by the time I stepped out, I felt almost like myself again.

Well, a really, really exhausted and worried version of myself, anyway.

When I finally emerged, Jesse stood up from the side of the bed, where he'd been staring down at his phone. He looked tired and grubby, and there was a smudge of dirt or ash on one cheek. He'd thrown the button-down shirt in the garbage can outside before we came in, and the muscles in his chest stood out against his gray tee shirt. He stood right in front of me, assessing me with worried eyes.

It kind of took my breath away.

"Are you okay?" he asked.

"Not really. Any word on Wyatt?"

Jesse shook his head.

There was a moment of painfully awkward silence, and then I blurted, "There's, um, only one bed." I immediately felt stupid. We'd shared a bed the night before, but that had been sort of an accident. This was a choice.

"Yeah," Jesse said, one hand lifting to scrub his palm through his hair. "They have some kind of convention here this weekend; there wasn't a double queen room. But I can take the pullout couch. Scarlett—" He stepped forward and grasped me around the waist, steadying me, and I realized I'd been swaying. "You should sleep," he said huskily. He sort of danced me over to the edge of the bed. When the back of my legs hit it, all the remaining strength seemed to leave my body. Jesse started pulling back the covers to tuck me in.

"Why do they want to kill me?" I said, to no one in particular.

"Best guess? Because you can stop whatever they're about to do," Jesse said, and his words chilled me. "But not without some rest. I'm going to take a shower now, okay?"

"Jesse." I caught his wrist, and he turned to look down at me, surprised. I tried to figure out what I wanted to say, but all that came out was, "Sleep in the bed."

He looked at me for a long moment, the light from the hallway casting a shadow on half his face. "I don't know if that's—"

Oh, God, how I didn't want to hear the end of that sentence. "Please?"

He bent and kissed my forehead, creating a spot of warmth that spread down to my stomach. "Okay."

Chapter 22

It was only a little after nine, but by the time Jesse came out of the shower, Scarlett was fast asleep at the edge of the bed. She hadn't moved.

The hotel phone rang, and Jesse hurried around the bed to answer it, although he doubted there was much that would wake Scarlett just then. It was Molly, as he'd expected. He gave her the room number, and a few minutes later, there was a soft knock on the door.

"Nice robe," she said as soon as he opened the door. She wore jeans and a tight tank top, her blonde curls bouncing against the large designer backpack on her shoulders. She moved past Jesse into the room before he could respond. "How is she?"

"Sleeping. Don't you have to ask permission to enter?" he said, slightly annoyed. Jesse turned and followed her toward the sleeping Scarlett.

"Har har. Not for a one-night stay. If you lived here for months and made it your home, maybe."

Molly's appearance changed subtly as she hit Scarlett's radius, but she was used to it and took it in stride. "Damn, she looks like shit. Aren't you feeding her?"

"Shh! You're going to wake her up."

"Nah. She sleeps like the dead. And I would know." Molly gave him a wide grin and a little *see what I did there* look, and took off the backpack. "Clothes for both of you. I guessed on your size."

"Thank you," he said, accepting the bag.

"Her new Batphone is in there, too. I texted the number to Abby so she can do her phone magic on it."

"Did you bring Scarlett's knife belt?"

Molly frowned. "Sorry, no. I was just told the clothes and the phone."

Jesse nodded. They'd figure it out in the morning. "What about you?" he said. "You know the cottage isn't safe right now . . ."

"It's okay. Dashiell has a safe house with a basement in Arcadia. I'll still be close if Scar needs me."

"You've changed," Jesse blurted, surprising himself. Molly raised her eyebrows, and he shrugged, a little embarrassed. "I mean, a few years ago, when Scarlett got herself in deep shit, you left town for a few days."

"That was before," Molly said simply. She was still looking at Scarlett, fierce love written all over her face. "She's my sister now."

Then she turned her gaze to Jesse. "Besides, I'm not the only one. Three years ago *you* would have tried to convince her to take this mess to the police."

Jesse expected the words to sting, but he realized she was right and gave a little shrug. "Maybe."

Molly was watching him carefully. "You're not going to ditch her again, are you?"

Jesse started. "I didn't—no. I'm not going to ditch her. I would never."

He regretted the too-honest words as soon as they left his mouth, but Molly just started shaking her head. "You two," she grumbled.

"What?"

Molly rolled her eyes and pointed both hands at Scarlett, then at him. "You're in love with her. She's in love with you. But you dance around each other like you're in orbit, because you're both too god-damned scared to do anything."

"Shh!" Scandalized, he looked at Scarlett, who hadn't moved. Jesse grabbed Molly's shoulder and ushered her into the hallway, snagging his room key on the way. The hall was empty, but Jesse still cinched his robe a little tighter, which made Molly smirk. He pulled the door shut behind them.

"You don't know what you're talking about," he told her. "There's that guy, Jameson—"

"Jameson is dead, and she was never in love with him," Molly interrupted. "She was in love with the idea of not being alone. But she never *was* alone. She's just an idiot. And so are you."

Jesse threw up his hands, exasperated. It probably didn't look very dignified, considering the hotel robe. "What do you care?"

"Human lives are short, dumbass," Molly said. She stabbed a finger toward the hotel door. "She almost died twice today. And knowing you, when she does die, you'll be right there dying too. Do you really want that to happen without finding out if you guys would have worked?"

Jesse just stared at her for a moment. He felt like he'd been ambushed into this conversation, and now he was rapidly losing control of his own position in it. "It *wouldn't* work," he said weakly. "Too much has happened. The timing—"

"The timing wasn't right before," she agreed. "But get your head out of your ass and look around. She's right here, literally in front of you, and you're in love with her." She crossed her arms over her chest, as though resting her case. Jesse wondered how long she'd been waiting to make this speech.

"Molly," he said wearily, "I love you, I do. You're my favorite vampire ever. But I can't talk about this with you right now."

"Fine," she huffed, raising her hands in an *I give up* gesture. "At least she wasn't pregnant," she muttered. "That would have *really* fucked things up."

Jesse froze. Scarlett had said not to mention the baby in front of Molly, but he hadn't realized that she'd actually convinced Molly that it was a false alarm.

Molly took his silence for shock. "Sorry," she said, looking actually contrite. "I probably wasn't supposed to tell you, but she had this pregnancy scare. It's all good, though." She shook her head. "Can you imagine? The entire Old World would be after that kid, and Scarlett thinks she's barely keeping her head above water now."

"She's stronger than she thinks she is," Jesse found himself saying.

"Well, duh," Molly scoffed. "That's not the point."

The elevator bell dinged, and a couple made their way down the hall toward them, giggling. They went quiet as they passed, giving curious looks to Jesse in his robe. He turned back to the hotel room door. "Good night, Molly."

"Tell Scarlett I'll call her at sunset," she said, turning to go.

"Molls?"

She paused.

"Thanks for the delivery. You're a good friend."

Molly just cocked an eyebrow. "So are you," she said, "but we both know that's not going to be enough for either of you. Not forever."

Jesse took the backpack into the bathroom and unzipped it. Molly had packed him brand-new clothes, still bearing tags from Nordstrom. She'd chosen dark pink boxers printed with little flamingos, just to be a jerk, but Jesse wasn't about to complain. He was lucky she hadn't packed him a thong.

He set the alarm clock and his cell phone alarm before climbing into the empty side of the massive bed, careful not to disturb Scarlett. Then he lay staring at the ceiling, running through it all in his head: Shadow being taken, the confrontation with Dashiell, all that fruitless running around searching for the bargest, and then, of course, the explosion at the Schmidt crime scene. Dashiell and his people would be busy cleaning up that mess tonight, but when they met in the morning, they would need a new game plan. Jesse had no *idea* what to do next. They'd failed to find Shadow, and they'd learned very little at the crime scene, probably because it had really been a trap. A damned good trap. The Luparii kept getting ahead of them.

Jesse rolled onto his side, looking at Scarlett's sleeping form. He'd left the bathroom light on, telling himself it was for her, but part of him knew the truth: now that things were finally quieting down, the fears he'd been fighting all day were seeping to the front of his mind. The memory of Sabine rummaging through his mind was so strong; it felt like greasy fingerprints had been left behind. Jesse knew that was ridiculous—whatever she'd done to him had been broken the second Scarlett got close—but he was pathetically grateful that Scarlett had wanted to share the bed. Partly this was so he could keep reassuring himself that she was alive, but there was also no way the Luparii could put him back in the twisted slumber while he was this close to her.

Not that they can put you in the slumber at all, he told himself. The witch, Sabine, had obviously needed to be nearby . . . right?

What if she'd taken a lock of his hair or something and could now use it to fuck with Jesse anytime she wanted?

He worried over this for a long time, and even went into the bathroom to check his hair in the mirror, feeling silly. He climbed back into the bed. He didn't want to touch Scarlett without her permission, but he found himself scooting closer and closer in the king-size bed, until he could just feel her back against his arm. His behavior reminded him of his parents' dog, Max, who preferred to sleep so he was *just* touching someone, to reassure himself that they were still there.

Only then was Jesse able to sleep.

Chapter 23

The next thing I knew, Jesse was nudging me awake. "Scarlett. Scar."

I grunted at him and cracked an eyelid. I'd rolled over in the night and was facing him; his brown eyes seemed to shine in the dim light from the bathroom. "Hngh," I said eloquently. "Time's it?"

"Just after four a.m. We're supposed to be at Dashiell's in an hour."

"What day is it?"

"Sunday."

"Traffic won't be bad. Sleep more," I mumbled. But then I remembered the night before and abruptly sat up in bed. "Wyatt?"

Jesse was already checking his phone. "Hayne texted. He said Wyatt is alive, but it's touch and go. They're feeding him blood as fast as they can."

I thought about that for a moment, then reached out my hand. "Gimme."

Jesse handed over the phone, and I scrolled through the contacts and called Lex, who sounded awake, thank God. The moment she answered, I said, "It's Scarlett. Your blood's, like, special, right?"

There was a pause, and then she said dryly, "I take it Jesse's alive?"

Oops. I had forgotten to update her the day before. "I'm sorry," I said, meaning it. "Yes, he's okay. Here, I'll put you on speaker."

I hit the right button, and Jesse said, "Hey, Lex."

"Hey. You okay?"

"More or less."

"Good." She cleared her throat. "Yes, Scarlett, boundary witch blood is unique in some ways. Why?"

"Could I . . . um . . . have some?"

Before she could answer, I explained about Wyatt getting shot and then getting a leg blown off.

"Someone *blew up your van?*" Lex said in disbelief. "What the hell are you into now?"

I couldn't really take offense at that. "Something big, I think. We don't know a lot yet, but we're working on it. Can you come donate blood to Wyatt?" I wasn't sure it would be enough to help him, but if Wyatt died and there was something I hadn't tried . . .

"I have my own life here, Scarlett, remember?" she said, clearly losing patience with me. "There are people who are under *my* protection, too. I can't just fly to LA at the drop of a hat."

"But then you must understand what I'm going through," I pushed. "Wyatt took a hit that was meant for me . . . right after taking bullets that were meant for me. Please?"

There was another moment of silence, and I started to think I'd gone too far. But then Lex sighed and said, "I could send Katia."

Jesse and I exchanged a surprised look. Lex's biological aunt, Katia, had come to LA a few months earlier as a sort of involuntary henchman for a man named Oskar, who had been seeking revenge against Molly. Oskar was dead now, and as part of a deal with Lex's boss, Maven, we'd sent Katia to Colorado. I hadn't thought to ask what had happened to her afterward, even when I was right there in Boulder. Stupid Scarlett.

But Katia did have boundary witch blood, like Lex. "What's she up to these days?" I said. Best to be cautious.

"Right now, Maven has her traveling around Colorado as a sort of vampire ambassador, checking in with various communities. She's in . . ." There was a pause, like Lex was checking a calendar. "Grand Junction today. But I could probably get her on a flight this afternoon."

I forced myself not to jump up and down quite yet. "Will that be okay? Will you get in trouble?"

There was a pause, and Lex cleared her throat. "Actually, Katia is—understandably—hesitant to swear an oath of loyalty to Maven, given what happened with Oskar. She helps with things on a freelance basis, but it can get . . . tense. It might be good for everyone if she takes a short trip to LA. Maybe she can clear the air there, too."

Oh. Right. Katia had kind of terrorized the city a little bit. I took about two seconds to ponder whether I'd get in trouble with Dashiell for bringing her back to town without consulting him, but decided I didn't care. If Lex trusted Katia, I did too, and if she could help Wyatt, it was worth the trouble.

"That would be amazing, thank you." I gave her Hayne's phone number and asked her to have Katia call him as soon as she arrived. I didn't know where they were keeping Wyatt, but Hayne could arrange the blood donation. Before we hung up, Lex said, "Listen, I was going to call you today anyway. Maven remembered something else last night, about the little girl in Azad."

"Okay . . ." Jesse gave me a curious look, and I mouthed, *Tell you later.*

"She and her grandmother both had specialties."

It took me a moment to parse that one out. Most witches were trades witches, meaning they could work with just about any kind of magic, but a small percentage had a specialty. Lex, for example, could only work boundary magic.

But if the female null in Azad came from a line of specialty magic, and she'd passed it on to her witchling baby . . . that meant that I needed to figure out whether or not my own mother's witchblood had been specialized or not. "Okay," I said at last. "I'll put it on my to-do list. Thanks, Lex."

As soon as I hung up, I threw back the covers. Jesse obviously wanted to ask about Lex's information, but I said, "I'll tell you about it in the car. We need to stop back at the cottage before Dashiell's."

Jesse looked at the clock on the bedside table. "We don't have time. And it's not safe."

"I know. But I need more knives. And my bulletproof vest."

As I'd figured, that made Jesse waver, but he shook his head. "We can buy you a new one. We've got the credit card."

"But it's a lot harder to replace my knives and my knife belt," I argued. My voice sounded firm, for maybe the first time in the past three days. "Look, if we're late, I can keep Dashiell awake past dawn, but who knows where he's going to send us today. I'm not going to feel safe unless I have my knife belt."

He sighed. "Fine. In and out, though, okay?"

I nodded. "Promise."

Half an hour later, we were heading into Marina del Rey. I had filled Jesse in on most of the trip to Boulder, including what Maven had said about the baby.

"Did she give you any advice?" Jesse asked when I'd finished. We were nearly at the exit to get to the cottage.

"No, that's when Kirsten called me to come rescue you from certain death," I said solemnly. Jesse rolled his eyes but didn't take the bait.

I had texted Dashiell to explain why we'd be late, and he had very succinctly texted back, "The Lexus has bulletproof windows." Which was *so* comforting.

Okay, fine, Jesse found it comforting. Personally, I thought the Lexus was a very nice car, but its plush seats made me feel like I was lying on my back, which made me feel exposed, which made me want my knives even more . . . not to mention my van.

My van. It was stupid to be so sad about a vehicle that was replaceable, but goddammit, I had loved the van.

Jesse made us cruise past the cottage a couple of times to check it out, but nothing seemed to have changed from the day before, and I didn't feel anyone with magic even when I extended my radius as far as it would go. Jesse still insisted on checking the house, gun in hand, before waving me inside.

I went straight to the bedroom closet and got out the bulletproof vest and my knife belt. My ex-boyfriend, Eli, had had it made for me by one of those companies that sells stuff at Renaissance festivals and comic-book conventions and stuff. It was sized perfectly for my upper waist, so I could still move and sit down and everything without knives stabbing into my abdomen.

I put on a tank top with a built-in sports bra, wriggled into the bulletproof vest, and strapped the knife belt on over *that*, adjusting the buckles to fit the vest's extra bulk. It was a little too easy—I'd lost weight. Opening the door so Jesse and I could talk, I went to the bucket of knives on my dresser and began loading them into the belt.

Jesse came in and sat down on my bed, watching me slide knives into the little loops. Then he asked in a too-casual voice, "Do you ever hear from Eli?"

My fingers fumbled, and I dropped a knife on the floor and cursed.

"Not really," I said once I'd recovered. "We've sort of agreed that I don't go to Hair of the Dog unless it's for work, and he doesn't come to meetings at Dashiell's unless Will orders it. I hear he started dating one of the new werewolves who came into town last year."

Jesse's eyebrows quirked. "Oh, really?"

"Yeah." I finished loading the belt, covered it with a soft, loose tee shirt, and plopped down on the bed next to him. "I've met her. She's tiny and cute and sort of obedient—not a dog joke, I swear. She worships Eli, which he . . . deserves, I guess? Frankly, I try not to think about it."

"That all sounds *very* emotionally healthy," Jesse said gravely.

I punched him in the arm. "Okay, why don't we talk about your quickie marriage and divorce?"

I expected him to back down, but he just gave a little shrug. "What do you want to know?"

Oh. Well played. I almost blew it off, but we'd never really discussed what had happened between him and the woman who'd ghostwritten his book, and if I was being honest . . . I was incredibly curious. "Why did it fall apart?" I finally said. I knew Jesse wouldn't have married the woman if he hadn't cared for her, and I wasn't so conceited as to think he was hung up on me, so something else must have tanked the relationship.

"It was my fault. She was nice and fun and easy to be with. I loved her, sort of, but mostly I was trying to *will* myself a normal life, or at least normal for LA. You know, working regular hours on a creative project, date night with the wife, Sunday evenings at my parents, everything orderly and on schedule."

"That sounds kind of nice," I admitted. The only thing I had that approached a schedule involved my DVR.

"It was, for a while. And there was no big fight, no cheating, nothing like that. We finished the book, and a couple of months went by with her taking these meetings for our next project." He shrugged, looking ashamed. "But I kind of just woke up one morning and knew I was kidding myself. 'Fake it till you make it' doesn't apply to everything. And she couldn't understand what had changed." He sighed, rubbing his forehead with the heel of his hand. "The problem was that *nothing* had changed. I'd changed my life, but not myself. And I'd been using her to make myself feel like a different person. I don't feel great about it."

I kind of understood what he meant. For a long time, I'd sensed Eli and I weren't working, that we were never really going to be able to fit together the way either of us needed. But I'd willfully ignored that because I thought I'd be happier with a compromised relationship than with no relationship at all. And I'd pretended to be fine with things that weren't.

I wanted to . . . I don't know, pat Jesse's shoulder or tell him it was okay or something, but it was just too awkward. He met my eyes again. "Does that answer your question?"

I nodded. "Ready to go?"

"Yeah." Then he froze. "Did you hear that?"

"What?"

"Someone just knocked on the front door."

Oh. I squinted at the clock. It wasn't even five a.m. Who the hell would be coming over? I couldn't see the Luparii deciding to knock. Well, not again, anyway. I got up and moved toward the bedroom door, starting to extend my radius.

"Hang on!" Jesse said. He was reaching for his gun in its side holster. "It could be—"

Then there was a familiar bark. Jesse and I locked eyes, and I could see him opening his mouth to tell me to wait, that it might be a trap.

I ignored this.

Instead, I threw the bedroom door open and ran for the front door, though I at least had the presence of mind to look through the peephole. There was a young man standing outside, bedraggled and exhausted-looking, but I barely glanced at him. My fingers scrabbled at the locks, and I threw the door wide. "Shadow!" I cried out.

The bargest knocked me flat on my back.

Chapter 24

Jesse couldn't help but smile as he watched the bargest slobber all over Scarlett as she laughed, tears running down her face. Shadow's fur—the little she had—was matted and filthy, and her dry, pebbled skin was obviously streaked with blood around her mouth and sides. The blood was coated in what looked like thick brown dust. Her tail, which naturally clubbed off at about ten inches long, was wagging back and forth so fiercely that Jesse was sure it would leave a welt if he stepped within its reach. A small cloud of dust was coming off her tail.

Then Shadow turned to Jesse, rearing up and putting her front paws on his shoulders so she could lick his face, too. "Ack! Down, please," Jesse said. When Shadow finally dropped back to all fours, Jesse turned his attention toward the young man, one hand going to rest on his gun. The kid was maybe eighteen, and he was even filthier than Shadow, covered in the same dirt. There was a strip of what looked like his shirttail tied around one arm, and a brownish-red stain had soaked through it.

"Um, hi," the kid said, shifting his weight from one side to the other.

Scarlett climbed to her feet. "Who are you?"

"I'm Owen? Um, your dog or whatever saved me, and then she was super insistent that we needed to come here?" He blushed. "She kind of herded me like I was a sheep, actually. Is this where—I mean, are you her owner?"

Shadow's head snapped around so she could give him a dirty look. Scarlett just smiled, reaching down to scratch behind the bargest's furry ear. She was practically radiating relief and joy. "Nobody *owns* Shadow," she corrected. "But I pay the rent and buy the dog food, yeah. I'm Scarlett." She held out her hand, which the kid shook.

"Okay. Shadow, that's her name. Okay. And you're Scarlett." The kid nodded to himself, like this was a really important mystery he'd just solved. "You're the one."

Scarlett's expression hardened a little. "The one what?"

The kid took a step back, scuffing his feet. "Um, the one they went to kill last night? We would have warned you, but we didn't escape till after, and then I didn't know how to find you . . ." He pushed out an anxious breath and tried for a smile. Jesse realized that beyond all the caked dirt and blood smears, his face was familiar.

"What's your name?" Jesse asked.

"I'm Owen. Owen Schmidt."

Jesse and Scarlett exchanged a look. "You're Karl's grandson," she said. "I saw you in the picture at his house."

The boy didn't actually fall down, but his whole body seemed to crumple, like someone had extracted all the oxygen from him. "Yeah. They killed him. But they wanted me alive, see, because I—"

"Because you have witchblood," Scarlett said quietly. "Luparii witchblood."

"Yeah," the kid said, looking at Scarlett with astonishment. "How did you know that?"

There was a heartbeat of silence, and then Jesse and Scarlett both started asking the kid questions at the same time. Owen Schmidt raised both hands and took a tiny step backward, giving Scarlett a pleading look. "Look, I'll explain the whole thing, as much as I can, I swear. But first—and I know I'm a stranger—but I would be really, really, deeply grateful if you'd let me use your shower? Please?"

There was a flurry of activity after that. While Scarlett found the kid some clean towels and sweats, Jesse fed Shadow ostrich steaks from the freezer. She gobbled them up still frozen, along with about two gallons of water, and Jesse knew that he and Scarlett had been right about the Luparii's plan to starve her to death.

Then Scarlett called Dashiell to explain the situation, and Jesse insisted on checking Owen's wound before the kid got it wet in the shower. When he untied the bandage, he let out a low whistle: it was a nasty-looking scrape on top of a deep bruise, but it didn't look like it would need stitches. "It's not as bad as it looks," Owen said, though he was wincing. "I just didn't want to leave a blood trail for them to follow."

"How did you get it?" Jesse asked.

"Getting off the cage rock," Owen said, as though that would explain everything.

Jesse shook his head. "Never mind. Get yourself cleaned up and you can tell us the whole story."

He left Owen in the bathroom, hearing the shower go on almost immediately. Scarlett wasn't talking in the living room anymore, but he found her in the backyard, sluicing muddy water off the bargest with a garden hose. A sponge and a bottle of dog shampoo sat beside her.

"I *know* it's cold," Scarlett was saying, "but we both know what would have happened if I let you use the bathtub again."

Shadow's lips drew open in a terrifying doggy grin. "What would have happened?" Jesse asked as he walked over.

"She would have shaken muddy water all over the inside of the house. *Again.*" Scarlett gave the bargest an exaggerated glare, but Shadow was unrepentant, dancing around in the spray of water, pleased as hell with herself. Jesse couldn't blame her. She was a hero.

"I can help," he offered. While Scarlett ran the hose, Jesse bent slightly so he could rub dog shampoo into the bargest's furry parts, gently cleaning her pebbled skin with the sponge.

"What did Dashiell say?" he asked as they worked.

"He accepts postponing the meeting. He wants us to talk to the kid and get the whole story, then call Hayne. We are provisionally allowed to wake Dashiell during the day, if it's an absolute emergency."

"Whoa." Jesse had some idea of how seriously Dashiell took his security. The one time Scarlett had woken him up during the day, he'd slapped her across the face. Jesse still ground his teeth a little at the memory.

"We are *not*, however," Scarlett went on, "to take Owen to the mansion. In case this is all a trap."

"Huh." It had occurred to Jesse that Owen's sudden arrival could be a ploy, of course, but he hadn't thought the possibility through that far. If Owen was with the Luparii, playing nice with them wasn't a bad plan. It could potentially get him into Dashiell's mansion during the day with a null in tow—pretty much the only way the cardinal vampire could be killed, short of an army.

Then again, in that scenario, Shadow would kind of have to be in on the betrayal, which made the whole idea laughable.

"Should we be worried that the kid will run?" Scarlett asked him.

Jesse shook his head. "I don't think he's going anywhere. He was limping when he walked into the bathroom, and he's scared out of his mind. Besides, where can he go on foot that Shadow here couldn't track him?"

Shadow licked the air near Jesse's face appreciatively. "What do you think, Shadow?" Scarlett asked the bargest. "Can we trust Owen?"

Shadow's head tilted sideways for a second, a perfect mimicking of "Let me think about it." Then she licked the air again and sort of pawed the ground in front of Scarlett.

"She *thinks* so," Scarlett translated to Jesse.

She rinsed the bargest one more time and then turned off the hose faucet. "I know you're gonna shake the water off," she said in a warning tone, mock-glaring at Shadow. "But if you wait until Jesse and I get back inside, I will give you one of those three-foot ostrich bones I've been saving."

Shadow's club tail waved, but there was something mischievous about it. Scarlett dropped the nozzle and grinned at Jesse. "Run!"

They dashed around the side of the house, Scarlett laughing breathlessly as they narrowly avoided an exploding grenade of water. For a creature only half-covered in fur, Shadow could really shake off water with the best of them.

Scarlett paused at the front door, leaning against the wall for support. She was still grinning, and her joy was infectious.

"I got her back," she said, her breathing finally slowing down. There were tears of happiness in her eyes. "I don't know what's going to happen with the"—she gestured at her stomach—"or the Luparii or whatever, but I got her back." Her face broke into a joyous smile. "I got you both back."

Without thinking about it, Jesse took two quick steps forward so he was inches away from her. Scarlett's grin faded, but she didn't move away. For once, she didn't even make a joke. She just gazed up at him seriously. When he slid his hands around her hips underneath the bulletproof vest, she reached up with both hands and entwined them around his neck—

And then Shadow came rampaging around the corner of the cottage, nosing her way between them in a total dog move. Jesse instinctively stepped back, but not before catching the look of relief on Scarlett's face. She was glad the bargest had interrupted them.

Shadow pawed at the doorknob, and Scarlett twisted it so she could barrel in.

"Let's . . . um . . ." Scarlett mumbled, and then she ducked past him into the house.

Jesse cursed himself. What the hell had he been thinking, trying to kiss her? This was Molly's fault, he decided. She'd gotten into his head. But if Scarlett could compartmentalize, so could he.

The shower was off when he went back inside. A moment later Owen emerged in a pair of Scarlett's baggiest sweatpants and a too-big Hair of the Dog tee shirt that had probably belonged to Eli. Owen was a bit older than Jesse had first thought, probably twenty or so, with light brown skin that nearly matched Jesse's own. His eyes were gray blue, same as his grandfather. He looked scared and a little scrawny, and Jesse wondered whether the Luparii had been feeding him. Scarlett must have had the same thought, because she ushered them into the kitchen and started making peanut butter-and-jelly sandwiches. "Is there someone you need to call?" Jesse asked the kid. "Someone who's worried about you?"

Owen tilted his head, thinking it over for a moment. "Yes and no. My dad's not in the picture, and Mom died three years ago. I've got lots of cousins—you saw the picture—but they're all at least an hour away. I was living with Grandpa until last year, when I finally started college at Cal State Long Beach."

He didn't so much trail off as nod off, and Jesse realized the kid was past exhaustion. "Owen?" he said.

The boy's eyes snapped open. "Right. Um, I'm in the dorms, but . . . I don't think it's safe to go back." He looked down at his hands, which bore a number of small scrapes and bruises. "They got my wallet, with my student ID card. That's the first place they'll look for me."

"Yeah, well, this is probably the second," Jesse said, looking at Scarlett. She handed him a sandwich and gave one to Owen. "We should move."

"You're not wrong," she said, "but to where?"

Jesse thought it over as they ate, standing around the kitchen or perched on stools. She was right; it was a problem. "If they've been watching us for a couple of months, they know all about Will and Dashiell and Kirsten. It'd be too easy to find us there."

"And Shadow is too memorable for an anonymous hotel," Scarlett added, giving the bargest a fond look. "If one guest takes a picture of her in the lobby and posts it to social media, we're screwed."

"True." The blinds in the kitchen were closed, but Jesse still had that itchy feeling, like someone was targeting them. "We still need to get out of here, though."

Owen was listening to the conversation with a kind of detached interest, like a kid whose divorced parents were determining where he would stay that weekend.

"What about Hair of the Dog?" Scarlett suggested. "I still have a key, for emergencies, and no one will be there for hours yet."

Jesse nodded and grabbed an extra sandwich for the road. "Let's go." He glanced at Owen. "You can explain on the way."

Chapter 25

We crammed into the Lexus. I told Jesse he should drive because I didn't like the car, but I think he knew I was nauseous again. Jesse and I had enough room up front, but Owen was smooshed in the back seat with Shadow, who immediately began fogging up the window as she hulked in the seat next to him. Jesse covertly hit the child safety locks so Owen couldn't bail out.

I had about a thousand questions for the kid, but first I had to call Will and let him know where we were going. He was awake, despite the early hour, and Dashiell had called him to say the meeting was off, so he knew about Shadow and Owen. Without saying it outright, I intimated that we were going to hole up at the bar for a few hours. The Luparii probably knew about Hair of the Dog, but hopefully they wouldn't expect us there before it was open. Plus, it was on a busy commercial stretch of Pico, which would be much harder to attack in broad daylight on a Sunday morning.

"Fine, that's fine," Will said distractedly. "I'm not sure we're even going to open today."

He sounded even worse than I'd expected. "Is everything okay?" I said cautiously.

To his credit, Will didn't respond with "Of course it isn't fucking okay, you moron."

"I'm still trying to get as many of my pack out of the city as I can," he explained, "but it's complicated because of territory. On top of that, half the wolves I talk to hear the word *Luparii*, and they want to stay and get their revenge for Drew and Terrence."

Oh. Trying to put a positive spin on it, I said, "Um, there's always the other half?"

Will sighed. "Many of *them* think running is the coward's way out, and I'm a bad leader for suggesting it."

So much for that positive spin. "I'm sorry, Will," I said, meaning it. Jesse gave me an inquisitive look, but I gave him a little headshake. "Hopefully we'll have some answers soon."

As soon as I hung up the phone, Jesse said, "How's he doing?"

"Not great." I glanced over my shoulder at Owen, who was making himself as small as possible. Jesse got the message: I didn't want to fill him in while the kid was listening.

Owen picked up on the attention and straightened up just a little. "Um. Okay. Where should I start?"

I was about to say something dumb like "at the beginning," but Jesse jumped in with "Start with yesterday morning, when they killed your grandfather."

Yeah, that was probably a better spot.

"Okay, well, I wasn't even supposed to be at Grandpa's yesterday, but I promised him I'd stop by in the morning and help pack boxes. He's . . . he was supposed to be moving from the house to an assisted-living place in a few weeks. Anyway, around ten there was a knock on the door. Grandpa had fallen asleep in his chair, so I went to answer it."

He paused, and I turned sideways in the car seat so I could look at him. "Through the little window I saw a woman, maybe your age, and an older man. He was probably sixty or so. And I . . . I opened the door." His voice broke, and guilt washed over his face. "I just thought they were lost, you know? I mean, this is Long Beach, in the middle of a nice suburban area in broad daylight. Hell, the woman had a yoga mat on a strap."

"I would have probably done the same thing," Jesse assured him.

I doubted that, but it was a nice thing to say. "Go on."

"The man pulled out a gun and made me back up, into the living room. Grandpa was just standing up to follow me to the door, but he saw the man, and his whole face turned white. I mean, Grandpa is—was—a pale guy anyway, but for a minute I honestly thought he was having a heart attack. But he knew the other guy. He called him Thierry." He pronounced it *tee-e-REE*. "And Thierry knew Grandpa's real name, Otto. He ordered Grandpa to give him the scroll."

Okay, that was a lot of information. I said, "What do you mean, his real name?" at the exact same moment Jesse said, "What scroll?"

Owen chose Jesse's question first. "It's a spell," he explained. "Grandpa stole it from the other Luparii a long time ago. That's why he left them. Changed his name and hid in Los Angeles."

Jesse and I looked at each other. Karl Schmidt had been a Luparii deserter?

Jesse told Owen to go on.

"Okay, well, Grandpa tried to play dumb at first, and the blonde lady opened up her yoga mat—it was actually a false compartment, kind of smart—and pulled out this"—Owen's voice dropped into an awed hush—"*sword.*

"I've never seen anything like it. It was shining. Not shiny—*shining.* I don't know if it was actually glowing or if it was designed to catch light weird or what, but when Grandpa saw it, he staggered and kind of fell back in his chair. Like he'd been shot or something. It seemed like he recognized it."

Owen's voice shook a little. We were getting to the worst part of the story. Shadow, to my surprise, laboriously turned herself around on the seat so she could rest her head on Owen's shoulder. He patted her absently, his eyes fixed on his car window as though it were a television screen and he was watching the whole scene again. "I was standing by the entrance to the living room, and the lady lifted the sword and sort of rested it on my shoulder. It only, like, *touched* my skin, no pressure at all, but I started bleeding." He raised one hand to a shallow cut on his neck. I hadn't noticed it earlier under all the grime.

"And Grandpa just . . . gave up. He told Thierry where to find the scroll: in an old trunk in the crawlspace. Thierry went up there, but the woman stayed where she was, with the sword on me. I wanted to punch her, to duck away or something, but Grandpa told me not to try anything. He sounded so scared, but I could tell he was scared for *me*. Because of the sword.

"But I knew Thierry was gonna come back down and was gonna kill us both, so I . . ."

He trailed off, looking ashamed. I saw Jesse open his mouth to ask, but I overrode him. "You tried magic," I said softly. The kid nodded.

He was a witch, but he hadn't used magic in a long time, and it weakened him. Owen had probably once been medium-powered, but magic is like a muscle: you have to keep using it to keep having much of it.

"I was so *stupid*," Owen burst out. "I thought . . . I tried to twist up her shoes, to make her stumble or fall down, so I could duck out from under the sword, you see? But it barely ruffled her. She laughed at first, but when Thierry came back downstairs, she told him I might be useful."

His voice sped up, like he was just trying to get the next part over with. "Thierry gave the woman the scroll and his gun, and she handed him the sword, really carefully. Then he told my grandpa to kneel down."

I'd had to turn all the way around again—sitting sideways was making me carsick—but now I snuck a look back at him. Tears were rolling down his face. "Grandpa knew they were going to kill him. I started to yell, but the woman hit me, and I shut up. I was crying. Grandpa asked them not to do it in front of me, but I said it was okay, I wanted to be with him, you know, so someone who loved him was there . . ."

The boy was openly weeping again now. Heartsick, I reached into the center console for tissues . . . and remembered that we weren't in my van. Beatrice's car didn't even have fast-food napkins.

Shadow solved the problem by licking the tears off Owen's face. He grimaced and then let out a little laugh. "We know what happened after that," Jesse said, trying to spare him.

But Owen shook his head. "No. You don't. Because when Thierry raised the sword and brought it down, he used *no* pressure. Basically just gravity. I don't know a ton about weapons, but I'm pretty sure the sharpest blade in the world can't do that."

Aw, shit. The sword was motherfucking magical. Like we didn't have enough problems.

"You're right, that was good for us to know," Jesse said gently. I knew him well enough to notice that as our conversation with Owen had gone on, Jesse's tone had changed from the one he uses with suspects to the one he uses with witnesses and victims. He believed Owen. So did I. "How did you get away from them?"

"Shadow saved me," Owen said, sniffling, shooting a fond look at my bargest. "Thierry and the woman tied my hands and put a blindfold on me. They drove for a while, maybe half an hour? When we got out, they wouldn't let me take the blindfold off. They marched me around this weird terrain, sort of up and down tiny hills. I stumbled a lot, and fell a couple of times, too." He lifted his hands to show me the cuts and bruises. "They finally had to take the blindfold off, and I saw we were on these weird sort of cliffs."

"Weird how?" I asked.

"They weren't really cliffs, exactly, more like enormous pieces of concrete that had been scattered around like Legos? And there was all this graffiti on them."

"I know where that is," Jesse said quietly.

Owen continued, "They had set it up like a little campsite with all this gear and supplies, but they also seemed to have taken over some of the houses that backed up to it, so they'd go in and out. Anyway, there was this one flat piece of concrete that was balanced on a tall, skinny piece, like a three-dimensional letter *T*. On top of it was a heavy metal cage, and Shadow was inside. There were spikes on the inside of the cage, about every six inches, so Shadow couldn't throw herself against the bars. And even if she did somehow escape the cage, they'd set up more spikes on the ground, like the kind that pop people's tires in movies. It was pretty brutal."

I couldn't help shuddering. I reached back and rested a hand on Shadow's pebbly skin. She turned her head to lick my wrist. *It's okay. I'm fine.*

"What happened then?" Jesse asked.

"They didn't know what to do with me because they weren't planning on taking a prisoner, see, so Thierry argued about it with the others for a while—"

"How many others?" Jesse interrupted. "How many people were there total?"

"I counted seven, but that might not have been all of them," Owen answered, then continued. "Anyway, they eventually decided to put me in the cage with Shadow. They didn't want to feed her, and some of them were afraid she'd eat me, but Thierry said it would be a couple of days before Shadow's will broke that far, and they would have left with me by then. They got this stepladder, and made me climb up into the cage. I've never been so scared in my life. I thought she was going to eat me."

I really couldn't blame the kid for that one. I had to be careful about taking Shadow for walks in public because people tended to cross the street to avoid us. Often they also crossed *themselves*. "But you escaped," I prompted.

The boy nodded. "We were there all day. I was so hot. I was really scared of Shadow, especially because she kept moving around." He smiled. "But after a while, I figured out that she was trying to position herself to keep me in the shade so I wouldn't get sunburned."

Okay, my heart kind of swelled at that one. Shadow had exposed skin, but it never burned because of her healing abilities. So she'd tried to protect an innocent.

Or maybe she'd just wisely decided the enemy of her enemy was a friend. I was never quite sure where Shadow stood, morally, when it came to people other than Jesse and me.

"There was this beige girl who would come out sometimes and sit on a rock nearby, watching the whole area. She would wave her arms around, and the pieces of concrete would lift into the air and move. She was *really* powerful."

I looked at Jesse. "Beige girl?"

He nodded. "Sabine. Even her hair is beige. Somehow."

"Is that her name?" Owen's brow wrinkled. "Okay, well, she was scary as shit. I think she came out there just so I would see what she could do, so I would be scared of her. It totally worked. Anyway, maybe an hour before sunset, Thierry came out of one of the houses with this guy who was even older, like seventy. They had a huge argument with the beige girl—Sabine, I guess—and this other guy with lots of guns."

"That would be Killian," Jesse said sourly.

"Whoa. Appropriate. Anyway, the old guy was *furious* with the two younger ones. I couldn't hear most of the conversation, but then the old guy started yelling and screaming about how they needed to kill Scarlett Bernard. And that's you." Owen nodded at me. "When Shadow heard your name, she kind of went apeshit. That's when I realized she could understand what everyone was saying. She tried throwing herself against the bars, but it obviously hurt her—she coughed up blood."

Ouch. I reached back to rest a hand on the furry side of Shadow's head. Her skin was basically impenetrable, but if something hit her hard enough, it was possible for her to get internal injuries. That explained some of the blood that had been matted into Shadow's fur. I had kind of assumed she'd eaten someone while they were escaping.

"I tried to calm her down, because I could tell the younger two were leaving, and it was getting dark. It was almost like they'd forgotten about Shadow and me, because they were sure we couldn't get out, and they didn't really care if Shadow ate me." He shrugged. "But see, *I* had plenty of room to put my hands on the inside of the cage bars, because the spikes were too far apart. They were sized to prevent a dog . . . thing from ramming into them, not a human.

"Eventually, we figured out that I could brace my feet on the bars, between the spikes, and Shadow could push on my back. We managed to slide the cage so it was hanging off the side of the concrete platform, and I was able to, like, dangle over the side and jump past the spikes on the ground. That's how I hurt my shoulder, when I landed on it. I moved the spikes on the ground out of the way, Shadow got loose, and we ran like hell."

Jesus. I wanted so badly to hug Shadow in that moment, but there was just no room in the back seat for me to do it. She saw my frustration and pushed her head and shoulders in between the front seats to lick my face. I laughed, hugging her head.

"And you walked all night?" Jesse asked Owen.

He nodded. "I tried to hitchhike, but no one would pick me up with Shadow, and I wasn't going to leave her. I didn't know where to go, but she was absolutely set on us walking along the ocean, so that's what we did, until we got to Marina del Rey."

Smart. The beaches were deserted at night, except for the occasional beach patrol, so no one would be bothered by a dog monster roaming free. And Owen wouldn't need to worry about his personal safety with Shadow there to protect him. "Good job, Shadow," I told her.

"Okay, time for the big question, Owen," Jesse said, taking the on-ramp for the 405. It had been a long time since I'd been on the west side of LA this early in the day. Everything looked so shiny and clean. "What's on the scroll?"

Owen shook his head. "I don't know. It was in German, or something sort of like German? All Grandpa would ever tell me was that it's old, bad magic, and it can't be destroyed. He said he even tried to burn it once, but it wouldn't catch fire. It can't be copied or even memorized, either, which is a big deal. To use it you have to have *the* scroll."

"But you must have asked him what the spell was for," I persisted.

"Grandpa just said it was a summoning spell. He insisted I was better off not knowing."

"And you left it at that?" I said in disbelief. "No follow-up questions at all?"

"You had to have seen him," Owen said. "He never meant to tell me about the Luparii at all, but . . . I found out."

"How?" Jesse asked.

Owen shrank into himself a little. "Look, my whole life, I thought Grandpa was just, like, a grandpa, you know? I mean, he was a retired crane operator! But he used to make these amazing leashes out of braided rope. They were super complicated and beautiful, so much stronger than any other rope I'd seen, and he worked on them all the time, the way other men might whittle or do crossword puzzles. But he'd just put them in a box or give them to his own kids, when they were grown, to use with their dogs . . ."

The kid winced, and I recognized the look of a shameful memory. "What did you do?" I asked.

"When I was sixteen, I worked at this shitty pet-supply store, and I stole a bunch of the leashes and put them out for sale. They were just sitting there in a box, and . . ." He shook his head. "They sold really quickly, so I took out some more. Eventually, I'd made a pretty good dent in the box, and I took the cash—minus a finder's fee, because I was an asshole—and I gave it to Grandpa in this envelope. I thought . . . I guess I thought he'd be excited. But he flipped."

"Why?"

"Because they were Luparii leashes," he said quietly.

Then I got it. "For controlling bargests," I said.

Owen nodded. "I guess his family had been making them for hundreds of years. They might as well have been trademarked. Grandpa demanded that I take them off the shelves, like, that night. He wanted me to look up which customers had purchased them and try to get them back, but I was too embarrassed. We got into a huge fight about it, and that finally pushed him to tell me the story. That he was born into a cultish family of witches who thought their life's purpose was to clear the earth of shapeshifter magic. The leashes were for the dogs they trained to hunt *werewolves*. It sounded so nuts." He shook his head. "Then Grandpa had me bring this trunk down from the attic, and it was full of photos and spellbooks and things. There were a couple of pictures of the werewolves, and they were"—he shuddered—"they were terrifying. So when Grandpa said knowing anything else could get me killed, I believed him."

That wasn't the end of the story—at some point, Owen must have tried messing around with magic, activating his witchblood as a teen—but just then, a tiny chirping melody came out of Jesse's jacket pocket, and I recognized part of the theme song from *Super Mario Bros.* Jesse made a face. "Sorry, that's Noah, texting."

Before Owen could continue his story, the phone chirped again. And then again. Annoyed, Jesse mumbled a curse in Spanish. We were a quarter mile from our exit, so he said to me, "Can you text him that I'll call him back later?"

"Sure." I dug the phone out of his jacket pocket and checked the screen.

Then I stopped breathing.

"Jesse," I said very softly. "I need you to pull the car over."

"What?" He gave me a sharp look. "We're on the freeway."

"Please, Jesse. Just pull over."

He started cursing again, but he cut across two lanes and slowed to a stop, nearly blocking off the exit lane to get on the 10. A car swerved in front of him to get on the on-ramp and blared its horn, but Jesse ignored it and slammed his thumb into the parking button. "What is it?" he demanded.

I didn't want to do it to him, but I handed over the phone, fighting the urge to vomit.

All three texts were the same picture: Jesse's brother lying on an inconspicuous patch of bare dirt. He'd been beaten. His shirt had been removed, probably to show off the deep blue bruises that covered his chest. His eyes were closed, but the skin around one eye was so puffed out that you couldn't even see it.

But that wasn't the worse part. With shaking fingers, Jesse zoomed in on the photo, seeing what I'd already noticed. Noah's hair was drenched, and his entire body shone with sweat.

"No," Jesse whispered.

From the back seat, Owen's alarmed voice said, "What? What is it?"

I didn't bother turning around. "It's the twisted slumber."

Chapter 26

I think Jesse was about to call his brother's phone, but his cell rang first. Jesse answered it, listened for a few seconds, and snarled, "I'm not doing shit until I know he's alive." Then his face clouded over with worry, and when I leaned closer, I could hear moaning. I'd only met Jesse's brother a few times, but even I recognized Noah's voice. It was so much like Jesse's.

A man's voice came back on the line. Jesse listened for a moment longer, started to talk, and realized that whoever it was had hung up on him. He threw the phone forcefully onto the dash, where it bounced up and thunked against the windshield.

"Jesse—" I began.

But he got out of the car.

That in itself shocked me, because we were on a *Los Angeles freeway*, which is basically certain death. It wasn't that crowded this early on a Saturday, but that actually made it scarier, because the cars were zooming past the driver's door at eighty miles per hour, so fast they looked like part of a video game.

But Jesse miraculously made it around the front of the car, and stormed over to the guardrail, placing both hands on the barrier.

"What's going on?" Owen said from the back seat. He sounded totally unnerved. I was right there with him.

"Stay here," I told him, unbuckling. "Shadow, you too."

She made a sound of protest, but I slipped out of the car quickly and walked over to Jesse. Slowly, I rested one hand on his shoulder. I could feel his back muscles bunch up as he leaned backward without letting go, rattling the railing as hard as he could.

"I'm so fucking stupid," he practically screamed. "I knew they were going through my brain, that they knew everything about my life, but it never occurred to me that—" His voice broke off, and he bowed his head, still clutching the railing.

"What do they want?" I yelled over the noise from the freeway.

Jesse finally let go and turned around, leaning his lower back against the railing. His eyes were red. "They want you," he said simply. "They want me to trade your life for Noah's."

I raised my eyebrows. "They said that?"

Jesse wiped at his face with the back of his hand. "Of course not. Killian told me you wouldn't be harmed, that they're just going to lock you up for a couple of days while they conclude their business. But they've already tried to kill you three different times. I'm an idiot, but I'm not *that* dumb."

"When do they want to do the trade?"

His eyes narrowed. "Scarlett—"

I held up a hand to say *Bear with me.* "When?"

"In an hour, at the caves in Griffith Park. They don't want us to have enough time to call anyone. He said they set a humans-go-away perimeter spell by the Canyon Drive entrance. They'll know when you break it, so we can't sneak into the park and go around them. If they see anyone other than you and me, he'll kill my brother."

"They're desperate," I said loudly, thinking it through. "Broad daylight on a Sunday morning? That's bold even for them. They probably came up with the kidnapping scheme five minutes after they realized Shadow had escaped. They don't know she's already with us, and they're hoping to get me out of the way before she finds me and goes into bodyguard mode."

Jesse reached out and took my hand, drawing me close. The freeway noise was still loud, but at least we could use our normal speaking voices. "Listen. I want you to take Owen and go to Hair of the Dog. Keep him safe."

"*Hell* no," I said. "I'm going with you to get Noah back."

He was already shaking his head. "Scar, they don't have to wait for us to get all the way into the park. They could have a sniper rifle pointed at the entrance, and the moment we drive up, your head explodes."

"How are you going to get into the park without me breaking the humans-go-away spell, huh?" I challenged. "They may have thrown this together last-minute, but they've thought it through. You need me just to get to Noah."

He lowered his head so it was right by my ear. "You're pregnant."

I flinched back, the wind whipping my hair around my face. "Nobody's perfect."

He didn't smile, so I pressed on. "And that doesn't make me any less right. If I don't go with you, Noah's going to die."

Jesse smoothed down my hair, cupping my face with his warm hands. "If you go with me, *you're* going to die." He pressed his forehead to mine. "I can't have that."

He looked so broken, so sad and terrified, that I began to get very, very angry. So I did what I usually did when I get angry.

I lashed out like an asshole. This time, physically.

My right hand snapped up and slapped Jesse lightly across the face. Just enough to wake him up. He looked appropriately stunned, but at least I had his attention. "*Fuck* that," I snarled. "We are *not* letting this happen. So get your head out of your ass and help me make a plan."

"Okay, Jesus. Did you really have to hit me?"

I steered him back toward the car. "Probably not."

While Jesse got us off the freeway, I used his iPad to pull up a satellite map of Bronson Canyon, where the caves were. Jesse pulled over in an empty parking lot and looked over my shoulder. "They're going to go high," he predicted, touching the screen to enlarge that section of the park. "It's not the most complicated trap. Killian and Sabine will be at the mouth of the caves, waiting for us, but they'll put a couple of shooters up in the hills. They can pick us off easily."

"How many, do you think?"

"I know Owen saw seven people," Jesse said, tilting his head at the kid, "but that seems low for a mission this big. They probably have a whole other shift, maybe two, that patrols and guards their base of operations. Let's say twenty, minimum."

"But they won't send everyone, not if they're busy preparing for some big summoning," I pointed out.

"True." Jesse glanced down at the iPad in my lap. "If it were me, I'd send three shooters to cover all the angles. Plus Killian and Sabine."

"Okay . . ." I stared at the map. I hadn't been to the Bronson Caves since a day trip to LA back in middle school, but I'd been in plenty of other parts of the park. "Isn't this basically loose dirt?" I asked, gesturing at the hills that formed the edge of the canyon.

"Yeah. Hard to climb up. Harder to climb down."

"Hmm." I checked the clock. It was still so fucking early: not quite seven in the morning. The Luparii had told Jesse to be at the park at 7:30, but we were already closer to the meeting spot than they'd anticipated. "I have an idea."

I dialed Will, who sounded just as distracted as before. "You know how you said some of your werewolves wanted revenge against the Luparii?"

There was a brief pause, and then Will said warily, "Yes . . ."

"Is now a good time?"

Chapter 27

We dropped Owen off at a Coffee Bean on Pico with forty bucks and Kirsten's phone number written on a scrap of paper. "Wait three hours," I told him. "If one of us doesn't come back for you by then, call that number and tell the woman who answers that you're a witch who needs sanctuary. She'll help you."

Owen made a few token protests, but he was obviously relieved not to have to face down the Luparii again so soon. As he was climbing out, he paused for a moment and looked at me sorrowfully. "Are you sure about this?" He gave a little shudder. "Don't you know what they can *do?*"

I turned in my seat, enough so I could smile at him. It was not a nice smile. "They can't do shit, Owen. Not with magic, not to me. And we're going to get some help with the rest of it."

Griffith Park is enormous. I looked it up when I first moved to LA, and at forty-three hundred acres, it's the second-largest park in California, about five times the size of Central Park in New York City.

Most of Griffith, however, is wild and untamed: steep cliffs, deep ravines, and brush that can't be navigated without a machete and a sacrifice to the god of cacti. There are a few roads and plenty of trails, but overall it's less of a traditional urban park and more of a wild space punctuated by small attractions. As long as you stick to the trails, though, you can make your way to a bunch of playgrounds and picnic areas, the Griffith Park Observatory, a theater, a couple of teeny museums, and the Batcave.

No, really. Bronson Canyon, in the southwest area of the park, is a former quarry that's often used as a filming location. The middle of the canyon has a rock formation with a couple of small caves, one of which served as the entrance to Adam West's Batcave in the 1960s show.

I'd made a frenzy of phone calls, and we now had three things going for us: first, Killian and Sabine had inadvertently given us a little more time than they should have. The time limit they'd given us would have been tight had we been at or around Marina del Rey, but we'd been well on our way to Hair of the Dog, which would cut our commute by half. Second, there was no way for them to know how far I could push out my radius, or how much time I had spent practicing.

Most importantly, they didn't know we had Shadow.

I had taken pains to make sure of this, with the help of one of Kirsten's witches, a reporter for a small Beach Cities newspaper. I'd texted her a few blurry photos of Shadow, and she'd immediately put up a web article about an enormous dog spotted loose on Redondo Beach. If the Luparii were monitoring news outlets—as any decent bad guys would—they would think Shadow was on the wrong side of town right now.

We deliberately delayed our arrival until 7:40 to give the werewolves enough time to get into place. Showing up late was a risk, but by LA standards, ten minutes late was practically early.

There wasn't really a gate or anything at this entrance to Griffith: we just had to go east on busy Franklin Avenue and turn left on Canyon Drive, which is a straight chute of residential neighborhoods that abruptly turns into parkland. Once inside the park, you just have to take a really sharp right on foot and double back deeper in for about a quarter of a mile to the cave entrance. Jesse and I had gone over it on the map. He thought the Luparii would have a spotter at the turn onto Canyon, so we'd chosen a bus stop on Franklin, a block before the turn, as our meeting spot.

There was a werewolf waiting for us: Astrid, a hard, rangy woman who always looked like she'd have no problem tearing off the head of a chicken and popping it in her mouth. Will had said he'd try to get a female werewolf, but I was a little surprised he'd chosen her: Astrid had never really warmed up to me. I wasn't sure she was actually capable of warming up to anyone, and we were asking her to put her life at risk.

But as she leaned in the window, giving me a slow, toothy grin, I realized that she wasn't here for me, and certainly not for Jesse's brother. "Howdy," she said with a smirk. She was wearing jeans and black motor-cycle boots with a plain green tee shirt, her hair knotted in a bun that went through a battered-looking USC cap. She pulled open the door and stood aside so I could climb out. I opened the back door and helped Shadow do the same.

Astrid passed me a plastic grocery bag and took my seat in the Lexus. "Should be everything you need. Walkie-talkie is at the bottom."

Cell service could be spotty in the park. "Thanks," I said. I handed her my sunglasses. Then, checking first to make sure no one was watching, I crouched down and emptied the plastic bag on the sidewalk: a blonde wig, a baseball cap, and cheap plastic sunglasses. My hair was already tied in a long braid that I'd run down the back of my shirt. I wasn't great with wigs, but I made the baseball hat tight enough to hold it on. When I was sure it was secure, I looked through Astrid's open door at Jesse. "Give us a two-minute head start."

He nodded, and opened his mouth to say . . . something. I knew it was going to be mushy and meaningful and might make me cry, so I said quickly, "Tell me later," and slammed the door. Jesse was probably annoyed with me, but that was better than dealing with sappy stuff.

Right?

I crouched down and looked at Shadow. "I love you," I told her. She wagged her club tail at me and licked the air in front of my face. The feeling was mutual.

"Look, I know that the werewolf smell drives you nuts, and I'm not going to be right there next to you to help," I said, looking into her eyes. They shone with unnatural intelligence and something else. I would have to call it happiness. Shadow loved violence against an enemy the way regular dogs loved walks. "I need you to remember that *these* werewolves are our friends. We want to hurt the bad witches, *not* the werewolves. Okay?"

She tossed her head like a horse, the bargest equivalent of rolling her eyes at me. "You know I had to say it," I told her. She licked the air in front of her face and wagged her tail again. We were good.

I put on the sunglasses, and Shadow and I began jogging toward Canyon. She left me behind almost immediately, sticking close to the shadows where she wouldn't be as noticeable.

We were in luck: as I'd hoped, there were a couple of joggers already out on Canyon. I slowed to a walk, watching them carefully. When they reached the last intersection before the park, every one of them stopped, turned around, and headed back the way they'd come. That was the humans-go-away spell.

I was still half a block away, but I ducked into a cluster of trees and lifted the walkie-talkie. "Okay, it starts at the corner of Canyon and Carolus. Let me know when you're in position."

We had to time this *really* carefully, because if Jesse wasn't in my radius, the spell would work on him and he'd stop the car, blowing the whole ruse with Astrid. At the same time, if I broke the spell too early and the Luparii were watching, they'd know I wasn't in the car.

I continued up Canyon at a brisk walk, keeping an eye out for the Lexus. A couple of family-type SUVs went by, and then I saw it. From a distance, there was no reason to think the woman next to Jesse wearing my sunglasses wasn't me. I was almost to the intersection, so I stopped, leaned against a tree, and closed my eyes, concentrating on the edges of my radius. When I was sure I was sort of holding the whole thing in my head at once, I thought as hard as I could: *expand.*

My eyes opened, and the Lexus sailed past the intersection, into Griffith Park. I sighed with relief, still holding my expanded radius. And I started to run.

Chapter 28

Jesse's stomach was tying itself in knots. He wanted desperately to hurry, to rush in there and get his brother out, but he forced himself to drive slowly into the park. When they passed the intersection and the spell didn't stop him, he sighed with relief.

"We're in her aura," Astrid said, shifting a little in her seat. It was less like she was uncomfortable and more like she'd just *gotten* comfortable. Jesse knew that werewolf magic was difficult: it sort of itched at their psyches. In theory, being near Scarlett was relaxing for them—but it never seemed to fully mellow Astrid. "How far can she make it go?"

"She doesn't know," Jesse admitted.

"Seriously?" Astrid was aghast. "How can she not know?"

"It's hard to test, because it expands when she gets worked up about something, and most of the situations where she's really needed to enlarge it are stressful," he explained. "But she's strong. She can do this."

Astrid settled back in her seat, adjusting Scarlett's black Ray-Bans on her nose. "I hope you're right. We might not get another chance at these fuckers."

Jesse was almost positive they were going to get another chance at the Luparii, if they survived this encounter, but he saw no reason to say that to Astrid.

"This is the lot," he said, pulling over a little ways past the entrance.

"How far are the caves?" Astrid asked.

"Not that far. Just keep your head down. They'll want to confirm it's us, so they'll wait until we're close. Remember to go slow," he couldn't help adding. Astrid just grunted.

They got out and walked up to the trailhead. It was unmarked, but Jesse had taken his parents' dog, Max, for a walk to the caves only a couple of months earlier, and he knew where they were going. They passed the small white gate meant to keep vehicles out, and the trail immediately widened, winding into the hills toward the canyon. It was at an incline, so anyone who wanted to take an alternate route to the caves would have to face a steep hill with very dense brush. Just looking at it made Jesse wince. He wondered for the first time if he and Astrid had the easier job.

They walked very slowly along the dirt road. Jesse scanned the hills that rose up all around them, trying to spot the glint of a gun or scope. There were just too many possible hiding spots. He'd put on his bullet-proof vest, and Astrid was wearing one too, but there were weapons and ammunition that could pierce it. The whole thing made his skin itchy.

"Where is she?" Astrid muttered through her teeth. "I could walk faster than this on my hands."

"Does Scarlett strike you as a really outdoorsy person?" Jesse said, in as low a voice as he could.

Astrid choked on a snort. "You think she's stuck on a cactus?"

Just then the walkie-talkie stuffed in Jesse's sock made a tiny blip. He bent down as if to tie his shoe, pressing the button with the side of his palm. "Go ahead."

"You were right," came Scarlett's breathless voice. "One on the ground, probably Sabine, and three in the hills. I felt the twisted slumber break, so she'll know 'I'm' close."

Witches were the only species in the Old World that Scarlett could feel without them knowing—unless they were using their power in that moment. "We'll hurry. Cue the others."

Jesse straightened up, slipping the walkie-talkie into his left pants pocket, and they began walking again. He was careful to keep the same leisurely pace, in case they were being watched through a scope.

Astrid's body sort of jerked for a moment, then she continued walking.

"Back to werewolf?" Jesse murmured.

"Yes."

Jesse carefully took hold of Astrid's arm, ignoring her quiet growl of annoyance, and the two of them hurried ahead. Scarlett would be contacting her werewolf friend Marko, who was currently in human form. He was waiting up the path on the other side of the caves. And he wasn't alone.

The wide path doglegged to the right, and suddenly the Batcave entrance was only forty feet away. The path continued to the left in an almost-circle around it, so the cave formation was right in the center. Killian stood at the mouth of the cave, wearing dark sunglasses and a sneer. Sabine was crouched behind him and to the side, but Jesse couldn't see what she was focused on.

"Hey, Cruz," Killian called. "Did you have a nice nap?"

Jesse felt a rush of anger. "Where's my brother?" he yelled, stepping forward. He didn't let go of Astrid's arm.

Smirking, Killian took one step sideways, revealing Noah lying on the ground. Noah's feet hadn't been in the photo, but even from a distance, Jesse could see that one of his ankles was twisted to the side at a grotesque angle. Sabine crouched near his head with a look of irritation on her face. Scarlett had popped the spell. She said something to Killian, and his sneering lips turned down. "My wife says her access to magic is already back," Killian called.

"Now?" Astrid muttered.

"Now."

With Jesse's body angled in front of her, Astrid reached into Jesse's pants pocket, fumbled for the walkie-talkie, and pushed the button twice. *Come on, Scarlett*, Jesse thought. She was going to have to come close enough to see them so she could expand her radius exactly the right amount. If she overshot it, they were screwed.

"Your wife?" Jesse yelled to Killian. "That's funny, I figured you guys for brother and sister. Then again, maybe we're both right."

Something flickered across Killian's face, and Jesse realized he'd actually been close. Considering their moral flexibility, the Luparii probably wouldn't be opposed to a little light inbreeding to keep up the strength of their magic. "What are you, cousins?" he called. "Second cousins?"

Killian stepped forward from the cave's entrance and took his sunglasses off, his face clouded over with anger.

It was obviously some kind of signal, because less than a second later, Astrid was shot in the head.

Chapter 29

I was panting by the time I came in sight of the turn to the cave. Panting and filthy, with scratches all over my arms and God knew what foliage in my hair. My boots were ruined, and there was a deep scratch across my cheek that I was trying to pretend didn't hurt and wouldn't scar. I'd had to break through a lot of brush to figure out how many Luparii witches were waiting on the edge of the canyon without being seen by said witches. I do not recommend going off-road in Griffith Park.

I almost cried with relief when I got to walk on the path again. Then I got the two-beep signal on the walkie-talkie, and ran to the side of the canyon wall so I could peek around the dogleg at the cave entrance. Jesse and Astrid had their backs to me, but I could see a prone figure a little past them. Well, okay, I saw legs. Good enough for me.

I was already tired, hurt, and—oh yeah—*pregnant*, so I had to close my eyes and concentrate as I expanded my radius to engulf a werewolf, then a witch—and I stopped, holding it right there. This was more intricate and fussy than I was used to—generally I stuck to "expand" or "contract," but I managed. Barely. I even opened my eyes so I could check on Jesse and Astrid again.

And then the fuckers shot Astrid in the head. And I realized that Jesse was going to be next.

My impulse was to run for them, of course, but almost immediately the rifle fired a second time. Instead of tearing into Jesse's head, it just kicked up a little burst of loose dirt near his feet. Far up in the hillside, I heard a terrified scream.

I forced myself to crouch down and focus on pulling my radius in and keeping it close. If Astrid was alive, she needed to be a werewolf to *stay* alive, which meant it was up to the wolves now.

A head shot? *Dicks.*

When I was sure I was calm enough, I looked around the corner again. Astrid was on her hands and knees, one hand clutching the side of her head, and even from where I stood, I could hear her cursing like a sailor. Jesse had his gun out and pointed at the guy who had to be Killian, who, in turn, was pointing a gun at Noah's still form. Killian looked scared, which gave me perverse satisfaction. The woman behind Noah looked more . . . dismayed.

"How is she not dead?" Killian yelled, glaring at Astrid.

It kind of felt like my signal.

I took a knife out of my belt, pulled my radius in more, and stepped away from the cliff wall so Killian and Sabine could see me. "Because she's not me, douche cannon."

Jesse glanced back at me and sort of goggled. "You okay?" he called.

Oh, right. I looked like I'd lost a fight with a mutant tumbleweed. "Fine." Keeping my eyes on Killian, I called, "Astrid? You good?"

"Took it at an angle," the werewolf grumbled. "Fine in a minute, and then I'm gonna eat that motherfucker."

It honestly took that long for Killian to put it together. "A *were-wolf*?" he said with a perfect combination of outrage and revulsion. Immediately, the female witch—Sabine, I presumed—began muttering something.

I couldn't expand my radius to stop her without hurting Astrid, and I was at the wrong angle to throw a knife, but luckily Jesse saw it, too. He yelled to her in French. I didn't speak the language, but I got the general gist of "Don't even think about it." She shut up, and Jesse began moving toward them.

"Stop!" Killian shouted. He was still kind of glaring up at the cliff walls, waiting for his snipers to act again. "If you take one more step, your brother dies. Your werewolf can't attack me before I get a shot off. Or my people." He gestured upward.

Jesse laughed. "Oh, man," he said. "I thought you guys studied werewolves. Do you not know that they travel in *packs?*" He nodded at the cliff side. "Take a look."

Uncertain, Killian handed the gun to the woman, who immediately pointed it at Noah. Killian stepped away from the mouth of the cave, craning his head to look where Jesse was pointing.

On cue, what was left of the first body slid down the cliff on a wave of loose dirt, trailed by a puff of dust. After what seemed like hours of falling, it finally tumbled to a stop at the bottom.

The body was red, so uniformly covered in blood that it looked like someone had painted a crash-test dummy and rolled it in a layer of dirt. Of course, that impression was somewhat ruined by the organs still shining through the holes. Well, the organs that hadn't fallen out on the way down. Yep, the pack was still pretty mad.

By the time I tore my eyes away and squinted at the top of the cliff, whichever werewolf had pushed the body over the edge had retreated out of sight.

Everyone else was staring at the body, which had landed less than eight feet away from the Luparii. Killian looked green, and for a second I thought even Jesse was going to puke. My morning sickness was oddly unaffected by disembowelment, which was a plus. Go, tapeworm.

We were frozen like that for a long moment, and then Killian turned to run away, back through the cave. Which was when Shadow stepped out of . . . well, the shadows.

Did I mention the cave is actually more of a tunnel?

Her teeth were bared—and stained red. She'd taken care of at least one of the snipers before running to the back of the cave. At least, I was hoping it was a sniper and not one of the werewolves. But I had faith in her.

Shadow focused in on Sabine, who dropped the gun in the dirt.

"If I were you," I advised, "I'd sit down and be very still. Shooting her will just piss her off."

Killian muttered something in French, and then he and Sabine both dropped to the ground, keeping their hands visible. Jesse rushed forward and knelt at Noah's side, touching his throat. Without waiting for me to ask, he called, "He's alive, but it's bad."

We needed to get him to the hospital. My radius was still pulled in tight around me. "Astrid?" I said.

She stood up all the way. Blood still ran down the side of her head, but it was visibly slowing. "Yeah, I can do it."

She went over to Noah and picked him up like he was a toddler. Jesse walked alongside her, stabilizing his brother's ankle. "I'll get him in the car and come back," he said to me.

"No, go with him to the hospital. I'll meet you there." Jesse glanced at the Luparii and gave me a worried look, obviously not wanting to leave me. "I got this," I promised.

He hesitated another moment before nodding. "Don't be long," he said, and then he and Astrid were moving along the path. When I was sure Astrid was well out of my radius, I let it relax to its normal dimensions and strode forward to stand just in front of Killian and Sabine.

"You can come down now," I yelled. "Stay about fifteen feet away from me."

We had ended up fairly close to the mouth of the cave, so Killian and Sabine had a nice view of the two werewolves skidding down the side of the cliff wall.

I knew from walking in other parts of the park that the ground was covered in loose dirt. If I had tried to climb up there, I would have fallen on my face, never mind going downhill. But the wolves were made for this kind of terrain. They seemed to be using the loose dirt like skis, floating down the cliff wall in a zigzag pattern. They both landed nearly at the same time, on either side of us.

I never got used to the size of werewolves. The conservation-of-mass principle remains true even in the face of magic, so a two-hundred-pound person becomes a two-hundred-pound wolf. Shadow weighed a hundred and eighty pounds, but she was so odd-looking overall that the size seemed to fit. The werewolves, on the other hand, looked like regular wolves who'd eaten giant mushrooms or something. They were beautiful. And terrible.

Sabine screamed, clutching at Killian, who also looked like he was shitting his pants. It occurred to me that the two of them had likely been raised on stories about evil, savage werewolves. And they were used to having a bargest to do their dirty work from a distance. Being up close and personal with a pair of werewolves was literally their worst fear.

Well. Good.

The wolves were about fifteen feet away on either side of us. With Shadow still at the cave mouth, that left Killian and Sabine surrounded on all sides. I knew I was the weakest link to use for escape—but I also knew how fast Shadow could move, and I had a knife in each hand now. I wasn't worried.

I crouched in front of them so we were at eye level. "Your snipers are dead," I said calmly. "Now you're going to tell me what Thierry and the rest of them are planning."

They both started when I used Thierry's name, but Killian tried for bravado. "You stupid bitch," he sneered in his haughty French accent. "Do you really think we're going to talk to you? We know you're going to kill us."

I shrugged. "I wasn't planning to kill you, no. I was going to take you to Dashiell. I can tell *you* don't have active witchblood, Killie Bean, which means he'll be able to press you and get all your secrets anyway. Easy enough." I paused, then acknowledged, "Granted, after *that* he'll probably kill you, but then it's not really my problem anymore."

Killian and Sabine exchanged a look. "Here's the thing," I went on. "I really only need one of you. And these wolves are *pissed* at you guys. All I have to do is back out of range, and one of you will be breakfast."

The Luparii man's eyes went wide. Sabine looked back and forth between us, not comprehending, and I wished I hadn't sent Jesse away. I didn't know how much of this she was actually getting. "I don't even really care which one. I mean, you speak English and Dashiell can press you, but Sabine here is powerful and would make a better hostage to trade with the rest of the Luparii. I'll probably just let the werewolves decide for me."

Okay, it should be noted here that I wasn't *actually* going to feed them to the werewolves. Even I'm not heartless enough to do that in cold blood. But I had no problem lying about it.

"What will it be, Killian?" I said pleasantly. "Bring you both to Dashiell for a merciful death, or let the wolves eat one of you?"

By now, Sabine had picked up enough of the conversation to start panicking. I felt her throwing spells at me, but of course it was useless while she was in my radius. I was kind of impressed with how powerful she was.

Then Killian said something very rapidly in French, and she became instantly calm, if sort of resigned. Shit. I didn't like that.

The smug look came back on his face. "Silly little girl," Killian said scornfully. "Everything is already in place. They ride tonight, and you won't stop them. All your friends will die, and the whole world will hear of it."

He dove sideways, toward the gun Sabine had dropped. I threw a knife, and Shadow pounced, but Killian rolled away from her, and the knife wound didn't slow him. He grabbed the gun and squeezed off a shot before I could even duck—

The bullet went straight into Sabine's head.

He lifted the gun to his own mouth, but Shadow had gotten to him by then, knocking the weapon out of his hand and tearing at his throat. "Shadow, stop!" I cried out, scrambling over to them. Shadow backed off immediately, but I could tell it was too late. Killian's throat looked like raw meat. He was already choking on blood, his face stricken.

Goddammit, Scarlett! I'd gotten too cocky. On either side of me, the werewolves were pacing, snarling with frustration. I covered Killian's throat with one hand, pressing down slightly to slow the bleeding without choking him. "Who?" I shouted at him. "Who rides tonight?"

Killian took in one wheezing breath, and the fear in his eyes turned into muted glee. "The Wild Hunt," he rasped.

Then he died.

PART III

Chapter 30

I stared at Killian's limp body in utter confusion. I didn't know anything about the Wild Hunt, except that it was literally a fairy tale. Like a for-real Brothers Grimm fairy tale. As far as I knew, the Grimm stories had very little to do with actual magic . . . well, except the ones that involved a big bad wolf. How was it possible that I'd finally gotten some information, and now I was twice as confused?

I got to my feet, pulling my throwing knife out of Killian's side. I felt like an asshole. Killian and Sabine had been our best sources, and now they were both dead. And that was my fault. I'd had one chance to find out what was going on, and I'd blown it because I'd been too cocky.

The two werewolves stepped into my radius, instantly becoming human. The wolves liked using my proximity for this, since the transformation was faster and less painful. I hadn't recognized them in wolf form, but the female turned out to be Esme, a short, curvy bartender at Hair of the Dog. The other wolf was a guy of about fifty who I'd seen around but didn't really know. He immediately began grumbling about my incompetence, and I couldn't really blame him. I'd fucked this up. They wandered off to find their clothes, picking their way around the rocks.

When Astrid came back, she found me crouched next to the two dead bodies, going through their pockets. She ran forward, looking crestfallen.

"You said I could eat them!" she complained. "What the hell?"

I blinked hard. "Um. First, I did *not* say you could eat them. And second, Killian went for the gun and shot Sabine. Shadow killed him before he could turn it on me."

She shook her head angrily. "You should have moved the gun farther away!"

"Well . . . duh."

Astrid heard the real embarrassment in my voice and huffed out a big sigh. She crossed her arms over her chest. "Did you find anything?"

I leaned back on my heels. "No. They were smarter than that."

"Is it over?"

"I don't know. I don't think so."

Another huff. "Well, shit." She dug in her pocket with one blood-stained hand and tossed me something. I caught it instinctively. Car keys. I looked at her, surprised.

"That guy Cruz wasn't kidding when he said it was bad," Astrid said soberly. "I'm not sure his brother's going to make it. You should go be with him."

My eyes landed on the bodies. "Oh, we'll take care of them," she added brightly. She pointed toward Canyon Drive. "Black pickup truck, two blocks down. There are baby wipes in the glove compartment."

I looked at my hands, which were stained with Killian's blood, and considered the offer. Dashiell would definitely not appreciate me handing off my job to a few werewolves I barely knew. But Dashiell wasn't here, and Jesse needed me. Fuck it.

Shadow trotted over to stand beside me. I hoped Astrid had enough baby wipes for her muzzle.

"Make sure no one finds the bodies," I reminded Astrid.

Her return smile was chilling. "That won't be a problem."

Jesse had texted: he was taking Noah to Hollywood Presbyterian Medical Center. On the way there, I called Kirsten, and gave her a rundown of what happened.

"The Wild Hunt?" she echoed, sounding intrigued.

"Yeah. Isn't that, like, fairies and shit? It can't be a real thing," I said, hoping she'd agree.

"I'm not sure," Kirsten admitted. "I know the fairy-tale story, of course, and I'd always assumed it was one of those myths that was started to hide real magical activity. But maybe it's the other way around. At any rate, we've been spinning our wheels on research, and at least this gives us a new place to start. Did Killian or Sabine give you anything else? Where are they now?"

"Um. They're both dead." I told her the rest of the story, still feeling guilty. But Kirsten wasn't a tactical person, and didn't bother to lecture me. She just said she would start researching the Wild Hunt—oh, and pick up Owen. She started to ask me more questions about him, but I hung up the phone. I had another call to make.

When I'd gone to Las Vegas, I'd met a few interesting people *besides* Wyatt. One of them was Grace Brighton's mother, Sashi, an outclan witch who specialized in healing magic. She could really only treat humans, but Noah *was* human.

Sashi didn't answer her phone—I had no idea what hours she worked, or if she was usually awake this early—so I left a message asking if she'd be willing to take an emergency trip to Los Angeles. I knew her rates weren't cheap, but I would borrow the money from Dashiell if I had to. I wasn't sure how crazy things were going to get the rest of the day, so I left Noah's full name and the name of the hospital on the voice mail just in case.

Shadow *really* didn't want to have to wait for me in the parking garage, but I hadn't gotten a chance to replace her service-dog cape, which had blown up in my van. She relented when I said she could hang out in the back of the pickup truck and keep an eye on the other vehicles. I pitied the car thief who chose that parking garage.

I jogged into the emergency room entrance, and spotted Jesse in the waiting area with his head in his hands.

The whole tableau was so eerily similar to the day Jameson had died that I actually stumbled and had to right myself. "Jesse?"

He looked up, his eyes rimmed with red. I don't remember closing the rest of the distance between us, but suddenly he was standing, and I was hugging him, and I felt his whole body shudder.

"Astrid lent me her truck. I got here as fast as I could," I babbled. I didn't know how to ask the question. "Is he . . ."

"He's alive, but his brain is swelling. They're cutting a hole in his skull, but they're not sure he's going to . . . I had to call my parents—" Jesse choked on the words. His whole body was trembling, and I could see that he was on the verge of breaking down.

"Do the nurses have your cell phone number?" I asked. He nodded, looking confused, but I just took his hand. "Come with me."

I pulled him down a hallway, searching for somewhere private we could talk. Medical shows always had plenty of broom closets where interns could make out, but I couldn't find a spot where we wouldn't be overheard. Finally, we reached a chapel with wooden chairs and a big stained-glass window. It was empty. I pulled Jesse inside and closed the door behind him.

"Talk to me," I said.

"It's all my fault, Scar," he said brokenly. "I left my own brother vulnerable."

"You know that's not true."

"*It is!*" He said it with such force that his breath blew my hair off my face. "I knew they'd rummaged through my brain, and I didn't even think about the consequences for everyone else in my life! If I hadn't had my head stuck up my ass, maybe I could have protected him!"

"Jesse . . ."

He seemed so defeated, and I couldn't think of a thing to say, because the déjà vu was overwhelming. He sounded exactly like how I had felt so many times, with so many people: My parents. My friend Caroline. Wyatt. My brother and his wife. And, of course, Jameson.

Jesse stood there looking at me with his desperate eyes, and I thought of all the times the people in my life had been made victims because of me. Suddenly the weight of their collective suffering anchored me to the floor. There was an actual roaring in my ears as I considered the sum total of the enemies I'd made and the pain they'd caused—

I shook my head hard. *"Enough,"* I said out loud.

Jesse just looked at me. I gazed into his warm brown eyes, and I felt the fiercest sense of love and protection I'd ever felt in my life. I was having a moment of perfect clarity. It was kind of heady.

"Enough," I said again. "We've had enough. This has to stop."

"What?"

I turned and walked a few paces away from him. I simultaneously felt perfectly calm and like I really needed to calm down. I shook out my arms for a moment and went back over to Jesse. "Why do the Luparii feel like they can come to LA and fuck with us?"

He was puzzled. "I . . . I don't know."

"Because they think peace is weak," I said. My voice was perfectly level. "All of them, all the assholes who've come to LA in the past five years and tried to tear us apart, they all think the way we share power is weak, and therefore we're fair game. And I've had enough."

"I have too," he said, still studying me. "But what do we do about it?"

"We make them afraid," I said matter-of-factly. "Starting with the Luparii. I don't know what this Wild Hunt is tonight, but I'm going to stop it. And then I'm going to make sure everyone in the entire Old World knows who I am, and that I am not a null with whom to fuck. And the next time someone thinks they can take your brother"—I touched my stomach—"or this baby or *anyone* else, they will think twice. I swear to you."

His gaze was intense, although I couldn't read it. I didn't remember moving, but somehow we had drawn toward each other. "You can't promise that, Scarlett," he said softly.

"Watch me."

And I went up on my tiptoes and kissed him.

Chapter 31

In that moment, I felt immortal and strong, and I wasn't afraid of anything . . . so I forgot to be afraid of the thing between us. Kissing Jesse wasn't just the right thing to do; it was the only thing to do.

That said, it wasn't much of a kiss, just a quick brush of my lips on his, but it sent currents of heat down my skin and into my abdomen. I pulled back, knowing the look of surprise on his face mirrored my own. I took a step back, suddenly remembering myself. We are in the goddamned hospital, Scarlett. "Jesse . . . I . . ."

But his hands gripped my hips and whirled me around, pressing my back against the wall next to the door. He paused then, resting his forehead on mine, his eyes asking a question. I lifted my chin, and all the feelings I'd ever had for him broke through a dam.

"Yes," I whispered. His mouth met mine, and his fingers tore at the flimsy tie in my hair, threading his fingers through it as it spilled down over my shoulders. He made a noise of pleasure, and suddenly I needed him *closer*. Which was impossible, but I needed it anyway. I pressed my body to his, and when that wasn't close enough I peeled his jacket back, but no, that wasn't close enough either. My mouth never left his as my fingers fumbled at the buttons on his shirt, starting at the bottom so I could slide my hands under his shirt and around his back.

He moaned into my mouth, and I felt almost light-headed. Weightless. The tremendous pressure I'd felt only minutes before was replaced by the light warmth of his touch.

Something in the air shifted, and an understanding passed between us, from my lips to his and vice versa. This wasn't a fluke or a mistake. It was solid. And it was inevitable.

People talk about getting lost in a kiss, and for the first time I understood, because my mind lost its grip on anything that wasn't the taste of him. Then he bent to kiss my neck, his fingers on the button of my jeans, and my eyes opened and saw the stained-glass window.

I remembered where we were.

"Jesse, stop," I gasped, pushing him away from me. Hurt instantly filled his eyes, and I felt like I'd been punched in the ribs. "No! I just mean . . . not like this." I gestured around at the little chapel. I was having a hard time catching my breath. "Not here. This . . . us . . . we deserve better." I wasn't sure how to say it, but he seemed to understand. He nodded and stepped toward me again, resting his hands chastely on my hips.

"You're right," he murmured, kissing my forehead. "Of course you're right."

I hated to do it, but I had to bring us back to reality. "There's something else," I said, and he frowned when he saw the look on my face. I took a deep breath. "When I thought you might die, while you were in the twisted slumber, I had Will hang out at the cottage on standby." It took a moment for comprehension to hit his face, and I rushed to add, "I didn't know if it would even be possible while you were under the spell, and the odds of a successful change haven't been great lately, but . . ."

"Noah," he said softly.

I nodded. "I called Sashi, the healing witch I told you about, but I have no idea if she'll even get the message in time. But we could try changing him. If—*if* it works, then I could turn him human again. Cure him."

He touched my stomach. "You shouldn't be doing that to your body right now."

I shrugged. "Either way . . . he would find out about the Old World. He'd be sucked in for good." Dashiell was historically not a fan of humans knowing about us, unless they had deep connections, like being the spouse of a werewolf, or a vampire's human servant. He had been seriously against Jesse finding out about us back when he was a cop, and considered having Jesse killed just to silence him. Jesse knowing had worked out okay in the long run, but it didn't mean I should run around town changing and then curing people.

To make matters even more complicated, Will was the only werewolf who could do it—if I was planning to change Noah back. He already knew about my ability to cure supernatural creatures. The rest of the pack couldn't find out or there would be anarchy. Some of them would camp out at my door begging to be cured, and some of the hardcore werewolves would likely try to kill me to protect the pack. Only Will could know, and Will was really, really busy today. He couldn't exactly hang around the hospital just in case.

Jesse knew all this as well as I did, and I could see him running calculations in his head. "Let me see what the doctor says when he gets out of surgery," he said at last.

He was taking a risk, one that could hurt him even more. I went on my tiptoes so I could wrap my arms around his neck, breathing in his scent. He hugged me back just as hard, and started pulling the phone out of his pocket. "What happened with Killian and Sabine?" he asked. "I mean, I'm assuming they didn't get away. Did you send them to Dashiell's house?"

I reddened. "No. I messed up." I told him about Killian shooting Sabine. I was expecting his face to fall, but he just nodded.

"You don't want to yell at me?" I asked.

"Of course not. I wasn't there, Scar. I'm not going to second-guess you now." Then a mischievous smile spread across his face. "Besides, I'm pretty sure Dashiell will yell at you enough for everyone."

I sighed. "You're so right about that." A thought occurred to me. "When we were talking to Owen this morning, before you got the text from Noah's phone, you said you knew where the Luparii were camped out."

He nodded. "I think so. I'm pretty sure he was talking about Sunken City. It's this development down in San Pedro that basically fell into the ocean in a landslide around 1930. Giant chunks of concrete and piping everywhere. Technically it's illegal to go there—they have a shitty fence around it—but it's really popular with hikers and kids and taggers. The city is kind of stuck, because it's both very cool and very dangerous. If they open it to the public, they open themselves up to lawsuits if people get hurt. And if they don't open it to the public, they've got to deal with trespassers and activists petitioning for access." He shrugged. "So the local government kind of ignores it. I've been there a couple of times just to walk around."

"So it's like an open secret?"

"Yeah. Hell, I'm pretty sure it's got a Facebook page." He pulled out his phone and tapped on the screen for a few minutes. Then he nodded to himself, reading the screen. "The hikers have been posting that the whole area has been closed off for the last three weeks, including the adjoining houses. There's a rumor going around that another landslide is expected. And another rumor that they're finally working on opening it as a public park."

"Sounds like a humans-go-away spell to me."

He pocketed the phone again. "But the Luparii aren't stupid. They'll have packed up and moved after Owen got away."

"I'm sure they did, but maybe they left something behind."

"Yeah, like a big-ass death trap." He looked skeptical. "Promise you won't go down there without me."

I shifted my weight from side to side. "Jesse . . ."

"*Scar*lett . . ." He mimicked my tone. "It's not safe."

"I'll have Shadow. And I don't know what else I can do to help. Will's evacuating the pack, and Kirsten and Owen are about to be neck-high in research. If I go over there and sit down in front of a huge stack of books, I'm going to pass out on it."

"Would that be so terrible?" he replied. "You could use the rest."

I shook my head. "If the Wild Hunt rides tonight, I need to be doing everything I can to stop them today."

Jesse put his hands on my hips, bending his forehead to touch it against mine. "I'll come with you then," he said.

"Your family needs you. What if . . ." I didn't finish the sentence. What if Noah died and Jesse wasn't here?

A look of terrible sorrow filled his beautiful face, and I reached up and kissed his lips again, gently this time. He kissed me back with intensity, but without the fevered lust that had almost carried us away before.

Then there was a loud buzzing sound from the direction of Jesse's pocket, and he drew a shuddering breath. "That's probably my parents, wanting an update. They're on their way back from a wedding in San Luis Obispo. I should call them back."

I nodded. "Right. Yes. Right." Why couldn't I stop talking? "That is a thing for doing."

A smile flashed across his gorgeous face, and it felt like something exploded in my chest. "Don't go to Sunken City without me," Jesse pleaded. "Please. Don't make me choose."

I took a deep breath. "I'll try my best. I have other stops to make first, anyway . . . How about I promise I will call you before I go down there?"

He nodded. "Look at us, all compromising and shit. It's like we're in a real relationship."

As soon as the word *relationship* left his mouth, a look of panic crossed his face, like he was afraid I was going to take it all back. I fought a smile. "Don't look now," I said seriously, "but I think we might be."

Chapter 32

As it turned out, the phone call Jesse had ignored wasn't from his parents. I waited while he listened to the voice mail, which turned out to be from the police, who had arrived at the hospital to interview Jesse about Noah's attack. Jesse's presence was requested back in the emergency waiting room.

The story he had come up with was pretty simple: Jesse had been planning to meet his brother at Griffith Park to go hiking. He was a little late, and when he arrived, he found that Noah had been attacked, probably for his car, and dumped near the parking lot. He'd decided to leave me out of the story so it wouldn't impede my movements for the day, which I appreciated.

I made a quick call to Hayne to make sure the car would, in fact, be stolen by the time the police started investigating, and we started back toward the waiting room.

"You can duck out the other door," Jesse said as we approached. We were holding hands. "I know you need to get to Kirsten and the others."

"It's not that," I said, stopping and turning toward him. "Hayne said Kirsten is making calls to all her witch friends, and they'll need time to do research. But I need to go talk to Jack and Juliet." If the Luparii had come after Jesse's brother, my own brother, his new wife, and their two kids could theoretically be in danger, too. "I *do* want to stay with you," I added, laying my hand on his cheek. I hadn't realized how much I wanted to touch him, all the time, until I was suddenly allowed to do it.

Goddamned baby hormones.

"I know," he assured me. He smoothed my hair behind my ears. I remembered him snapping my hair tie and shivered with pleasure. "If Noah stabilizes, I'll try to get away tonight." He hesitated. "You don't think the Luparii will try something here, do you?"

I considered it. It seemed really unlikely, but I could understand why he was worried. "Tell your folks that Noah's new girlfriend is going to come to the hospital as soon as she can, probably around seven. You can come meet me then."

"Noah doesn't have a girlfriend," he said, confused.

"Sure he does. Molly." I grinned. "I'll call her now and leave her a message to come here after sunset to keep an eye on them."

A smile spread across his face, but he hesitated. "Don't you need her?"

I shook my head. "I don't have anything for her to do that would be as useful as this."

He kissed me again, and I pulled him closer, prolonging it. It seemed obscene to have joy bursting in my chest when so many things were going wrong all around us, but I couldn't help it. When we finally came up for air, I pushed him toward the waiting room. "Go."

If Shadow hadn't been waiting for me in the back of Astrid's pickup truck, I might never have found it. I was so distracted that I was keeping an eye out for the White Whale.

She barked lightly when she saw me wandering around, and I remembered what I was driving and my name and stuff.

Jesse.

I smiled to myself.

Shadow could undoubtedly smell him all over me. Her tail wagged madly as I walked up, and I didn't think I was imagining the playful glint in her eye. She hopped down—not waiting for me to lower the tailgate—and practically pranced over to the driver's side door so I could let her in. I laughed. "Okay, okay," I said. "But we've got to get it together. People are depending on us."

Stop smiling, Scarlett.

Stop. Smiling.

My first stop needed to be Jack's house, and I was brought back to earth when I realized I was going to have to think of a story to tell him. Shit. It wasn't even ten a.m. yet, and I was operating on very little sleep. I had no idea what to say.

When I rang the doorbell of Jack's condo in Sherman Oaks, my brother answered the door in boxer shorts and a white tee shirt, holding what looked like a bowl of Lucky Charms. His red hair was jutting up at odd angles, and his eyes were bleary. And yet the first thing out of his mouth was, "What the hell happened to you?"

"Good morning, sunshine," I said, grinning. "Fell down in Griffith Park. And I'm pretty sure I still look better than you do right now."

He glared at me. "Don't be perky. It's weird when you're perky." He stepped aside so Shadow and I could come in.

As I walked past, I got a good whiff of him. "Holy crap, Jack! Are you . . . *hungover?*" I'd never known straight-arrow Jack to have more than one beer. The little sister in me was kind of delighted.

"It's not my fault," he groused. "Some buddies from work came over last night to play Magic: the Gathering, and one of them brought this raspberry moonshine . . . it got ahead of me."

"You're such a *weird* nerd." Jack led me back into the living room, where he leaned against the arm of the couch and ate more cereal. I looked around at a scary amount of empty chip bags and beer bottles.

Yep, it definitely looked like things had gotten ahead of him. "Where are Juliet and the kids?"

"In San Jose visiting her parents," he said, yawning. "Until Monday."

God bless weekend traveling. "You should probably start cleaning now."

"Bite me." He took another spoonful of cereal. "What's up? I haven't seen you in . . ." He blinked, his eyes focusing. "Wait, it's been like two months. Juliet said you're not returning her calls."

Right. Whoops. "Can we sit down?" I asked.

He nodded. "You want some cereal?"

I was about to say no, but the baby felt differently. "Actually, yes."

A few minutes later, we were seated at the kitchen table with our bowls of cereal. I was having flashbacks to being eight. "Jack, listen . . . you know how I work for Dashiell."

His eyebrows went up. "Yeah."

"Well . . ." I pushed the cereal around with my spoon. "I don't just clean houses for him."

Jack finished chewing a bite, swallowed, and said, "I kind of figured."

Now it was my turn to look surprised. "What do you think I do?"

"Honestly, I have no idea. But you're smart and tough, and you make too much money." He shrugged. "I figured it was something legally questionable but morally sound, like helping illegals get fake IDs. Or fighting crime at night in a cape. Something along those lines."

"That doesn't . . . bother you?"

Jack put his spoon down and pushed the bowl away. "Scarbo, when Mom and Dad died, I ditched you. We didn't have much money, you couldn't focus on school, and you were just . . . out there in the world. In LA. I'm your big brother, and I let that happen." He reached across the table and touched my hand. "What right do I have to question the choices you made in order to take care of yourself when I couldn't?"

Tears pricked at my eyes. Was it possible that I *wouldn't* need to blatantly lie to my human brother? "Listen. You're right. Dashiell does some iffy stuff, but his heart is in the right place. He takes care of people. And that's made him some enemies."

Jack's eyes narrowed. "Go on."

"I haven't been calling Juliet back because I was afraid there might be blowback on you guys for what I do to help Dashiell."

He pulled his hand away and toyed with the spoon, looking unhappy. "I didn't realize your work was like, *dangerous*."

I pushed out a breath. "It usually isn't. But today, there's something going on, and . . . well . . . the bad guys know I have a brother."

Jack leaned back in his chair and crossed his arms. "How much trouble are you in?"

I faked a smile. "No more than I can handle," I said lightly, hoping it was true. "But can you go somewhere else for a day or two? I can pay for it," I added quickly. At this rate, I was going to need to start taking a lot of freelance jobs.

Jack shook his head. "It's not that . . . I don't like this, Scarlett. Shouldn't you just go to the police?"

I almost laughed. "That . . . would not be a good idea at this time, no."

"So quit," he said, like it was the easiest solution in the world. "Get another job. We can help you, if it's about money—"

"It's not that." I actually considered the idea for a second, but of course it was hopeless. Nulls were valuable. I needed to be under someone's protection, and I was never going to get a better offer than I had here. This was my home. "I can't quit, Jack."

"Why not?"

"It's complicated."

He stood up then, pacing away to look out the window. I waited him out. Finally, he turned around and looked at me. "Do you really think they'd come after me?" Fear hit his face. "Or Juliet? The kids?"

I considered telling him about Noah then. I really did. But that kind of confirmation could be dangerous down the road, especially if Noah recovered and we needed to press him. "It's not a chance I'm willing to take. Will you go somewhere?"

"Fine. I'll call in sick for tomorrow, and drive up to San Jose to join Juliet. But . . . I need to think about this whole thing, Scarlett. About"—he hesitated for a moment, obviously upset, then pushed on—"about whether you have a place in the kids' lives, if you're gonna keep doing what you're doing."

My heart sank, but . . . wasn't this exactly what I'd expected? Jack had a family now. They needed him more than I did. "I understand, Jack. Really, I do."

I got up, the cereal forgotten, and headed toward the front door. Then a thought surfaced from way in the back of my mind, and I turned around again. "Hey . . . do you remember any of our grandparents?"

Jack looked surprised. "A little. Why?"

"Just something I've been thinking about lately. Grandma Rose lived the longest, right?" She had been our mother's mother.

"Yeah, she died just before Mom and Dad. But she and Mom hadn't talked for a long time before that."

I nodded. "I remember how upset Mom was, but do you know why they stopped talking?"

"Uh . . ." He looked at the ceiling, his eyes going distant. "No, I guess I don't. I remember Mom screaming at her on the phone once, when I was supposed to be in bed. She was mad that Grandma had never told her about something." He shrugged. "I never got the details."

He spread his hands, not saying it. *And now they're all gone.*

"Okay . . . thanks, Jack."

"Goodbye, Scarbo."

He sounded oddly formal, and I knew what it meant. Fighting back tears, I added, "I love you."

"I love you, too."

I left the condo wondering when I'd next see my brother.

Chapter 33

After I left Jack's house, I checked in with Kirsten, who got a little snappish as she told me that she had calls out everywhere and was *working on it, Scarlett.* It wasn't that she couldn't find information; there were apparently hundreds of different stories about the Wild Hunt, in English alone. The problem was sifting through and figuring out what was real and what was classic Old World misdirection. I asked after Owen, and she paused and said, "Actually, he's been a lot of help. He seems . . . invested."

"They killed his grandfather in front of him," I pointed out.

"Yeah. Hey, what about *your* contacts?" Kirsten said suddenly. "Aren't there nulls or someone you can ask about the Wild Hunt?"

Huh. I hadn't really considered that. I had already left a message for Lex asking her to talk to Maven, but I'd need to wait until after sundown to hear back, and it sounded like whatever was happening would start at nightfall. But I did know a few other people. "I'll make some calls," I promised Kirsten.

We agreed to meet in another two hours to pool our findings. As soon as I hung up, I opened an e-mail on my phone.

It's hard to reach out in the Old World, because it's so much like Fight Club, and because it's not organized into governments or anything. There are no embassies, no tourism boards. It's sort of a feudal-system-meets-the-Wild-West kind of scenario, which makes it hard to communicate in the modern world. You can't just google "nulls in Japan" and get anywhere.

About five years ago, however, my former mentor and fellow null (and, as it turned out, psycho hosebeast), Olivia, had made a concentrated effort to find other nulls. I never really got all the details, but she managed to dig up five more of us: two in Europe, one in Japan, one in Russia, and Jameson, who was now dead. It was one of the only useful, non-evil things she'd ever done, and I'd inherited all the contact information after her death.

I didn't have much of a relationship with most of them—we had all needed to pledge loyalty to some faction or another, which made us wary of each other. But years ago, when Olivia was threatening Jack, I'd gotten desperate. I'd sent him to spend a few days with a Scottish null named Rhys.

I hadn't actually spoken to Rhys on the phone since then, but we sent the occasional e-mail just to check in and . . . well, make sure the other was still alive. Mostly it was him making sure *I* was still alive. He had the most normal life of any null I'd ever heard of: he was in his forties, and he and his wife had adopted a couple of children, now in their early teens. Rhys lived in a fairly small town that didn't have much of an Old World presence, so he worked a day job as a carpenter and only did null stuff when called upon. I got the impression from him that this rarely happened, partly because there were no werewolves in the British Isles.

Because of the Luparii.

He was obviously the right person to ask about this. I did the math, determined that it was only early evening there, and placed the call. I would have called either way, but at least I didn't have to apologize for waking him up.

The phone rang twice, and as soon as I said hello, a thick Scottish brogue said, "Scarlett Bernard, lass, what's the matter now? Are ye sending Jack my way again?"

That gave me pause. "Hi, Rhys. Why do you think something's the matter?"

"Oh, because ye only call when ye world's fallen in. What is it this time?"

I'd been planning to ease in with some small talk, but hey. "The Wild Hunt," I said, as evenly as I could manage.

There was a long silence, and I checked the phone's screen to make sure the call hadn't dropped. "Rhys?"

"Aye. I'm here."

"Do you know anything about it, besides the Grimm brothers' folklore and the stuff on the Wikipedia page?"

"I know it's very old, and that it doesn't happen anymore, for which we should all be bleedin' grateful," he said.

"Um . . . it's happening here, in LA. Tonight, I think."

He chuckled. "Someone is pulling your leg, lass. The spell for the Wild Hunt's been lost since—"

"Rhys, the Luparii are here," I interrupted. "I'm told they found the scroll."

Another long silence. Then, in a shaken voice, he said, "That's impossible."

I told him about Karl Schmidt and his flight from Europe.

"The Wild Hunt in the modern world?" Rhys said, sounding amazed. In an *Oh no, we're all going to die* kind of way that made my stomach twist.

"Why? What *is* it? There are hundreds of different stories, and we can't figure out which are real."

He sighed. "It's a spell—a very, very old spell, likely predating Christianity. It transforms a group of riders and their hounds into spectral warriors."

"Spectral warriors?" I repeated, because . . . come on.

"Aye. I know how it sounds. But the Wild Hunt was how witches went to war against other Old World groups, including other witches. My own great-great-grandmother claimed she heard the Wild Hunt go by once. She had nightmares about the blowin' of the horn and the bayin' of the hounds, to her dying day. It's evil magic, lass."

"I thought magic wasn't inherently good or evil," I said.

"Maybe it isn't," he amended, "but this particular spell is evil. It alters a group of witches so that they canna be killed or harmed. The full spell changes their hounds and horses and everything, so the riders are able to pass through structures and kill anyone with ties to magic."

Wait, that wasn't what I was expecting. "Not humans?"

"No. Humans can't even *see* it without special ointment. Only witches, werewolves, and vampires can see the Hunt, and only they can fall victim to it. And it doesn't affect the physical world, other than the bodies of its victims. You say the Luparii came to Los Angeles to recover the scroll?"

"I believe so, yes."

"All right." Relief had crept into his voice. "You should still be okay . . . so long as they don't get the sword as well."

Oh, *shit*. "About that," I began.

"Scarlett," he groaned. "Don't tell me they have Durendal too?"

"Okay, I won't . . . unless Durendal is a magic glowing sword that can cut through anything?"

There was another long silence, and then I heard voices in the background—children and an adult woman. She must have asked who he was talking to, because he said, "Hang on a minute, lass," and then the phone was muffled. I had a bad feeling I needed to prioritize my questions.

When Rhys came back, I hurried to say, "Rhys, wouldn't nulls be able to undo the Wild Hunt magic?"

"I don't rightfully know. The Wild Hunt spell predates us. But listen to me: I can't help ye with this no more."

That brought me up short. "What? Why not?"

"This is Scotland, girl!" he said defensively. "The Luparii have eyes and ears here."

"I thought they were in France." Dashiell had also said Portugal and Romania, but I wanted separate confirmation.

Rhys groaned. "Their headquarters are in France, but they have outposts in England, Germany, Romania, and Portugal," he said. "They need room out in the country to train the dogs. They know about me, but they think I'm nothing, just a low-power null who picks up the occasional vampire job. If I get on their radar . . . I've got kids, Scarlett."

I closed my eyes. "Rhys, can you just tell me—"

"I can't. All I'll say, and I say it with the best of wishes for ye: get out of Los Angeles. Wherever the Wild Hunt is, don't be there."

And he hung up the phone. I looked at it for a minute in amazement. Well . . . shit.

Chapter 34

Kirsten hadn't wanted me to come to her house, not that I could blame her. Her place is warded all to hell against intruders, and if I stopped by she'd have to redo all her defenses. Her daughter with Hayne, Ophelia, was at the house too, and the last thing I wanted was to put a toddler in danger.

We could have crashed Dashiell's place, but Kirsten had apparently just redone all the wards there, too. Being a null is a pain in the ass sometimes. She and I debated it for a bit before deciding to meet somewhere non-warded.

Kirsten had suggested a place called the Los Angeles River Visitor Center, which turned out to be a sort of half-park, half-museum just northeast of Dodger Stadium. It consisted of fancy Spanish Mission–style grounds with rooms for conferences and a few exhibits on the history of the LA River. Mostly, it seemed like a really pretty place to have staged wedding photos or catch Pokémon or something.

But I had to admit, it *was* pretty, all wrought-iron fences and fountains and creeping ivy on stucco walls. As Shadow and I walked in—she probably wasn't allowed in there, but I'd wait for someone to yell at me—I saw a handful of people wandering around taking photos or chatting next to a large map of the LA River. For the most part, though, the place was pretty empty. Apparently, this was not a popular destination if there wasn't a wedding, which was probably why Kirsten had picked it.

I'd texted Kirsten upon arriving, and she'd replied that she would meet me in a little side alcove.

"You're early," she said with a frown as Shadow and I rounded the corner.

"I took your advice and called a null in Europe," I explained. "I have a little new information."

"Oh goody," she said with a brittle smile. "*More* information." She led me down an open-air corridor to a small building entrance. "One of my witches volunteers for the River Center," she said over her shoulder, pulling the exterior door open. We went through a short, wide hallway to an unmarked door. Kirsten knocked five times, and I heard a bolt slide over.

Owen's face appeared in the crack. "Scarlett!" He swung the door wide. Then, to my surprise, he threw his arms around me for a moment. Almost immediately, he ducked away, embarrassed. "I'm glad you guys made it," he mumbled. The bargest trotted over to him and inclined her head so he could scratch at her favorite spot, behind her furry ear. He obliged.

"Um, thanks," I said, feeling a little guilty. I hadn't really thought about it at the time, but it must have been really scary for Owen, to escape the Luparii's clutches and then watch his would-be rescuers walk right into a Luparii trap.

But now we were both obviously desperate to change the subject. "Uh, what's going on here?" I said, looking around. The room turned out to be a surprisingly plush-looking conference space, with one of those superlong tables. Three-quarters of it was covered in papers and books, many of which looked old and kind of crumbly. *Oh.* This was why she'd made the joke about more information.

"Owen has been helping me with research," Kirsten said simply.

"Where did you get all this?"

"Most of it was from my collection, but some of it came from Owen's grandfather." Kirsten gestured at on old-timey trunk lying open at the foot of the conference table.

"You took it from the crime scene?"

"Remember how I was helping my grandfather move?" Owen put in. "I'd already moved his trunk of Luparii stuff. I just went back over to the nursing home this morning and picked it up."

"Smart," I said.

Owen's face fell a little. "Yeah, well, I think they were glad to get rid of his stuff. Make way for someone else."

"You were saying about talking to another null?" Kirsten reminded me.

"Yeah! Rhys. He knew a little bit about the Wild Hunt spell, like the name of the stupid magical sword," I offered. "'Durendal.' Don't ask me how to spell it."

"No need," Kirsten said, sifting through one of the stacks. This one looked like regular computer printouts. "I've heard that before. Here." She picked up a page. "Durendal was a sword of legend in France. Mostly known for belonging to Roland, one of Charlemagne's famous knights." She shrugged. "I haven't seen it connected to the Wild Hunt, but there *were* rumors that Roland was a witch."

"Well, according to Rhys, to run the Wild Hunt you need the sword and a magic scroll. Maybe that's something we can use."

"I read about a scroll," Kirsten began, but her phone buzzed. She frowned down at the screen. "Hang on, Will is here. Let me go get him."

When she left the room, I turned to Owen, determined to try again. I had my own shit going on, but this kid had been through a lot. "How are you holding up?" I asked.

He shrugged. "It's just . . . surreal, you know?"

So far that day, I had seen two people die, made out with my best friend, and said goodbye to my brother, possibly forever. And that was just today. "Believe it or not," I told Owen, "I kind of do." I let a moment of silence pass before adding cautiously, "It's good of you to help us with this."

He focused on petting Shadow, avoiding eye contact. "The way I see it is, stopping the Luparii is the only way I get my life back. I won't be safe until they're dead or gone."

There was something he wasn't saying. "So it's not about revenge?"

"That's the thing." He looked at me then, and I realized that his brown eyes were terrified. "I'm from a long line of murderers and torturers," he said quietly. "What if I like it?"

That brought me up short, but only for a moment. "Magical specialty isn't the same thing as destiny, kid. I know a boundary witch who could tell you all about that."

His eyes widened, but Will and Kirsten came through the door before he could respond.

Will looked worried and haggard, wearing the same clothes as the day before. "How is Jesse's brother?" he asked me.

I held up my phone. "Jesse just texted. The doctors are putting him in a medically induced coma until the swelling goes down. They won't know anything else for a bit." I looked at Kirsten. "Is Hayne coming?" I asked.

She shook her head. "He's staying with Ophelia," she said shortly. "This is it until Dashiell wakes up for the night."

"Okay." I couldn't exactly blame her for wanting her husband to protect her kid. Besides, if what Rhys told me was true, they'd be safer together—away from anything supernatural.

"Tell Will what you told us," Kirsten instructed me.

"Right. I called my null friend in Scotland," I began, and this time I walked them through the whole conversation.

Will looked surprised. "Hang on," he said. "You're telling me the world's most powerful witch magic has been locked up for the last fifty years in an attic in *Long Beach*?"

"That's what *I* said," I exclaimed.

"Has the spell always been with the Luparii?" Will asked. "I mean, they didn't actually invent it, did they?"

Owen and Kirsten shook their heads. "I've been speaking with my aunt about the scroll Owen mentioned," Kirsten said. "It's fallen into the hands of any number of people over the centuries—it was even in Sweden at one point—which is partly why the spell is called different things in different countries."

Owen looked through a stack of notes and pulled out the one he wanted. "In Germany it was the Furious Host, in England it was Woden's Hunt, Mesnée d'Hellequin in France, and so on."

"We think," Kirsten added, looking at Will, "the Luparii got ahold of the scroll shortly after Charlemagne asked them to kill werewolves. The Wild Hunt may have been how the Luparii originally cleared Europe. They used it to kill werewolves for around three hundred years.

"Then, in the early twentieth century, one of the Luparii witches decided that the Wild Hunt magic was too powerful and destructive, and they hid it away," she went on. "I can't find any evidence of it having been used since then."

"So how did your grandfather find it?" Will asked Owen, reasonably.

Owen puffed his cheeks full of air, then blew it out. "He . . . okay, well, during World War II, a bunch of the Luparii men signed up to fight for the Nazis—"

"Of course they did," I muttered.

"And as they traveled around Europe, they kept finding signs of werewolves. They were *pissed*. When the war ended, all any of them could think about was how to cleanse Europe of the werewolves again."

Owen was fidgeting, and I realized he'd skipped this part of the story earlier, when he'd talked to Jesse and me. Or maybe we just hadn't had enough time for him to get to it. We had kind of rushed off to save Noah. "Just tell us," I commanded.

"You asked me why I never bugged my grandpa about the scroll," Owen said in a rush. "It's because he was so obviously ashamed of belonging to a family that had willingly joined up with the Nazis. His own father—my great-grandfather, I guess—was a soldier. My grandpa was still a kid when his dad got back, maybe thirteen or fourteen, but he was really smart. Grandpa wanted to impress his dad, this badass soldier, so he threw himself into research. And he found the scroll. It had been hidden in some German library for almost forty years."

Kirsten rested a hand lightly on Owen's shoulder, which surprised me for a second. But then again, Kirsten's whole job was taking care of wayward witches. I felt a little spark of hope. Maybe if we all survived this, Owen could actually join her group, if that was what he wanted.

The touch seemed to give Owen courage. "Grandpa didn't tell me what the spell was about, but he did say he showed it to Werner—that was his father's name. Werner was super happy. He told Grandpa how proud he was.

"But then, later, Grandpa overheard the Luparii discussing what they were going to *do* with the spell, and he realized what a terrible mistake he'd made. That night, he stole the scroll and ran, all the way to Los Angeles, where no one would ever think to look for him."

"He didn't give you *any* details about this part?" Will asked, looking frustrated. "What they were going to do with the spell?"

Owen shook his head, looking miserable. Kirsten took over the story. "But from what we've been able to find, it looks like Werner didn't just drop the matter, even when Karl couldn't be found," she said. "Werner was an active Luparii witch, and although he couldn't replicate the full Wild Hunt spell without the scroll, he was able to re-create one small part of it. They already had plenty of dogs, because even after the scroll was lost, they kept training dogs to hunt werewolves."

"Wait, you lost me. Which part of the spell?" I said, like an idiot. Because it was so obvious.

Kirsten gave me a pitying look. "The hounds," she said softly, her eyes dropping down to Shadow. "Werner used his knowledge of the scroll to re-create the bargest spell."

Chapter 35

I completely tuned out the conversation then, as the size of this whole thing threatened to overwhelm me. You know that feeling, when you're watching a TV show and they air a flashback that suddenly makes the last five episodes fit together in a new way, and it's so obvious that you're mad at yourself . . . and simultaneously impressed with the people who made the show? That's exactly how I felt in that moment.

Because it had been practically staring me in the face. Three years earlier, when the Luparii had first come to Los Angeles and I had learned about their anti-werewolf efforts, I'd wondered how they had managed to clear all the wolves out of mainland Europe. Our best source, Sashi's mother, Dr. Noring, had known a little about the history—how the ancient Luparii had spent hundreds of years using bargests to *control* the werewolf population, meaning they used a bargest to hunt and kill any werewolves who tried to enter their territory. That made sense, once I'd met Shadow, but I'd never understood the logistics of getting all the werewolves out of Europe to *begin* with. You wouldn't be able to control more than a few bargests at a time, and even with a handful of them, how could one group cover enough ground to clear that much area?

But if they'd initially used the bargests as a part of the Wild Hunt, a massive hunting party of legend that would keep supernatural creatures away by fear alone . . . it made so much more sense. I'd just never made the connection between the bargest and the Wild Hunt, mostly because the folklore I'd found didn't necessarily reflect it.

But I should have realized that at some point, the legends must have gotten twisted up—after all, it wasn't exactly the first time that had happened. Just as the Wild Hunt had different names, so did the bargests: I'd seen Shadow's kind referred to as devil dogs, black shucks, hellhounds, and about half a dozen more. The only reason I used *bargest* was because it carried the least amount of negative connotation.

Then it sank in how screwed we now were. This was about more than an evil witch clan, or even the bargest spell. The frickin' *Wild Hunt* was real, and it could be used to hunt and kill the people of the Old World. Right here in Los Angeles.

No wonder Rhys had told me to leave town.

I felt panic clawing at my chest—and then Shadow reached over and took my hand in her mouth, biting down just a tiny bit.

I jumped, looking down at her. She wagged her clubbed-off tail at me, then lay down on her back and put her paws in the air, asking for a belly rub. I blinked.

She'd only ever done this when the two of us were alone, because showing your belly is a sign of weakness. But she wanted to remind me that, at the end of the day, she was real. A creature of legend, maybe, but real. I smiled and leaned over in my chair so I could scratch her tummy.

I tuned back into the conversation. Owen was saying, "It wasn't famous until Jakob Grimm wrote about it in 1835, but most scholars believe that it predates Christianity."

"Rhys thinks it predates nulls," I put in.

"Does that mean you can't stop it?" Will asked.

I shrugged. "The Luparii seem to think that I can—hence their deep and thorough commitment to killing me. But I don't really know."

"You've dealt with magical objects before," Kirsten reminded me. "The Transruah was powerful, and you zapped that."

"True," I conceded. "But the Transruah was a witch spell; it came from a conduit. What if the Wild Hunt spell comes from a time *before* conduits? From creatures that came before?"

Will stared at me. "Are you talking about fairies? Actual fairies?"

"It's not impossible," Kirsten said thoughtfully. "We've all seen enough of the Wild Hunt stories to know it was usually connected to the fae, and there have always been rumors that conduits weren't the first magical creatures. So . . . why not?"

I had kind of hoped the others would contradict me. "Well . . . shit," I said, which seemed to sum up the feelings of pretty much all of us.

"So we don't know if Scarlett can stop it," Will concluded. "But what *do* we know? What actually happens?"

"According to Rhys, a group of witches, their horses, and their hounds—or bargests—turn into spectral warriors," I informed him. "Who can kill supernaturals. But he says the spell doesn't affect humans. They can't even see what's going on without a special ointment on their eyes. Which we don't have."

"How do the riders make the distinction?" Will said doubtfully. "When I run as a wolf, I can only tell people apart by smell."

"The riders only *see* witches, vampires, and werewolves, like they're wearing special heat-imaging goggles," Kirsten explained. I pictured a cat in a whole roomful of mice. "And they kill everything they see. When the Luparii first used the spell, I'm guessing they called and warned the vampires and friendly witches about their route beforehand."

"How do we stop it?" I asked.

Kirsten shook her head. "According to all of this"—she gestured at the table—"you can't. You can only run, or hide, and hope they pick someone else instead. If you hear the oliphant blow, you're already too close."

"Oliphant?" I said, confused. "I swear that's the name of an unreasonably attractive actor."

"It means a horn," Owen said, miming blowing on his closed fist. "It was a medieval instrument made from elephant tusks. The Wild Hunt uses at least one. When you hear it, it's a harbinger."

"What kind of damage are we talking about here?" I asked. "How many people can they kill?"

"Theoretically?" Kirsten said. "Hundreds each night."

Great. Just fucking great. "Can we evacuate?" I looked back and forth between her and Will. "I mean, I know Will's already been getting the pack out of town, but what if we just sent everybody out of LA County? No victims, no Wild Hunt." I kind of liked the idea of the Hunt riding around LA all frustrated because there was no one to kill. It would be like Spiderman stuck in a meadow.

Kirsten and Will exchanged a look. "For how long?" Kirsten said to me. "And how will it look?"

"Seriously?" I said, surprised. That was the kind of question I expected from Dashiell, but I'd thought Kirsten cared more about her people than that. "You're worried about *optics*?"

"I have to be, because *they* obviously are," she countered. "The Luparii could have come to Long Beach, quietly killed Karl Schmidt, and returned to Europe with the scroll. No offense," she added to Owen, who shrugged. "Instead, they are making this as big and splashy as they can. They want to look like they're putting us in our place. Have you thought about what happens if they succeed?"

Oh. "No, I hadn't," I admitted.

"The Luparii have been collecting power in Europe," Will said quietly. "They're expanding with terrifying speed. I can think of only one reason why they'd come here now."

"Because we embarrassed them," I said, understanding. I thought of what I'd said to Jesse, about how the Old World saw peace as weak.

"You did?" Owen asked, looking between me and the others. "When?"

"Three years ago," I answered. "They sent a scout on a mission to check out the nova wolf, and we bitch-slapped her and stole the bargest. No offense," I added to Shadow, who gave me a *not amused* look.

"Yes, we embarrassed them. And if they want to keep collecting power, they have to get a foothold in the United States," Will put in. "Taking us down is the perfect way to do it. If we run and hide, we're giving them what they need."

"But what do they want with all that territory, all that power?" Kirsten pointed at me. "Great question."

"One we should be asking Dashiell," Will reminded us.

"I don't disagree," Kirsten said. "But I can't shake the feeling that waking up Dashiell and taking him out during the day might be exactly what they want."

She was right. Unless there was imminent death on the line, I wasn't going to pull Dashiell out of the safety of his mansion. I checked my watch and groaned. How was it only noon? "We've got seven hours until sunset. What do you guys want to do?"

Will looked at Kirsten, and they exchanged some kind of complicated leadership look that I was glad I didn't have to interpret.

"We evacuate the weakest among us," Will said finally, "and prepare the strong to fight."

Chapter 36

That sounded suitably dramatic and all, but contacting all the city's witches and werewolves wasn't really something I could help with.

What we needed to know was where the Luparii were now, although I'd settle for where they intended to start the Wild Hunt. Owen would keep doing his best with the book research.

I had a different idea for how to spend my afternoon.

Jesse wasn't going to like it much, but I had Shadow for backup. And the bargest seemed to be spoiling for a fight.

Will agreed to contact Astrid and make sure I could keep using her truck, promising to provide her with a spare vehicle if she needed it. While Shadow and I walked out to the parking lot, I called Jesse's cell phone, but there was no answer. He was probably talking to the doctor, or maybe Noah was out of surgery and had been moved to intensive care. I left him a voice mail, not sure if that was making it easier or harder for either of us.

When people from other places talk about Los Angeles, they're really referring to the greater LA area, a massive territory that includes incorporated towns like Santa Monica, Beverly Hills, and Pasadena. It's all LA to someone from Michigan, but residents might actually take offense if you accuse them of living in LA when their actual home is within the Beverly Hills limits, and vice versa.

I know. It's weird. Then again, most people in LA can't tell you the difference between Minnesota and Wisconsin, so whatever.

But although *Los Angeles* is often a blanket term for places outside the city, San Pedro technically *is* within the LA city limits, though it's crowded by other cities on two sides, and the ocean on a third. It's large and independent enough to be its own town (in fact, it used to be), but now it has something that LA wants: the Port of Los Angeles, which brings like a million jobs into California. So San Pedro stays in the city limits, even if it requires some creative border-drawing to make it so.

And at the southern tip of the southernmost part of the city lies a big chunk that fell into the water. I'd looked up Sunken City before leaving Kirsten and Will, and Jesse had been right: it was a condemned oceanfront area that had once contained a fancy new development—or however fancy developments got in the 1920s. At about forty thousand square feet, it wasn't even that big, but it was dangerous as hell: a bunch of people had died exploring the area, sometimes as many as five in one year. And yet its location was still easily available on Google Maps and Yelp, with handy tips for parking and sneaking past the fence.

Oh, Los Angeles. I love you.

Even with light Saturday afternoon traffic, it took me over an hour to get down to San Pedro, shoot south on Pacific Avenue to the shore-line, and park on the corner of Pacific and Shepherd. I turned the truck off and leaned forward to peer over the dash. You couldn't actually see Sunken City from the street; it was pretty well hidden behind a stretch of perfectly normal-looking houses. The only clue from this distance was the tall, wrought-iron fence that ran along the back of those proper-ties to keep people away from the wreckage.

I closed my eyes to concentrate and pushed my radius outward. Almost immediately, I felt some kind of major-league witch magic go *pop.* I wasn't sensitive enough to know what kind of spell I was breaking, but it felt a lot like the one at Griffith Park, which in turn had seemed similar to Kirsten's standard humans-go-away spell. Like the other one, though, this had a sort of sickly cast to it. I was guessing it was some kind of Luparii signature. Gross.

I sat there for another five minutes, concentrating hard on my radius. If I felt the slightest hint of witch magic—or any magic, really—I was going to peel out of there and get help.

But there was nothing. No active witches, no other spells.

I looked at Shadow. "You sure you're okay with going back there?" I asked her. She actually licked her chops, obviously hoping we would get a chance to revenge-maim someone. What a cliché. "Okay, then."

We got out of the truck. Shadow was on high alert, ears and nose twitching as she surveyed the area. "How do we get in?" I asked her. She immediately began trotting down Shepherd Street, along the row of houses. I started following her, then stopped. Shadow paused, too, and turned to me inquiringly. "What happened to the people living in these houses?" I asked, gesturing at the row of buildings that faced back onto Sunken City. "They were all inside the humans-go-away spell."

Shadow tilted her head at me, which meant she either didn't know or the answer was too complex for her to communicate with body language. But she made no attempt to stop me as I started up the walkway of the nearest house. I rang the doorbell, but nothing happened. I put my hand on the knob, and it turned.

A dozen different scenes from horror movies flashed through my head, and I pictured myself opening the door on a neck-high pile of dead bodies.

I cracked the door open a few inches. "Hello?" I called. The house smelled a little musty and closed up, but there was no hint of *eau de* decaying bodies, a scent I was unfortunately very familiar with. I stepped into the house, knife in hand, and Shadow barreled past my leg so she could check it for threats. I waited in the living room for her, but I didn't expect her to find anything. It *felt* empty.

When Shadow returned, wagging her tail, I wandered into the kitchen and found empty takeout trays stacked on the counters—not cheap fast food, but heavy foil or cardboard containers that bore the logos of some of LA's nicest restaurants. I followed a hallway to the bedrooms and found that the beds were still made, but topped with sleeping bags. Each room had at least one duffel bag. I went through one of them, but it contained only clothes and a handful of toiletries: shampoo, deodorant, toothpaste.

I held up a handful of clothes to Shadow. "Were the Luparii witches staying here?"

She didn't bother to sniff, just licked the air in front of her face.

Hmm. They must have left in a hurry after Shadow and Owen had escaped. "What would Jesse do?" I asked myself.

The answer was obvious: he'd be thorough. So I painstakingly went through every single duffel bag, hoping they'd left behind something about where they planned to start the Wild Hunt, or how to stop the spell itself. But I found nothing other than clothes and toiletries: no personal items, no maps or diaries, no discarded burner phones. There was nothing else of interest, so I checked the neighboring house. It contained more or less the same situation.

One by one, Shadow and I searched all seven houses on that stretch of Shepherd Street, counting sleeping bags. Every time I opened a new door, I was afraid that this one would reveal a pile of bodies, but it never happened. There were twenty-one sleeping bags, but no signs of the houses' actual owners. "What did they do with them?" I asked Shadow. She just wagged her tail slowly, the bargest equivalent of a shrug.

"Okay, how do we get past the fence?"

Shadow led me between the houses to a place where two welded chunks of fence were supposed to meet. A whole twelve-foot section of fence had been detached and tipped forward onto the ground, and there were dusty lines on the metal where truck tires had passed over it. This was how the Luparii had gotten supplies in and out of Sunken City.

Shadow led me over the downed fence, past some tall grass, and I could see scratches in the dirt that had probably been pallets and tents holding supplies. They'd taken the time to pack this stuff up, leaving clothes and other replaceable items behind. We wove along a little path in the grass that had obviously been made by feet rather than a machine. It looked old, and I realized this wasn't a Luparii addition: this was the path that hikers used to get to Sunken City.

Then we went past the tall grass, and suddenly there it was.

It looked as though a giant had picked up several concrete buildings, crumpled them in his hands, and flung them onto the jagged side of a cliff. And then some pretty spectacular artists had done the decorating. It was kind of breathtaking. I understood why hikers and sightseers continued to sneak in here, despite the potential for injury or trespassing tickets. I had never been to Stonehenge, but something about the formation of the concrete chunks reminded me of it: a humungous visual marvel that had been simultaneously created by humans and by nature. I wanted to take photos, to climb up and down the structures and admire the graffiti.

But that wasn't why we were there. Shadow was already moving, leading me down the inclined path toward a formation that looked like a giant letter *T*—just like Owen had described. There was nothing on the top, but I could see scratch marks where the metal bars of the cage had dragged. "This is where they kept you?" I asked. She wagged her tail. "Do you see anything they might have left behind?"

She lowered her nose to the ground and wandered away, looking for clues.

I wandered a little myself, but the only thing I noticed was straw scattered around, likely by the breeze coming in off the ocean. It didn't look like the tall grass, or anything native to the coast. It seemed like the kind of thing you'd feed to horses. "Shadow?" I called. The bargest trotted back to me. "Were there horses here?" I asked.

She took off, which surprised me, but she just led me to a different spot on the cliff's edge. I peeked over—and the reek of horse poop hit my nostrils. "Ugh!"

But I made myself look back over. "That is one big pile of shit," I said aloud. Shadow didn't laugh. Every bargest's a critic.

It looked like a lot of poop to me, but I didn't know enough about horses to determine how many would have been required to create such a mess. Probably however many they were planning to use tonight for the Wild Hunt. This was not good.

Shadow's nostrils flared, and she wandered off again, leaping to the top of some of the stone structures. The whole area was wildly uneven: peaks and valleys created by concrete, mounds of dirt, fallen trees, and decades of wind. I picked my way down to the bottom of the U-shaped valley, checking the crevices for scraps of paper. There was some trash, but it looked like the kind of things teenagers might leave: cigarette butts, the occasional soda cup or beer bottle. I sighed. There was nothing here. It was pretty and interesting, but this had been a huge waste of time.

I turned to climb back up, but my thoughts shifted to Jesse. It was kind of surprising that he hadn't called back by now. We'd already been there for over an hour looking through the houses, and it had taken us an hour to get here in the first place. I pulled my cell phone out of my pocket and checked the screen. I only had one bar, and even as I looked at the screen, it faded away, returned, faded out again. Shit.

Suddenly, my screen lit up with a bright red circle. I squinted, adjusting the angle of the phone, and realized the glow extended from a small dot. And it was moving. What the hell? Could phones get viruses? But then the little red dot slid to the bottom of the screen, went down my wrist, skimmed over my arm, and stopped on my chest.

Chapter 37

My insides froze. "Shadow," I called, wondering if I could duck behind the nearest concrete chunk before whoever it was got the shot off.

The bargest had been standing on a massive horizontal chunk of concrete about twenty yards away, but she turned to hop down—and a voice boomed through the air, courtesy of some kind of megaphone.

"Stay on that ledge, bargest," said a male voice with a French accent. "Or we will shoot her."

I heard Shadow snarl, her nails scratching on rock as she shuffled anxiously, but she didn't come closer.

I was still thinking about moving away—I had the bulletproof vest, after all—when two more dots joined the first. One of the three slid up my chest. I couldn't follow its progress past my collarbone, but I figured it would end up somewhere around my forehead.

The tall grass at the top of the incline seemed to ruffle, and a man appeared on the dirt path, making his way down toward us. He looked to be about sixty, but I'd lived in LA long enough to know well preserved when I saw it. He was probably upward of seventy. There was a sound amplifier in his hand, but no weapon. He didn't need one.

"Miss Bernard," he called as he approached me. "I thought it was time we spoke in person."

I expanded my radius to get him inside it sooner, and felt the immense tug of a powerful witch. A Luparii witch.

He stopped about a dozen feet away and stood to the side, staying well out of the line of fire. "So good to finally meet you," he said, as though we were at a fucking college mixer. "My name is Aldric."

The name rang a bell. "You're the head of the Luparii," I said, a little awestruck. He had come himself, in person? "Don't you have minions for this kind of thing?"

He gave me a pained smile. "Come now, Miss Bernard," he said cheerfully. "You don't think I'd miss the opportunity to lead the Wild Hunt?"

"Plus, squashing your insolent enemies doesn't carry the same weight if you have a lackey do it."

The smile faded from his face. "Really, you should be honored," he said. "It shows great respect to the soon-to-be former leaders of Los Angeles that I came for them in person."

I snorted. "Yes, that's just what we've been feeling these last few days. *Respected.* How did you know I was here?"

"You tripped the spell I had placed around the houses. When I stopped feeling my magic, I knew you must have arrived."

Stupid, stupid. Served me right for not learning enough about witch magic. Karl Schmidt's house, Noah's kidnapping, and now this? I was getting really fucking sick of these guys setting traps in my own damn city. And even sicker of falling into them. I had underestimated these people, which was stupid. They'd spent three years preparing for this, and at least part of that time watching me. Of *course* they'd had contingency plans in place.

"So why am I not dead?" I said bluntly.

"Because in this moment, I do not desire your death."

Oh, goody. We were going to play word games. "So what *do* you want?"

He smiled mirthlessly. "They did tell me you were direct. I want to go for a car ride, young lady. But first I'll have you remove your knife belt and vest and toss them aside."

"I don't think so."

He must have been wearing some kind of communication device, because he just said, "Roland," and a chunk of dirt kicked up six inches in front of me.

"The next shot will go through your left upper arm," Aldric said in the same maddeningly calm tone. "After that, your right upper arm. Then each hand. At that point I may lose my temper and simply let you bleed out, but who knows? You'll certainly be incapacitated enough for us to do anything we want."

Gritting my teeth, I pulled my tee shirt over my head and unbuckled the strap of my knife belt. I could hear Shadow whining and scratching behind me, so I called, "Stay, Shadow."

I tugged at the Velcro straps of the vest, ripping them apart harder than I really needed to. Aldric watched me pull the vest over my head, but he didn't smirk at my skintight tank top. "You may put your blouse back on," he said, as though he were being hugely generous.

I scowled, but picked up the shirt and slid it back over my head. "Toss me your cell phone," he instructed. Crap. He could use that to text someone as me. I thought about dashing it against a rock . . . but Jesse could track the phone. As long as I had it turned on, I had a lifeline.

Aldric turned his body sideways and held out a hand for me to walk up the path. "After you. Stay six feet away from me, please, or Roland might grow . . . uneasy."

As I started up the path, Aldric glanced at Shadow and yelled, "Bargest! I'm leaving behind a watcher. If he does not call every twenty minutes and tell me you are still on that platform, she dies. If you get off the platform, she dies. Sit if you understand."

I couldn't resist looking at Shadow. She looked terrifying, literally drooling with rage, but she sat. Only she did that insolent dog thing where her back haunches barely skimmed the ground.

"I'll come back for you, Shadow," I called. "Me or Jesse, okay?"

That made her relax into an actual seated position. She licked the air in front of her.

"She seems to respond to you," Aldric observed, like he was doing a clinical study. "Interesting." He turned his back on Shadow and motioned for me to continue up the hill.

Aldric directed me past the downed fence and through the path between houses. There was a strange-looking black Mercedes waiting at the curb: shorter than a limousine, but longer than a sedan. As we approached, a uniformed male driver climbed out and rushed to open the door. "After you," Aldric said, gesturing me into the car.

I balked. The one thing everyone always says about kidnapping is don't let them take you to a second location. Don't get into the window-less van—or in this case, tinted luxury vehicle. But the driver pulled a Glock out of a side holster and stood with it pointed at the ground in front of us. The implication was clear.

I climbed into the car.

It was definitely the most luxurious vehicle I'd been in, all plush leather seats and glossy fixtures. There were two sets of seats in the back, and they faced each other for conversation. Aldric slid into the seat across from me, his knees cracking a bit. Before I could come up with a decent plan other than punching his stupid face, a hard-looking man with pale eyes and hair opened the opposite door and slid onto the seat next to me. Neither of them buckled their seat belts, so I didn't either.

"Miss Bernard, this is Roland, my bodyguard," Aldric said politely.

Roland didn't speak. Or deign to look at me. He simply adjusted his suit coat in a way that fully displayed the handguns he wore on shoulder holsters.

"You know," I said conversationally, "only a few years ago, you'd never see guns in the Old World. They were considered . . . uncivilized."

"You don't strike me as a particularly civilized person," Aldric responded. "Personally, I happen to agree that they are gauche, but unfortunately, that seems to be what you bring out in people. Why did you tell the bargest you'd return for her?"

I blinked. "Excuse me?"

"You told the bargest you'd come get her, you or Mr. Cruz. To what purpose?"

"I . . . so she wouldn't be as upset," I said. Did he really not understand the concept of lying to make someone else feel better?

"Why does it matter if she's upset? She's a monster."

I gave him a look. "Well, isn't that Dr. Frankenstein calling the Creature black?"

It was his turn to say, "Excuse me?"

Obviously, I had always expected to hate this guy, but even so . . . I was really starting to hate this guy. "Forget it. Could you just tell me what I'm doing here?"

I was back on script, which seemed to put Aldric at ease. "I want to make you an offer."

I probably should have seen something like that coming, since I wasn't dead and all, but that genuinely surprised me. "You want me to *work* for you?"

"Don't laugh." He said it politely, but with an undercurrent of *Seriously, I'll fuck you up if you laugh.* "This is a very real offer."

"Okay . . ." I forced myself to take a deep breath. "What would be in it for me?" I said carefully.

He smiled. "Better. As you said, I'm deeply interested in 'squashing my insolent enemies.' One way to do that would be to terrorize your city with the Wild Hunt, an option that's certainly very appealing."

He waved one hand. "Then again, I have already gotten so much of what I want. Petra is free and has learned the cost of her mistakes. The city leaders have been embarrassed. Perhaps it would be enough if their prize null defected to the other side."

I stared at him. He wanted me to trade myself for everyone he was planning to kill? The idea was horrifying, but at the same time . . . what was my happiness compared to the lives of hundreds of people, many of whom I considered friends?

It might have been a very tempting offer—if I believed for one second he'd stick to it. I glanced at Roland to see what he made of all this, but he didn't seem to have moved.

As if reading my mind, Aldric said, "You're thinking I would go back on my word because I would need to prevent them from coming to save you. But I'm not talking about a kidnapping, Miss Bernard. There would be no manacles, no chains. I'm talking about you leaving them of your own free will. You can even say goodbye if you like." He shrugged. "We could be on a plane or a ship this evening, and you can start a new life working for me in France."

"Doing what?"

"Why, the same thing you do now, but on a much larger scale." He smiled in an indulgent, grandfatherly way. "The world is changing, Miss Bernard. Four hundred years ago the Vampire Council fell, and the Old World has had to make do without leadership. But as technology advances, we need better strategies to remain hidden. We need new leadership. A new council."

"The Luparii," I said. That was why they wanted so much power. They were literally going after world domination. Well, Old World domination, at least. I would have laughed if it weren't so fucking terrifying. "You want to be . . . what? The new government?"

"Someone has to lead," he said patiently. "Now is not the time for supernatural factions to be divided. Now is the time for working together."

Now I did laugh. "Says the guy who came here to kill a bunch of us."

"But you can *stop* all that," he said, so serious that it scared me. Well, scared me *more*. "All you have to do is say yes."

I stopped laughing. "What's to stop me from running away once we get there?" I asked. I wasn't even sure if I was just playing along now, or if I meant it.

He looked as if he'd expected the question but was still disappointed by it. "Do you have any idea how easy it would be for me to have Mr. Cruz killed? Or Mrs. Hayne? Hell, I've wanted to kill Will Carling for quite some time. And I've had people in this city for years. If you tried to run, how long do you think it would be before your friends no longer drew breath?"

I tried to keep my breathing even, to keep the stricken look off my face. "Why me?" I said. "There are other nulls."

"None as powerful," he replied. "And you've proven quite resourceful."

"I killed Killian and Sabine," I pointed out.

"And if you hadn't, I likely would have," he said casually. "Once we understood your inherent worth, Killian was instructed to take you alive. Instead, he planted a bomb in your vehicle." Aldric shook his head. "Sloppy."

I had a sinking feeling in my belly. "What do you mean, my inherent worth?"

He shifted in his seat. "Oh, pardon me. The deal I'm offering isn't only for you. It also includes the child you carry."

Chapter 38

I was too shocked to respond. How did they know about the baby?

How did they know about the baby?

Jesse. The twisted slumber. They'd taken it out of his brain, and then pretended not to know.

"Of course, I can see why you might be hesitant to accept an arrangement of this nature," Aldric said, smoothing nonexistent wrinkles from his pants leg. "But please understand, you will not be a prisoner in a castle tower. You will have minders, but you can come and go as you please. Most importantly, your child will want for nothing. She shall have money and doctors and nannies. Anything you need. Anything the child needs. All you have to do is work for the Luparii cause."

For a moment, I tried to picture it: Having the baby in a foreign country, surrounded by strangers paid to be there. Endless resources, endless security—and none of the people I loved. They would probably never know what had happened to me.

"And if I say no?"

Beside me, Roland made his first noise of the car trip: a quiet scoff. Aldric leaned forward, looking incredulous. "If you should make that mistake, the Wild Hunt will ride tonight, as planned, and many, many people will die. No humans will be harmed, so Mr. Cruz may survive, but consider the many who will be lost. Our world will see Los Angeles fall, its leadership crumble."

I had to clench my teeth to keep from screaming at him. "Then you will still come back to France with me," he went on, "and spend the next, what, eight months as a prisoner. After the baby is born . . . well, an uncooperative prisoner is of no use to me." He gazed at me with a look of pleasant inquiry.

"I see." Despite my best efforts, my voice came out shaky, goddammit. I took the time for a couple of deep breaths, forcing my fists to unclench. Finally, I said, "You're not leaving me much of a choice here."

His smile was almost sympathetic. "I understand, of course, that you may be inclined to lie now and promise cooperation you don't intend. That's what Roland, and some of my other employees, are predicting. But I have faith in your ability to do the right thing for your child." He held up my cell phone. "So I'll make this very easy. Call Mrs. Hayne and Mr. Carling. Hell, call Mr. Cruz. Tell them you're with us now, and I'll drive you straight to the airport. Give them any hint that it's involuntary and we'll go with plan B. You will spend this evening on our airplane, locked up in the cargo hold where you will be safe and out of the way, while the Wild Hunt decimates this ghastly mess of a town."

I looked at the phone in his hand for a long moment. I didn't have to fake the tears that began to spill down my cheeks. This was just ridiculous. How could this old man with his fancy car and absurd accent get to have power over me? He was batty as fuck.

I won't say that I made a choice, because I never really had one. I took the phone, looked Aldric straight in the eye, and said, "You've got a deal. But I want to make the hardest call first, and that's Jesse."

Aldric nodded, waving his hand and relaxing back into his seat. I dialed the phone. Roland didn't appear to have moved, but something about his body language suddenly screamed *on alert*.

Jesse answered on the first ring, traffic sounds in the background. "Oh my God, Scar, where are you? I've been—"

I tried to make my voice sound as calm as possible as I cut him off. I was *not* going to cry on the phone, goddammit. Aldric wouldn't get that out of me. "Jesse . . . listen . . ."

He heard my tone and went dead silent. "I love you," I said simply. "I'm sorry it took so long to . . . but I love you."

Aldric's eyes narrowed, but he wasn't sure where I was going with this yet. I held my hand up to signal that everything was fine, that I was getting to it.

And then I leaned as far toward the window as I could and said into the phone, "I'm in a long black Mercedes on the corner of Seventh and Pacific—"

For an old man, Aldric could move fast. He ripped the phone out of my hand and slapped me across the face. I lunged across the seat after him, but Roland was instantly on top of me, slamming me back against the seat and fastening my seat belt to keep me in position. He had a nasty, smug look on his Aryan poster-boy face, but at least he didn't say "I told you so" to Aldric. He was smarter than *that*, anyway.

Aldric, for his part, composed himself, gestured to the driver to roll down his window, and tossed my phone out of the car. By craning my head, I was *just* able to see my last link to Jesse and the rest of my life explode against the pavement. "That was a poor choice, Miss Bernard," Aldric said. "I hope you won't regret it when your friends' and colleagues' heads are rolling in the streets this evening." He made a sad clucking noise. "And I tried to help you."

I narrowed my eyes at him. "You tried to subjugate me. It's not the same thing, you dumbass third-rate Bond villain." I shook my head. "Jesus, you idiots have been watching me all this time, and you've learned nothing about me. But I've learned about you. I know you're scared."

Aldric glowered. "*Excuse* me?"

"You heard me." I mimicked his tone. "You believe I can stop you tonight. And you think Dashiell and the others, our whole way of life, is a threat to your plan. So you kidnap me and try to dress it up as a decision I get to make. I call bullshit, you sanctimonious piece of sister-fucking Eurotrash garbage. Fuck you and the horse you think you're going to ride on tonight. I will *crush* you."

For one second, something like fear flickered in Aldric's eyes, and then he chuckled. "Oh, Miss Bernard. I think I'm really going to enjoy the process of breaking you."

His voice was chilling. I opened my mouth to deliver what I'm sure was a scathing rebuttal, but none of us ever got to find out what I was going to say, because at that moment a certain red Lexus T-boned the Mercedes and knocked us off the road.

Chapter 39

Jesse had lucked out with the cops who came to interview him: they were from the Northeast division of the LAPD, far away from his own former precinct, and if they recognized him from his book, they didn't mention anything. It helped that the story was simple and short: he had arrived to meet his brother, but Noah was already lying there, beaten up. That was it. They told him they'd be investigating the attack, but said in all frankness they didn't have a lot of hope unless witnesses came forward, they found the car, or Noah woke up and identified his attackers. Jesse told them he understood, and they promised to be in touch.

The rest of his morning was occupied by a flurry of doctors' updates, nurses' updates, pacing the waiting room, and talking on the phone to his parents. By the time they arrived around noon, Noah was out of surgery and in intensive care.

Jesse's mom, Carmen, came rushing into the hospital room first, her makeup running down her face. She was a short, solid woman with glossy dark hair that was graying at the temples. She was wearing a green velvet dress for the wedding, but she'd swapped whatever shoes she'd had on for Keds. *"Mijo,"* she cried out, throwing her arms around Jesse. "What happened?"

"Hi, Mom." Jesse bent down to accept the hug. "Is Dad parking the car?"

"I'm here," said Robert Astin, puffing his way into the room. Jesse's parents had made a deal before their sons were born that both boys would take Carmen's last name, and Robert had chosen their first names. He was a few years older than his wife, medium height, with silvering blond hair and warm blue eyes. "Your mother's just faster. What'd I miss?"

Jesse stepped aside so they could see Noah in the bed. His brother was nearly unrecognizable, his face swollen and bruised, and most of his exposed skin seemed to be hooked up to machines. Jesse had spent a lot of time in hospitals, but he only recognized half of them.

Carmen cried out, and the two of them rushed to Noah's side. Jesse gave them the same story he'd told the police. "Where is the doctor?" Jesse's mother asked anxiously. "I have so many questions."

Jesse checked his watch. "He should be stopping by again in a couple of minutes," he said.

Carmen turned her full attention to him. "You look so tired, *mijo*. Why don't you go get something to eat? We'll be here."

Jesse wasn't really hungry, but he wanted to check his phone and figure out what was happening with Scarlett. And he wouldn't mind some non-hospital air. "Yeah . . . okay. I'll be back in a few."

Jesse left Noah's room and headed down the hallway, already pulling out his phone. There was a new voice mail from Scarlett. He was just about to listen when he heard his brother's name and looked up.

"No, I'm not technically family," said the woman who'd spoken. She was Indian, a couple of years older than Jesse, pretty and harried-looking with a light British accent. "As I said, however, they're expecting me."

"Sashi?" Jesse asked.

The woman turned, blinked, and said, "Oh my. You must be Jesse."

"Yeah." Over her shoulder, Jesse smiled at the nurse. "This is Noah's girlfriend. She's also a . . ."

"A physician's assistant," Sashi filled in, showing the nurse some sort of laminated credentials. "In Las Vegas."

"Yes," Jesse said. "Right."

The nurse looked a little skeptical, but Jesse gave her his best smile. "Would it be okay if we let her in to see Noah?"

He led her back down the hall to Noah's room, and said under his breath, "Thank you for coming. Scarlett wasn't sure you'd even get her message."

"Yes, well, Scarlett sounded very upset on the phone, so I caught the ten o'clock flight. I tried to call her when I landed, but her mobile went straight to voice mail."

They'd reached the right door, but Sashi stopped short. "Give me a quick rundown of his injuries," she instructed.

"I don't remember all the medical terms, but his left ankle is broken, he has a massive concussion, and his brain is swelling. Lots of bruising. They've already done surgery to fix internal bleeding and removed a chunk of his skull to help with the swelling. He's in an induced coma."

She took it all in for a moment, nodding. "Is the ankle a compound fracture?"

"No, just a simple break."

"Right. When I speak to his body, I'll focus on the brain and internal injuries. Those are the most life-threatening. The ankle should heal itself in time, and it will look too suspicious if the bone suddenly knits back together."

Jesse was a little thrown by "when I speak to his body," but he just said, "Whatever you need; whatever you want."

She nodded, checked whether anyone was coming down the hall, and unbelted her trench coat. Underneath, she was wearing a conservative gray dress and a white lab coat. Anyone passing by would just see another doctor in a busy hospital. Jesse was impressed, but then, this was what she did. "I need time with him. An hour would be best."

"My parents are in there."

Sashi wrinkled her nose. "That will complicate things. Can you get rid of them?"

"We're going to have to stick to the girlfriend story."

"Fine. What do I need to know?"

Jesse told her a few things about Noah, including where he lived and his job. "All right," Sashi said. "We've been dating long distance for six months, but it's only started to look serious in the last two. I'm a PA, and I want to check his chart myself."

"Got it." He held the door for her. "Let's do this."

Jesse made the introductions. His father took the news in stride, but Carmen was fascinated to learn about Sashi, the girlfriend Noah had never mentioned (and did not, in fact, know about). Jesse had to do some tap-dancing, but he eventually convinced his parents to go to the cafeteria with him for lunch, giving Sashi a little time alone with Noah. "But we just got here," Carmen protested again as Jesse ushered them out. "And I have so many questions!"

He scrambled to think of something to say that would temporarily divert her attention from Noah's condition, preferably without lying too much, and finally said, "There's something I want to tell you about anyway. I'm seeing someone, too."

That got Carmen to turn her head away.

As they walked back down the hall, Jesse had a sense of déjà vu and remembered he hadn't actually checked the voice mail from Scarlett. "I'm just gonna pop into the restroom, then we'll go get lunch," he promised his mother.

In the single-stall bathroom, he played Scarlett's message: "Hey, it's me. I know you don't want me going to Sunken City without you, but I'm out of other ideas, so I'm going to run down there. Shadow's with me, and I've got my knives and bulletproof vest." Scarlett paused, probably wondering if she needed to say something relationship-y now. She added in a softer voice, "We're gonna be fine, Jesse."

He cursed and called her cell. It went straight to voice mail. Jesse tried again, with the same result.

He cursed longer and louder, in Spanish and then English. Sunken City could be dangerous even if you weren't being pursued by an evil witch clan, and she'd gone down there anyway.

Jesse debated with himself for a moment. He knew that Scarlett's last relationship had failed partly because Eli had been controlling and overprotective: the werewolf had been so obsessed with Scarlett's safety that he'd ignored what she actually wanted. Jesse didn't want to make the same mistake, especially now that they were finally on the same page about dating. At the same time, she was pregnant, she was being hunted, and she was outnumbered. And, maybe most important, she hadn't actually said she *wanted* to go by herself, or that she wanted him to give her space.

Jesse decided that he would take the risk of Scarlett accusing him of smothering. This was too important.

He sighed. Now he just had to figure out what to tell his mother.

Twenty minutes later, Jesse was practically flying down the 110. He'd given his parents a hasty excuse about Scarlett being in a fender bender—he'd talked about her many times—and ducked out before they could ask questions. He was definitely going to pay for that later, and Sashi might get annoyed if they went straight back to Noah's room, especially if they saw or heard something they shouldn't, but Sashi was a pro; she would figure something out. In his gut, Jesse was sure something was wrong.

He tried calling her again, but Scarlett still didn't answer her phone. Next, Jesse called Abby Hayne, the woman in charge of all of Dashiell's technological needs. Abby usually worked a pretty pedestrian

Monday-to-Friday schedule, but he hoped that with the Luparii in town, Dashiell or Hayne would have put her on high alert.

Sure enough, she answered immediately. "What's up, Jesse?"

"Abby! Can you trace Scarlett's newest phone for me?"

There was a brief pause, and then Abby said dryly, "There's this thing called Find My iPhone now . . ."

Jesse reminded himself that Abby was employed by Dashiell and didn't actually owe him anything. "I know, I know, but I'm driving, and I don't know if it'll work with the newest phone. Please?"

She heard the urgency in his voice and said, "Okay, okay. I gotta put the phone down while I get to the computer." Abby had cerebral palsy and usually used a wheelchair at work. A couple of minutes went by, and then she was back. "Okay, I'm tracing it now. She's in San Pedro, right on the ocean."

"Thank God." Maybe he really was overreacting. Jesse would be happy to take that particular hit, though. "I'm headed down there now. I may need to have you check again, okay?"

He could practically hear her eyes rolling. "I live to serve."

Forty minutes later, the 110 was about to dump him onto Gaffrey Street in San Pedro, about three miles north of Sunken City. He tried Scarlett first, and this time the phone rang, but she didn't answer. Frowning, Jesse called Abby back. "Do you still have her location?"

A pause, then: "She's headed north on Pacific."

"Okay, good." Pacific ran parallel to Gaffrey, one block east.

"Do you—" Abby began, but Jesse's call-waiting beeped.

It was Scarlett. "Thanks, Abby, call you back!" he said in a rush and clicked over. "Oh my God, Scar, where are you? I've been—"

"Jesse . . . listen . . ."

He shut up. Her voice was all wrong: sad and resigned. She told him she loved him, and he knew, he *knew* something terrible was happening.

"I'm in a long black Mercedes on the corner of Seventh and Pacific—" she started to say, and then the phone call was abruptly cut off.

Fear seemed to pulse through all of Jesse's extremities like a jolt of adrenaline. He was still on Gaffrey, but he took his eyes off the road to check the map on his phone, which was incredibly dangerous and stupid. Then he topped that by cutting across two lanes of traffic to take a screeching left onto First Avenue, speeding a block east to Pacific Avenue. He turned right and leaned forward, craning his neck, looking for a Mercedes.

In some parts of Los Angeles, finding a single Mercedes might have been impossible, but this area was San Pedro's answer to a commercial district: Chinese food and liquor stores and Laundromats. He didn't see any Mercedes.

Jesse was just beginning to despair when he had to stop at a light on Pacific. Oncoming traffic had the green, with a left-turn arrow, and Jesse spotted a weird-looking black car, sort of halfway between a limo and a sedan. It was turning left, trying to get off Pacific Ave. He saw the Mercedes logo on the grill and, without really thinking it through, pressed his foot on the gas.

He wasn't flooring it, and the Mercedes wasn't going very fast, but Jesse's airbag still popped as the Lexus's bumper hit the side of the Mercedes, just in front of the passenger seat. His head snapped back and forth, but he was already unbuckling and tipping himself out of the car when the driver of the Mercedes stepped out with a handgun raised. Disoriented, Jesse pulled his own gun and crouched, duckwalking to the back door of the Mercedes.

He tugged it open, and a gunshot instantly whipped past his ear. He half-stood and peeked through the window into the car.

The shot had come from a bodyguard-looking man who lay on his back on the floor of the car. Scarlett was in the seat closest to the door, facing backward. There was also an old man lying halfway across the seat, partially tipped off it. Jesse's quick impression was of a turtle trying to right itself.

"Get back!" Scarlett yelled to him, and she kicked the hands of the bodyguard, sending his gun tumbling away. The man started to rise, but Scarlett stomped down hard, right on his nuts. It looked excruciating.

Meanwhile, the driver of the Mercedes had come around the nose of the car, climbing and sliding over the point where it still connected to the Lexus. He had his gun out, but Jesse raised his own weapon before the driver could shoot. He put two bullets in the man's chest, realized he was wearing a vest, and shot him in the head.

Scarlett fell out of the still-open car door, kicking it shut behind her. One of the two men must have been reaching for her, because there was a scream of pain. Jesse struggled to his feet.

Scarlett's eyes were huge and panicked. "Run!" she yelled.

Chapter 40

The moment the cars impacted, there was some part of my hindbrain that started doing my job. *Camera phones, traffic cameras, witnesses* . . .

But like it or not, cleaning up a supernatural mess wasn't currently my problem. The problem was surviving one.

When I tumbled out of the back seat of the car, Jesse took my hand, and we dashed away into a crowd of onlookers. No one followed us. Aldric was too old, Roland was too injured, and the driver, as it turned out, was too dead. No one in the crowd was interested in pursuing people with at least one gun.

A big part of me wanted to stay and fight, to hold my ground until Aldric was dead or at least really, really hurt. But for one thing, there were way too many witnesses, and for another, I had to get back to Shadow before the Luparii could. If Aldric gathered his wits enough to send his guy after Shadow, there was a possibility that she'd let herself be captured again, thinking it might save my life.

The car accident was two and a half miles from Sunken City. At first, as we ran, I was looking for a cab, but traffic was picking up, and it was only going to get worse now that we'd blocked off a huge chunk of Pacific Ave.

Then I figured we could just run the whole way there—I ran five miles, three days a week, so three wasn't out of the question. But I got a stitch in my side, and my boots were hurting my feet, and at one point Jesse looked over his shoulder at me and skidded to a stop. "Scar? You okay?"

"I'm great," I said, breathing hard. "Let's go get Shadow."

"We need a pit stop." Jesse glanced around for a moment. There was a 7-Eleven on the west side of the street, and he walked me over there and went straight to a cooler of bottled water.

"If you try to give me any fucking crackers, I'm going to feed them to you, and I don't mean through your mouth," I warned him.

He flashed that heart-stopping smile at me, but it disappeared right away. "I want you to stay here," he said, his eyes pleading. We were standing in the back of the store, away from the windows "The Luparii don't know you're here, and if they did, they wouldn't attack you in the middle of a convenience store with video cameras. I'll get Shadow and Astrid's truck and come back for you."

I nodded. "Okay." I pulled out the keys and handed them to him. He looked shocked. "Okay?"

"Jesse, I'm exhausted, and I feel like crap, and we've got a long night of trying to stop the Wild Hunt ahead of us. Shadow trusts you. I trust you. So bring back my dog."

"I'm gonna tell her you called her that." He leaned in and kissed me, hard and fast. "I'll be right back."

"Be careful," I yelled after him. I wasn't too worried, though. When I'd expanded my radius back at Sunken City, I hadn't felt any witches besides Aldric. Whoever he'd left behind was human, and Jesse could handle himself against a human.

While I waited, I went to the counter with an armful of snacks and a new disposable cell phone, since mine had gone out the Mercedes window. As the clerk rang me up, I said bluntly, "Listen . . . my boyfriend went to change our tire, a couple of blocks away. Would you have somewhere I could sit down? I'm six weeks pregnant, and I feel like crap."

The clerk, a Middle Eastern woman in a hijab, glanced up from the register and really looked at me for the first time, taking in the scratches on my face and arms and my general air of exhaustion. Then she smiled and came out from around the counter with a folding chair and told me to help myself to a magazine.

It took more than an hour, but finally Jesse returned, looking as tired as I felt. He entered the store alone, and I jumped up from my chair. "Is she—"

His face broke into a smile. "We don't have her little assistance cape, remember? She's in the parking lot."

I practically ran for the door, yelling a thank-you in the general direction of the clerk.

Shadow was waiting just on the other side of the glass, her breath creating a foggy spot. She backed up so I could come out, then reared up on her hind legs, rested her front paws on my shoulders, and began licking my cheek. She let out a soft, happy bark.

I laughed and pushed her gently away. "I've never heard her do that," Jesse said, sounding amazed.

"That's because the Luparii trained enthusiasm out of her," I said, rubbing vigorously at Shadow's neck. She dropped down to sniff all around me in a circle, and Jesse took the opportunity to step closer.

"Are you okay?" he said, studying my face.

"More or less." I reached up and draped my arms around him, leaning some of my body weight on him. I closed my eyes. All I wanted was to fall asleep like this. Or at least have another serious make-out session.

When she was satisfied that I was in one piece, Shadow sat down and looked up at us, head cocked to one side as if to say, "Now what?"

"It's time to go wake Dashiell," I told her. First, though, I looked at Jesse. "What happened to the Luparii guy that Aldric left behind?"

He snorted. "There was no guy. Aldric just said that to keep Shadow from coming after you."

God, he was a dick. "How's Noah?"

Jesse's face lit up. "He's great, actually. Sashi showed up around one."

"What? Really?"

"Yup!" He told me about Sashi arriving at the hospital from Vegas. "She called while I was on my way back here with Shadow, and Noah is out of the woods. His ankle is broken, and he's banged up, but the doctors are decreasing the sedatives. They think he might wake up as early as tonight. Your friend Sashi is *really* good."

I felt my whole body unknot a little. "We're gonna have to figure out what to tell him."

"What did they want with you?" Jesse asked, meaning the Luparii. A couple of kids chose that moment to practically gallop past us in their rush to get into the 7-Eleven. I made a face.

"Come on, let's talk in the truck."

Shadow hopped into the back of the pickup, looking positively gleeful about getting to ride with the wind in her fur. I warned her to stay down so she didn't draw attention, but we both knew I wasn't going to enforce it. When I climbed into the passenger seat, I saw that Jesse had grabbed my vest, boots, and knife belt from Sunken City. "Yesssss," I said out loud.

Jesse drove, and we started the hour ride back toward Pasadena. It was already 4:30, and the sun would set at 7:36. Before I got sucked into the Wild Hunt situation, I called Molly and left a new voice mail telling her to still go to the hospital and keep an eye on Noah and Jesse's parents, but with a different cover story. She would come up with something. Then I called Will and Kirsten and arranged to meet at Dashiell's house at six. It was cutting it close, but we would need at least an hour to get up to Pasadena, and Jesse wanted to stop at his house for clothes—and, more importantly, lots and lots of weapons.

On the way, I filled him in on everything I'd learned from Aldric. I debated not telling him about Aldric's offer, but if the Luparii was after the baby, that was something Jesse needed to know. He was upset when he realized they'd pulled it out of his brain, but I told him we didn't have time for his guilt hysterics, and that got him to smile.

Jesse lived in a tiny apartment in the Echo Lake district. It was the kind of place you usually stayed in for just a year or two while you were figuring things out, but he'd had his lease forever. He found a parking spot on a side street and turned the truck off, pausing to look at me. "Do you want to come up?" he asked.

There was an intensity to his tone that I didn't understand right away, because I am naturally very dense.

Then I got it.

We didn't really have time for . . . me to come up. But there was also a decent chance that one or both of us would die tonight, or that I'd be taken by force and shipped to France. So I didn't overthink it. I just got out of the truck.

Shadow came up to the apartment too—she didn't really give us a choice in the matter—and made her customary search for danger before she'd let me cross the threshold. Then she pointedly went into the living room, climbed on Jesse's couch, and flopped over with her head in the direction of the front door. She made every effort to look asleep.

I wanted to laugh, but I was too nervous. Wordlessly, Jesse took my hand and led me past the tiny kitchen and into the tiny bedroom. It was messy and unpretentious, just a box spring and mattress covered by a light quilt with a design like Spanish tiles. I'd seen into this room plenty of times from the hallway, but I'd never actually stepped inside. We'd been too busy being afraid of each other for that.

Jesse closed the bedroom door and turned to me, resting his forehead on mine. "Scarlett," he said, his face troubled. "When I was in the twisted slumber . . ."

He seemed to choke on the words. I reached up and put my hands on either side of his face. "What?"

"I saw you dead. It was . . . bad."

Ah. I was immune to the Luparii magic, but if it was as good as everyone seemed to think, what Jesse had experienced would have felt so much worse than a dream. "I'm right here." I took his hands and put them on my waist so he could see. "I'm fine."

"I know, I just wanted to . . . it made me realize I . . ."

I tilted my head up so I could kiss him. This time it was tentative and light, as though I was afraid to hurt him. Maybe I was.

He was the one who broke the kiss, craning his head back to look at me without moving away. "Did you mean what you said on the phone?" he asked.

"Yes." I lifted my chin so I could look into his eyes. "I'm in love with you."

He grinned that thousand-watt smile that always made my insides melt. "Yeah?"

"Yeah."

"I'm in love with you, too."

"I know." Then I took a tiny step back, and my hand fluttered to my stomach. "But we're going to need to work out some . . . logistics." I chewed on my lip. "I'm keeping the baby."

His grin widened. "Good."

"Does that . . . bother you?"

"Scarlett . . ." Slowly, he got down on his knees in front of me, lifting the hem of my shirt to uncover a few inches of my stomach. He kissed it, his warm lips making me shiver. "How many adventures have I followed you into?" he said into my skin.

"A lot," I admitted. "Although I'd classify most of them as 'misadventures.'"

"I wouldn't." He looked up at me with searching eyes. "Why do you think this would be different?" I caught my breath, unable to speak as he whispered, "I'd follow you anywhere."

That wasn't enough, of course—not for a baby, but it was enough for today. My fingers tangled in his hair. I wanted to kiss him, but he didn't get up. Instead, he kissed my stomach again and unbuttoned my jeans, pulling the zipper down with exquisite slowness. I knew I should tell him to hurry, we didn't have time—but at the moment I didn't care. We were stealing this time together, whether anyone else liked it or not.

I sat down on the bed, and Jesse pulled off my jeans. Still kneeling, he pulled his shirt over his head, and I immediately ran my fingers over the muscles on his chest, making him shiver. He closed the distance between us and kissed me on the lips, his momentum carrying me back onto the bed.

His tongue slid into my mouth like it'd been made specifically for this purpose, and there were suddenly so many things I wanted to do that I'd never been allowed, a bucket list that applied exclusively to Jesse's body. I wanted to run my tongue along his collarbone, and trace my nails on his back. I wanted to bite the muscle in his shoulder and slide my hand into his pants until he cried out.

So I did.

I did all those things, mostly while I was still kissing him. And then he was lifting my shirt over my head and kissing the top of my breasts, and I really needed him to have more access, so I pulled the sports bra top over my head while he made appreciative noises, his fingers tracing the muscles along my sides.

And then his mouth closed over my breast, and I was gone, gone, gone.

Chapter 41

I was late to my own war council. Embarrassing.

I sort of expected the ride from Jesse's apartment to Dashiell's house in Pasadena to be embarrassing too, but it just . . . wasn't. Whenever traffic allowed, Jesse would reach over and take my hand, and I caught him smiling randomly. I might have teased him about it, but I was doing the same thing. With Shadow in the truck bed, her tongue lolling out with great happiness, this was the most at peace I'd felt in . . . I didn't know how long.

At Dashiell's, everyone was waiting for us. Kirsten and Will looked exhausted and impatient, and even the usually quiet Hayne seemed antsy. I had a terrible thought, and the first thing out of my mouth was, "Ophelia?"

A tiny smile flickered across Kirsten's face. "She's safe," she said shortly. "Abby took her out of town a few hours ago."

"I sent Cliff with them," Hayne added.

Cliff was one of Hayne's daytime guys, and he'd accompanied me on my ill-fated trip to Vegas. I'd only seen him a couple of times since then, but I had to smile at the thought of the reserved ex-military bodyguard shepherding sharp-tongued Abby and a two-year-old on a road trip.

"You're late," Kirsten said, looking annoyed.

"Sorry," I said, not meaning it. "Are Dashiell and Beatrice still downstairs?"

"I moved them into Dashiell's office," Hayne said pointedly, "when you were late."

I refused to take the bait. "Okay, then." I expanded my radius to include most of the mansion, feeling the two vampires wake up a few rooms away. "They'll be here in a minute. Where's Owen?"

Kirsten's face took on a certain stubborn look. "I sent him away, too."

"What?" Dashiell stood in the open doorway, dressed in his "day-time casual" clothes: jeans and a wrinkled white dress shirt. He looked aghast. The last he'd heard, Owen had just knocked on my door. "We could have used him!"

"For bait?" Kirsten countered. "I won't allow it. The poor kid has been through enough."

"We need fighters!" Dashiell argued. "And he's certainly motivated, from what you've told me."

"His magic is basically useless for the near future, and I will not have you dangling him in front of the Luparii." Kirsten crossed her arms. "He's a witch, in my city, so he falls under my protection."

Dashiell grumbled a little, but he finally had to concede that Owen was Kirsten's responsibility, not his.

It took a while to bring Dashiell—and to some extent, the others—up to speed on the events of the day, from Owen's story to Noah's attack to Aldric's attempt to kidnap me at Sunken City. I knew we were short on time, so I went through the story as quickly as I could. When I got to the part about Aldric taking me instead of killing me, Dashiell frowned. "Why would he need a null so badly?"

"He must believe Scarlett can stop the Wild Hunt," Will said thoughtfully.

"It's not just that," I said, feeling suddenly nervous. Jesse squeezed my hand under the table, and I nodded at him and turned to face the others. "It's because I'm pregnant."

The whole room seemed to go still. You know that expression "You could hear a pin drop"? I swear, if I'd had any bobby pins in my hair at that moment, I would have yanked one out and tossed it on the table in front of me.

"That's not possible," Kirsten said, at the same moment Beatrice began, "Scarlett, honey, I think you've made a mistake."

"No mistake," I told her. "Jameson is the father. Two nulls?"

I wasn't sure I'd ever seen Dashiell quite so shocked. He's usually stone-faced about everything, even in my radius, but his whole face had gone slack. I admit, there was a tiny part of me that was finding this awesome.

"This . . . this is what your trip was about?" he said in a slightly dazed voice.

"Yes. I went to see Maven, the cardinal vampire in Colorado. I hoped she might know more about nulls because of her age, and I was right. She told me that the baby would grow up to be a powerful witch. Powerful enough to boost something called ley lines, which will boost all of magic."

Everyone glanced at Kirsten, who held out her empty hands. "Ley lines are where witch magic is strongest," she confirmed, "but only one line even touches the LA area, and it's not very strong."

Both Dashiell and Will started asking follow-up questions, but I said, "Look, guys, we can talk about what this might mean if we all live through the night. Bottom line?" I put a hand on my stomach. "This is my baby. Not a bargaining chip, not a hostage, and definitely not a threat to any of you. I'd like to make sure we're all *very* clear on that."

My voice was mild, but I stared at them until, one by one, they all nodded. Even Dashiell, although of course he was last, just to be a dick.

Only then did my shoulders relax, and I realized how tense I had been. "Meanwhile, the Wild Hunt is coming. What do we do?"

"I've evacuated nine of my pack members," Will began. "Leaving thirteen who will fight."

"There are a few dozen vampires whom I would trust to go into a battle," Dashiell said. They both glanced at Kirsten, who looked uncertain.

"We don't have many witches with combat experience," she explained. "Few of them are powerful enough, and those who are, mostly fear that power. I've sent nearly two hundred witches away, with their families. Of the ones who are left, I could count on maybe forty. They're all on standby, but I'm not sure what to do with them."

That was nowhere near all the Old World members in Los Angeles, and I wondered about the rest. Did we just not trust them, or were they an actual threat? I knew there were plenty of backstabbing vampires who would be happy to see Dashiell lose power.

Still, that was nearly a hundred people, all told, and the Luparii had between nineteen and twenty-one, depending on whether or not Killian's and Sabine's sleeping bags had been among those I'd counted at Sunken City.

"I sort of have a plan," I told them.

"How much of a plan?" Jesse asked beside me.

I flashed him a grin and said under my breath, "Twelve percent." To the others, I said, "But we need to know where they're going to be. I need help with that."

"Do you have a map of the city?" Will asked Dashiell.

Beatrice got up and retrieved a map of the greater-LA area. Trust vampires to still have paper maps. Will took it and handed it to Kirsten. "Where is this ley line?"

She shot him an appreciative look and pulled a pen out of her purse. She drew a curving line from the Simi Valley southeast through Canoga Park and Burbank, curving around and south all the way to

Long Beach, not too far from Sunken City. Even from the other side of the table, the line looked familiar, and I got up and went over for a closer look. "It follows the river," I declared, pointing at the blue line whose course was almost identical to the pen line. "I saw it on a map this afternoon at the River Center."

"I'd never paid much attention, but I suppose that makes sense," Kirsten said thoughtfully. "Ley lines often follow natural landmarks, and that river's been there in some form or another since the Tongva." The Tongva were the Native American people who had occupied the LA Basin before the first Spanish settlers. "Staying near the ley line would likely boost the Hunt's strength."

"It's not just that." Jesse leaned forward to trace his finger along the line. "They can use the riverbed itself to get around the city."

He was right.

"That's good to know and all, but 'they'll be somewhere along the river' isn't enough for us to go on," Will pointed out.

"No, it isn't," I agreed. "Unless we could predict exactly where they're going to turn up and be waiting for them."

Every head in the room turned to look at me. "How fast can you guys assemble your people?" I asked.

Chapter 42

I started laying out my plan—or my 12 percent of a plan—and the others spent another fifteen minutes poking holes in it. The biggest question was whether or not I would be able to stop the Wild Hunt magic. We would have to bet everything—every*one*—on the theory that I could.

"How sure are you?" Kirsten asked, looking worried.

I chewed on my lip for a moment. "Mostly sure?"

The other three Old World leaders exchanged looks. "That's not overwhelming me with confidence," Dashiell said.

"Okay, let me show you something. Please just humor me for a second. Bea and Dashiell, can you come stand by me?" They raised their eyebrows, but pushed their chairs back and came toward me. I looked at the wall, where Shadow was curled up next to the door so she could ambush intruders. "Shadow, can you come here?"

The bargest stood and trotted over to me. I asked her to sit next to my chair, and then I stood up and went to the other side of the room, positioning her between myself and the others. I brought Beatrice and Dashiell with me so they wouldn't turn into dead vampires again. "Be very still," I advised Will and Kirsten. "Will, fight your instincts."

Before anyone could react, I pulled in my radius. Almost immediately, Shadow stood up and ran straight for Will, her teeth bared. He followed my advice and held still, while she stood three feet away from him, the hair on the back of her neck bristling straight up. Her whole body was tensed, waiting for the command to rip out his throat.

Carefully, I extended my radius until it encompassed Shadow—but not Will.

The bargest calmed down. She did a little dance in place, whined, and then retreated to stand next to me. "But I'm still a werewolf," Will said, confused.

I released my radius back to its usual area, and we all went back to our seats. Jesse, who had watched the whole demonstration with disinterested calm, grinned at me. "The bargest magic is Wild Hunt magic, and it works on two levels," I explained. "There are the permanent physical effects, which give her strength and speed and the impenetrable skin, but there's also the . . . mmm . . . nonphysical component of the magic that lets her heal quickly and forces her to want to hunt and kill werewolves." I gestured to Will. "The physical stuff is permanent; I can't undo it. But the nonphysical stuff is affected by me." I shrugged. "'Spectral warriors,' to me, implies nonphysical. Definitely not permanent. So . . . I'm mostly sure I can stop the Wild Hunt."

They all looked at me thoughtfully. "What about the animals?" Kirsten asked. "In all the lore, there are horses and dogs, at the very least."

"That's what I'm not sure about." I checked my watch. We had twenty minutes until sunset—though I doubted that the Wild Hunt would begin the moment the sun went down. That kind of complex magic would require a whole ritual to begin. "That's why we need fighters."

"And another thing," Jesse added, looking inspired, "I don't suppose any of you have access to animal tranquilizers?"

A couple of minutes later, the conference room sort of became the situation room, as everyone began talking or texting, trying to assemble their people.

I expanded my radius so Beatrice and Dashiell could move around the mansion, and kept an eye on Will as he made his calls. Many of his weaker werewolves had already left town, so he didn't have as many calls to make as the others. When he finished, I asked him if we could talk in the hall for a minute. He looked surprised—the two of us didn't really do much one-on-one time, especially since I had broken up with his second-in-command—but he complied.

"What's up?" he asked after I closed the door behind us.

"Listen . . ." I began, not really sure how to begin this conversation. "Uh, you know we're probably all gonna die tonight, right?"

He shrugged. "Yeah. But we've been probably going to die before."

"That's not . . . grammatically sound, but yeah. Anyway." I took a deep breath.

It was stupid of me to interfere, of course, but hey. Sometimes I do stupid things. Will had a daughter he didn't know about. Sashi had never told him about Grace, and now it might be too late.

When I'd called her on the way to Dashiell's place to thank her for saving Noah, I'd asked if I could tell Will she was in town.

"Do you think that's really necessary?" she'd said in a panicky voice. "I'm going back tonight. He doesn't need to know I was ever here."

"Sashi." I'd tried to think of the right words, and finally just said, "I'm pregnant."

She'd gasped. "That's not possible."

"Apparently it is. Do you remember the guy I lost in Vegas? The other null?" Despite what was happening with Jesse, it still hurt to think of Jameson. It probably always would.

"Yeah," Sashi had said, and then, "Oh."

"Yeah. He died not knowing he was going to have a kid. And Will . . . there's a good chance we won't make it through this tonight."

"I see," she'd said in a small voice.

"Look, I'm pretty sure I'm going to be the world's shittiest mom, and I have no right to give you advice. But maybe if Grace met Will . . . maybe if she understood why you couldn't marry John . . ."

There was a long silence, and I was sure I'd overstepped. But all Sashi had said was, "What do you have in mind?"

Now that I was standing across from the alpha werewolf, I struggled for the right words. "This morning, when Noah was attacked," I said finally, "I made a call to a healing witch I met in Las Vegas. She took a late-morning plane and got here in time to save him."

"A healing witch," he echoed.

There really wasn't any way to sugarcoat this. "Will . . . it's Sashi."

His face changed. Actually, his *everything* changed. His body language went from loose and relaxed to sort of defensive and prepared. Like he thought I was about to kick him in the teeth, and there was nothing he could do to stop me. "My Sashi?" he said, in a voice that sliced at my heart.

I nodded. "She's in town, although she's on a late flight back to Vegas in a few hours. If . . . you know. You wanted to talk to her."

He stared at me. "Why did you . . . I mean, how did you and her . . ." He drifted off, and then sort of shook himself. "Does she want to talk to me?"

Not really. But Sashi felt that the news should come from her, which I had to respect. "She thinks it might be a good idea," I said carefully. "But it's up to you."

"How do I . . . should I call her?" The alpha werewolf of Los Angeles suddenly looked like an uncertain kid on his way to pick up his prom date.

I checked my watch again. "She should be parked out on the road."

He turned and started toward the door before pausing. "Thanks, Scarlett," he said quietly.

I felt like I should add something. *Wait until you learn what I've been keeping from you.* But I just nodded and headed back into the conference room, shutting the door behind me.

Dashiell called me over. He was standing with Beatrice and Hayne, who looked a little guilty. "Did you invite a boundary witch into my territory?" Dashiell said, his face clouded over with annoyance.

Oops. With everything that had happened, I'd completely forgotten that Katia was coming to help Wyatt. But she would have called Hayne when she arrived . . . and Hayne would have felt obligated to tell Dashiell. I couldn't really blame him for that. "Uh, a little bit?"

Dashiell frowned, and I rushed to add, "Look, it didn't seem like a big enough thing to wake you up over during the day. But yeah, I thought if Katia had any chance of saving Wyatt, it was worth a phone call." And, okay, I'd forgotten about it.

Beatrice laid a hand on his arm, and he sighed. "Sometimes," he said tiredly, "I honestly think you're trying to drive me insane."

"It's really more of a fringe benefit than an overall goal," I said helpfully.

Beatrice shot me a look. "I'm sorry," I added, more contrite. "It's been an intense week."

Dashiell just waved me away.

Chapter 43

When most people think of rivers, they think, you know, "large body of quickly moving water." But the Los Angeles River is different. Mostly, it's a gigantic concrete trough that usually has a trickle of filthy liquid running down the middle. You know the big race at the end of *Grease*, where they're in the wide concrete channel that's completely dry except for a tiny bit of water? Yeah, that's the LA River. It's littered and polluted, and until very recently, it was one of many ugly things in Los Angeles that people just sort of averted their eyes from, like homeless people, graffiti, and the condition of all public bathrooms.

In the last decade or so, however, activists had made serious efforts to "rebrand" and revitalize the river, starting with removing the concrete bottom from many sections so native plants could grow in again. New parks had also sprung up along the river, and bike trails, and there were places where you could even kayak.

The vast majority of it, however, was still a wide, dry channel. And if you weren't concerned with being seen, or facing possibly violent homeless squatters, you could use it to move through most of the city. There was no traffic, no crowds of distracting humans. And, best of all, no one paying attention.

Kirsten had called in the witch who did volunteer work for the LA River, and she'd arrived at Dashiell's house within fifteen minutes, which was pretty damned impressive. Her name turned out to be Paloma Greene, which really, really sounded made up, but then again, that could just be LA for you.

I was expecting some variation on "New Age hippie," but Paloma arrived in jeans and a button-down shirt, smelling of fertilizer. She was about fifty, with short, sensible black hair and the look of someone accustomed to running four lives at once. A mom look. "I was working in the garden," she said, unconsciously scrubbing her hands together, though they didn't look dirty. "What do you need?"

Kirsten explained, and Paloma went over to the map still spread across the conference-room table. She stood there for a few minutes with her hands on her hips, looking over her options.

Part of the recent revitalization project had included setting up a bunch of new parks along the river, or sprucing up existing parks to encourage people who wanted to use the channel for bike or walking trails. Paloma pointed at a green spot very close to Long Beach. I squinted to read the name: Maywood Riverfront Park. "This one," she said. "There are residential homes around the park, but most of it is fenced and contained. And the entrance from the river forms a choke point."

"Thank you, Paloma," Kirsten said. "Will you join us? We could use your expertise."

Paloma bowed her head. "I'm not sure how useful I'll be," she said. "But I will do my best."

After that, it was a matter of getting everyone the park's address and telling them to head down there immediately with whatever weapons they could carry . . . except for two of Dashiell's vampires, who were out trying to press a noted veterinarian who worked with the LA Zoo to get some serious tranquilizer.

The idea was simple: if the witches of the Wild Hunt could only see the supernatural, we could draw them to wherever we wanted by gathering all of LA's remaining supernaturals in one place. Instead of riding through the city lopping the heads off witches and werewolves who might be trying to hide or run, they would be drawn to the hunting ground we'd chosen.

It sounded easy in theory, but Kirsten and Dashiell, especially, had a hard time persuading their people to come be . . . well, *bait* wasn't quite the right word, but it was probably the closest one. We needed to reach critical mass, and only by threatening and cajoling were the leaders able to convince everyone to join in. Dashiell could have *ordered* his vampires to come, since they'd all sworn loyalty to him to be allowed to live in his city, but he couldn't do it over the phone, and he said that soldiers who were being forced to fight were not the kind of soldiers anyone wanted.

Happily, convincing other people to join us had been Will, Kirsten, and Dashiell's problem, not mine. In the end, I think the tipping point was that those who refused would be taking their own kind of risk: after all, a werewolf on his own would still be vulnerable to the Wild Hunt.

I went down to the park with the first wave of people—including Jesse and Shadow, of course—because I needed to get inside the territory so Kirsten could set the humans-go-away spell.

She had offered to give Jesse a witch bag, which would have protected him from the spell, but he'd shaken his head firmly. "Then I couldn't go near Scarlett," he'd pointed out, taking my hand. "Where she goes, I go."

Kirsten had looked from him to our joined hands, to my face, which was turning red. She'd given us a wide, sunny smile. "About damned time," she'd said.

Dashiell must have called his contacts at the LAPD or the Highway Patrol, because Jesse raced the truck down the freeway doing nearly ninety, and we weren't the only ones.

As soon as we arrived, I could see why Paloma had chosen this particular park. It was sort of wedge shaped, with one edge formed by busy Slauson Avenue, and the other by the river. The park itself formed the curved part of the wedge, enclosed (mostly) by an iron fence. That made me hopeful: many of the legends suggested that the Wild Hunt riders weren't able to pass through iron. It was worth a shot, at least.

Speaking of which, Jesse had two guns in hip holsters, and he'd convinced me to take his Glock, which I'd put into a small-of-the-back holster. Under that I had my knife belt, and under *that*, the bulletproof vest. I felt bulky as hell, and I couldn't see how the Luparii would be able to carry guns anyway—spectral guns?—but I wanted to be prepared. And as much as I disliked the things, I wasn't at all opposed to bringing guns to a sword fight.

Shadow was trotting along on my other side, and I sort of wanted the three of us to start walking in slow motion; we were so obviously ready for a fight. We jog-walked into the center of the park, surveying the territory. "How do you want to do this?" Jesse asked me.

"Humans-go-away spell starting on the other side of that bridge," I said, pointing. "And closing off this section of Slauson Avenue."

"That includes the bridge." He grimaced. "It's gonna piss people off."

I sent him a sweet smile. "What's the point of having city officials in your pocket if you're not gonna take them out and mess with them once in a while?"

"What about the riverbed itself?" he said. "Are we closing off a section?"

I shook my head. "They might be able to feel the spell, or they might bring humans along for the specific purpose of feeling out traps. Let's close the bike path, but leave the riverbed open." That gave me another idea. "We should actually get a couple of human servants to hang out in the riverbed, a quarter mile in either direction. Like spotters." I could ask Dashiell to get some of the human servants on it.

"I thought humans couldn't see the Wild Hunt," Jesse commented.

"Not the hunters, but if the Wild Hunt includes bargests, they should be able to see them." I didn't know about the horses.

I turned around. "The residential area is going to be a bigger problem." There weren't a ton of houses facing the park, but there were some. "Kirsten can set another humans-go-away, but when the vampires start arriving we should still have them go door-to-door."

"Agreed."

With that, there was not much else I could do except stay away from the edges of where Kirsten was planning to set spells. Jesse hurried off to talk to the people who were arriving, and I sat down on a bench in the middle of the park. Shadow jumped up on the bench beside me, causing it to quake, but when it didn't collapse, she lay down, allowing me to lean on her like a pillow.

Within the next half hour, Kirsten—and the big group of chanting witches following her around—had almost finished setting spells on the edges of our target area, and the vampires were clearing the neighboring homes. Everyone in this part of Long Beach was going to have a sudden desire to go to the movies, or a bar, or whatever the vampires felt like telling them.

Meanwhile, the wolves—except for Will—were in wolf form, prowling around the edges of the territory. They were bouncing around a little, and I figured they must be excited about this additional chance to change into their wolf forms, when it wasn't the full moon. They steered clear of me, and vice versa. Mostly this was so I didn't turn them human again, but I also didn't want to tempt Shadow by dangling werewolves in front of her nose. Okay, fine: my ex-boyfriend Eli had turned furry so he could lead them, and I was pathetically grateful to stay away from him.

Jesse came over and plopped down on the bench next to me. "Kirsten needs me near you now," he said. "She's going to make sure there aren't any humans still in the area."

I nodded, lifted my head off Shadow, and turned to face him. "I wish we had some of that ointment Rhys mentioned," I said. "It would be really helpful if you could see the Hunt, too."

He shrugged. "There just wasn't enough time." He had draped one arm along the back of the bench, and now he lifted his hand to smooth back my hair. "How are you doing?"

"I'm okay. Tired, but okay."

A beat, and then he said, "How are you doing . . . about earlier?"

I squirmed, still surveying all the activity in the park. "Um. On that matter, I would say I am doing exceptional."

"No regrets?" he said, and I stopped watching the witch crowd and turned to find him studying me.

"No regrets," I said softly. He gave me a quick, chaste kiss, and then it was back to waiting. Everything took a lot longer than I'd anticipated—but then, there was no sign of the Luparii yet. I only hoped their prep was taking as long as ours.

I felt a vampire hit my radius, and Dashiell nodded to us as he and Beatrice sat on a nearby bench. A few minutes later, Kirsten and Hayne sat down, hands clutched together. Will appeared out of the shadows and loomed against a nearby tree. His eyes were red. "You okay?" I asked. He had been late to arrive because he'd been talking to Sashi.

He just gave me a look. In a low voice, he said, "You should have told me."

There was no reason for that to sting, but it did. "It wasn't mine to tell."

Will just shook his head and stared into the darkness, like he was too angry to even look at me. I decided to shut up.

We sat there like that for a few more minutes, just waiting. It occurred to me that this had never happened before, the seven of us together in one place at the same time. Usually it was smarter to divide your resources—and Dashiell himself rarely joined in a fight. Actually, now that I thought about it, I wasn't sure this group had ever faced a straightforward fight before.

I sat up straight and looked around. The park was full of small groups of people talking in hushed tones. I knew if I expanded my radius, I would encounter witches, vampires, and werewolves of all ages and strengths. This was our community, brought together to face a common enemy.

It was kind of nice, if you didn't think about the part where we might all die.

Around midnight, Dashiell flinched suddenly, lifting a hand that was already holding a cell phone. He read the text and looked up—right at me. "The spotter to the north," he said, standing up. "They're here."

Chapter 44

I pulled in my radius, and Jesse and I ran to the corner of the wedge, through the gate leading down to the riverbed. Most of the Old World could see just fine in the dim light from the city—at least, for now—but Dashiell's vampires had set out powerful camping lanterns along each bank, spaced every hundred feet or so. From the air we probably looked like a bizarre runway. I'd never really looked at the river at night, but the dry concrete bed seemed even bigger somehow, and alien, like the concave surface of the moon. It really was an enormous amount of space.

I turned right, crossing the narrow bike path and climbing down into the riverbed with Jesse and Shadow alongside me. The other leaders followed behind us, out of my radius, as we'd planned.

"You ready?" Jesse murmured.

"Nope."

Then we heard the horn.

What was the real term for it again? Oliphant. I had expected something sort of flutey, but it sounded more like a hollow foghorn with a sense of dread. I thought it was a little loud, but all around me, I saw people drop to the ground, covering their ears. Jesse and Shadow seemed unaffected, but when I turned to look, even Beatrice had fallen to one knee. Dashiell was bent over her, looking worried. Will's hands were clamped over his ears. Kirsten's lips were moving in some sort of protection spell.

Then the sound finally faded, and I faced forward again. Before anyone could speak, I heard a galloping sound, like hooves striking concrete. Hooves and claws.

It sounded like a whole horde of them, ominous as fuck, and my stomach turned into a rock. What if I was wrong about all this? What if we were all just lined up here waiting to die?

Then they came around the bend, and into the light of the farthest lanterns. The Hunt rode toward us as a single organism. There was no jostling for position, no veering off course, no confusion. They moved like an enormous, rolling black wave: terrible and inevitable.

Beside me, Jesse said something low and scared in Spanish. The people of the Los Angeles Old World, God bless them, held steady, waiting for a signal from me.

My eyes went to the horses first, because . . . well, the horses were horses the way that Shadow was a dog. They were all ink-black, their hides covered in pebbled armor, galloping and snorting like something out of a nightmare. I didn't know much about horse breeds, but they looked like Clydesdales or something similar. Each one probably weighed twenty-five hundred pounds, and despite the dim light and the distance, I could see that their hooves set up little sparks on the concrete, like metal ax heads. There were too many for me to count quickly, but probably close to twenty.

"Oh, shit," squeaked Kirsten's voice behind me.

"What are they?" I heard Hayne ask her.

"Hellhest."

It didn't sound like English, but it was as good a name as any for the equine equivalent of bargests.

I couldn't make out much about their riders, because all the lights were sitting on the ground, but running at the hellhest's feet, I saw a pack of terrifyingly massive black dogs.

Bargests. *Five* of them.

I recognized an Irish wolfhound mix and a couple of Great Danes, all with the trademark inky darkness of the spell. Each and every one of them was bigger than Shadow.

And it was only in that moment that I realized what had happened to the people living on the edge of Sunken City. Permanently changing dogs into bargests and horses into hellhest would require a human sacrifice . . . for each one. Which meant that something like twenty-five humans had been killed, and judging from the bedrooms I'd seen, some of them had been children.

I felt righteous anger build up in my rib cage. The humans of Los Angeles weren't technically under my protection, but that didn't mean these assholes could show up and kill entire families in *my fucking town*.

I stepped forward, and when the Wild Hunt was a hundred yards away, I held up my hands in a stop gesture.

Truthfully, I wasn't sure they were even capable of stopping. The law of inertia didn't seem to apply here. But the leader pulled on his reins, and the entire group pulled up short behind him.

I walked forward.

Only now that they were close could I make out anything about the riders. Dressed in black robes and metal masks, they were both terrifying and glorious, like something out of Guillermo del Toro's personal happy place. The leader moved his snorting, stamping hellhest closer, but stopped a good twenty yards away from me. He had a massive sword slung onto the saddle. They all had swords, but only his seemed to emit its own gentle glow.

"Dashiell?" I said over my shoulder. "You're up."

The vampire came up behind me and slowly passed me, stopping ten yards from the silent rider.

Then I closed my eyes and pushed my radius out until it encompassed the entire Wild Hunt.

It felt . . . astounding. I was used to Shadow's power, and this felt similar, but magnified by the sheer number and size of the different animals. Something still felt wrong, and it took me a moment to realize that I hadn't actually *broken* the spell. I'd only subdued it, like holding your foot down on a cockroach. The magic was still *there*, so powerful that it staggered me. Jesse appeared beside me, putting out a hand to subtly support my elbow.

Dashiell was talking, trying to negotiate, but I couldn't focus over the intensity of the Wild Hunt magic. "Scarlett?" Jesse murmured, glancing down at me. "What's going on?"

"I don't know," I whispered. I looked at the riders, who had instantly transformed back into humans. They were all blinking and looking around with obvious disappointment. Their black robes and masks had disappeared, revealing regular street clothes. The majority of them were women, which shouldn't have surprised me—statistically, nearly all witches are female. I just never expect women to do the really evil stuff.

The Wild Hunt's leader was, of course, Aldric, now dressed in jeans and a red button-down shirt. There was black cloth showing under the shirt, and I figured he was also wearing Kevlar. Like the others, he blinked a couple of times, looking around, and then a smile spread across his face. "Intoxicating," he said, lifting one hand from the reins and studying both sides of it. "Just as I hoped."

I forced myself to tune him out. I had to figure out what why the Wild Hunt spell hadn't broken. I closed my eyes again so I could pick out the different sensations that were swirling in my radius. It was hard to separate and identify them, like picking out different ingredients in a smoothie. Only the magic was trying to blend together into a fucking force of nature rather than a delicious beverage.

My eyes popped open again. The witches didn't feel like witches. That was the answer. Whatever magic drove the Wild Hunt was the same substance that all witches used—but Kirsten and her kind *channeled* magic, pulling it out of the air and letting it run through them. These Luparii witches had done something different. They'd summoned the Wild Hunt magic into *themselves* and kept it there, something no one was supposed to be able to do. So they felt less like witches and more like magic incarnate: densely concentrated and borderline unstable. This was stronger than witch magic. It was elemental.

And it was exhausting. I could do it—I could keep them human—but for the first time in my life, nullifying magic was slowly tiring me. Then I realized that it wasn't just the riders, their hellhest, and the bargests, although that was plenty. It was also the sword, Durendal, hanging at Aldric's side, and something else. There was something on Aldric's person that felt practically radioactive.

Jesse squeezed my hand. The conversation had been getting tense. I tuned back in.

"You need to leave my town now," Dashiell said to Aldric. I had to admire the vampire. He was currently in my radius, but he spoke with such bracing authority and command that even *I* kind of wanted to get a plane ticket out of there.

Aldric just smiled. His street clothes should have looked comically weird against the black, unearthly hellhest, but the old man looked completely at ease on its back, like he'd been riding horses since birth. I recognized the witch flanking him on his left. It was Petra Corbett, her spine perfectly straight as she smirked down at me from her horse. I managed not to spit at her, but it was a close thing. "Why would I do that?" Aldric said coolly. "Because of the *connard*?" He gestured at me. Jesse's hands curled into fists, and I had the impression that I'd been insulted.

"If you want me to be human, you'll have to be as well," Aldric continued. "*Le anneleur* or no, my Hunt can decimate your pathetic numbers. And if she dies, the Hunt returns. No matter what you do, the spell will last until sunrise."

Dashiell said something back, but I had closed my eyes again, trying to figure out the source of that extra pulse of magic in my radius. So I never saw Aldric's mount sidle a little to his left, making room for a rider in the back of the pack, holding a handgun. I *did* hear Jesse scream, "Scarlett, down!" . . . but not before the rider pulled the trigger.

Chapter 45

Jesse had argued with Dashiell for a long time about the gun thing.

The Luparii had showed before that they were willing to use modern weapons, so Jesse's feeling was that they should be prepared to raise guns the moment Scarlett turned them human. But Dashiell was old-school enough to think firearms didn't have a place in the Old World, and he didn't want to be the first one to break that unspoken rule.

"Why does it matter?" Jesse had countered, back at the mansion. "They came to your town and are planning to kill your people. Who cares about archaic rules?"

"It matters," Dashiell had insisted. "Their whole objective is to come here and prove that our previous resistance was a fluke, and they can exterminate us whenever they want. People are watching how we handle them. If we resist with honor—or what passes for honor in the Old World—it matters to people. And if they beat us dishonorably, that matters as well."

Jesse kind of thought it was bullshit, but they didn't have enough time to keep arguing about it. They'd agreed that Jesse would bring guns, but he wouldn't take the first shot.

Jesse was really regretting that compromise when one of the Luparii witches shot Scarlett in the chest.

He was flanking her when she fell, and he managed to half-catch, half-lower her to the ground so she didn't hit her head. Shadow immediately began nosing at Scarlett, checking that there wasn't any blood and the bulletproof jacket had done its job. Jesse said a silent prayer of thanks that the werewolves and Shadow had taken out the Luparii's snipers at Bronson Caves. If they had been with the Wild Hunt, they could have killed Scarlett with a head shot.

Jesse really wanted to yell at Dashiell for his boneheaded "resist with honor" plan, but after making sure Scarlett was alive, the cardinal vampire had run straight into the fray.

The gunshot was a signal to the rest of the LA community, too. Dashiell had never really thought talking to the Luparii would get them anywhere, but he'd suggested using it as a cover, so their own people could circle around to the back of the Wild Hunt's group undetected. Now the Luparii group was surrounded. Several of them tried to run out of Scarlett's radius, likely hoping to become the Furious Host once more, or at least circle around to the LA people, but the sight of the snarling werewolves patrolling the edges kept them where they were. These people were afraid of werewolves.

Most of the LA's vampires and witches surged forward to clash with the Luparii—though a few of the physically weaker witches backed away under the bridge. Jesse couldn't see the whole battle, but Dashiell was currently just a little ways in front of him, dodging Aldric's sword as he tried to pull the Luparii leader off his mount without being struck by the hellhest's terrible hooves. The beast—it was really the only term for it—seemed sort of confused, like it suddenly couldn't remember what it was doing, but Aldric was spurring it on.

"Scar?" Jesse said, looking back down at her. "I know that hurt, but are you okay?"

She didn't answer him. Her eyes were open but unfocused, like she was struggling to concentrate on something. He figured it had to do with her radius and the Luparii and stopped trying to get her to talk.

She probably couldn't hear him anyway: there were a number of people shooting guns on both sides. Several of Kirsten's people were down, but the Wild Hunt witches must have been wearing Kevlar, too, which just seemed . . . unfair. Jesse kept his head down and made sure his body was between Scarlett and the gunfire.

Then Shadow suddenly sprinted away from his side.

She had been glued to Scarlett's prone form, but when Jesse looked up, he realized that three of the bargests had broken off from the fight and were coming toward them in a triangle formation. All around him, the Los Angeles Old World was fighting the Wild Hunt, but Aldric had likely told these animals to focus on Scarlett. If she died, LA would fall.

Jesse helped Scarlett lay down on the ground and stood up, pulling out his Glock. He knew from experience with Shadow that gunshots couldn't really hurt the three snarling bargests, but they would heal more slowly in Scarlett's radius, and he could at least slow them down and scream for help.

As a cop, Jesse had broken up two different dogfights, and he wasn't eager to see the bargest version. The closer they got, the more Jesse's hopes sank. Each of the new animals had a good fifty pounds on Shadow, and there were three of them. Still, Shadow raced toward them, obviously determined to meet them as far away from Scarlett as possible.

He expected them to start circling each other like any other big dogs, with added power and healing, but instead Shadow charged straight at the lead bargest's front leg. Jesse didn't even see the attack so much as hear the leg *snap*. The new bargest snarled, but Shadow was already attacking another leg.

Only then did Jesse realize what Shadow had figured out: the new bargests were obviously well trained, but they moved with hesitance, like they weren't quite used to their new speed or strength. Shadow was experienced, and she was taking advantage.

As she snapped a third leg on the lead dog, one of the flanking bargests closed her teeth around Shadow's neck, which would have been a great strike if Shadow's skin hadn't been impenetrable. By the time the second bargest realized it couldn't rip out Shadow's throat, she had turned, somehow managing to catch and rip out the second bargest's tongue.

Oof. Apparently those weren't invulnerable.

Jesse winced, but he couldn't look away. The second bargest yelped, pawing at her mouth, and the third approached Shadow more warily. Shadow planted all four feet and snarled, a deafening sound—and then the third bargest completely shocked Jesse by flipping over on its back, showing its belly.

Slowly, the two injured bargests did the same, showing submission to Shadow, who began stalking around them in a circle, snapping her jaws. It was like watching an angry teacher trying to discipline her students in the middle of a hurricane. Finally, Shadow backed up—and two of the three bargests stood up and followed her. The bargest who'd led them before was still healing two broken legs, but it rolled onto its stomach and held its head in submission.

Jesse choked out a laugh. Shadow had just taken over a pack of bargests.

But there were two still missing. He looked around. The gunfire had ended, and the Los Angeles group within Scarlett's radius were now fighting hand to hand with the members of the Wild Hunt, led by Kirsten and Hayne. At first it'd been chaotic, but now they were clearly focused on a single objective: getting the Luparii off their hellhest. Eight of the riders were already down, and five of those were clearly dead on the concrete riverbed, with little streams of black-looking blood trickling toward the tiny channel of sluggish water. The remaining three witches on the ground had abandoned their guns and were fighting with swords and fists.

Jesse saw that a half-dozen of Kirsten's witches were focused on the riderless hellhest, who seemed disoriented and confused. Several of them were reacting violently, but a few of the witches must have been horse lovers, because Jesse saw a couple of women standing in front of one of the beasts with her hands up, talking in soothing tones.

Finally, he spotted the last two bargests. They were creeping around the sides of the channel, headed for Will, who was shouting orders to some of the werewolves prowling the edge of the riverbed. His back was turned to the bargests.

"Will!" Jesse yelled, and the werewolf alpha turned around just in time to see the nearer bargest leap for his throat.

Then there was a flash, an agonized noise from the bargest, and the creature backed away from Will with its tail tucked between its legs. The other bargest tried to pounce, but Will extended what looked like a short metal pole, about two feet long.

A cattle prod?

Jesse stared, his mouth open, and Will shot him a grin. "I've had to get creative over the years," he shouted, shocking the first bargest who'd attacked as it came in for another round. Will backed up until his shoulders hit the side of the bridge support, and he was able to fend off the two bargests without much trouble. Eventually the cattle prod would run out of power, though.

The other four bargests streaked down the channel to his aid. Shadow looked completely in her element: confident and sure and in control. Jesse wished Scarlett could see it.

He crouched down again to check on her. Her eyes had closed, but he could see her breathing. "Scar?"

When she didn't move, he turned on his phone flashlight and gently used his thumb to raise one eyelid. "Shit!"

Her eye was bloody.

Jesse had actually seen this before. Years earlier, Noah had gotten a concussion doing stunt work, and ended up having a subconjunctival hemorrhage, meaning the little blood vessels in his eye had burst, and blood became trapped between the eye's clear cover and the eye itself. Jesse had seen a couple of cops end up with the same thing: once after a boxing match and once after taking a punch from a suspect.

But Scarlett hadn't been in the fight, and he was pretty sure she hadn't hit her head.

He checked the other eye—that one was clear. "Scarlett?" He bent closer to her. "Scarlett, honey, wake up. Talk to me."

Her lips moved, and he put his ear next to her mouth to hear. "Not sleeping. Trying . . . to hold them."

Jesse looked up. The fight was still raging, although nearly all the Wild Hunt riders had been pulled off the hellhest. That was something, anyway.

But Scarlett was scaring him. Jesse reached into her pants pocket and took out her phone, a new one she'd collected at Dashiell's mansion. He was relieved to find that Abby had found the time to transfer all her contacts. He scrolled through and found Sashi's phone number.

It took a few rings for a sleepy voice to come on the line. "Scarlett?" Then: "What's happening? It's so loud."

"It's Jesse Cruz," he shouted, plugging his other ear. "Something's happening to Scarlett." As quickly as he could, he described the Wild Hunt and the burst blood vessels in Scarlett's eye.

"She's hypertensive," Sashi said immediately. "Her blood pressure's rising. Tell her she needs to calm down and relax."

Jesse rolled his eyes. "She can't do that! If the riders turn spectral, they can't be killed."

"I don't know what to tell you!" Sashi sounded upset. "She's too stressed. If she keeps it up, she'll lose the baby. And she could die."

"Shit. Call you back." Jesse hung up the phone and looked around for Shadow. If he couldn't get Scarlett to stop pushing, Jesse would have to find a way to reduce the pressure.

Several of the lanterns had gotten kicked over, and he couldn't find her in the chaos. He brought two fingers to his lips and whistled hard. "Shadow!" he hollered. Maybe ten seconds went by before she appeared at his side—with a line of panting bargests behind her like a dogsled team from hell. She'd converted all five.

"Scarlett's in trouble," he told her. "I have to help with the fight, okay? Can you watch her?"

Shadow turned her head around, some sort of unspoken communication passing between her and the other bargests. Instantly, they all hurried to form a circle around Scarlett, facing outward. There was some part of Jesse that longed to take a picture to show her later.

Instead, he got to his feet and ran down the channel, pulling out his Glock. From what he could see as he waded into the chaos, the Los Angeles side appeared to be winning, but very slowly. Three Luparii witches, including Petra fucking Corbett, had come to Aldric's aide, and were fighting Dashiell, who—holy shit, Dashiell could *fight*?! He was currently human, but he whirled and spun around the Luparii's sword strikes, knocking Petra down with an open-handed punch to the throat, kicking another calmly in the knee. The third, male witch was hanging back, looking for an opening so he could catch Dashiell off guard, and Jesse recognized the guy who had first shot Scarlett. He raised his own Glock and fired a round at the man's head.

The Luparii member crumpled to the concrete channel, and Dashiell looked up, surprised. He nodded his thank-you and turned back to Petra, deflecting an overhead strike with some sort of flashing blade. He wasn't using a gun—he'd been paranoid about hitting his own people in the fray. Dashiell didn't exactly spend a lot of time at the range in human form.

But Jesse did. He looked for other openings in the chaos, and realized that all the witches still on their hellhest were easy marks. No chance of accidentally hitting the LA people. He put down three of them before one of the Luparii members figured out who was shooting and came for Jesse.

Jesse started to line up the Glock—but he hadn't heard the Luparii witch coming up behind him. She kicked the weapon out of his hand with her thick work boot and danced away, her hands up like a boxer. Jesse started to reach for the Beretta in his other holster, but she darted in first, landing a quick jab to his solar plexus before he could move away. Even as a human, she was fast as hell. She ducked his next swing—aimed at her head—and danced sideways. He got his elbow up to block her next punch, but it had been a trick. She'd wanted to get close enough to grab the Beretta out of his holster. Jesse fumbled to take it back, but she was quicker—and her movement had put her between him and Scarlett. With a gun. The woman smiled viciously and lifted the handgun, pointing it at his head. Jesse braced himself.

And then the most bewildered look came over the witch's face. She dropped the gun, and sort of half-heartedly tried to reach over one shoulder. Instead, she flinched again and dropped to her knees, finally falling forward.

Only then did Jesse see the three throwing knives sticking out of her back. And just beyond, Scarlett, standing and swaying in the middle of a circle of bargests. Blood was trickling out of her nose. She gave him a woozy smile and crumpled.

Chapter 46

Despite the pressure in my radius, I managed to struggle to my feet long enough to stop Jesse from being shot by a mean-looking female Luparii. I made a mental note to tease him about letting someone steal his gun . . . then I was falling back down, and I figured I probably wouldn't remember it.

I managed to sort of catch myself on my hands and knees, rather than face-plant. I was dimly aware that there were other bargests near me, but they weren't even looking at me, and I figured if Shadow was cool, I was cool. At some point my undershirt must have torn, because the Kevlar vest felt itchy and constraining. I wanted so badly to unstrap it that it was probably good I needed my hands to support myself. I lowered my butt to the ground.

I looked around as best I could, with a huge part of my mind focused on my radius. The fight was starting to wind down, but it wasn't over. The Luparii witches on their hellhest kept coming to Aldric's defense, and any number of our people had fallen near his hellhest's feet and been dragged to safety by the others. Two of the vampires were running around with honest-to-goodness squirt guns, trying to shoot tranquilizers into the hellhest's mouths.

The squirt guns had been Jesse's idea, and it seemed to be working: four hellhest were down, and I could see one actually swaying.

Some of the Luparii witches must have tried to run, because there were three naked people trading punches with Luparii witches on the ground. I figured the werewolves had leapt at the riders trying to escape my radius, turning human as they did. I hadn't even felt the change. It had probably been pretty awesome-looking.

I noticed with grim satisfaction that Petra Corbett was lying on the ground, unmoving. I couldn't tell from a distance, but I was pretty sure she was dead. I didn't even care how it had happened. Dashiell, meanwhile, had stopped fighting Aldric long enough to help Hayne, who was holding on to the reins of one of the hellhest as it gnashed its teeth at Kirsten. The creature finally settled down, and Dashiell immediately turned back toward Aldric, who was snarling and kicking at his hellhest, trying to head under the bridge and escape in the other direction. I watched Will step into his path and then—

"Scarlett?" Jesse had dropped down by my side, his guns back in their holsters. Why did he sound so worried? "You're bleeding, sweetheart."

I looked down at myself, confused. I hadn't been shot—well, not anywhere the vest didn't protect me. Then a couple of bright red drops hit my shirt, and I realized they came from my nose.

"I called Sashi, she said it's high blood pressure—if you don't calm down, you could lose the baby," he said.

I felt the pressure on my radius ease up some more, but I wasn't sure how much longer I could hold it anyway. That was too much to say out loud at the moment, though, so I held up a finger to Jesse and took stock of my radius. The bargests and hellhest were still buzzing at me, but only four of the Furious Host remained.

I zeroed in on Aldric. Will had done something to cause Aldric's hellhest to rear up, and I watched Aldric slide off the hellhest's back, landing on his feet with a nimbleness that seemed strange for a man his age. Then he pulled and brandished the sword, Durendal, and I suspected it was helping him somehow, or maybe protecting him.

No, not the sword. There was something else on Aldric's person. The thing I'd sensed earlier.

The scroll.

I looked at Jesse, who bent close to hear me. "Aldric has the scroll on him," I whispered. "It didn't short out, but I think I could destroy it."

He nodded and stood up, running toward Aldric. I looked at Shadow. "Help him?"

She looked from me to the other bargests surrounding me, and I could see her decide she needed to stay and keep them in line, just in case their loyalty to her wasn't absolute. Shit.

Jesse pulled one of his guns and aimed it at Aldric, but the shot hit him in the back of the Kevlar. Aldric snarled and swung around to face Jesse, which left Will an opening to jump on his back, choking him. Aldric roared and swung the sword up, but I could practically see him decide not to swing it—he would risk burying the magic blade in his own shoulder. While he was distracted, Jesse tried to shoot him in the head, and when Aldric ducked the blow, Jesse shot him in the leg instead. It collapsed, causing the Luparii leader to go down in a tumble, with Will still clinging to his back. Jesse had been smart enough to stop a good fifteen feet from them, where Aldric couldn't swing the sword, but that meant he couldn't get in another shot without possibly hitting Will. I stood up and staggered closer to them, pulling a knife out of my belt.

Even on the ground, Aldric would not let go of the sword. He rolled sideways and swung it at Will, who instinctively put up his left hand to protect his head—and the blade sliced clean through his forearm, just below the elbow. Will's hand dropped with a meaty sound. He cried out in pain and fell back on his butt, cradling the stump.

"No!" I bellowed. Suddenly, the pressure of keeping everyone in my radius seemed to lift, as my range exploded outward with my emotions.

Kirsten's humans-go-away spells began popping all around us, and a bunch of werewolves turned human again. I didn't even notice. I was trying to crawl toward Will.

Jesse turned to look at me when I yelled, and behind him I saw Aldric's face light up with an idea. He might be losing this battle, but he could at least take out Will—and possibly run away in the chaos.

"You. Will. *Not*," I screamed, and without any thought at all, I raised my right arm and pointed the flat palm at Aldric.

I was already really in tune with my radius, and I immediately felt the buzz of his magic—not just the Luparii witch powers, but the concentrated magic of the Furious Host that was currently possessing him. Fairy magic, quite possibly. I studied that magic for one heartbeat, because it was big and scary and nothing I'd ever played with before, and then I pulled on it. I called it toward me.

This was more or less what I'd done each of the times I'd "cured" someone of being a vampire or werewolf. Usually I called it into me and then let it dissolve away, like sand through my fingers, but this time the magic was too strong, too big. I wrestled with it for a moment, trying to let go of it, but it was like letting go of something you'd accidentally superglued to your hands. I couldn't stop feeling, tasting, the Wild Hunt magic, and it was twisted and wrong, an intricate structure built on the corpses of sacrifices. But I couldn't let go.

My body started to shake, and I vomited green-tasting . . . something.

Then there was a tearing, and everything went still. The last thing I saw was Jesse standing over me, holding two pieces of torn parchment paper.

Chapter 47

"Shh! I think she's waking up."

"Scarlett? Sweetheart?"

I felt feverish, but a cool hand smoothed sticky hair off my fore-head. I caught a smell of Armani cologne and oranges and felt myself smiling. Jesse.

My eyes opened, and I processed the most immediate and obvious new information: *hospital room*. I was in a fairly plush private room—someone had obviously pulled strings—with Jesse in a chair on one side of the bed, holding my right hand. There was an IV in the other one. Sashi stood on the left side. She looked exhausted, her hair mussed, her clothes wrinkled. The first time I'd cured someone of magic, I'd lost my powers for a few weeks, but to my surprise, I could feel Sashi in my radius.

Holy shit. I was getting stronger.

Although it *really* didn't feel like it at the moment.

"Hello again," Sashi said when she saw me looking.

"You came back?" I croaked, in a voice that had obviously not been used for a while.

She smiled. "I never left. When Jesse called the night of the fight, I was at a hotel in Burbank, crying my eyes out. Didn't want to fly home like that."

It started coming back to me. I'd sent Will out to talk to Sashi. Will.

I tried to sit up, but I didn't do more than lift my head an inch, and even that was exhausting. "Will?" I asked instead.

A peculiar look crossed her face. "He's alive," she said.

I looked at Jesse. "The baby?"

"Also alive," he assured me, and I breathed out a sigh, my numb body somehow filling with relief. "You had a seizure in the riverbed, and by the time we got you to a hospital, you had a pretty serious fever. The doctors were worried," Jesse added. "But they've been giving you fluids around the clock."

My eyes drifted to the IV in my left arm.

"They did an ultrasound about two hours ago, and the heartbeat was going strong," Sashi put in.

"You guys heard the heartbeat?"

Jesse grinned. "It was amazing. Fast, like a tiny locomotive."

I smiled, then their words caught up with me. Sashi had said *the night of the fight*. That was late Sunday night. "What day is it?"

"Tuesday afternoon," Jesse said. "It's . . . well, there's a lot to catch you up on."

Sashi checked her watch. "I should get back to Will's room."

"He's here? In the hospital?" My brow furrowed. Werewolves didn't go to the hospital. They didn't need to, for one thing, and for another, they'd be identified as medical anomalies. "Why?"

She glanced at Jesse. "Scar," he said gently, "when Aldric was going to kill Will, you took his magic."

"Yeah . . ." I sort of remembered that part.

"Will was kneeling just behind him. You took his magic, too."

I blinked at him for a long moment. I'd . . . *what?*

My first thought was that "curing" Will would prevent him from ever being able to grow his arm back. And that was on me. Tears pricked my eyes. "I'm so sorry!" I wailed. "I didn't mean to!"

"It's okay," Sashi soothed. "Scarlett . . . he's human now."

I stared at her, uncomprehending, and then finally I understood.

Werewolves can't heal injuries sustained *before* they become werewolves, so there would be no going back for Will. Even if he went through the change again, he would only have three legs, and that would make him too slow and weak to be alpha. There was no reason not to stay human.

"You guys . . . you're going to be together?" I asked Sashi.

"We're going to try." She smiled at me with tears in her eyes. "Thank you. Stopping Aldric saved his life."

I just stared at her, openmouthed, as she kissed my cheek and left.

Then I tried to focus on Jesse, although I was already getting drowsy again. "Hi," I said.

He smiled, bent down, and kissed my lips. "Hi."

"How's your brother?"

"He's going to be okay," Jesse said. "Molly stayed at the hospital that night, and pressed Noah when he woke up. He was discharged this morning."

"That's good," I said, my eyelids getting heavy, "I think I'm s'posed to sleep more."

He kissed me again, this time on my forehead. "Rest."

The next time I woke up, it was dark outside, and Jesse was sleeping hunched in a chair. His head was at practically a ninety-degree angle. I slid sideways in the nice hospital bed. "Jesse," I said softly.

He woke up with a start. "What's wrong?"

"Nothing. I'm fine. You should go home and get some sleep."

He shook his head, as I'd expected. "I'm staying."

"Then come in the bed."

Jesse hesitated for a minute, then got up and walked around the bed so he could climb in on my right side, where there was no IV. It was an odd re-creation of when we'd shared my bed after his attack, only a few days earlier. We spent a few seconds awkwardly trying to find positions that would fit together, and I fell back to sleep with Jesse holding my hand.

The next morning I woke up feeling stronger. Almost back to myself—or at least the pregnancy version of myself. After the nurse's rounds and my breakfast, I pushed away the tray and said to Jesse, "Have you been getting updates?"

He nodded. "Hayne or Sashi call every couple of hours."

"Okay. Fill me in."

So he did. Well, I kept falling asleep, but every time I woke up, he picked up where we'd left off.

The Los Angeles Old World had lost twelve people: six witches, two werewolves, and four vampires. Of the dead, Jesse only knew the two werewolves: Travis Hochrest, who had required my cleaning services a couple of times, and Rosarita Hernandez, whom he'd interviewed briefly during the first Luparii case. I felt a surprisingly sharp pang of sorrow for Travis, who had been a little dim and silly, but a really nice guy overall. There had been lots of injuries, but most of them had healed after I shorted myself out. The remaining ones were handled by Matthias and, later, when Will was out of the woods, Sashi.

Aldric had survived the night only to find all his minions dead and his magic gone—all of it, permanently. He was now susceptible to vampire press, so Dashiell had been extracting all kinds of juicy information from him for days, more than enough to squash any remaining Luparii operations in Europe. Apparently this was quite upsetting for Aldric, because he had tried to hang himself in one of the cells in Dashiell's basement. They'd stopped him in time, and pressed his mind so he wouldn't try again. Dashiell was working on a way to execute him that would send a message to anyone back in Europe who might still be toying with the world-domination plan. A nicer, more humane Scarlett would probably have felt sorry for the old man, or tried to talk them out of killing him in cold blood, but I just couldn't find it in me to care when or how Aldric died.

"Did Aldric say anything about why they wanted three years to come back here?" I asked Jesse.

He nodded. "Because of the animals," he reported. "They needed time to train new dogs, specifically to go after Shadow. And the horses, too." He shook his head a little. "But they couldn't do the spell until they got the scroll, so the animals weren't really used to their new forms. That probably saved us during the fight."

Speaking of the scroll . . . "How's Owen doing?" I asked.

Jesse told me he was back at school, trying to get his human life on track again. I wondered if it would take, or if he would find himself sucked back into the world of witchcraft. I had a feeling Kirsten would keep a close eye on him. Meanwhile, he was also helping a couple of his aunts organize a funeral for Karl, whose murder would probably go unsolved. I hoped that Jesse and I would be able to go to the service. Whatever family he'd been born into, Karl Schmidt had saved a lot of people by keeping that spell away from the rest of the Luparii.

As for the Wild Hunt magic itself, it had been completely destroyed, thanks to Jesse. He'd ripped the scroll containing the spell in half while it was in my radius, which had released the pent-up magic. The sword had short-circuited at the same time I'd "cured" Aldric. It now appeared to be just a regular sword, without the creepy glowing. Kirsten and her witches were studying both objects to try to figure out how they'd managed to contain such power.

"What will happen to the animals?" I asked, worried about Shadow. I already missed her. Again.

He grinned at me. "Remember the end of *101 Dalmatians*?"

"Oh no. We are not starting a dalmatian plantation."

Jesse laughed and said, "No, but it kind of feels that way." All six bargests were currently staying at the cottage, overseen by Molly and *Astrid*, of all people.

"Wait, a werewolf? Aren't they trying to kill her?"

"That's the funny thing," Jesse said. "When I ripped the spell, all the animals lost their . . . well, their urge for evil, I guess? Physically, they look the same, but the bargests aren't driven to kill the wolves, and the hellhest aren't trying to hurt anyone either. They're basically just smart, bulletproof horses now. It's just like when Shadow is in your radius: all the permanent physical changes stay, including the intelligence. I'm guessing they won't heal fast anymore, but none of us are willing to experiment on them."

"Good call. What's going to happen to them?"

"Well, Dashiell wanted to try to kill at least the hellhest, but Kirsten convinced him that they could be a show of power to our enemies. He's probably going to buy a ranch in the mountains and hire a couple of the witches to stay there and take care of them."

I noticed that he'd said "*our* enemies" instead of "their enemies" or "your enemies."

"That sounds like the best sitcom ever," I commented. "What are we going to do with the new bargests?"

"Believe it or not, Astrid thinks Eli should let the werewolves adopt them. Regular pets are scared of the werewolves, but the bargests aren't affected, and they're powerful enough to run with the wolves on full-moon nights. If they can be sort of incorporated into the pack, it will increase LA's power base, too. But the others are still discussing it." He held out his hands, palms up. "It's a work in progress."

That was good and all, but . . . "Eli?"

Jesse's face sobered. "He's the new alpha."

Oh. It made sense, of course: Will had been effectively forced into retirement. Scratch that: *I* had effectively forced Will into retirement.

But having my ex-boyfriend back in my life as someone I regularly had to work with? "That's awkward."

I watched Jesse carefully for signs of jealousy, but he shrugged, tucking my hair behind my ear. "We'll deal with it."

That night, I had a very welcome visitor. "Wyatt!" I cried out as the cowboy vampire hovered in my doorway, hat in hand. He looked good—pale and drawn and leaning hard on a cane, but good. I waved him in. "Your leg?" I said as he limped his way in. "It . . . came back?"

"Yes, ma'am." Jesse gave Wyatt his chair, and the vampire nodded gratefully. "And it's an experience I cannot recommend less." He regarded me in the hospital bed for a moment. "I leave you alone for one day, and you end up in the hospital?"

I waved it off. "I'm okay, really. Mostly they're keeping me here to . . ." I trailed off, then shrugged to myself. What the hell? I trusted Wyatt. "To keep an eye on the baby," I finished.

Wyatt's enormous mustache spread into a smile. "The . . . Miss Scarlett, you're expecting a child?"

"Well, it better not be a dinosaur," I replied.

"I don't know, I think a triceratops would be pretty cool," Jesse commented.

For a second, Wyatt looked like he might cry. "That's . . . golly, that's just wonderful. Congratulations to you both."

Jesse and I exchanged a look. We had already dealt with this from a dozen different doctors and nurses, and I, for one, was tired of it.

"Thank you," I said simply. I hesitated for a second, then forced the words out. "Are you angry with me? About . . . Katia?"

"That she saved my life?" He gave me a gentle smile. "I was, a bit. I still want to be with my Ellen. But . . ." He gave a little shrug. "I swore to Mr. Dashiell that I would look out for you for a year. I reckon I need to stick around for it."

"You . . . wait." I'd known that Wyatt had sworn loyalty to Dashiell, of course—every vampire in the city had to do that. "He asked you to look out for me?"

Wyatt's smile widened. "I volunteered. He agreed that you seem to need some extra help." He glanced wryly at the cane. "Or maybe just a straw man. I can work with that."

Jesse squeezed my hand. I didn't know what to say.

Wyatt started to shift his weight to leave, then gave a little start. "Oh! I almost forgot." He leaned his cane against the bed so he could reach into his jacket pocket. "This is for you." He handed me a set of keys. I looked at him in confusion.

"Dashiell, Kirsten, and Will all went in on it together," Wyatt explained. "It's a Mercedes Metris cargo van." His eyes twinkled. "Now I know why they were so obsessed with getting all the safety features."

I looked down at the keys, and back up at Wyatt. "I . . . I . . ."

"It's all paid off," Wyatt added. "They wanted you to know how grateful they are. And I imagine it's something of a baby gift, too."

I looked up at Jesse with tears in my eyes. He smiled and kissed the top of my head. "Thank you," I said to Wyatt.

The following morning, I went through a whole series of tests on me and the baby, and eventually the doctors pronounced me well enough to go home. The ones not on Dashiell's payroll were mystified, but they eventually decided that I'd caught some sort of weird flu bug that had caused high blood pressure and a seizure. I was too busy being grateful that the baby and I were healthy to care what they called it.

The next morning, Thursday, I was discharged. Jesse, who hadn't left my side except to shower and fetch clean clothes, got to wheel me out of the hospital.

"Don't get used to this babying-me thing," I warned him.

"Yes, Miss Scarlett," he sang.

I made a mental note to punch him when he wasn't pushing my wheelchair.

Epilogue

December 25 (eight months later)

"Elizabeth," I suggested, tossing a kernel of popcorn.

    Jesse caught it in his mouth, because he was better at this game than I was. He had an unfair mobility advantage. "Too Victorian. How about Posy?" He threw a kernel of popcorn toward my mouth, which I completely missed.

    I made a face. "How many times do I have to tell you, we are not going to be those LA people who give their kid a weirdo name just to be different."

    We were sitting in my living room at the cottage, on opposite ends of the sofa, attempting to catch red- and green-dyed popcorn in our mouths. Jesse's Christmas playlist was on the stereo, and he'd put up a little tree that glowed in the corner. I hadn't helped, because I was so huge by then that I felt like Jabba the Hut. It was seriously affecting my popcorn-catching game. There would have been kernels covering my lap if not for the helpful bargest making sure we kept the floors clean.

    "So that's a no on Khaleesi?" Jesse teased.

    I grabbed a whole handful of popcorn and chucked it at his face, which was stupid because he caught most of it in his mouth and managed to give me a smug grin while he was chewing. Shadow happily snapped up the popcorn that had fallen on the floor. Half the time it didn't even touch the ground before she got it.

Jesse was trying to keep me distracted, I knew. I'd tried to call Jack the day before to wish him and the kids a Merry Christmas, and my brother had let the call go to voice mail. In the last eight months, we'd had one phone conversation, in which he told me that he'd be happy to welcome me back into his life—whenever I quit working for Dashiell. Jack had quit his position with the cardinal vampire a few days after he'd learned about Dashiell's "criminal activity."

Jesse had tried to convince me to tell Jack about the baby, but I'd kept it to myself. I didn't want my brother to compromise his (valid) principles because I'd extorted him with guilt. But I missed him and Juliet and my niece and nephew. I'd thought about sending gifts, but it seemed manipulative.

Jesse and I had exchanged Christmas gifts the night before. I was tired all the time now, so mine was lame—an enormous tin of popcorn and a book. But Jesse had surprised me with a thick manila file. He had hired a private detective in New York to investigate Jameson's background. His mother had died three years earlier, it turned out, and afterward his father had moved down to Jamaica to help a distant cousin with a boat business. The file did include a phone number for Jameson's older sister, Diana, who I planned to call in a few days, once the holidays were over. I just wasn't sure yet what I would say.

The private detective had also managed to dig up several photographs of Jameson, which was a small miracle considering he'd worked for a security-conscious vampire. Jesse had framed the nicest one, and I'd already set it out in the baby's room. I was deeply touched by his gesture, especially since he had every right to be jealous.

"What about your mom's name?" Jesse suggested. "Sarah?"

"I like it, but it seems a little rough to name her after two, you know . . . dead people," I said ruefully. I had already decided that the baby's middle name would be Jamie, to honor her father. If I thought it wouldn't make me want to cry every time I shouted at my kid, I would have made it her first name. But I wasn't strong enough for that.

"You'll figure it out," Jesse assured me. "You've got another week and a half yet. Molly will be back tonight, right? You know she'll want to add her two cents."

Molly was visiting her friends in San Francisco again, bringing them some Christmas presents. I'd been seeing less of her the last month, since she'd been busy buying furniture and decorating her new place. The little guest cottage wasn't big enough for three adults, a bargest, and a baby, and before I could even raise the subject, Molly had insisted on moving out.

I'd protested—I wasn't ready to be far away from her, especially when I was feeling fat and useless. But Molly had a surprise for me too: she had contacted the vampire who owned the mansion adjoining the guest cottage, and arranged to buy it. Vampires are *stupid* rich. Anyway, she was going to be living just a few dozen feet away, and she had insisted on setting up a nursery in the big house, too, so she could babysit when I had to go out on jobs. In true Molly style, her nursery was ostentatious as hell.

I put a handful of popcorn in my own mouth and took the Batphone out of the pocket of my hoodie—which was actually one of Jesse's that I'd taken to wearing around the house like a bathrobe. I checked the screen, but there was nothing to see.

Jesse was watching me. "Tonight is the thing, isn't it?"

"Yeah. I kind of wanted to be there, but they didn't invite me." I tried to put the phone back in the hoodie pocket, but it fumbled and fell on the floor under the coffee table. I sighed, leaving it there for now. Reaching for it would make me fall off the couch, and I'd already done that many times. This was exactly why Jabba the Hut had so many servants around. Jesse didn't pick it up either, having learned the hard way not to run around fixing things for me. "I guess I keep waiting for someone to change their mind and call me," I admitted.

"I get that. You spent a long time making it happen."

I shrugged. "I owed her a favor." Then I had to put a hand on my huge belly. "Oof."

"Kicking?"

"Yeah, watch." I moved my hand, and we both stared at my shirt as it visibly moved.

"I'll never get used to that," Jesse marveled. "It's so . . ."

"Gross?"

He laughed. "It's not gross."

"You wanna feel?"

He scooted closer and rested his flat palm on my huge stomach. Of course, the baby chose that moment to stop kicking. Jesse started to pull back, but I grabbed his hand and held it in place. "Just wait," I told him. "She loves high-fives."

We waited for a minute, two, and then the baby kicked or pushed with her hand or whatever, and Jesse's face crinkled with delight. Then he went quiet, looking at me for a long moment. "What?" I asked.

"You know what we haven't really talked about?" Jesse said, in a tone that was almost studiously casual.

"Why you think it'd be okay to name a child Posy?"

"What's my role in the baby's life?" he asked, his eyes meeting mine.

It was true; we hadn't actually discussed it. It had gotten down-right awkward during Christmas Eve dinner at Jesse's parents' house the night before. He had told them the baby wasn't his—it would be pretty obvious when she came out looking part black—and that we'd gotten together for real after I was already pregnant, but his folks and brother had still looked at me with confusion.

I didn't really care what they thought, though; Jesse was the one who mattered. He had come to every doctor's appointment and birthing class with me. He'd painted the nursery, and put together the car seat. He'd driven halfway across the city to buy me the one sandwich that sounded good to eat, and had made any number of late-night trips to the pharmacy for antacids when I had heartburn. And he loved me. In many ways, the last eight months had been the best of my life, and Jesse was a huge part of that—not just as my boyfriend or lover, but as a partner in this bizarre . . . endeavor.

"Well," I said finally, "I don't want to erase Jameson. Whatever I know about him, I'll tell the baby, and it'd be nice if she can have some kind of relationship with this Diana." I blew out a breath and gathered my courage. "So, yeah, Jameson is always going to be her father. But I was kind of hoping you would be her daddy."

Jesse's face broke out into a smile of pure joy, and I felt my eyes fill with unexpected tears . . . something that was happening a lot these days. "I can't give you your own biological child, you know," I reminded him. His hand was still on my stomach, and I covered it with mine. "This is it for me."

He looked into my eyes and said softly, "This is it for me, too."

On the floor in front of the couch, the Batphone began buzzing. I tried to lean forward to pick it up, but, Jabba the Hut–style, I couldn't reach. Jesse laughed and grabbed the phone and glanced at the screen. "It's Kirsten," he said, holding the phone to his ear. "This is Jesse."

He had taken over my cleanup work for the past three weeks, since I'd gotten too huge to do it myself. If the job was really bad, I would come along just to provide magic cancellation, but most of them had been easy for an ex-cop to handle. I called him my unpaid intern. Corry was also home for the holidays, if we needed extra assistance, but her I would pay.

Jesse listened for a second, rolled his eyes, and nodded. "I'm on my way," he told Kirsten, and hung up the phone.

"Bad?" I asked. "You need me to come?"

"Nah, just some witches who messed up a love spell again."

"Help me up before you go," I commanded. "I gotta pee again."
I *could* stand up by myself—really—but it would take a pathetically long time.

Jesse stood and reached both hands down, bracing himself to pull me up. I couldn't really blame him for that one.

I stood up, and at the same time felt something inside me loosen. Oh, shit, had I finally peed my pants? I looked down. "Uh, Jesse? I think you better call Corry to go on that job."

"Why?"

"My water just broke."

Twenty-four miles away, at a mansion in Pasadena, Dashiell was straightening a portrait on the wall that had not, in fact, been crooked.

"I don't know when I last saw you this nervous," Beatrice said behind him. She sounded amused—and a little worried. They had sent all the staff home for the night on full pay, claiming it was a Christmas gift. Generally they kept at least a few security guards, even on holidays, but Dashiell doubted they'd have any difficulty with attacks from outside the mansion. And if they came under attack from inside the mansion, well, no security guard in the world would help.

When the doorbell rang, Beatrice started forward, but he rushed past her to answer it himself.

The young woman on the doorstep wasn't at all what he'd expected. She was young-looking and beautiful, which was fairly typical, but she had neon-green hair and wore a baggy red sweaterdress that disguised her figure. Layers and layers of costume-jewelry necklaces covered most of her chest. "Maven?" he said, not entirely sure.

The young woman took off her large spectacles, shoving them into her handbag pocket. She smiled. "I'm glad we could finally do this."

Dashiell stepped aside. "Please come in."

They sat down in the living room, and he introduced her to Beatrice, who offered to call in a refreshment from the guesthouse in the back, but Maven declined. "I'd prefer no one knew I was here, at least not yet." She looked around the mansion. "You have a beautiful home. Do you sweep it for bugs?"

"Just this afternoon," Dashiell assured her.

She nodded and crossed her legs. "I'll get right to the point, then. After you allowed Scarlett Bernard to fill me in on the Luparii attack last spring, I looked into the Luparii and their activities in Europe. They came very close to creating a new order."

"I know." He had done his own investigation, in addition to the information from Aldric. The old witch had put all his bets on the Wild Hunt, allowing his best people to come to LA to participate. As a result, there were no strong leaders left to take over the organization after the Furious Host was wiped out. The Luparii group had limped along for a few months, but Dashiell had used Aldric's information to make some calls to a few well-organized werewolf packs. The Luparii was now officially extinct.

"Their methods were selfish and violent, but their motivations weren't entirely without merit," Maven went on. "The modern world *has* been changing quickly. As a result, the Old World has gotten out of control."

Suddenly Beatrice gasped, immediately clapping a hand over her mouth. Dashiell and Maven both looked at her. "I'm sorry!" she said. "I just realized . . . I saw a portrait of you once."

Maven smiled. "Not very flattering, is it?"

Dashiell looked back and forth between them, missing something. Maven took pity on him. "I was born Gunhilda of Denmark, in the year 1020," she told him. "I am the last surviving member of the Vampire Council." She paused for a moment to let that sink in, and then she added, "And I believe it's time for the council to rise again."

Acknowledgments

This book was the culmination of many years of planning, and I'm so happy that you guys finally get to read it! Many thanks to the team at 47North for trusting me with this story line, especially my acquisitions editor, Adrienne, and my development editor, Angela, who always makes my books better. Thank you, also, to my husband and family for all their support and encouragement, and to all the LA friends who helped me with information or tagged along on my bizarre research outings: Mark Wheaton, Tracy Tong, Kate Maruyama, and Emma Hassan. If I'm forgetting anyone, I apologize; it's late, and the book was due yesterday.

As with many of my novels, *Shadow Hunt* features a lot of real-life locations, and I encourage you to check out Griffith Park and the LA River Center. The revitalization of the LA River is a fascinating project and you can learn more about it here: lariver.org. Legally, I cannot recommend you visit Sunken City, but if I allegedly were to ever go there, I would hypothetically tell you that it's really frickin' cool. As usual, I have taken a few liberties with location details in order to tell a better story in a reasonable amount of time. Any mistakes are mine and made with the best of intentions.

Shadow Hunt is the end of an arc, but not the end of Scarlett's story. I don't believe your life ends when you have a baby, and I don't see why Scarlett's would, either. Look for her to pop up in future Boundary books and hopefully another trilogy of her own.

About the Author

Melissa F. Olson was raised in Chippewa Falls, Wisconsin, and studied film and literature at the University of Southern California in Los Angeles. Melissa is the author of nine Old World novels for 47North as well as the Tor.com novella *Nightshades* and its two sequels. She lives in Madison, Wisconsin, with her husband, two kids, two dogs, and two jittery chinchillas. Read more about her work and strange life at www.MelissaFOlson.com.

Made in United States
North Haven, CT
10 May 2023